THE WILD MAN

PATRICIA NELL WARREN

The Wild Man

WILDCAT PRESS
wildcatpress.com

Printed in the United States of America. Inquiries should be addressed to: Wildcat Press, 8306 Wilshire Blvd. Box 8306, Beverly Hills, CA 90211, 323/966-2466 phone or 323/966-2467 fax. Email address: wildcatprs@aol.com.

Jacket design: Jay Fraley, Tyler St. Mark, Patricia Nell Warren
Typesetting: Lee Look
Sword by Bermejo

First printing: April 2001

10 9 8 7 6 5 4 3 2 1

==

**Library of Congress Catalog Card Number: 98-91095
ISBN: 1-889135-05-4**

==

To Daphne, Rio and Gensie

The light that blinds us is not art,
Rather it is love, friendship, crossed swords

— Federíco García Lorca,
"Ode to Salvador Dalí"

Other Titles by Patricia Nell Warren

Fiction

Billy's Boy — Wildcat Press, 1997
Harlan's Race — Wildcat Press, 1994
One Is the Sun — Ballantine/Random House, 1991
The Beauty Queen — William Morrow, 1978
The Fancy Dancer — William Morrow, 1976
The Front Runner — William Morrow, 1974
The Last Centennial — Dial Press, 1971

Nonfiction

Ukrainian Dumy, co-translated with George Tarnawsky — Canadian Institute of Ukrainian Studies and Harvard Ukrainian Research Institute, 1979

Poetry

Horse With a Green Vinyl Mane — Novi Poezii, 1970
Rose-Hued Cities — Novi Poezii, 1966
Legends and Dreams — Novi Poezii, 1962
A Tragedy of Bees — Novi Poezii, 1959

The Wild Man

****

Author's Prologue

In the autumn of 1991, two gay men asked me if I'd been to Numbers. I had just moved to Los Angeles, and my new friends were taking exuberant charge of introducing me to the local turf. "Honey, you've got to go to Numbers. It's one of the best places on the West Coast for a writer to see elegant men and working boys."

For a while, the three of us stood at the bar, having a drink and discreetly tracking that night's re-invention of the sex industry. In the mirrored walls and ceilings, men's greed and men's need were xeroxed into millions. The sellers were young and perfect nobodies — old enough to be in a place that sold liquor, expert enough to look sun-splashed indoors at midnight. All they needed was a shower, a dash of after-shave, clean jeans, and fingers run through palomino hair. The buyers were some-bodies, but decidedly imperfect. They needed designer slacks, brand-name cologne, gym membership and a deep breath to get themselves to this establishment on Sunset Boulevard. Agreements made, buyer and seller departed for a more private venue.

At around 1 a.m., an older Hispanic man came in alone, cutting through all those healthy Anglos with a purposeful limp that he didn't try to hide. His eyes searched the throng warily. His gaze was that of an old soldier, or an ex-convict, or a war refugee of yesteryear. Yet his seamed handsome face revealed such a self-possession and dignity, that every other gaze in the place pulled away from the perfect boys, and veered to him.

The newcomer's face was vaguely familiar. But I couldn't remember what movie or news flash I'd seen him in.

The moment he took one of the best booths, a Latino waiter was at his elbow. I cocked my ear to hear their voices. To my surprise, the new customer was speaking Spanish with that lisping dialect that turns the Spanish hero El Cid into "El Thith". The lisp might have stamped him as Peruvian or Colombian upper class, but something in his enunciation told me he was from Castile, ancient homeland of the lisp. As a young working journalist, I had spent the 1960s in and out of Spain, when that country was still ruled by the fascist regime of Generalísimo Franco that took power in 1939. I had lived in Santander, in northern Castile, so I spoke Spanish with that same lisp.

The Castilian was in his mid-50s, about five foot nine, with the arthritic grace of an old leopard. His close-cut grey curls, and sloe eyes, and sun-bronzed skin, all had a steely gleam. He was that quintessential Iberian hybrid, with a millennium of war and trade roiling in his blood — Roman, Arab, Berber, Sephardic Jew. But right now he wore a dark conservative English suit. His right little finger flashed a gold pinky ring with an ornamental bezel where a cabuchon gem was missing. Diplomat? Businessman? The clothes said he was upper class, or pretended to it. In Spain you can never judge by clothes alone. His were several years out of date — he either didn't care about fashion, or couldn't afford new ones.

That face — hadn't I seen it in the Spanish press long ago?

I questioned the Latino bartender, switching to Los Angeles Spanish, no lisp.

"*Sí,* I know him," the bartender replied in the singsong Spanish of northern Mexico. His own sloe eyes rested impassively on the customer. Most Mexicans hate the lisp — to them, it is the accent of arrogant invaders who raped, enslaved and murdered their Indian ancestors. "The Spanish Don. We don't know his name. When he comes, it's usually on Wednesday. He buys dinner for some boy, and then he always leaves alone."

So I sent the waiter back to the Don's booth with a message. That the *señora* at the bar had overheard him speaking Castilian. That she was a journalist who had lived in his country. If the moment was not inconvenient, she and her friends would buy a drink for him and his companion.

The Don glanced over at me, hesitated, then nodded his head.

In a moment, we were seated in his booth.

When he learned that my Iberian beat had included bull-fighting, his eyes sparkled with amusement. For a moment there, he pegged me as a foreign camp-follower of the bulls. But by the next drink he had to unpeg me. I'd grown up on a big cattle ranch, so fighting cattle had always fascinated me. The Don agreed — he thought that *Bos ibericus* was the most wonderful of wild animals. Did I know that *Bos* once roamed free across the Iberian peninsula and southern France?

As the Spanish Don unbent a little, we chatted for half an hour. He was a good coffee-house talker — a human species almost extinct in the U.S. His dry wit, his power to say a lot with a few words, beguiled all three of us. But he didn't volunteer his name, and we didn't ask. Shortly we excused ourselves, so the Don could get on with his evening.

The following Wednesday, overcome with curiosity, I wondered if he'd be at Numbers again. Carrying a copy of my best-known book about gay life, I dropped by the club at midnight. The Don was there, having dinner with a new blond beauty. When he saw me at the bar, he sent the waiter to invite me over.

"Woman, what kind of lovers are you seeking here?" he teased, with the smile of a Spanish fox.

"My lovers are good stories," I smiled, returning an American coyote grin. "What are *you* doing here, man?"

"I walk," he said. "One foot in front of the other."

The hard-eyed boy ate hungrily, while his client smoked a cigar and talked with me about Spanish wildlife. We spoke English, so the boy could understand. We discussed the wild animals of Spain — ibex, chamois, boar, red deer, lynx, and wild cattle. My new acquaintance had an idea that would seem radical to the traditional Spaniards I had known. He thought that the *toro bravo* *, the wild bull, should be returned to its wild state, and no longer be killed in the ring. He had heard of American reserves where buffalo ranged free, though he had been so busy that he had never seen a buffalo herd yet. He spoke feelingly of the industrial ruin of his wild Spain, of the wild places of the world. He talked about how state religions speed up that ruin, because they teach reverence for a set of rules, but no reverence for the Earth.

"The war against wild animals and against the Earth is a terrible symbol of the war against human individuality," he said.

At this point, the boy's eyes softened. He mentioned that he had hiked in the Tetons and seen a few mountain goats. The beauty had made his heart falter.

"Yes, I would like," said the Castilian softly, "to see some buffalo."

It was almost closing time. The boy's eyes hardened again, and met the eyes of his client. Next on the agenda was a motel or apartment where he'd service this old raider in whatever way was demanded. Young men like this one went for $200. The under-age ones who worked the street went for $50 — or less, if the hour was late.

The Castilian hauled two 100-dollar bills out of his wallet.

"Here," he said. "From someone who used to get $10,000 a trick. Put this to the acting classes you say you need. Next time I see you, you'd better be able to tell me you're being serious about a career."

He riveted the boy with those merciless eyes of his. In the booth next to us, two gay men were arguing about Bill Clinton's chances to escape investigation of his womanizing.

"Ten thousand dollars a trick?" The boy's hustler cool was melting.

"Promise me you'll do this. Beauty fades quicker than you think. Do you swear this? Word of honor?"

"I...uh...I swear." The young man wasn't used to talk of honor.

"Good. Off with you now. I have to talk to this lady."

The boy walked out alone, with the bills in his hand. At the door, light glanced off his perfect sunlit hair as he threw a puzzled look over his shoulder. Then he stuffed the bills in his jeans pocket, and plunged away into the Hollywood night.

I stared at my new acquaintance. Coming from a macho man of his culture, his remark about turning tricks was astounding. Surely he was talking in symbols.

"What are you...some kind of morals crusader?" I asked, as I gave him my card, and my book.

The Spanish Don just chuckled, pocketed my card and flipped curiously through the book. Since he still hadn't told me his name, I hoped to learn it by a ruse. Getting out my pen, I said, "How would you like me to autograph it?"

"Just say, To a friend from Spain," he said.

Two weeks later, my phone rang, and I heard his familiar voice. *Sí, sí,* he had read the book. Would I meet him for dinner that Wednesday evening at Cafe Boheme? My journalist antennae were twitching. Something told me that there was an interesting story here.

This time no boy was tagging along. We had dropped the formal *usted,* with that speed of Republican egalitarianism that I had found lingering even in fascist Spain, and were calling each other by the familiar *tú.* I was Paty or Patrí, not Patricia.

"You have chosen an unusual subject for a woman reporter," he said as we looked at the menus.

"Men write about men. Men write about women. Women write about women. Not many women write about men. Especially gay men. I think my perspective is needed."

"You must have men friends who trust you…who tell you their secret things."

As we ate, the conversation was still general — about the international shock-wave that the U.S. gay and lesbian movement had set off. He said little about himself. But he spoke of his country as one where state religion had existed for so long that, in some of its citizens, the human heart became the state. "In such a country," he said drily, "these citizens no longer need an Inquisition to tell them to burn *maricones*. **
The people themselves wear the hood of Inquisition, and believe that God has told them to wear it. And those who tear off the hood, find that their skin comes off with it. Yes, yes, Franco is dead and we have a democratic government...for now. But the Old Catholics have not given up."

He spoke of his country as a laboratory where the most violent human and political extremes could be intelligently studied, even tracked like a hurricane.

"Your American civil war was terrible, Paty, but not as total as ours. Our entire country was destroyed. The enemy took our greatest poet, Lorca, and killed him with two bullets up his ass because he was gay. You must imagine that kind of death being inflicted in public on Walt Whitman. But the United States is catching up to us...you too are becoming that kind of dreadful laboratory for your Old Protestants."

As the waiter brought our espresso coffee, he said:

" Many Americans think of my country as backward. Oh yes, oxen still plow in a few rural areas! But we are ahead of the United States…five hundred years ahead…into the great experiment. The one of learning whether a modern state religion can control every citizen and every family. It is no accident that Fernando and Isabella chose the ox yoke as their symbol five hundred years ago, when they established state religion in our country."

"But the wild bull wears no yoke," I said.

"Exactly."

This was when the Castilian finally gave me his card.

"My apologies for being so cautious. It is an old habit, from a lifetime of fear. My family and I have a ranch near Escondido," he said. "As a writer, you must come and see what we are doing there — for the wildlife."

His card said:

Antonio Escudero
Rancho Diana
14144 Camino Los Ciervos
Valley Center, California

"Your name sounds familiar," I said to him.

"No doubt."

"Escudero... There was Antonio Escudero, the matador."

He paused a beat before answering. "I am he."

"Well, I saw you in the ring many times! I traveled the country to see Diego Puerta, El Viti, Jaime Ostos...and you."

Antonio chuckled. "You had good taste in toreros."

"When did you come to the United States?"

"In 1969."

So Antonio had left Spain before Franco died. He and his family must have been political refugees. Franco's regime, and the Old Catholics of Spain, had a hatred of homosexuals that was equal to that of the German Nazis, but rooted more in Old Catholic terror of heresy. It was said that Generalisímo Franco had personally seen to the ruthless elimination of "vice" among cadets in Spanish military schools. One of his most faithful long-time ministers, Serrano Suñer, had fallen from power because of Franco's anger at a gay scandal involving Suñer's secretary.

After dinner, Antonio and I migrated around North and West Hollywood in his BMW. We had drinks at one bar after another — a social habit that I remembered from Madrid in the 1960s. I was enjoying Antonio's company, feeling myself sliding from "disinterested journalist" to "friend". He was one of those gay men who understand and appreciate women in a way that one would wish in straight men — even fight and die for women if they had to. Anything but sleep with them. Often I think that perfect friendship between the genders can only happen between a gay woman and a gay man. And he had a dry humor, affectionately tweaking my feminism by calling me *muñeca* (doll).

My mind was casting back to the mid-60s.

Antonio Escudero's young image was still sharp in my memory. While he was never an international celebrity like Manuel Benítez "El Cordobés," he was considered by some to be the best "classic torero," and had his fanatic following. Others would argue, saying that El Viti or Diego Puerta was the best of the "classics." A few critics accused Antonio of being technically brilliant and boring. But sometimes he caught fire with a splendid rage that transcended technique. I had seen him on a couple of those afternoons when he edged his leg terrifyingly close to the horn. He was gored often — one of those called "cannon fodder" by the fans. For all I knew, he sent the boys home alone because he was impotent from old wounds. The fans called him *El Bravo* — Wild Man, wild as the bull.

Contrary to what Americans think, the word *bravo* does not mean "brave." It means "wild", like the wild cattle used in the ring. It also means a temperament, a rage against captivity — a kind of savage will that never steps back from pain and punishment, ever seeking a way towards freedom.

I also remembered Antonio as a scion of some threadbare clan of minor aristocracy that clung to a tiny estate near Toledo. The Franco regime had favored bluebloods. How did he become a refugee from Old Catholic fascism? Why was it better for him in the U.S., where our Old Protestants warred on homosexuals?

"You started by fighting on horseback, didn't you?" I asked. "Then you switched to doing it on foot."

By now, we were at Capote's, drinking a brandy. He smiled sadly, and said: "My father was a cavalry officer in the Nationalist army, but he missed most of the civil war because of a wound. He taught me that a nobleman of today must earn his place in society by doing something useful. When I was at military school and told him that I hated the army, that I wanted to be a torero, he was surprisingly agreeable. But he said I had to do it on horseback, like a gentleman. I also had to get a university degree, and retire from the ring at 30, into a useful profession."

He paused, remembering, then went on:

"I made the promise, but my young mind was waking up, and I didn't care to be a gentleman. I had a great passion to end the arrogance that has made Spaniards so hated in other countries. One day when I was 18, I jumped off my horse, and killed the bull on foot. My father almost disinherited me on the spot...to the delight of my brother Paco, who was next in line. But before my father died, he came to respect my decision. You see...he loved me. And in spite of our differences, as I grew more liberal over the years, I loved my father. My greatest dread was that my parents would find out about me. Not because of shame. I have grown past shame. But because of the horrible censure and sneering that they would have suffered if my fact had been known in Spain."

"You saw being a torero as *useful?*"

"At the time. Very useful...for my heart."

"And your university degree?"

"Biology. The family's land had been ruined. My father knew it had to be rescued. He knew that our agriculture, our management of our country's resources needed to be modernized. But he was old, and lacked the will to do it. Study was hard...I had to do it between contracts. But I finally graduated."

Now we were at The Palms, jostled by gay women, a few men, as we drank another brandy, trying to talk over disco noise. "So a torero says the bull should go back to the wild," I yelled.

"Exactly." He was yelling back.

8

"For humane reasons?" I probed relentlessly.

"Humanity to animals helps people be human to each other."

"You *are* a rebel."

"So you lived in Santander. Did you happen to see me there in May 1969?"

"I did. You had been out of the ring for a while."

"For a year. I had been badly gored."

"I remember that afternoon. You stood my hair on end."

"Ah…" he said softly. "You saw me on the day I met Juan Diano."

For some reason, my hair stood on end again. In the disco, the D.J. slid one song into another. Against that background of pumping young bodies, Antonio's stern profile softened, his eyes misted, and he blinked once. Suddenly that look of distant death moved to the front of his eyes. Spanish men aren't afraid to cry openly. That I knew. Unlike American men, they consider that manhood can be enhanced by manly tears.

Now we were outside, walking along the Santa Monica "strip". Young lesbians and gay boys in street fashions jostled us in their eager hunt for partners and thrills. Many of them were Chicano or Latino or Mexican-American kids, brushing past this older man who spoke their language but had grown up in such a different universe. We were unnoticed, two elders absorbed in their talk. Antonio rubbed away his tears, and took my arm.

I hardly dared to ask the big question. We were speaking of things that happened a quarter-century ago. The world had seen massive changes since the mid-60s, not the least of which was something that our government termed "the AIDS epidemic."

"Is Juan...still alive?" I asked.

The shadow was in Antonio's eyes again. "You must visit Rancho Diana," he said. "And I will tell you about Juan."

Maybe Juan Diano was dead. Maybe he had died in a Franco prison. Clearly something terrible had happened. I felt a wrench of sadness, as if I had known this Juan personally. My emotion was definitely a friend feeling, not a detached journalist kind of feeling.

It was one of those autumn days when the weatherman predicts a santa ana, and Californians nervously await the fabled winds.

At first glance, Rancho Diana was not spectacular. My pickup passed an ordinary stretch of irrigated pasture, perhaps 200 acres, with a game-park type of fence around it. The pasture looked grazed, but no animals were in sight along the creek, fringed with brush in yellow leaf.

My eyes followed the stream back to a canyon in the boulder-strewn hills. As I parked near the barn, four half-bred Arabian horses raised their heads in the pipe corrals. Antonio was in a corral alone, wearing faded Levis and a straw Stetson. Using a shovel and wheelbarrow, he was scooping up horse turds. A grey horse followed him, mooching at his hip pockets for treats. The ex-torero looked like an old Chicano rancher doing his chores. He came to greet me pushing the wheelbarrow. Today the limp wasn't too noticeable, as he gave me a warm Spanish-style hug and a kiss on the cheek.

"Hello, Paty," he said. "The rest of the family are out doing things," he said. "You will meet them later."

Family? Was he still halfway in the closet, then? I saw no bicycles, basketballs or other kid clutter about.

"No children, Antonio?"

"The land is my child."

As he introduced me to the horses, we were pestered by two brindle greyhounds — retired racing dogs, he said. He'd adopted them so they wouldn't be destroyed. California quail were everywhere, running between the horses' feet, pecking tamely at grain.

"I have learned to appreciate foreign animals," he said drily, scratching the horses' ears, petting necks.

The subtle spirit of this place touched me. One hears many stereotypical things about the Spanish — how proud they are, how stubborn, quixotical, cruel, passionate, enigmatic, etc. One seldom hears about Spanish love of land.

Rancho Diana's buildings were early 1900s stucco structures, built in a former olive orchard. Most of the olive trees had been bulldozed for pasture by previous owners, but one belt of 400-year-old olives still shaded the stables. I suddenly realized what a lure those trees might have been, to Spaniards looking for California real estate. Well-watered young fruit trees sheltered a kitchen garden overflowing with the last vibrant vegetables and herbs. At feeders everywhere, hummingbirds swarmed like bees. Autumn roses bent heavy along the walks. Clearly the family worked like dogs to keep the place so beautiful.

Then, as the morning got hotter, a herd of magnificent elk-like animals with reddish coats came drifting out of the brush by the creek. They moved toward the canyon. Most were cows, calves and young males. Among them was a mature stag, with vast pink antlers shedding the last of summer velvet. He stopped to pound his antlers in some bushes, cleaning them more.

"You know what those beasts are, of course," Antonio smiled proudly.

*"Huuy...*I have not seen red deer since I was in Spain. Where did you get them?"

"Surplus from an Argentine hunting park. A bloodline that we don't have in Spain now. Rancho Diana has a California permit as a private wildlife facility. We scour the world for any Spanish wildlife that's out there...zoos, dealers. From here, once we know the animals are healthy, they go back to Spain. That bull has world-class horns. But of course we will never shoot him. We have a pair of Spanish lynx here too...the pens are over there."

At the tree-shaded lynx pens, we watched the two cats padding restlessly around in glimmering dappled light, their golden eyes watching us warily, stubby tails curled over their backs.

"So," I said, " toreros change careers after they retire from the ring. Domecq raises Andalusian horses. El Cordobés went into real estate. El Viti and Mondeño wanted to be monks. Dominguín does film importing. And you are... a conservationist?"

"Time for shade and wine, *muñeca,* " he said.

So we walked through more glimmering shadows, to the stucco house that was couched like a deer in a dense grove of eucalyptus and live oak. In the hallway, hung a framed newspaper clipping from a 1975 Los Angeles *Times*. It read:

SPANISH LEADER DEAD AT 83.
*Dateline: Madrid. Francisco Franco Bahamonde
died today after a long illness...demonstrations
by left-wing factions filled the streets of the
capital, demanding...*

The cool silent rooms were modern, Californian — cane furniture, a few jute rugs. The family's tastes in art ran to the inexpensive, with young Latino painters and Sierra Club wildlife prints. I did not see any Spanish antiques, nor a single memento of the *fiesta brava****. No stuffed bull-heads or swords hanging on the wall. Not a single photograph of Antonio in the ring, doing one of his trademark passes. One bullfight critic had called him "the Goya of the cape."

In the living room, I stopped before a carved Mexican chest, where a small framed picture of the Blessed Virgin stood — candles burning around Her, roses dropping their petals before Her. It appeared to be a photograph of a late-medieval painting. She was seated between the horns of the sickle moon, guarded by a cow and a bull, surrounded by a forest teeming with deer, boars and other wild animals. Beside Her were framed old photographs of two pretty Spanish women.

"Who are the ladies in the photos?" I asked.

"My sister and my ex-wife."

"I thought all toreros prayed to the Virgin of Macarena."

Antonio was pouring two glasses of California chardonnay. "Toreros pray to whatever Virgin keeps them out of the hospital," he said drily.

As he handed me the glass, he added, "That is Our Lady of the Mercies. She belongs to the Escuderos. Every afternoon of bulls for nine years, I prayed to Her in my hotel room. The times I landed in the hospital, it was not Her fault."

"In your house I see nothing else from those times," I said.

He handed me the glass of wine. "We were yanked out of the jaw of Spain like a tooth," he said.

As he sank down on the sofa, he winced a little.

"The old wound?" I asked. "The one you got in...Jaén, was it?"

"It was in Écija," he said. "I still have to walk a step at a time. Old wounds...yes. *Cornadas* of the heart too.**** I was one of those men who wasn't gay. The guy who obliged me... who took it like a woman...he was the gay one."

Antonio's discreet sharing of his story stretched over the next two months. I didn't dare use a tape recorder. Going home, I would work like a dog to make notes in my best English translation of his words.

Intimate biography of the kind that Americans buy so avidly did not exist in traditional Iberian letters. Even the post-Franco openness, the fact that Spanish literature and film and pornography were now the most outrageous in Europe, had not affected Antonio's reticence. Now and then he would be astonishingly frank. Other times he reared battlements of stone in front of certain things. Often I had to lay siege to his hints, to scale the castle wall and try to glimpse what had really happened. Antonio's story, as it emerged on paper, was palaeontology in prose. He gave me a heel-bone and a bit of skull. From it I reconstructed a life, and a love.

Escudero knew that it was his function in Spanish society to be a lightning-rod for the libidos of both men and women. No wonder that, on his most powerful afternoons in the ring, the sand melted into smoking glass where he walked. I began to understand why he spoke of whoring for $10,000 a trick — the equivalent in dollars of his fee for a single appearance. "They all got to fuck me with their eyes," he said. A nation had publicly exalted him for his power over both sexes, yet some had condemned him to a living death for possessing the secret of that power over men. A nation that, for an almost unbroken 500 years, had condemned every form of open sexual expression except the cold begetting of children.

As he shared the story, I felt dread, rage, surges of tears. How was I going to keep my professional distance? Everything about this story challenged things I had believed about love, relationships, loyalty, family. As a writer I had always framed a conflict between individual freedom and the repressive state. In Antonio's story, the family itself had became the state.

The way he said "Juan" reminded me of the loving way that Spanish people say the names of rivers, in that land where water is so revered. Short names, ancient ones, like Tajo, Arga, Duero, Genil, Deva, Ebro, Pas. To speak of Juan was to speak of water, trees, light and shadow, the Earth herself.

"Juan," he said with hoarse tenderness. "Juan…my wild one. Wilder than me."

Bravo — wild, as in wild animal.

**Maricones* — homosexuals.

***Fiesta brava* — translates literally as "wild fiesta." A common way for Spaniards to refer to bullfighting.

****Cornada* — wound caused by a bull horn.

Antonio's Story

1

My second bull of the afternoon fell over on his side, with my sword in his heart. He was finished, and so was I.

By then I'd killed almost 500 bulls in my 9-year career. Yet I remember that moment and that bull, because I was in such a shocking state of mind. He was an ugly bull, black and white pinto, with horns like little bananas. My sword-hilt cast a shadow across his bloody shoulders. As the light died in his eyes, his legs still vibrated, and his tail flailed as he voided helplessly, the runny shit of death. The wet tongue trailed from his wet muzzle, caked with sand.

It had been a quick, clean kill — my best since the goring in Écija. The curving blade had cut the aorta behind his heart. No blood showed at his mouth, but a hot spurt had jetted up the blade, bathing the inside of my sleeve. That was the way it was supposed to happen — red spurt into satin sleeve, the perfect symbol of making love. It was what my fans expected of me... what I demanded of myself.

Now, only now, the fierce trembling hit me.

It was that last Sunday in May 1969 on the north coast of Spain. Springtime coolness should have refreshed me and given me strength — sea breezes and mountain airs, there in the green Spain. Dry Spain was my motherland — the central plateau, where fields already fried in African breezes at that time of year. But today the cool weather hadn't helped at all. My satin suit of lights weighed on me like a suit of armor, and sweat stung my eyes now. I blinked, trying to see.

"Two ears!" "No, the tail!" "The tail!" Fans were arguing about what trophies I should get.

The worst thing was my bad leg — it felt nerveless and spastic, and hurt like the devil. But I didn't dare show weakness. Each step I'd made in front of the bull had been fiercely willed. As I pulled my sword out of the carcass, the light weapon felt heavy as destiny. I didn't dare wipe my face on my sleeve. Standing there alone, with everybody's fluttering handkerchiefs dizzying me, the rich folks on the shady side of the bullring and poorer folks on the sunny side, I noticed that my hand was empty. My sword-man had taken the weapon from my hand. Was time playing tricks on me?

I felt alone, and naked.

A torero does what he does while dressed from head to foot in heavy silk and embroidery. In a world inured to nude celebrities and pornography, I have my way with a crowd without even opening my fly. At most, the crowd gets to see a bit of skin through torn clothes, if the bull catches me. They may see me vulnerable — wounded, in shock, carried to the infirmary in other men's arms. At worst they see the occasional matador dead in a black coffin and the traditional blaze of candles. But naked? Never. Juan Belmonte* had scandalized everybody by posing nude for a sculptor, back in the bad old days of the Second Republic, but few cared to remember he'd done that. So why did I feel so naked that day?

Now, up in the officials' balcony, the mayor was signaling for trophies. The grinning ringman went to work with his knife, and held the severed things in front of me. Two ears and the tail.

Pull yourself together, Antonio, I told myself.

From bleachers and balconies of the bullring, the crowd's roar poured over me, suffocating me like a sandstorm. It was their first afternoon of bulls that year, and they were eager for excitement. For once, they were giving me the crazy roar, like they'd done for Manolo Benítez on the previous bull. My sensational colleague from Córdoba had cut two ears and tail too, and the crowd had gone mad. Now they had gone even crazier for me.

"Give him the whole bull," some guy was screaming.

Two ears and the tail, man. It might rate a few seconds on the TV news. The EFE wire service would say *Antonio Escudero also triumphed* in smaller type, under the big headline EL CORDOBÉS TRIUMPHED IN SANTANDER. God knows I needed publicity. My comeback had fallen flat so far. The goring in Écija 13 months ago had taken more out of me than I'd thought. The comeback started at Jaén — I was terrible there. Then the Sevilla fair, where I got one ear. Sevilla fans were exacting — one ear was a major concession. Then the San Isidro fair in Madrid last week, where I felt frozen and couldn't deliver. The Madrid fans whistled and threw beer bottles at me. Every afternoon, I was as depressed and tired as now.

And there were questions haunting me. How long would the bad leg obey me? Could I stop the downdrift of my career? My profession was my lover, my Muse. I was losing my one passion and inspiration — the only thing that I had ever been able to possess and adore completely.

Step forward, leg.

That's it. Step again.

Today, from somewhere, not even Earth but from somewhere in the universe, I'd pulled the old *bravo* rage back into my heart, and willed the leg to work. Desperate and angry, facing a slow bull with little banana horns that would allow me to do some filigrees, I gave the crowd everything. The stripper takes off her clothes, but the torero takes off his safety margin. I had stood a few centimeters from the horn, and held the little cloth behind me, and provoked the bull with my thigh. Only at the last second, as the pinto monster lurched into motion, did I move the cloth forward to catch his eye and pull that banana past my thigh, letting the blood on his shoulders rub off on my fly. Even the bananas can kill you. Like the movie stunt-man, the torero must calculate his chances intelligently. Chaos always lurks in every bull.

How much longer could I do this? I was almost 30, a full matador for nine years. Already too old and too rich to feel the hunger for bulls any longer. Other hungers gnawed me now. The hunger to stay off the horn, for sure. The hunger to retire, and spend all my time improving my land. The hunger to enrich my life. To know the world better — to travel more outside of Spain. To see more of what people were doing out there in the great world.

And to feed the big hunger. *That* one.

Now I threw back my head and forced myself to stand proud and wild-looking. To look very torero. Wasn't that why they wanted me here in the ring? To be the symbol for all those ecstatic, shouting men? To be the dream for the women? But I wasn't in the ring for other people...was I? No. I was here for myself. I was here because of the hunger. One of the hungers, anyway. The craving for a destiny of my own — a life of risk and freedom, instead of the suffocatingly safe heritage of the Escuderos.

My trembling hands held up the trophies to the crowd.

"Wild man! Macho! *Machote túuuu!*"

The loud yell came from a young woman right in the front row in the shade. A girl of these yeah-yeah times. Her embarrassed friends were trying to shut her up.

Her bold shout, the kind of language that only men were supposed to use, was as shocking to the old folks in the bullring as the "yeah yeah" of rock and roll music that now invaded our borders. The Beatles weren't allowed to perform in Spain, but their smuggled recordings were heard everywhere.

Now the horse-team was skidding that pinto hulk out of the ring. Shortly, in the municipal slaughterhouse next door, a crew of men would hoist it by the hind legs, skin it and gut it, saw it in half along the spine. Tomorrow morning, in the municipal market, butchers would advertise wild bull meat. Bars would offer appetizers to their male customers — bits of fried testicle on toothpicks. A few yeah-yeah women would daringly nibble them.

Behind the barrier, the tanned faces and narrowed eyes of my crew questioned me. Bigotes and Manolillo Vandilaz, brothers in their 30s, two of the best subalterns in the business, failed matadors who were good at rescuing me with their capes. Santí and Fermín, the picadors, just as good in their own specialties — broad faces taut in shadow under their big tasseled hats. Braulio, my sword-man and valet. They could see how I'd strained. Beside them was Isaías Eibar, my manager and lawyer. He was worried too.

Now it was time to make the victory round of the ring.

Jesus, my right leg really hurt. I'd probably pulled a nerve when I extended my body doing that last breast-pass before the kill. In Écija the horn had entered my upper thigh, torn the artery, penetrated my pelvis, damaged nerves. If Manolillo hadn't yanked off his tie for a tourniquet, I would have bled to death before they got me to the bullring infirmary. People had stood in line outside to give blood — eight transfusions. The fact was, the doctors had wanted to amputate my leg, but I screamed at them and Isaías screamed at them till they gave me a chance. I was in the Sanitorio de Toreros for four months. Then a year of recovery and therapy, even some help from a soccer trainer, to get back in the ring. And the effort to free myself of need for morphine. Even now I sometimes hungered for the white goddess of ease.

So I motioned to Bigotes and Manolillo. When they entered the ring, I put my arms across their strong shoulders. These two subalterns had campaigned with me for 8 years, sat at my bedside, helped me get off morphine. They were like brothers. I loved them the way I never loved my one blood brother. Everyone would think I was honoring them for their good work that day. And I was. But the hug had a second purpose: I could lean on them.

Walk, Antonio. One satin shoe in front of the other.
Make the damned leg work.

Slowly we three made our way around the ring, from the shade into the sun. I must have been a sight. The suit of lights was a brand new one from the second-best bull tailor in Spain, costing 25,000 pesetas*. Now it was ruined, streaked with blood. And the right sleeve was absolutely soaked. Everybody likes to see that ejaculation of blood on the torero's satin. Except Braulio — he would have a fit. And he would try to clean it because he knew how short of money I was.

As the municipal band was thumping out "El Macario," I threw the trophies up into the seats. One woman put a bloody ear inside her white silk blouse. A German tourist grabbed the pinto tail out of the air, and got green shit on his hand. Men pelted us with cigars. Bigotes thriftily picked up the cigars. Women tore carnations out of their hair, and threw them at my feet. Manolillo picked them up, and I saluted the crowd with the growing bouquet. Toreros are the only Spanish men who dare to carry flowers in public — any other male would find his manhood compromised by the deed.

Then a pair of dainty lace underpants fluttered down. They landed on the sand, right in front of me.

The entire bullring went into a frenzy of lustful delight. Young women screamed like girls did at a Beatles concert in London or New York. Men howled and pounded each other on the back. Ahead, some of the slaughterhouse crew were standing behind the barrier, bellowing innuendos.

"Ass-tounding!"

"They must belong to a cunt-ry miss!"

"Hey, wild man — let's see you cape with these!"

My fans were careful not to yell the real words. Otherwise the police could grab them. In spite of recent liberalization of our Press Law, you still couldn't say the natural, honest words in public. There were many natural little things that men and women couldn't do, like kiss on the street, the way you could in France or Italy. Even men's shorts were still illegal on the Spanish street. Perish the thought that some woman — or even some man — would lust after your bare knees.

Here in the bullring, state police were posted, glowering in their grey uniforms, to make sure that no social crimes were committed here. Right now the Greys were squinting around, trying to locate the monster of depravity who'd thrown the panties. Yet we toreros were allowed to flaunt the bulge of our manhood in these skin-tight satin pants of ours.

Now Manolillo bent over, pants creaking. He had gained a little weight in the year I'd been inactive, and we were always afraid he'd burst his rear seam. Carefully, respectfully, he picked up the panties and gave them to me.

Just then, out of the blur of lewdly laughing men's faces, one of the slaughterhouse men leaned over the barrier.

I noticed him because he was so serious — the only one who wasn't yelling things about the panties. Broad knotted tense shoulders told me he had grown up at hard labor. His bare dirty arm reached out to me, holding a drink in a shot glass. In the shadow of his sunlit blond forelock, his somber blue eyes held mine briefly. Even in my exhausted state, I briefly noticed those eyes. They were blue as wild cornflowers that bloom in summer along lonely Castilian country roads. Yes, he was sad, strangely studying. Envious, maybe. Wishing he was me, probably. I'd seen the look before. I was weary of seeing it.

Then a dark lightning flashed in his eyes, so quickly that only a man like myself could catch it.

Not daring to meet his gaze, I looked down at that powerful naked arm, which was still patiently holding the drink. His skin was nicked by scars, smeared with animal dirt and blood. The veins along his arm were big, like the ones that lace the belly of a large grass-eating animal, a horse or cow.

As I took the glass, our fingers touched. The glass was not too clean, but I didn't care, and swallowed the drink whole. It was *orujo,* the fiery full-proof stuff made from grapeseed that they drink in these northern mountains. When I handed the glass back, I croaked a thanks.

Then, walking on, I forced myself to do the expected thing with the panties. Tucked them inside my jacket, next to my heart.

Another wave of delighted screams went up.

Some toreros make the crowd scream even louder by kissing those panties that fell from heaven. For me, that was going too far. In these changing times, a classic torero like me was supposed to symbolize a grip on tradition. Strange that I stood for that...because in in my heart, I was the king of heretics.

When I got back behind the barrier in the shade, my work was over for the afternoon. The trumpeter blew a fanfare to announce the fifth bull. Fortified by the *orujo,* I stared through the sweat stinging my eyes, as the bull trotted into the ring.

This one had another set of bananas on his head. The rancher bred them that way, so he could sell bulls to the new wave of sensationalists like Manolo Benítez, who had more flash than foundation in their art. This bull was not too eager to get his little horn into anything. An underage overfed animal who charged nice and straight. Benítez could do all kinds of filigrees with him. Naturally he was dangerous anyway. Even the underage bulls carry chaos inside, and they can kill you if you get careless.

Benítez fell on his knees in front of the charging bull, and whirled the cape over his head. It was a *farol,* one of his trademark flashy passes. His Beatles haircut whirled with it.

The crowd was primed by his earlier triumph and mine, and they instantly screamed a tremendous OOOOOOOLÉEEE! that shook the bullring. Listening to them, one would never know that 30 years ago, this convenient municipal structure had been used as a prison camp after the fall of Santander. Republican prisoners were herded into this very ring, and machine-gunned by fascist soldiers sitting in the seats. Somewhere under the layer of new sand we'd walked on, one could probably still find traces of human blood.

Meanwhile, a few people reached down through the railing to pound my shoulder, congratulate me. If I shook hands they'd feel me trembling. So I kept my back turned to them and stared into the ring. Manolo was on his feet now, doing more flashy stuff, passing the banana at a safe distance. The crowd didn't give a fig — he did it with such explosive style.

My manager slipped me a handkerchief. Now that nobody was watching, I could finally mop my streaming face with it.

"Good work," Isaías said.   "Pull yourself together, *hombre*…you look like a boxer who just got KOed."

His hand gave me a comforting fatherly rub on my back. It felt good through all the silk and gold embroidery. For eight years, this barrel-chested old Basque businessman had been my manager, lawyer and second father. When I'd decided on the bulls, my blood father had found me a relentlessly fascist manager, but I ditched that one for Isaías after my father died. Isaías and his delightful wife Teresa — we called her Tere — were blessedly more liberal. My family despised the Eibars, because they were Basque and came up from nothing — their forebears worked in the sardine fleet.

Isaías could feel me trembling through all the tailored layers of torero flummery. The old man said:

"You just got an offer from the Syndicate. Sótano's up there in the third row. He sent a message down."

"So the old bastard remembers that I exist?" I croaked.

Out of the corner of my eye, I could see impresario Miguel Sótano sitting in the second row, smoking a cigar, looking like a dapper gangster in an English-tailored suit that was too tight for him. He was one of the three *grandes* ...controlled a chain of 12 northern bullrings. But I was strangely unexcited at the offer, and didn't want to be seen gawking at Sótano like a kid getting his first major contract. So I grabbed the clay jug of water and spewed a stream between my lips, then over my close-cut hair. Northern water, to cool a dried-out man from the south.

Across the ring, the young slaughterhouse guy was standing apart from his coveralled companions. He was not watching Manolo's fancy cape-work. He seemed to be looking in my direction. I wanted to grab a lady's fan, and ease my parboiled face with a little northern air. But this would be seen as weakness. People would talk.

Isaías still had his mind on business.

"Sótano wants you for Big Week in Bilbao," he said in a low voice. "You'll be substituting for Zamora, who's still out with his wound. Sótano is offering 750. I'm trying to get him up to a mil."

A million pesetas for one afternoon. I had been in the one-million category before, so my comeback was assured. All I had to do now was strain myself more, and more, to keep the momentum going for another 20 afternoons in Spain, plus a few in France and Portugal. Then spend the winter killing bulls all over Mexico and South America. For the first time in my life, that year of future contracts looked terrifying.

"We'll talk about it later," I mumbled.

"Your sleeve, Antonio," came Tere's voice.

.   Through my haze of sweat, my second mother was leaning under the railing, holding out her own lace-trimmed hanky. Tere was sturdy and high-busted as the prow of a Basque fishing trawler, her iron-grey hair twisted into a bun. She had tweaked Spanish social dogma by traveling with her husband and helping with his business. She ran his office, kept his books. The couple had no children. How many times I had prayed to the Virgin that, in our next life, Isaías and Tere would have children and I'd be one of them! I had dedicated the pinto bull to the Eibars, so my glittering parade cape was spread on the balustrade in front of Tere.

Tere took my wrist, discreetly wiping a big clot of blood off my sleeve. Her motherly touch steadied me, and my eyes cleared.

Beside Tere sat my twin sister José, frowning down at me with loving concern. She'd been born first, by five minutes; at moments like these, she always reminded me of her seniority. José was there in Tere's social lee, chaperoned, like a rowboat tied to that stately trawler.

The fact of chaperonage said much about my sister, baptized María Josefina Carmen, known to me as José. She had declined to be a yeah-yeah girl. There was a difference between being yeah-yeah and just being "modern." José had grown out of a brief tomboy time, when she shocked the family by wanting to kill bulls like I did, and was now a respected *moderna.* In a changing Spain where some unmarried girls secretly took the black-market pill smuggled from France, José had never done the unthinkable — declared her sexual freedom. At 30, she still publicly wore the yoke of upper-class restraint — chaperoned even to mass on Sunday. She talked of marriage, and dated men who were acceptable to the family, boredly entertaining an offer or two...and rejecting them. My mother and aunts complained that María Josefina was more finicky about men than they'd ever been. Her Berhayer linen trousers and jacket were safely within the Spanish canons of conservative fashion, considering that in our Mamá's eyes, no decent woman wore those foreign things called "slacks". No reek of yeah-yeah scandal had ever trailed in my sister's perfumed wake.

Only I, her twin, knew the untamed tomboy that still lived deep underground inside her, and the restlessness that drove her lately. To me, she looked like an exiled Egyptian priestess sitting there in a fantastic red wig. Her thick hair was as curly as mine but red — that copper-red Berber hair you still find in Spain, a genetic relic of North African invaders 1500 years ago. Her curls fought the constraints of hairpins, and bushed loose in the humid sea air.

A few years ago, José started doing *moderna* things that threw the family into turmoil. She shouted at our mother that she wanted to do something with her life. In defiance of Spanish law, she left our Toledo home still unmarried and went to Madrid to find work. If our father had been alive, he could have had her arrested. As the senior male now, it was my place to stop her, but I didn't.

Next, José had stepped into one of Spain's most macho professions — journalism. Her pedigree, and some string-pulling by me, got her hired at the monarchist daily *ABC*. Here, she did another *moderna* thing, and became the first female bullfight columnist in history. *ABC's* old columnist had died, and José submitted samples of her work to the editor-in-chief. It was so good that he couldn't resist. Besides, he was a liberal monarchist who didn't care for Old Catholicism. Having a female reporter was a good way to tweak the nose of the regime.

At first, toreros, managers and impresarios had laughed at José. But these days they trembled when she sat down at her little Olivetti portable typewriter in her hotel room. José knew bulls. She didn't need to take bribes because she was already rich. She made open hints about corruption in the fiesta, about horns being "shaved" for some of the yeah-yeah toreros. Best of all, José knew how to sting with scorpion wit. On afternoons when I was bad, she even stung me. Many people bought *ABC* just to howl with laughter over her latest barbs. In fact, her willingness to sting her own brother won her a reputation for incorruptible honesty. By traveling around Spain in company with Tere, whose reputation was without stain, my sister had kept her own reputation shiny.

Right now, José knew enough to see the strain in my eyes. She leaned under the railing, and I could smell her favorite French perfume, Le Dé.

"Dig your toes in," she said.

I managed a smile, and squeezed her hand. She had always said this when we were children climbing the mulberry tree by the house, and my fingers were slipping and I was about to fall.

On José's left, sat Paco, my younger brother. He was 29, slick and slender and excruciatingly well-dressed, with his air of history professor and curator of family glory and his job as secretary to the Minister of Culture and Education. A solid paterfamilias, he was raising his three sons to be as insufferable as himself. Paco was the type of Spanish historian who insisted that the Inquisition killed only a few people. He felt that the patrimony of the Escuderos was wasted on me, and prayed nightly for a bull to kill me so he could step into my shoes. Failing that, Paco wanted me to retire, get married and go into politics.

Now Paco sat edged away from José, as if he was afraid that her *moderna* air would rub off on him. He smiled down at me, showing his pointed white teeth, which gave him a ferret look.

"Two ears closer to marriage," he said.

Manolo Benítez' picador was in the ring now, on a well-padded cart-horse. Impassively the big man waited for the charge with lance ready. As the bull slammed against the padding, the picador sank the iron point down into that swollen neck-muscle. Feeling the iron, the bull slammed the big horse against the barrier like it was a feather pillow. As the iron kept jabbing, the bull's rage grew — he might be young and stuffed with corn, but he was truly *bravo,* and kept fighting the pic as blood bubbled out of his hump.

I remember thinking, at that moment, that you can't cowe the wild ones. Neither the wild animal, nor the wild human. No, *señor.* The deeper you push the iron into them, the harder they fight you.

Not too soon for me, the *corrida* was over. Carrying our parade capes, we three matadors trudged across the ring and out to the gate, amid a final storm of applause and thrown flowers.

Outside, in the shadow of the bullring wall, fans crowded at our cars. The biggest, noisiest crowd jostled the Mercedes sedan belonging to El Cordobés. I saw Manolo's yeah-yeah hairdo go bobbing wearily through the crowd. From here Manolo would go to the airport and his private plane, back to his home in Córdoba. Manolo was the only torero who could afford a private plane. The rest of us still traveled around the country by car, the old way.

A batallion of Greys stood nervously. Their rubber truncheons were ready to crack skulls. Their eyes shifted this way and that.

These were confusing, volatile times. As a former Republican stronghold, Santander was seething with rumors. The Basque left-wing separatists, the ETA, planned a new bombing to avenge some arrests last week. The Christian Democrats were wringing their hands. A new right-wing terrorist group, the CYS, was forming. Its full name was Caballeros del Yugo Sagrado, or Knights of the Sacred Yoke. The ox yoke was adopted by Fernando and Isabella after their "cleansing" of Spain. They lived by the New Testament teaching "my yoke is sweet." That symbol had been revived by the Falange, our fascist movement, which had controlled Spain since our long civil war broke out in 1936. Now the yoke was CYS. Anything that smacked of foreign ways and foreign immorality was hateful to the CYS. They seemed to be more rightist than the Falange. Judging by their flyers, printed on somebody's old mimeograph and scattered around Santander, the CYS felt that our dictator, General Franco, had gone soft in his old age.

These days, most rumors started with the question "What will happen when *He* dies?" Franco was old and sick — at public functions his hands trembled and he often nodded off. The rumor was that he might restore the monarchy. Prince Juan Carlos de Borbón might return to the throne. But five centuries of state religion, broken by two short-lived Republics, was finally ending in revulsion against official religion. Many people's patience with the Catholic Church, and its indifference to human rights, was wearing thin now. Since the Civil War, slump in church attendance had been drastic. Spain, it was said, was ceasing to be Catholic. Would our country tolerate a restoration of the throne?

To rescue the situation, Franco and his governing coalition had liberalized a little. Even the Spanish bishops were belatedly seeing that it was time for the Church to lighten up. But demands for faster change were piling up, thunderous as *olés* — workers, students, women, even outlaw priests. So Franco was clamping down again. Political arrests were up. The trial of leftist leader Julián Grimau had shocked the world. Grimau had been tortured and thrown out of a window before he was finally executed. No matter. The CYS was scattering leaflets announcing their intention to restore Spain to her "primal moral destiny".

"Manolo! Ayyyy, Manolo!" fans were shrieking.   Hands jerked the gold tassels from Benítez' jacket.

"Shit...this might get nasty," said Isaías in my ear.

Next to my Cordoban colleague's car was my own dusty black

Mercedes, a 1957 model. Ahead of us was my youngest picador, Santí Hijuelos. Like a bodyguard, Santí used his broad shoulders to bull a path through the mob. Behind me, Bigotes was trying to divert people by giving away the cigars that he'd picked up.

Just as we reached my Mercedes, a man's strong voice at my elbow said, "Antonio?"

I turned. It was that slaughterhouse worker.

The owner of those blue eyes had fought his way out here, to waylay me. Now he was so close at my elbow that I could smell the cheap tobacco of his half-smoked cigarette. He looked to be in his late 20s. He was a few centimeters taller than me — those extraordinary eyes stared straight down into mine. His blunt, open face was not exactly handsome, but its intense expression held my attention. He wore no wedding ring. Probably he helped his father support a large family, and this was his second or third job. Probably he wanted a hand-out. It was not a good moment to approach me, but men who were poor and desperate seldom thought about timing. My valet always had a bank note ready for these moments, and now Braulio pulled it out.

But the slaughterman drew himself up proudly, took the cigarette from his lips.

"No," he said. "I don't want a single *pesetuca.*"

He spoke a quaint kind of Castilian, the Montanese dialect of these northern mountains. His race was our northernmost strain, a mingling of Celt and Visigoth. Surely his cantankerous pagan mountaineer ancestors had rolled rocks down on the Arab troops at the battle of Covadonga — and probably a few rocks on Christian troops too. Under his faded beret, that straight hair was the dark gold of ripened cornsilks in his native fields of La Montaña. He had shaved early that morning, but already a bronze stubble glinted on his jaws.

His refusal of money was odd. Probably he was a refugee from some dying mountain village. The kind of rural bachelor who went looking for work in the city and sent most of his pay home to relatives.

Braulio insisted, holding out the bank note. But the slaughterman looked into my eyes with that fierce, anxious stare.

"Antonio, are you all right?" he asked.

Not "Don Antonio." No servility. I liked that. There was a presence, an egalitarian pride, about him. Fans seldom asked me how I was. Usually they wanted to know how much money I made, how many girlfriends I had. This man had seen through the white satin armor. He'd seen the trembling. That's why he offered me the shot of *orujo.*

Paco and José were heading for José's car. Santí pulled urgently at my arm.

"Thanks for your concern. Do you need anything?" I asked the slaughterman.

He dragged calmly on his cigarette, hesitated for a beat.

"I need to be a torero," he said.

Most hopefuls were so poor that buttonholing you outside the bullring was the only way they could get to you. Among the thousands of hopefuls, there was always one who had the gift — the one you could train. I'd never had a protégé. Isaías had been urging me to train one before I retired. It was my duty, Isaías said, to make sure there would always be classic toreros.

Suddenly an ugly eddy surged through the crowd. El Cordobés was in his car now, and disappointed fans rocked the vehicle. My party were flung against the side of my Mercedes. I was actually pinned between the slaughterman's thighs, bathed in his smell of bull-guts and sour sweat. His face was against my cheek, close enough for a kiss. My flat-soled satin shoes slipped — the damn things are made to walk on sand, not sidewalks. To keep myself from sliding down between his legs, into the trample, I dropped my parade cape and grabbed him around the waist. He seized hold of my red sash, hauling me back up against him.

No one saw what happened next. It was one of those things between strangers in a puritan country where the state bids to control the smallest sexual urge. Deep in that crush of bodies, his crotch "accidentally" pressed against mine. He was aroused — I could feel it.

Caught by surprise, I felt my own surge. As a Spanish man, I was eternally awake to any chance for sexual larceny. Even in these strange circumstances, my senses responded. A hard-on is painful in those tight satin torero pants. But my hands "accidentally" grasped his hips, holding him hard against me. Under my palms was the hard flex of his buttocks. He caught his breath in surprised excitement.

Then the crowd surged again, grinding us cruelly together. I felt a white-hot pain in the old Écija wound. Instantly my hard-on melted.

"*Ayy* ...my leg," I gasped.

"Hold on, *majín*," he panted. "I'll take care of you."

Bracing his hands against the frame of the car, and his feet against the curb, the slaughterman pressed back as hard as he could. With a fierce protectiveness, he now had me guarded between his arms and his knees. Straining like a weightlifter, he forced a few people back, to open a tiny space around me. Even so, the crowd pushed him back against me a few more times. His hoarse voice deafened my ear, as he yelled at everyone that I was being hurt. Nearby spectators started helping him push the crowd back. Then Santí, the human tank, surged to our side.

In another moment, a few Greys were there. Batons swung. Heads were bloodied. A couple of unfortunate men got dragged off to the black police vans.

Now the crush eased. As Santí yanked the Mercedes' back door open, the slaughterman pushed me into the car. I hauled him in after me, to make sure the Greys didn't arrest him. Braulio rescued my trampled parade-cape from the pavement and threw it on top of us.

Panting, we all fell in a heap on the back seat.

"Are you all right?" the slaughterman asked.

Majín, ** he had called me. It was Montanese for "handsome guy." This slaughterhouse rough had felt me up in public. Majín. Majín. What an adventurer.

"Yes, thanks to you." I was saying *tú* to him. "And you?"

Now the rest of the crew piled into the Mercedes. We were a hot male bio-mass of sweaty satin and metal embroidery. Braulio threw the sword-case in the trunk and jumped in. Car-doors slammed shut. Our driver and my crew stared at the slaughterman, who was now staring down at his lap, overcome by sudden shyness. No doubt he was aghast at his impulse in the crowd, wondering if I would have him arrested and charged with an indecent act.

"This guy risked his life for the boss," Santí explained to the rest of the crew. "Antonio was almost squashed like a bug."

As our engine started, the crew grunted their approval of this heroic deed. Isaías reached across Fermin's broad chest and shook the slaughterman's hand.

"To the Roma Hotel," I told the driver. "And drop our friend a few corners away. So he doesn't get nabbed by the Greys."

"Curses on the Greys," Santí growled.

With the police opening a narrow corridor, our car crawled laboriously through the crowd, onto the main avenue.

Briefly I glanced at the slaughterman. Now that he knew I was going to keep his secret, he recovered his composure, daring to lift his head again but not meeting my eyes. His hard profile — keen eyes, good mouth, strong chin — stood out against the welter of torero satin around him. From a face among thousands, this young migrant suddenly shone as an intriguing individual. I wanted to take him back to the hotel with us. Legitimately I could thank him by making him part of my retinue for the evening — taking him to drinks and dinner with us. But that was all I could do. People would talk. Especially in this profession where male adoration of males is stoked to white heat. Every torero is the object of advances from men. I'd had my share of discreet gropes at parties and unsigned love letters.

Talk is a sharper horn than marriage. Liberalization had never dented the core of moral iron that was forged in so many Spanish hearts from birth. People who'd only been to church twice in their lives would throw rocks at me. Talk could lead to the quiet death sentence of ridicule and loss of my career. Years in prison on some trumped-up charge (since it was tricky to mention *maricones* in the press, even though vice laws made them criminals). Torture by the police, if political charges could be made serious enough. I knew how the great *maricón* poet García Lorca had died. I knew about that torero that Lorca celebrated in the poem "Llanto." Ignacio Sánchez Mejías was also a *maricón*. Lucky for Mejías that a bull killed him before the Civil War — otherwise somebody would have bullet-holed his bullfighter ass.

So I would give this slaughterhouse guy the hint that every sidewalk hopeful got from me. If he was smart, he'd take the hint and I might get to see him again very soon in the future.

As our car braked at the corner, I said: "Well, good luck in the bulls. Isaías, one of my cards, please, and a pen."

My manager complied. The card bore my address and telephone in Toledo Province. "Your name?" I asked.

"Juan Diano Rodríguez."

On the back I wrote, "Juan Diano Rodríguez is a good man. Do me the favor of helping him in any way you can," and signed it. At the least, it would help him find a better job.

"Will you take some advice?" I asked, handing Juan the card.

"Sure."

"Pick your master carefully. Go ask him if he'll train you. And do it now. Don't wait. You're old to be starting."

"Thanks," Juan Diano said.

Clutching the precious card, he crawled over Fermin's massive knees, and got out of the car.

The car-door slammed. I felt like some bronze cathedral-door of fate had crashed shut on my fingers.

As we pulled away, the young man's blue jumper had already vanished into the dense evening crowd. He would be forging along the sidewalks, putting the card in his pocket — heading back to the big echoing municipal slaughterhouse where six bull carcasses were now strung up on hooks. All I could see now was strolling mothers with baby buggies. Perfectly dressed parents with their perfectly dressed children. Tourists looking lost. Boy-girl pairs walking decorously, not touching hands in public. Two Spanish girls in mini-skirts, leaving a wake of Spanish boys who turned to stare after them and murmur illegal compliments.

"Antonio, you weren't very kind," Isaías grumbled. "You could

have invited the kid to dinner. Good publicity. Fan protects Escudero
from mob. Very good publicity."

Isaías was always such a predictable Christian Democrat.

"He looks like he could use a good meal," Bigotes added.

"I'm too tired for publicity tonight," I said, sounding as heartless
as I could.

"He rescued the boss on purpose," Braulio put in dourly. "So he
could get to him. He just wanted money."

"No," Bigotes countered. "His deed was genuine. I saw it. He
didn't plan for the riot."

As my crew bickered, the Mercedes picked up speed, heading along
the harbor drive towards El Sardinero, the ocean-front district where our
hotel was. One would never know that, 30 years ago, this harbor lay
bombed to ruins by Franco and his Italian allies. Now it was splendidly
rebuilt by wealthy commercial families of the city. Cruise ships docked
along the waterfront. Yachts were mooring for the night at the Royal
Yacht Club. We slowed for happy spectators leaving a soccer match
between Santander's Racing and the Royal Madrid.

My head was whirling. What an extraordinary encounter! Yes,
Juan Diano hadn't known the crowd would surge. But he'd taken impul-
sive advantage, like any man in a crowded subway car. He'd pressed
himself against me. He hadn't fought to prevent our faces from touching.
He had breathed a hot compliment in my ear. *Majín. Majín.* I could
still hear the tone of his husky voice, feel his warm breath against my
cheek. How much had he guessed about me? Or was he winging it?

Others had stolen tassels from El Cordobés's jacket. This guy
had stolen a feel from me. What a risk he'd run! What a guy!

But he was gone.

"Isaías," I said, "get in touch with the police. See if you can get
those three men released. The ones who were arrested at our car. I
don't want anything bad to happen to them because of me."

---

*Juan Belmonte — one of the greatest matadors of all time, active in the ring before
the Spanish Civil War.

**Peseta* — unit of Spanish money. In the late 1960s, the peseta was very inflated because of rapid Spanish economic development.

*** *majo* — goodlooking man. *Majín* (pronounced mah-HEEN) is a typical Montanese variant of this expression.

2

It felt like I had been a starving wild creature all my life. Ribs showing, I hunted for food in the blowing dust of a wasteland.

There are many kinds of hunger. In the bullring, hunger is what drives a man. Only famine can drive him to be so valiant and so stupid...to stand in front of a galloping bull, and risk being a pinwheel on the horn. As a torero, I have the right to say the truth about the art of tauromachy — it is beautiful, stupid, cruel, and reveals much about human nature. Some, like the young man I'd just met, grow up in poverty and physical hunger. These stand in front of wild bulls so they can feast on quick money. Others, like me, hunger to kiss the virgin lips of risk.

The mind can crave too — new ideas, wild new challenge.

My family had tried to bring me up tame. They intended to castrate my spirit. For them, I would be a human ox wearing the oaken yoke of Old Catholic. But they had failed. They knew I was only going through motions to please them. They'd failed to domesticate my twin sister too.

As soon as they saw what a single rebel mind linked José and me, our parents separated us. They had already crushed her childhood tomboy urges — she hung around the bulls with me, wanting to be another Conchita Cintrón* galloping her horse to plant a lance in the bull. Worse still, they caught her reading forbidden books. "You two take after your Republican greatgrandmother," my father told us in disgust. Even after my father died in 1959, my mother went on trying valiantly to keep the two of us apart.

But my sister and I were drawn to that greatgrandmother of ours.

32

It was Doña Carmen who told us the hidden heterodox side of the family history — the side that Professor Paco didn't know. Before she died in 1961, at the age of 95, Doña Carmen shared a family secret with José and me. She gave us directions to the location of an archeological treasure that most of the Escuderos had believed was lost for 500 years. We went where Doña Carmen sent us, and found where the old Crypt of the Mercies was hidden.

Unlike that young man in Santander, I'd never known physical hunger. For me, the hunger was in the mind, emotion, spirit. My heart was a wild bull starving for love in a worn-out pasture with no gate. I'd gnawed the grass-roots of fantasy and paid sex partners right down to the dry ground. My hungry tongue was ready to curl itself around thistles.

That night, my retinue stayed in Santander and dealt elegantly with physical hunger.

Santander had always been elegant. In the Sixties, as in bygone royalist times, high society and government people fled there in the summertime to get away from Madrid heat. As our Mercedes rolled into Sardinero, the last Spanish families were leaving the beach to take a trolleybus home, then go out for tea or drinks. I tried to imagine myself as one of those young husbands, with my obedient children and my wife in her modest one-piece bathing suit. On the trampled sand, a few tourist girls still lolled in bikinis. The police pretended they didn't see the bikinis...but only because of the government's hunger for tourist money. Sardinero's 19th-century bathhouse loomed as a stark reminder of times when both men and women wore bathing clothes that were far more prudish.

That evening, I had to walk a gauntlet of elegant social dangers, worse than the bulls.

After I showered and changed at the Hotel Roma, the car took me to Villa Carmen on a quiet nearby street. There, behind garden walls, camellia trees smothered the air with pink blooms. A portly overdressed mother and her daughter sat in this suffocatingly opulent setting, waiting for me with high tea spread on a table. The girl silently, unsmilingly let me kiss her hand. She was María Serafita Cordoblillo del Monte, my sister's best friend since childhood, and the girl my family were pushing me to marry.

"Oh Antonio, you *are* all right, aren't you?" Her mother, Doña Margarita, was pouring coffee, doing her usual gushing. "Yes, you are all right. I can see that. We heard that you had a great, great afternoon! Congratulations!" as I offered the wilted triumphal flowers from the ring.

"They're a little bruised," I apologized.

Sera and I exchanged cautious glances. She could see I was limping, a little bruised like the flowers I'd brought her.

"Are you all right, 'Tonio?" she murmured anxiously, using the childhood nickname. "We heard —"

"It was nothing," I lied, sipping the coffee that Doña Margarita handed me.

For a second I remembered that taste of *orujo,* those wild blue eyes staring at me. Then they faded, and I was staring into the troubled dark eyes of Sera.

Twenty-seven years old, dainty and dark, somber and unsmiling, Sera was the picture of traditional Spanish girlhood, living an ornamental but useless life at her widowed mother's home, putting up with her Mamá's baroque wiles and whims, waiting for a marriage set in filigrees. Sera had not gone to school past convent academy in Toledo. I couldn't remember ever seeing Sera laugh out loud, even in our wildest childhood games. Lately she had a strange shadow in her eyes. This humorless girl was a strange companion for José, whose raucous laugh embarrassed everybody in the family but me.

Sera and I were third cousins, actually. Her family were titled small-fry like mine, well-placed with the government. Franco loved aristocrats — many of his biggest fascist supporters were Counts of This or That. Both families were waiting for me to quit the bulls and marry her. I had promised my father on his deathbed that I'd be retired and married by age 30, and my 30th birthday was five months away. Like my sister, Sera was getting long in the tooth — her family had prevented her from accepting other marriage offers. She was not allowed to attend bull-fights, since her mother believed that the brute spectacle and natural anxieties of a fiancée-to-be would overwhelm her. But Doña Margarita had dragged her to Santander on the train, to coincide with my contract, in hopes that I would finally pop the question.

"Come now, you two — a little animation!" her mother chattered. "Is this a funeral?"

"Mamá, he's tired," Sera said.

A rich pastry sat on my plate. If I ate it, I would probably vomit. I still felt swelteringly hot, and loosened my tie.

"I can't stay long," I said. "Isaías has me booked everywhere this evening. I just wanted to pay my respects."

Doña Margarita cried out, "But you just got here! You're *always* on your way somewhere!"

"Mamá, it's his work. Let him be."

Sera and I had never talked about it, but I sensed she was as unhappy about this marriage as I was. Hopefully she loved another man.

Sometime in the next few months, I'd have to find out who he was. Maybe I could help her oppose our families and get her wish. Imagine marrying a woman who never smiled! But if I didn't tie the knot with some woman after retirement, my overripe bachelorhood would become the object of unwelcome gossip.

Marriage was a bull with a sharp horn.

In the Hotel Roma dining room, no one bothered me much. Most of the Spanish diners let me have a little incognito. Foreigners didn't run after me the way they did Benítez.

First, a dinner and many toasts with my tiny local fan-club, the Peña Escudero. I had recovered a little. Amazing what a shower and clean clothes can do for a torero — even one who trembled uncontrollably when the bull was dead. I was the picture of traditional bullfighter — dark suit, ruffled white shirt, diamond studs, the gold pinkie ring with its diamond cabuchon that was a gift from Doña Carmen. The diamonds added a bohemian detail. I'd always been amazed at today's belief that "classic toreros" somehow represented political conservatism. The horseback torero may have been an aristocrat, but the old-time matador who fought on foot was viewed as culturally indispensable trash, like an actor. One went to see him kill bulls, but one didn't socialize with him unless one was slumming. My beloved Juan Belmonte hung around with actors, pimps, courtesans, poets and painters, which was how he came to let himself be sculpted in the nude.

Amid cigar and cigarette smoke that layered its blue archeology in the air, I made a short speech, thanking my Peña for their loyalty during my convalescence. Their adoring eyes felt like groping fingers.

But my appetite still flagged. I ate only half the filet of beef. The potatoes were fried in oil that was a shade rancid. Nobody could fool me about oil — I owned 3000 hectares** of the best olive groves in Spain. All the while, those blue eyes floated in my thoughts, ghostly as a curl of smoke in the air. Under the perfect clothes, my body glowed secretly from the memory of that intimate nudge in a crowd.

Then we adjourned to the Roma bar, crowded with more overlaid histories of smoke, more Spanish ladies in Balenciaga cocktail dresses, more tourist men in nylon suits. More obligations awaited me. While the four bachelors of my crew sat drinking with some tourist girls they'd picked up, Isaías and José and Paco and I joined two Yankee*** journalists who had arranged an interview. José had swept up her hair and changed into her own Balenciaga cocktail dress. Tere had gone upstairs to bed.

At a quiet corner table, I faced the journalists warily.

Why did we always end up dealing with Yankee scribblers who probed political problems in Spain when they had problems in their own country to write about? These Yankees could have interviewed El Cordobés, but they wanted to talk to me. José and I knew it was going to be a long night, so we ordered a bottle of sherry. My sister could hold her liquor better than a Basque steelworker. Paco frowned as she expertly poured the first shot.

"So," said Bob in English, "you're different from most guys who fight bulls on foot. You're a blue-blood in a blue-collar profession. Right?"

"Blue collar?" I asked.

My English was learned at the University of Madrid in the late 1950s. It hadn't included a glossary of Yankee social terms.

"Blue collar means workers," offered the other Yankee. His name sounded like Chorch.

"Foot bullfighters come up from poverty, right?" said Bob. "They get rich fast. Right? Like baseball players in America. Especially niggers and spics."

"Spics?"

"Hispanics."

I pondered the slur, and swallowed a glass of sherry whole. It reminded me of that gulp of *orujo,* and my body glowed briefly.

"So how do you explain your popularity?" asked Chorch. "You're the Count of Mora. Why are you fighting bulls on foot? How do you get the blue-collar fans hot like today?"

Chorch switched to limping Spanish. "You're a *señorito*...the idle rich. Spanish people hate *señoritos.* Right?"

These guys knew my language well enough to know the dangerous word *señorito* ****. I thought about this long enough to cue Isaías. My manager was supposed to answer questions that I couldn't answer without looking immodest.

So Isaías jumped in with Basque bluntness.

"When Antonio goes wild," he said, "and passes the bull with the fly of his pants, the fans forget what color his blood is. A man's fly is always the fly. No matter what social class of… underwear is inside it."

At this, José burst into her famous laugh. She had a husky contralto voice like that Yankee actress I'd seen in the movies, Tallulah something.

The journalists were delighted with my manager's quip and wrote it down.

But Paco scowled again, sipping his one brandy of the evening. He didn't like my manager's bawdy quip, and he didn't like José laughing at it. On the road, José sometimes overheard the kind of he-talk that would get us arrested if we said it to her on the street. She didn't mind hearing it — in fact, it amused her.

I tried changing the subject.

"So…you Yankees are less *señorito* and more humanist these days," I said.

It was always interesting to hear Yankees talk about their own country.

I had first visited New York City five years ago, on a detour from fighting bulls in Mexico, supposedly to look for a U.S. importer for my oil, but really to pay a secret visit to Doña Pura, my greatgrandaunt. Pura was another family heretic, my greatgrandmother's younger sister. She had quietly left Spain in 1928, when she saw the fall of the Second Republic coming, and settled in the growing Spanish emigré colony of New York. My family called her "the Red traitor." My aunt wasn't a Communist, of course — just another family member who was an Old Pagan instead of an Old Catholic. And she knew about the Crypt of the Mercies from her sister Carmen.

The United States intrigued me. Aunt Pura never wrote me, because Paco would surely get his hands on her letters, but I managed to visit her two more times, under cover of olive-oil business. Her American husband had died years ago, and left her comfortable, among mementos of Spanish notables who had visited her, including García Lorca. We had long talks about her new country. The U.S. pretended to have religious freedom, she said, but it was hard to be anything but a Protestant there. She explained that after the American Revolution, Tomás Jefferson and other free-thinkers had pulled their heads out of the ox-yoke of Protestant state religion, which ruled most of the colonies. But Yankee right-wingers had put the yoke back, even in the schools. By the time General Eisenhower became president, they had succeeded in disguising the wolf of Protestant empire in sheep's clothing of democracy.

But no intelligent person was fooled, Aunt Pura said. Especially in the 1950s, when right-wing Yankees had jailed and killed liberals, Socialists, Communists and atheists like we did in Spain, she said. Only they used a barbaric method called the electric chair, instead of our barbaric Spanish garrotte. The Yankee Catholics had tried to take control of this state religion, only to have their first President, Juan Fitzgerald Kennedy, be assassinated. Now student riots and anti-Vietnam demonstrations were shaking their land. It looked like as many Yankees as Spaniards were sick of being oxen for the church.

To my emigré greatgrandaunt and my Republican greatgrandmama, there was little to choose between Catholic and Protestant ox-dom. Both yokes had callused a lot of necks. Both sides had tortured and terrorized a lot of people. Pura had talked bitterly about García Lorca's murder by Franco's troops.

"Oh, we're getting so liberal it's scary," said Chorch.

"We're freeing the niggers, of course," put in Bob.

"That is a wonderful idea." José nodded wisely. "Someday we will invite our Jews to come home. Some still have the keys to their old houses in Córdoba, you know."

"Shut up, María Josefina," said Paco in a low voice.

Ignoring Paco, José lit a Turkish cigarette and blew smoke luxuriously in Paco's eyes.

So I opened my silken cape of words, and maneuvered us back onto safer ground. "What else are you Yankees liberalizing?"

"Music," shrugged Chorch. "Drugs. Birth control. Abortion. War. I guess you know about Vietnam, right?"

"We read about Vietnam in smuggled copies of the London Times," Jose said cheerfully. "The pill is smuggled from France."

Paco winced.

"Did I mention hair length on men?" Bob added in. He paused, racking his brain. "Oh, and women's lib."

"We don't want feminism here," drawled José. "If we jail every Spanish girl who already takes the pill, we will have to rent prison space in Portugal."

Paco ground his teeth.

"As for hippies," José added, stubbing out her cigarette, "we simply kill them on sight."

"Yeah, we know," Bob replied drily. "When we were in Benidorm last week, we saw some Spanish guys grab this tourist kid. They cut his long hair off right on the street, with their pocket knives. Man, that must have hurt."

"Everyone is a policeman here," said José cheerfully.

"And I suppose you people don't have any *maricones* either," said Chorch.

The table went silent. Paco blanched. No one could pretend that the terrible word hadn't been said in a woman's presence.

José raised her eyebrows. "Absolutely not," she said. "Our country rid itself of *maricones* during the Civil War."

Heads turned at the next table, hearing the forbidden word from a woman.

"We're about to liberate our *maricones*," said Bob gloomily.

"Liberate…them?" my manager repeated, trying not to say the dreadful word again. His eyes bugged.

With the force of a blow, memory of that grope in the crowd

came back on me, like a bull wheeling to charge again. But I was shocked to discover that I couldn't remember that slaughterhouse worker's face, though I could remember the feel of his fingers, and his hard-on against me, with surreal heat.

"Yeah," said Bob. "In New York, there's a quarter where only *maricones* live. A few months ago, they had a riot at a *maricón* bar called the Stonewall. The damn *maricones* actually fought with the police. Ever since then, they've been demonstrating and demanding civil rights for *maricones.* Unbelievable."

Bob had actually said the word four times in one breath. The people at the next table swallowed their drinks hastily and left.

To a Spaniard, it was inconceivable that fags might go political, like Asturian coal-miners demanding the right to unionize. Paco was beside himself. In his 500-year-old world, *maricones* were the most forbidden of the forbidden, an ancient and terrifying force that must be thrust under the yoke at any cost. They were unwholesome reminders of foreign things in our history — Greek trade, Roman army, Egyptian and Celtic rite. Today, tiny coteries of female and male homosexuals — their secret nightspots, their meeting-places in private homes — stayed one jump ahead of the Greys, living underground like French resistance fighters.

The effeminate man is visible, so he is easily identified and crushed. But machos like me stir the deepest revulsion, because of the belief that we couldn't possibly be attracted to one another. This belief is the cornerstone of Spanish church civilization. As I'd learned, the same belief is held in Protestant civilizations like the United States. Men like me are considered invisible traitors because of our power to hide within the very fortress of society. We are the family man, bachelor, fiancé, widower, soldier, teacher, politician, prince or king, even priest. We are the virile citizen who might dare to stare from under his hat brim, through his drifting cigar smoke, at the mighty crotch of a peer. Citizens like Paco would happily carry firewood to burn all of us at the stake, if he still could. The Inquisition had burned more than a few *maricones.* Nowadays, the garrotte or firing squad had to do.

"Speaking of fags," said Bob, "what *did* happen to García Lorca?"

Now Paco smiled broadly. "That pig in human form was killed in the War of Liberation," he said. "They should have given medals to the ones who did it."

"What about liberalizing in Spain?" Bob asked me. "What happens when *He* dies?"

"Antonio is a torero," said Isaías. "Not a politician."

"Are you Protestants?" Paco broke in, glaring.

"Damn right," said Chorch. "I'm a Baptist. My sidekick here is a Presbyterian."

"Only a Catholic can understand our country," said Paco.

"A good reporter can understand anything," Chorch scoffed.

"Only an *Old* Catholic can understand us," Paco added relentlessly. "Not a yeah-yeah Vatican Council kind of Catholic."

Isaías looked like he wanted to strap adhesive tape over all our mouths.

"It is vital to keep liberalism at bay," Paco proclaimed. "Spain has always needed the strong hand. We must avoid the anarchy that is happening everywhere. Look at the hippie anarchy in your own country. Your students out of control...your soldiers refusing to fight in Vietnam..."

Behind the bi-focals, his black eyes flamed with fervor. But Paco was not a gifted orator. He was a schoolteacher, his mind always trapped in some gloomy invisible classroom with hard oak chairs. The Yankee scribblers listened impatiently, looking bored. The rest of us slumped in our chairs. The ashtray was overflowing with butts. José recklessly poured herself another drink.

Paco's voice droned on and on.

"....But we will stay conservative and Catholic. And, I might add, it's time for the old Spanish nobility to burnish their armor. To take an active role."

My tired mind wandered. My brother and I had suckled at the same breast, but we had spent boyhood bloodying each other's noses. As I got older, I always bloodied his nose first. When our father died, I got the title and the palace in Toledo and the game reserve, while Paco got a little townhouse in Madrid, where he lived with his envious wife and three priggish sons. But my brother's anger went deeper than that. Hundreds of years ago, something had gone wrong for the Escuderos. We had lost our high place, and slid to a place of obscurity. Our house was divided into two warring factions, he said. Why? Paco had taken to studying the family archives, a collection of documents going back to the 11th century. Some documents were missing — he was sure our Red aunt had taken them to New York.

José swallowed the next sherry like it was fair week in Sevilla. The journalists finally gave up the interview, and left.

I stared recklessly into Paco's eyes. "And the 70 percent of our people who don't go to church any more — do they understand Spain?" I asked him.

Paco flushed with anger.

"Maybe," I added, "they remember how many of us were murdered in the name of the faith."

Paco could not believe his ears. "Brother, do you cross swords with *me?*" he demanded.

"You don't even own a sword," I said.

"I've watched you edging to the left for years," Paco said. "Are we nursing a Marxist freemason in the bosom of the family?"

"I've been too busy supporting you," I retorted, "to be subversive."

Paco's knuckles went white, and veins swelled in his forehead. This was a sore point with him. By the time our father died, there was no Escudero money, just some rundown land and a few dusty art treasures. Paco's salary barely stretched to support his growing family. It fell to me and José, the black sheep, to support our mother and Aunt Tita. A couple of times, when Paco had sick children and no money, I had paid his doctor bills.

"One day, brother," he said, "you'll go too far."

With gallant desperation, Isaías tried to change the subject. "So," he asked me, "are you really going to give that slaughterhouse guy a chance?"

"This province isn't exactly a cradle of toreros," I said. "He probably won't show up."

"But if he does? A protegé would be good publicity. I've told you that for years. Speaking of your sword — a good person to give it to. A classic torero like you — your wisdom must be taught to the young. Or everything that is real in the fiesta will die. And we'll be left with nothing but performers like El Cordobés."

I pretended vaster boredom, and pushed away my empty sherry glass.

"The young have to ask to be taught," I said. "Why didn't he ask me, right there? I guarantee — he'll be back in the slaughterhouse tomorrow."

"Of course, of course," said Isaías. "And —"

Paco cut in, with an awful glare at Isaías. "I disagree. It's a terrible time for Antonio to take on a protegé. Brother, you'll be 30 in a few months. It's time to get your mind out of the bullring, and keep your promise to our father. Time to do something noble and useful with your life."

Isaías growled, "Your brother will do what he wants."

Paco now turned on Isaías. "That's because you have tainted my brother with your liberal views. If he had stuck with his first manager, Antonio would not have strayed. Surely God has punished you and your wife by denying you any children."

Isaías and I were astounded at this slur. But the old man was too seasoned to rise to Paco's bait. He simply stood up and threw a tip on the table.

I stood up too. "Paco, you insult this faithful friend and colleague of mine."

"You're a swine, Paco," my sister added.

The three of us walked out, leaving Paco sitting there alone.

Back upstairs, my hotel suite was still full of fans and reporters, half-empty glasses, cigarette smoke, and loud talk. José excused herself and went to her room.

For a little while, I held court in my room, with a last dozen admirers. I was in shirt-sleeves now, holding my liquor well. My diamonds sparkled with manly bohemian fire. I was insufferably polite. The object of my patience was two women — another kind of sidewalk hopeful. Woman No. 1 caressed my arm. Woman No. 2, a blonde foreigner of indeterminate nationality, ran her hand down my back. Both viewed my body as a public place...which it was. My body belonged to the mob. Which female would I invite to view my showy monument to manliness? Which one was less likely to give me clap, or steal from my room?

I decided on Woman No. 2, because her hair was the same color as Juan Diano's hair. At least with her, I could fantasize. My glances, my arm over her shoulder, advertised to everyone that she'd made the cut. By morning, every aficionado in town would know that I'd taken her to bed.

Braulio caught my glance.

"Get everybody out of here," I said quietly. "Except the blonde. Tell her to stay in the bathroom till I'm ready for her."

"She's the one I would have picked for you, boss," Braulio whispered, with a conspiratorial grin.

Instantly my valet cleared the room. While room service cleaned up the mess, Isaías wrote checks and paid my crew. He had my fee of 700,000 pesetas ($10,000 in U.S. dollars). Seventy percent would go for my men and expenses. I would bank what was left. Out of this chicken scratch, collected 30 or 40 times a year if I wasn't in the hospital, I kept my tiny taurine enterprise going. El Cordobés had earned 2 million pesetas that afternoon.

"Boss, are you okay?" Santí asked, pocketing his check.

Santí was 28, had come up the hard way, from day-laborer on a cattle ranch near Huelva. All his life he'd dreamed of moving from foot to horseback, and working for me. When I finally gave him his chance, he never forgot it. While he was not my bodyguard, he was fiercely loyal and protective, like a kid brother. He never failed to put his bulk between me and danger, whether it was social danger or sinking his pic in the neck of horned danger. I knew he had the Yankee girl waiting in his room.

"All I need is a little quiet," I said.

"I'm going then. Enjoy yourself, boss."

"And you, Santí. The benefits of tourism, eh?" I slapped my picador on the back.

Santí grinned. "The peseta rises against the dollar," he said.

He left.

I peeked into José's room, which adjoined mine. She had a glass of sherry on the night table. Still frowning and tense, she curled on her bed in her Chinese silk robe. Phone in one hand and typed page in the other, she was dictating the last words of her column to someone in the *ABC* office. Her portable typewriter still sat open, and the room smelled of Le Dé and alcohol.

"...Yes, I'll get the next one in earlier," she barked into the phone. "I'm sorry I was late this time."

As she hung up, I sat on the bed beside her.

"What's going on with you?" I demanded. "You drank too much tonight...and you talked too leftist."

"You said a few leftist things yourself." She swigged the sherry.

José and I had been allies against Paco since childhood, when we conspired to knock our hated third sibling out of trees. These days Paco's objections to José's morals started with the *ABC* job. Why (he argued) didn't she start a nice little feminine dressmaking business? That was when Paco learned that his sister was as *bravo* as me. She charged him like a wild cow. Told him to go ahead, have her arrested and dragged home. Dragged through the courts and the press. Naturally Paco didn't want to risk a public scandal. So he came to me. Why (he demanded) wasn't I controlling her, as the family's elder male? That was how Paco learned that I lack the fine moral sense that every good Spaniard is supposed to have. I told Paco to leave my sister alone.

Yes, José was my ally. I knew a lot about her, and she knew a lot about me. But she didn't know about the Big Hunger. It was the only secret that I had from her. Sometimes I wondered if she had ever sensed it. It was making me so lonely that I wondered if I should tell her.

"Screw Paco," I said. "I've never seen you so edgy."

"Things are happening..." she said evasively.

"Boyfriend things? Confide in me."

"Brother things. You have me worried."

It was hard to stay angry at José. I melted. "Did you write the usual mean things about me today?" I teased her.

She laughed, slid one satiny arm over my shoulder, and pulled me to her. The forgotten page of bullfight column crackled between us. For a while I lay with my head on her shoulder, face in her neck, nostrils bathed in her fragrance. I wanted to go to sleep in my sister's bed. Perhaps the only reason I found women halfway appealing was that I had dreamed in my sister's arms for nine months, in our mother's womb. What did José know about me? As children, we had often crawled into each other's beds at night when we were frightened or confused or lonely. It was one of the reasons why the family had separated us.

"Today," she said, "I could praise you without being accused of nepotism."

"I'll have the column framed, and hang it on my wall."

"Along with your sword, I hope."

I sat up, shocked at her words. "You too, José?"

My sister stuffed the crumpled column into her empty sherry glass. "Every time I see you in the ring, you are pushing the edge harder. Today, if the leg had failed you..."

"The leg is better every time. I command it more."

"*Uy,* you can't fool me, 'Tonio. I have never seen you look so tired."

"Occupational hazards."

"You should have that tourist girl just give you a back rub, then send her away."

I got up. "She's one more ear I have to cut in Santander. And I have to go...the poor thing is waiting in my bathroom."

"Haven't you proven your manhood enough?"

"Good night," I said, kissing her forehead.

She sighed. "See you tomorrow," she smiled drunkenly, touching my cheek. "Enjoy the lady."

Alone in my room at last, I turned out the lights. Before I let the girl out of the bathroom, I threw open the shutters and leaned out the casement. Night air poured over me, into the smoke-filled room. Outside, a delicious shower had wet the street. Hungrily I drew the scent of water into my dry lungs.

This northern air was so wonderful that the Santanderinos had a joke about selling tin cans of it to tourists. Sixty or seventy centimeters of rain fell here every year. To a man from the dry central plateau of Spain, all this lush northern vegetation was overwhelming, sensual — a rain forest. The nearby municipal park was bursting with juicy lawns and fat palms. Tamarisks and camellias fountained over with pink blooms. Inland, millions of hectares of lusty emerald corn fed the famed dairy herds of this province, known since medieval times as La Montaña. In the mountains, wild oak and chestnut and eucalyptus filtered the ocean winds, making the air as bracing as cough drops. Somewhere in that Spanish rain-forest, my young man had suckled at the breast of his Montanese mother. Long live that mother.

On the dresser was the portable altar where I'd prayed in the morning. The Virgin of Mercies smiled reassuringly at me from Her gilt frame. One candle still guttered in its votive glass.

Reflected in the mirror over the altar, I saw the Wild Man.

In 1961, that face had shone with a youthful grin and unscarred arrogance. That was the year its 20-year-old owner cut his first ears as a full matador. Alas, the eyes of a tired gladiator now stared back at me from the hard face.

The diamond ring came off, and lay on the dresser — worn by generations of Escudero men who'd known the secret. Diamond studs came undone, snow-white shirt opened to reveal the Wild Man's torso with its old scars of horn wounds. Hunger and rage had driven him to risks that few toreros now took. One light scar, souvenir from a Pedro Romero bull in Jaén, cut right through the mat of black hair between his breasts. A light scar from the Guardiola bull in Salamanca who hammered him on the sand and broke three of his ribs.

The big scar of Écija, gotten on April 23, 1968, couldn't be seen in the mirror. It was hidden inside the Wild Man's expensive English-tailored trousers. If I may speak so frankly, this was a wound that taught the Wild Man to feel compassion for raped women. Pinned to the sand, he heard himself cry out, his hands trying to push the horn out of him. The Lara bull had spared his genitals, but spiked the horn deep between his thighs, up into his pelvis. He sustained damage to certain nerves that led to his leg. As always, the surgeons' report was published in merciless detail by newspapers that couldn't tell the truth about political jailings and tortures. This was the tradition when toreros were gored. Our bodies and our wounds belonged to every citizen.

Having survived this close call, the Wild Man's manhood now wanted to do something besides cite bulls. It wanted to be pressed against another human being with love, with love.

The Wild Man was hungry. Now and then, he took a discreet vacation in another country, supposedly to view art and culture. Out there, incognito, he had gorged on the sexual food forbidden by law in Spain. He could count the times like trophies. Once in New York, six times in France, twice in London, three times in Germany. No boys. No drag queens who hid the surprise inside their lace panties. A boy or drag queen was a scrap of anchovy, for a man who wanted to eat a whole tuna. The Wild Man preferred adult hustlers, scarred and hard-faced as himself— foreign *putos* ***** who walked like men, smelled like men, and tasted like men when you got their men's belts unbuckled. These experiences gave a fleeting relief, and left the Wild Man paralyzed with lustful regret as he went home to don the yoke again.

During the Second Republic, fag life had sprung up in Spain, like poppies and cornflowers along the potholed highways of old belief. A wild meadow of poets, writers, musicians, playwrights, painters, sculptors, who all stood for humanization and change. Aunt Pura told me that Federico García Lorca planned to launch a movement for the right to love whomever you chose. No wonder they shot poor Fede in the ass. Today, right-wingers considered the word *maricón* to be a synonym for "Red", "freemason" and "traitor." The Wild Man yearned to graze on those wildflowers of love. But he had been discreet. He had done the bits of theater with women, and never touched a man's body inside Spain. In his professional life, he'd even been careful to surround himself with loyal men who didn't attract him, so he wouldn't be tempted into folly — men like Santí and the Vandilaz brothers.

Yes, this was the most honest answer to that Yankee journalist's question. The answer to why, on a good afternoon, with the right bull, a blueblood Wild Man could drive the crowd crazy. He could open a chink in his armor and force them to glimpse his sexual dilemma, the slow death of his spirit, the sword through his own heart. But only in the ring. Outside the ring, the Wild Man of the bulls was just another ox with his neck in the yoke.

Feeling tired, I locked the diamond studs and ring in my suitcase, and stuffed the suitcase key under the mattress. Then I went to the bathroom door. The blonde girl was sitting slumped on the edge of the bidet, wondering if I had forgotten her.

"Speak English? *Sprechen Sie Deutsch? Parlez-vous français?"*

So here I was, between the sheets with a naked woman. No full intercourse tonight — I was too tired. Just a blow job. I could lay back and relax.

Walk.

I sent my exhausted imagination in search of the blue-eyed man. To get it up for a woman, I had to think about men. There was no cure for this. One time, on my French travels, a French priest admitted to me that some men might be willing to go to bed with women, but they still had to think about men to get off. He had heard this truth a thousand times in the confessional. Somewhere in Santander, Juan Diano was laying awake, maybe in some tiny basement that he shared with other migrants. Was he fondling himself and thinking of me? Was he fondling a roommate and thinking of me?

My imagination drew Juan Diano to the hotel. He got on the trolleybus and came out to Sardinero, looking for me with his own hunger. The door opened, and there he stood — tense with his young raw wildness. Almost before the door closed, we were in each other's arms. My hungry hands pushed the bloody coveralls off his shoulders. Meanwhile, he was trying to pull down my sweaty satin torero breeches. They are hard to get out of — it's the kind of detail that makes a fantasy good. Panting, grappling, we tried to keep quiet so no one in adjoining rooms could hear.

But just as the fantasy was getting good, my energy collapsed. Woman No. 2 was working me hard, but nothing would happen.

"A thousand pardons, *señorita,*" I mumbled. "Some other time, perhaps?"

Woman No. 2 thought I didn't find her attractive. Angry, she dressed and flounced out. The door banged shut, telling every guest on that floor that the torero's lady had left his room early.

Shakily, I got up and opened the door, hoping that Juan Diano might be standing outside, with that hunger in his eyes. But the corridor was empty — a pitiless vista of locked doors.

In another minute, I was sleeping like the dead.

Next morning, my entourage left Santander. Nobody mentioned the slammed door last night. Paco had swallowed his pride and apologized to Isaías. Isaías and Tere headed for San Sebastián in their own car, to meet with Sótano about my Bilbao contract. The sleepy crew rode off in the old black Mercedes. Paco, José and I threw our luggage in José's Citröen.

"I won't ride with you," Paco snapped at José, "unless you put on decent clothes." He was staring at José's bellbottom jeans, a brand called Levi Strauss that I had brought her from New York.

"It's my car," José replied coldly. "And you can take the train if you don't like my clothes."

José adored her car — she was the first Escudero woman in history to have a driver's license and buy a vehicle with her own money. Grumbling, Paco got in the back seat. Wearing sunglasses and sport clothes, I slumped in the front passenger seat while José drove hung over and yawning. On the seat was that morning's *ABC,* with her column stating that Antonio Escudero had been "tremendous, for once."

As we gunned through the municipal park, crews of workers were busy mowing lawns with their razor-sharp scythes. In this country of

God, we still didn't have lawnmowers. Outside of Santander, we crossed a few stone bridges. Under them, smoke drifted from cooking fires of migrants. These days, the country was full of them, mostly young and male, leaving their frayed-out villages for the cities where they hoped for jobs, money, modern high-life. No doubt the young man I'd met was one of those wanderers. I wondered if he felt up any of his brother migrants.

An hour out of town, José got sleepy and almost ran off the road into a sycamore tree. So she let Paco take the wheel.

Paco drove like an old maid. At a sedate speed, we climbed towards the Reinosa Pass, avoiding the work-crews who were forever filling potholes in those antiquated two-lane highways of God. We passed endless cornfields, and endless emerald pastures with black and white Holstein milk cows. While Franco made speeches about the evils of foreign ideas, our dairy farmers were quietly junking the old Spanish breeds and importing dairy cattle that were bred to produce impossible amounts of milk. Sadly I studied every cow, every chestnut tree, every bank of fern and heather and wild geraniums that went past, saying good-bye to them.

Soon we were on the pass, which crosses the high rocky summit of the Cantábrico mountains. There we left behind those cooling mists of La Montaña. Before us was the dry vastness of the central plateau. For some reason, I felt deeply depressed at losing the geographical close-ness with a young man I didn't even know.

All the while, Paco kept talking, driving with one hand and waving the other like a lecturing professor. Today Paco was trying to be more reasonable, more the concerned family member.

"Your physical condition is shaky," he said to me.

"Are you a doctor?" I parried.

"Everyone in the stands could see it."

"Everyone but Sótano."

"Sótano is blind to everything but ticket sales. But I have eyes. I'm your brother! You'll get yourself seriously crippled, or killed. Our mother, the rest of the family, want you to stop this foolishness and retire. Retired and married at 30. You made that solemn promise to our father. You swore this on his deathbed, in front of the Virgin of Mercies. I will hold you to that promise."

"Death, or the altar," I said drily. "Is that how you see it?"

Paco ignored my sarcasm.

"For a man of your social standing," he reminded me, "the bulls can only be a bohemian pastime of youth. Yes, yes, we all know why you did it. You had to have your youthful rebellion. But *hombre*...you're about to be 30. Youth is over. A torero as broken-up as you — a year, maybe two, if a bull doesn't catch you, you're finished anyway. Will you be happy messing around with your olive trees and your game animals? I don't think so. You have a great mind...you'll want to use it."

Paco's approach was an old one. Today, my exhaustion made it a shrewd one.

"Time for a new career," Paco went on, "that you can put your heart into. What better than a political career? A Senate seat in the Parliament. Maybe a high government post under the king, if Franco brings the throne back. You will have no trouble achieving these things. You have always been a torero of honor. Your name is untouched by scandal. Not like your sister —"

He scowled in the rear-view mirror.

"Leave my sister out of this," I said coldly.

"Your fans will become your enthusiastic political supporters," Paco went on, as if he hadn't heard. "If you and I work together, the Escuderos will move back into the mainstream of Spanish history."

José stared out the back window.

But Paco's pedant plan for me had me frantic. Maybe he knew he was boring. This was why he was so eager to seat me in the Cortes. A speech by him would put our Parliament to sleep. Paco had seen me speak at torero banquets. He knew that I could make people laugh, think, using words the way I used my cape.

"You know I don't give a fig for the king," I said. "When Franco dies, Spain will become a democracy."

This morning, Paco was trying hard to stay calm. "You know democracy will never work here," he said. "The technocrats in the government now...the ones who are pushing all this capitalist growth...they will ruin it for democracy."

"Democracy never got a chance here."

Paco darted a glance at me, and smiled eerily.

"One day you'll go too far with me," he said.

"How can I go too far with a bookworm?" I retorted. "You live in books, Paco."

"If that peasant shows up and tempts you, remember what I said," Paco added.

I felt a flash of fear. Had Paco sensed something? My brother had always seemed too insensitive for that. If my sister had never sensed anything, then surely Paco was oblivious to my sexual dilemma. But I'd better not underestimate him.

"The peasant will have to show up first," I said casually.

There was a long silence. Turning away from Paco, I leaned my head against the window and closed my eyes. José was nodding off too.

"By the way," said Paco, "in one of the old books, I've found a clue to the location of the Crypt."

In the darkness behind my eyes, a rainbow flash of nervousness went through me like lightning. I didn't open my eyes, but sensed that José felt the flash too.

"Oh God, the Crypt again," José grumbled sleepily. "Who cares about a hole in the ground full of bones?"

"The tombs of our fathers should matter to us," Paco intoned. "The Crypt...*ayyy*, it must have been a magnificent creation...a pantheon of our service to the Catholic Kings. If we can find it, and open it to the public, it will reveal our true past greatness...inspire the king to give us a high place once again. Who knows," he added wistfully, "tourists might come to see it."

"Bones are only good for fertilizing trees," I growled, and let myself fall asleep.

When I woke, nursing a stiff neck, the green coast of Spain was far behind us. Through the car's open window, that familiar furnace breath of the high central plateau was buffeting us. I stared out at wheatfields, and more wheatfields. Lonely rows of poplar trees bent in the wind against a cloudless sky whose very color seemed to bend through space. We passed a narrow highway that led away into the vastness. There, in a dust cloud, five gypsy wagons toiled along, with a few loose horses and colts. Only here in the north did you see the occasional caravan now. The gypsies, like all other things wild, were being herded into cities, into modern conformity.

I looked at that sweep of dryland wheat, and felt my heart closer to breaking than ever. Dry Spain — where my own mother had suckled me. Long live my own mother, even if she didn't know my heart. Juan Diano's hair was the color of ripe wheat. I willed that he come, like I willed my crippled leg to move.

---

*Conchita Cintrón was probably the greatest woman torero in history. She fought bulls on horseback. In Spain, women were not allowed to fight on foot.

**Hectare — metric land measurement. One acre equals 2.5 hectares.

***Yankee — among Spaniards, it was a common term for citizens of the U.S.

*****Señorito* — contemptuous word for a young aristocrat, especially one with an attitude.

*****Puto* — male prostitute.

3

We stopped for lunch in La Granja. By late afternoon, we were far south of Madrid, in our home country — that wild sparsely populated region known as the Montes de Toledo. Paco carefully negotiated the narrow highway — an ancient route that had led merchant caravans and foot troops through these ancient rounded mountains of granite and gneiss and shale for two thousand years, south into rolling farmlands of the Mancha, then across the Sierra Morena into Andalucía. Rounding a curve, Paco narrowly missed hitting a man on a mule who was ambling grandly along in the middle of our lane.

"Peasants!" he cursed. "Why don't they learn about cars?"

A few kilometers farther, our two vehicles lumbered across a Roman bridge over a gully, and into my first olive groves.

While Paco listened to the stock-market report on Radio Madrid, I stared out at the groves. They were a hardy old variety called *cornicabra*. After I became a matador, I had expanded the inherited groves by a thousand hectares. Isaías and Tere had insisted. "It will give you enough for a good business when you retire," they had said. "Spanish olive oil is going to give Italian oil a run for its money." I had paid for the trees by selling a 14th-century altarpiece to a rich Catalan art collector. The family had been furious. Selling off my patrimony! How could I? Now I was glad I'd listened to the Eibars. Among those youthful trees that I'd planted a decade ago, were gnarlier specimens that dated to an earlier expansion during Philip II's time. And a few arthritic ancients still clung to life here — trees that remembered my Arab and Berber forebears, maybe even the Roman ones that family tradition mentioned.

Like me, the groves were still healing horn-wounds gored into them by storm, drought and war. Many trees had been destroyed during fierce fighting in September 1936, when Franco's army rolled through here on their way north to Toledo. When my village work-crew rooted out dead stumps, they found shell casings and metal buttons, even bits of bone. I gave the olive burls to an artisan in the village, so he could start a shop.

But now the evening was quiet, with bark growing back over gouges in trunks. The creamy-white blossoms had changed to tiny fruit. Between the trees, anywhere that wildflowers bloomed, colorful bee-eaters were winging in search of their supper.

"The crop looks good," José remarked.

I grunted assent.

On a granite hill east of the highway, loomed the familiar hulk of our small castle — nothing grand like the one in Ávila. From those walls, we once taxed trade on the road, and guarded the southern approaches to the Catholic throne in Toledo, which Sanches had sworn to protect — hence our name, "shield-bearers"*. In 1936 a Republican command had holed up in those walls, where they were blown to bits by Franco's artillery. Now, in its tumbled state, the castle was nothing that even a foreign Hispanofile would want to repair and live in, as they were doing elsewhere. José and I had never played here as children, but Paco had dared its resident vipers to daydream of medieval glories.

A solitary griffon vulture circled high above the castle, like Nature's comment on the death of these glories.

Next, the road wended us to the dusty village of La Mora, which serviced the castle in olden times. Dwindled to 550 souls by my father's time, it had no electricity or sewer, and scratched out a living by grazing sheep and goats in the hills. In 1936, as Franco's Africans advanced on Madrid, local Republican militia and villagers made a stand here. Some were women, defending La Mora with scythes and shotguns. After the town was occupied, men were massacred and women raped. Nine months later, it was said, a few brown babies were born in La Mora. But they had vanished during the war and the famine afterward, so great was a woman's shame.

Now, along the pinched cobblestone street, pock-marks of bullets were still visible in house and stable walls. Some houses were empty. But emigration to Madrid had stopped, thanks to my efforts to keep people employed on my projects. The remaining homes sported a few new roofs and TV aerials. Vespa motor scooters, window-boxes of geraniums, diggings for the new sewer, were signs of prosperity. At night, most homes were lit by the new power-line. The mayor was even talking about getting a telephone. But the fire-scorched Gothic shell of a church was still abandoned. On its silent bell-tower, a mother stork flapped wings, settling onto her enormous nest of sticks. There hadn't been a curate here since the one who was crucified by surviving villagers in 1936, in furious retaliation for the fascist massacre.

As we bumped along the main street, passing a mule train loaded with charcoal, the old driver yelled, *"Olé-olé* Antonio!" I waved at him.

On the outskirts rose the oil-processing plant, metal buildings lettered ESCUDERO S.A., that I had built with torero earnings. The workers, a skeleton crew this time of year, were strolling out the gate, on their way home to eat lunch. They waved. I waved back, wishing that they would stop thinking of me as the feudal lord returning from the Crusades.

Beyond the plant, hazed in hot yellow light, rose the wild and lonely summits of the game reserve. This was the Coto Morera, the part of my inheritance that I had loved most since childhood. The *coto* ** was almost 120,000 hectares. This is around 50,000 acres by the United States measure, meaning 10 Yankee miles long and 8 miles wide. It was very large for a private holding in a country the size of Spain. If it had been good farmland, the government would have frowned on us for not keeping it in cultivation. As it was, the *coto* was too rugged for olive trees — good only for a crop of wild creatures and wild trees and brush.

Till I inherited the patrimony, the *coto* had suffered from absentee ownership. The Escuderos made their seat in our drafty 16th-century house in Toledo. They paid no attention to the *coto,* except to shoot there a few times in autumn and winter. My father put up our blue-blood friends at Las Moreras, the hunting lodge at the *coto.* He had even gotten Franco, an avid hunter, to come and shoot partridge. Old family photos showed phalanxes of adults posing with shotguns and gun-bearers. We children peered uncertainly from the sidelines, staring at braces of dead animals laid on the ground like trophies of war.

The Wild Man's first fascination with wildlife was born in those hunts. A Wild Boy could be glimpsed in those photographs, sadly fingering the bloody tusks in the jaws of a wild boar. He touched soft spotted bellies of lynx. He watched antlers of red deer being measured for records. He examined the limp iridescent bodies of endless partridge. Bags of 500 partridge to every six guns had been taken at Coto Morera. The old gamekeeper died in 1950, and wasn't replaced. By the time my father died in 1958, not a pig or red deer or wolf or lynx could be found anywhere in the *coto.* Partridge were so few that I stopped the hunts. Centuries of cutting wood for charcoal had wiped away the old belts of broadleaf and pine.

My heartbreak over the *coto* went so deep that I abandoned the drafty Toledo mansion to my mother, Aunt Tita and Paco, and turned the hunting lodge into my home. Here, between public appearances, the remoteness of the place made it possible for me to have the life I wanted. Business was handled by Isaías' office in Madrid. This was José's home too, though both of us had flats in the capital. Both of us loved Las Moreras, the harshness and honesty of its life.

There was a second reason José lived here with me. Out in the *coto,* the Crypt of the Mercies was hidden. We two were now its keepers, the only ones who knew its location.

Paco must have read my mind.

"Sí ...the Mercies," he said. "It's out there somewhere."

I stretched, yawned. "You and your fantasies. The family crypt is where it's always been. Under the chapel at the house."

"No, no, that one isn't the real Mercies. And I'm going to find the real one," Paco said grimly. "It's very important to help our family reclaim its place in Spain."

One kilometer past the village, still following the new power-line, we pulled off the paved highway into Las Moreras, the parcel where the hunting lodge stood. Here, unpaved traces of the Roman road took us past the lodge, then angled away through the pastures, between stone walls. Two kilometers farther along the road was the actual entrance to the *coto,* and a small farm where the present gamekeeper lived. Beyond, the ancient road lost itself in the strong glare of afternoon as it went switchbacking over a natural pass on the summit of the *coto,* then headed south towards Andalucía.

At the lodge, barking dogs and clucking chickens scattered before the two dusty cars. The small homes of my housekeeper-cook, gardener and three guards had their TV aerials and gardens bursting with onions and flowers. A SEAT 600, the little Spanish-made FIAT that was fast becoming the "people's car," had just braked in a cloud of dust. Everything else was old, built of lichened native stone pillaged from the castle and other ruins in the area. Here too, machine-gun fire had pocked the walls of stables and granaries.

Among these familiar scenes, Juan Diano's blue eyes seemed far away — something I'd seen in another life.

"Don Antonio!" a village woman shouted at me, getting out of the SEAT with three other women. She was Candalaria López, once a goatherd, now manager of the oil plant. She gave me a big strong handshake, like a man.

"The olives look good, eh, Don Antonio?" she said.

Candalaria's strong bugle voice still had the old edge in it. Her mother was among the women massacred by Franco's troops in 1936. Her family had blamed all churchmen and aristocrats for this atrocity, though lately she had shown signs of making an exception in my case.

"Yes, they look very good," I replied, hoping that one day she would stop calling me *don.*

"You were enormous, Don Antonio!" shouted Eustacio, the gardener. "We watched you on the *tele!*"

"We're glad you're all right," his wife called.

I waved at them, and walked on. Even in the midst of my depression, it felt good to come home.

Ahead jutted the two-story manse. José and I had planted a belt of pines and mulberries around it, to break the winter winds and soften its grim silhouette. The architectural style reflected a time when the family adopted a stout post-Inquisition puritanism. The main quadrangle grafted gracelessly onto a small austere 13th-century church next door, forcibly annexing it as the house chapel. Now it had electricity and indoor plumbing. No central heating yet — we still relied on butane heaters on wheels, rolled from room to room as needed. Our own TV aerial poked bravely from the lichened tile roof, near a vast stork-nest on the northeast corner. We let the nest stay as a sign of our wish for wild creatures to come back. Stork flappings and noisy calls brought life to the house.

The church's weathered door stood open, and the four women went in. One was carrying some garden flowers she'd picked. I'd encouraged the La Morans to pray here — another effort to bridge the gulf between my family and the village. They hadn't asked for a priest to come on Sundays, and I hadn't offered to bring one. But they had adopted Our Lady of Mercies because the *coto* was feeding them. Inside, the women would dust and fuss around, re-light blazes of candles in front of Her and arrange the flowers around Her.

As the three of us got creakily out of José's car, that heat and stillness hit us like a blow, after hours on the highway.

My eyes went to the *morera,* an ancient Persian mulberry tree thirty feet tall, that shaded the house's south wall. In spite of my sadness, I felt the familiar surge of love for her. Her golden berries would nourish every bird in those parts, from our chickens to songbirds arriving from Africa. The lodge's name suggested that a whole grove of mulberry grew here in medieval times. But only this one survived. Her roots drank from the same deep seep that fed our well, and gnawed minerals from our very walls. Like the Escuderos, she had been here forever. José and I, in turn, had fed off her. We had grown up playing in her branches, sitting hidden in her leaves, till the family grew perturbed at our unruly comradeship. Who knows what they feared — whether incest, or the simple threat of shared rebellious thinking. At any rate, José was packed off to a convent school in Toledo, and I to the same military school in Toledo that Franco had attended. The officers were so watchful for "vice" that I never knew if other boys shared my lonely hungers.

José's eyes caught mine. She remembered too — the way we'd stayed in touch by secret letters carried by the family driver. Eventually the commandant booted me out, and told my father that I was not officer material. But José was stuck in her school till she was 18. Sera was boarded there too, so the two girls became chums.

I took José's hand, and she squeezed my fingers.

The crew unloaded my gear and left immediately, piling into Manolillo's and Bigotes' car. They were off to work for a new kid that Isaías had billed in Ciudad Real in a few days. My dwindling contracts had forced the men to scratch around for other jobs.

"Good luck," I told them.

They waved, and were off in a cloud of dust.

The tall coffered door, with its elaborate rusty iron hinges, loomed ahead. My valet, Braulio, always such a dourly correct soul, swung it open. José and I walked into the patio.

When my sister and I had occupied Las Moreras, this patio was empty, its stone pavement littered with broken roof-tiles blown off in winter storms. But José and I had made twin magic here. We hired Eustacio, a villager, as our gardener. Now this arcaded space was filled with sunlit trees and rose shrubs, growing in huge terracotta jars. Their freshness hung in the still air, casting gracious shadows across the center fountain where war-horses once drank. Now the marble basin was mossy quiet — filled from the medieval well beneath, in whose depths a new German-made electric pump purred. I'd brought the pump home from one of my erotic rovings to Hamburg, so we had all the water we wanted. That well had never failed us.

Under the sheltering arches, amid hanging pots of red geraniums, was a comfortable clutter of rattan chairs and divans, Moorish rugs and cushions, and our outdoor dining area. In summer we practically lived in the patio, retreating to the upstairs rooms only at night, or during the winter.

"'Tonio my boy!" my mother Doña Elena cried out.

My mother and Aunt Tita sat bolt upright in their rattan chairs, looking like a Victorian photograph of court ladies. They were obvious sisters in identical black silk day-dresses from Crippa's, the stodgiest salon in Madrid. I had never understood our national obsession for wearing black (even the British have sense enough to wear white in hot countries). Being widows, Mamá and Tita avoided flamboyant jewelry. Their tiny gold watches were Spanish made, since they considered the Swiss to be foreign, Protestant and therefore immoral. Both ladies flapped their fans — a traditional amenity that some older Spanish women were not ready to surrender in favor of *moderno* air conditioning. The late spring heat was a good opportunity for an Old Catholic to do a little penance.

Mamá and Tita had been watching the news on our new TV, which cast its eerie silver flicker on the lichened vaults above. Across the screen our great cyclist Bahamontes flashed, pedaling furiously. The "eagle of Toledo" was better known than I — why wasn't Paco courting *him* into politics? Yes, times were changing. Soccer and bicycle races were more popular than bullfights now.

The two ladies spent as little time as possible at Las Moreras. To them, my village and torero associates were barbarians. But today they had motored up from Toledo, and I braced myself for trouble. They never watched me on the *tele,* for fear of having heart attacks with every pass, but news of my exhausted state had surely reached their ears via Sera's mother.

"*¡Canastas!*" my mother proclaimed. "We will be so thankful to God when all this is over."

"Baskets" — *canastas* — was the strongest swear-word that Mamá and Tita used. By "all this", they meant my career in the ring.

"You look very tired," Tita added accusingly. She worked her fan too. "When will you rest?"

"When I'm old," I said.

Mamá fluttered her fan at her sweaty face. Her sharp eyes had already moved on to José, noting that my sister was wearing heretic clothing, namely the Yankee blue jeans.

At one time, I had dutifully willed myself to love my mother. But love had sun-faded to annoyance and pity. She was the archetypical woman in the cartoons of Mingote, overbearing yet trapped in tradition, the kind of woman whose sons did exactly what she wanted...and what she wanted was for men to rule the roost. In truth, Mamá had no power, beyond whatever scrap of privilege she'd accept from the family males. Since I did little to stiffen her spine, she had turned to Paco for a prop.

When Braulio went upstairs with my bags, my mother's voice dropped to a conspiratorial tone. "Well? Did you talk to Serafita? Did you settle things?"

"An afternoon of bulls," I said, "is not a good time for proposals."

"But you saw Serafita after the bulls," accused Tita.

The electric fan stood blatantly unplugged by the TV. I started it, and turned its breezes pointedly at my mother and aunt. They ignored it, and kept flapping their fans. On the TV screen, General Franco was making a speech somewhere, in that high feminine voice that his enemies derided behind his back. "Freemasons and Communists are deadly threats to Spain," he ranted. He was 77 now, thirty years in power, hand shaking as he gestured.

Supper was informal, but stressful. To escape the heat, we ate there in the patio, at the oak table under the arcades. The menu was veal chops from one of our own calves, marinated in our own oil and garlic, washed down with La Mancha red wine. The cook, Marimarta, grilled the chops masterfully over a twig fire in the opposite corner of the patio. Smoke roiled up past the arches, carrying a fragrance of burning native brush, to lose itself in the evening sky.

Silent, drinking wine, my sister and I listened to Mamá and Tita lecture me. Paco said not a word — the two women capably picked up the harangue where he had left off. Bla bla bla...the wife, children, new blood, new life for the struggling family tree. José would surely do nothing to further our Escudero destiny. In any case, José was only a woman. Everything depended on me. I had to stop living dangerously and settle down. Serafita was the perfect match for me. Two great families grafting together, as they had once before in the past, when they worked together to support Philip II. Bla bla bla... Sera's family great? They were as faded as the Escuderos.

The iron door of fate was swinging shut on me. My comeback could stretch for a few more afternoons, maybe. But my career in the ring was finished. And the Montanese peasant wouldn't come. It was a thing between strangers. A fantasy. The most passionate and painful moment I'd known — a graze of bodies in a crowd. And it was over. Why argue with Mamá and hold out for my right to marry for love? I had never felt that way about any woman. I might as well get it over with — get married, and continue my erotic rovings in secret, as I had always done.

I heaved a deep sigh.

"All right," I said wearily. "I have four more afternoons. Marbella, Bilbao, San Sebastián. Then Arles in the last week of August. After Arles, I'll retire."

"Where is this Arles?" Tita demanded to know.

"Arles is in France," I said patiently. "An ancient center of Roman culture."

"The Romans were barbarians," Tita sniffed.

"You can cancel," Paco said. "Send them a telegram."

"I signed contracts. I'm a man of honor. So I'll finish my obligations the right way."

"And after Arles..." Mamá prodded relentlessly.

"After Arles, I'll marry Serafita. If it can be settled. You don't even know if she wants this."

"She does."

"How do you know?"

"Her mother says so."

Mamá's and Tita's faces glowed with delight. Paco smirked in triumph. They had finally brought me down. I lay at their feet like a dying bull, with a sword through my heart.

Unsmiling, José studied me. She pulled out her silver cigarette case, and extracted a Turkish cigarette. For the moment, my mother ignored José's smoking. Marimarta came from the kitchen with a bowl of her famed chilled custard for dessert, and served us.

When the family was alone again, Mamá grandly gave me a gift that she must have hoarded for years, waiting for this moment. My shaky fingers opened the little box to find a pair of gold wedding rings, filigreed in the most elegant Toledo style. Mamá had ordered them from some hoary artisan in town. Right in front of the other family members, she dared to lecture me further. I was to put the rings in the chapel, before the Virgin of Mercies. She said I was road-hardened. Serafita was innocent, unspoiled. I was to pray that the Mother of Mercies would guide my crass male heart, she said.

Sitting half-turned away, José smoked in silence, listening. Keeping my face expressionless, I put the box in my pocket.

"Yes, Mamá. Of course," I said.

Made bold by victory, Mamá and Tita now turned their cannons on my sister.

"And you, María Josefina, you know as well as we do where smoking leads," Mamá said.

"Mamá," José replied patiently, "smoking has never led me to indiscretions. So let me have my one little *moderna* vice."

"María Josefina," Tita said loftily, "you will not smoke in our presence."

"Then I'll smoke somewhere else," said José, getting up.

As my sister strode out of the patio, narrow hips moving rhythmically in her jeans, Mamá called after her: "And those kinds of pants are only fit for foreign men. Remember that."

"Pants," José shot back over her shoulder, "are armor. That's why men wear them."

The great door banged as she went out.

"Leave José alone," I blazed at them.

"Don't call her José," Paco barked at me. "It isn't fitting."

"I've called her José for twenty years," I barked back, "and I'm not going to stop now."

Getting up, I followed my sister out the door. It boomed shut a second time. Outside, we both had a smoke under the mulberry tree. Depressed, we listened to the first calls of the nightjar, that bird of Castile who makes the night so sweet. Its single piercing notes went ringing across the rocky slope above.

Early next morning, while it was still cool, José and I headed for the olive groves. Here, on a pretext of inspecting the crop, we could talk privately. My sister was mounted on our grey stallion, Faisán. She was wearing the jeans, chaps, a man's Cordoban hat and vest, and had a cigarette gripped grimly in her lips. Because my doctor had said that walking was good for my leg, I was on foot, with my four greyhounds at heel. *Walk, Antonio,* the doctor had said. *Walking will heal you.*

The 18-year-old stallion was a relic of my early torero days, when my father hoped I'd fight bulls on horseback like a gentleman. Faisán was a purebred Carthusian — his pedigree almost as long as ours. My father had traded a small El Greco painting for Faisán because he didn't have the cash for such a horse. When I went to fighting on foot, José took over Faisán. She was in her tomboy glory then, and spent one passionate winter training for her own debut as a horseback bullfighter, before the family put a stop to it. Faisán hadn't been in front of a bull for eight years, so the finer points of his dressage training had gone rusty. He was now a family pet — a complete waste, as Paco kept saying. But Faisán still flexed his powerful neck into the basics, and obeyed my sister perfectly. She lined him away at a collected canter, smoke drifting over her shoulder, along a row of richly woven shadows cast by olive trees. Then she turned and cantered back to me, making the horse change leads. Faisán's bountiful silvery mane rose and fell with each stride.

José looked so dashing in men's riding clothes! Yes, a *marimacho***, a tomboy, was still there behind the cultivated feminine facade. Now and then I'd wondered if she was — well, like me. Probably she was not. She was always talking about men. "If only I dared to go out with more interesting men!" she always said. "The right men are all so boring!" I yearned to tell José my secret. Why couldn't I tell my sister, who had grown into life with me, holding me against her heart for nine months?

José halted Faisán in front of me. I stroked the horse's forehead, and he nipped me. "He's getting bad manners," I said.

"He's bored. He needs something to do."

"You still look good on a horse. Better than I ever did."

"Yes," she said wistfully. "I did dream of being the next Conchita Cintrón."

"The horse is still sound and strong. We could get a trainer in here...have the two of you back in shape in no time. The family can't stop you now. *Canastas*...you can support me when I retire."

"Nobody will buy a ticket to see a 30-year-old lady lancing bulls," she scoffed. "Yes, it's too late for me."

Too late. Too late. The words rang in my ears.

"Content to be an old-maid journalist, eh?" I asked.

"Why not? It's a good life."

I walked on. She walked Faisán beside me. One of the hounds, Miki, put up a rabbit. All four dogs chased off over a hill.

"'Tonio, I've never seen you so sad," she finally remarked.

"Is it that obvious?"

"Braulio keeps looking at you. Marimarta asked me what's eating you. Tere is out of her mind worrying about you. Of course nobody but me will ask the right questions."

I sighed. "Then ask."

"Do you really want to marry Sera?"

"No."

She drew a deep breath, and looked away to the west, at the skyline of the *coto*. "Do you want to marry anyone?"

"No."

"Why not?"

While I anguished over the answer, she wheeled Faisán and cantered away from me again. I watched the horse's magnificent haunches flexing as he moved along. Instantly my imagination leaped to picture a man's haunches flexing as he made love. Juan Diano's narrow butt, humping me in his slaughterhouse coveralls. The feel of him against my leg. Being frenzied and alone with this thing for so many years was making me crazy. Yes, some friendly counsel was needed. If I couldn't trust José, who could I trust?

The next time José came cantering back, she halted Faisán and pressed me: "Why not, 'Tonio?"

I looked around to make sure no one was near.

"Because," I said, "I am in the throes of desire."

"This is unusual for you?" she scoffed.

"This time, yes."

"So...you're worried about managing a mistress *and* a wife?"

"It's more serious than that."

José stared down at me. The dogs were returning rabbit-less from their chase, panting.

"What can be more serious than a mistress?" José demanded. "Two mistresses? Three?"

I was silent again.

She laughed. "Is your mistress a cripple? Does she have hair on her upper lip?"

"Worse yet."

"A German lady? A Yankee?"

I could hardly get the words out. "A man," I said.

Did the trees have ears?

José's mouth didn't fall open, like I thought it would. She just stared at me for a long moment. I couldn't meet her eyes. When she threw away her cigarette and dismounted, I turned away, afraid to face her.

"Darling," she said softly, holding the reins with one hand and seizing my arm with the other. "Look at me."

I summoned my courage and faced her. José's wonderful eyes met mine with a man's frankness and strength. "Darling brother," she repeated. To my relief, she hugged me with one arm, enveloping me in her fragrance of Le Dé. I hugged her back so hard that her dashing hat fell off and rolled on the dusty ground. The horse tried to nip us both, and we fended him off blindly.

She rocked me in her arms, mother-like. I could hardly speak, choked by intense emotion and relief.

"For years, I've wondered," she said against my neck. "I've watched men caress you with their eyes."

Finally we drew apart. I brushed her hat off, put it on her head. As we walked, she put her arm through mine, leading Faisán.

"Well!" she said in her best sherry voice. "Don't tell me you're chasing after a boy flamenco dancer with silver heels. Or some impossible drag queen in Barcelona."

"A man of Castile."

"*Huuuuuuy,*" she said in awe.

By her expression, I knew she understood exactly what I was saying. I was going to step off the accepted path. A man like me, if he sinned in this manner, might keep within the barest bounds of acceptablility by doing it with boys or drag queens, because they were "women" who gave it up to "real men." A deep shiver went through me.

Now she too shivered, very visibly. "Yes, this is serious."

"To see him again, I'd give a finger off my right hand. The finger I use most."

She gripped my arms. "Darling, be careful."

"I've been careful all my life."

"You're obsessed." She fended off another Faisán love-bite.

"I am. This thing is going to change my life somehow."

"May I know who he is?"

"The man in Santander."

She stared at me. "The slaughterhouse guy? Are you mad?"

"I have never been more sane."

"You don't know him," she pointed out. "How do you even know he's..."

"I know enough to know."

"But he's rabble." My sister did have her social prejudices.

"Maybe he'll make a great torero."

"Then how can you bear to put him in front of the horns?"

Seeing my despair, she laughed. "Don't worry. Even for a slaughterhouse guy, I'll be your ally," she said.

Suddenly she was brimming with good advice.

"Training him as your protegé is a good cover. What the devil— even if he doesn't make a torero, you can set him up somewhere nearby. Find him a job that would let you visit him. See him when you can. I'll run messages if you need it."

My courage started limping back, cautiously.

"I have to find him first," I said.

"Yes, you didn't encourage him," she said. "You gave him your card and showed him the door. Why didn't you just invite him here...for a tryout?"

"My crew...Isaías...they might sense something."

"Bah. You are a master at hiding things. You fooled me all these years. Toreros invite novices for tryouts all the time. They all would love to see you with a protegé."

"I know," I said, despairing. "Fear made me stupid."

We walked for a bit.

"Look," I said. "Let's you and I take a trip. I'll tell everybody I need a few days' vacation before my next contract. We'll run back to Santander and try to find him."

"Good idea. If he's interested in you, we'll give him train fare. He can show up at Las Moreras like he came on his own. If he's intelligent, he'll see the need for intrigue. If he doesn't understand, well...you should stay away from him."

"We have to be careful about Paco."

"Have you ever wondered if he has us watched?"

"Sometimes. But I never notice anything. He's so wrapped up in his Sherlock Holmes thing about finding the Crypt."

She shivered. "It's no Sherlock Holmes story any more. I hear things in the *ABC* office. These days they have got all kinds of *moderno* spy equipment. Paco could have a spy put one of those little things in the phone, that can listen to us..."

My own paranoia was tweaked by this.

"It was odd how Paco talked about García Lorca the other night," I said.

"Yes. People have not forgotten that. My boss was talking about Lorca at lunch the other day. He knows somebody who knows somebody who knows where they shot him."

"Where?"

"Outside of Granada. Near the Fountain of Tears."

---

escudo — Spanish for shield. *Escudero* — shield-bearer. Synonymous with *hidalgo,* meaning noble.

**coto* — game reserve.

***marimacho* — tomboy.

4

The next day, José and I raced north in her Citröen. We had a wonderful trip — a reconfirmed oneness. As the Cantábrico mountains rose before us, and our tires screeched around curves, I lounged in the passenger seat and told lightly censored stories of my ventures into foreign tenderloins. José howled with laughter, eyes always on the road, driving like a professional trying to win at Le Mans.

All the while, a less conversational part of my mind held its obsessive images of Juan Diano. My body vibrated in anticipation. With every kilometer ticked off on the dashboard, I was closer to him again. When we crossed the summit at Reinosa, descending back into that bracing coastal air, my vibrations reached frenzy level. With luck, if we found Juan soon, I could bed him discreetly in a hotel on the way home.

In Santander, near the slaughterhouse, I hid behind sunglasses and waited nervously in the car, while José put on scuffed flats and tied a village kerchief over her head. Pretending to be a big-city relative looking for her cousin Juan, she inquired at the slaughterhouse. The boss told her that Juan quit the day after the bullfight. Too bad — good worker. Smart kid too. No, he didn't know where Juan lived. Maybe some workers' boardinghouse on the edge of town. He did recall Juan mentioning that his father was a stock-raiser in Santillana. Or maybe it was Santilla. Or Umbrilla.

Next we tried boardinghouses that catered to emigrant men, and their neighborhood bars.

After that, we went to the edge of town and walked gingerly through the migrant shantytown. We were shocked at its squalor. There were half a million Juans in Spain, and several of them might live in these tin shacks...except few people would talk to us for fear we were police spies. The one we found was a wobbly old wino. He was accompanied by a wobbly old dog named Syphilis who was infested with mange.

"As you can see, I'm not your cousin," the old man declared with great dignity. "Come, Syphilis." The pair wobbled off.

"So," I told José hopefully, "let's look for his village."

At a tourist shop, we bought a map of La Montaña. It showed Santillana and Santoña, but no Santilla. There was an Umbrilla in the wild area known as Picos de Europa. So we left the capital and jounced west, along tiny highways honeycombed with potholes. We bored through moldering mountain villages, past the occasional abandoned 16th century manse whose gentry owners had emigrated to Mexico or Peru. We wended past chokingly lush cornfields and steep cow-pastures, along stone walls overgrown with ferns and tiny wildflowers. Every man at work in some steep field, cutting hay with a scythe, could be Juan Diano.

Once, on the road ahead, I was sure we'd spotted him. A tall blond man, with shoulders like a steel-worker, was walking beside his team of oxen — a dun breed typical of the province, with an oaken yoke lashed to their horns. The wagon was piled precariously high with a jiggling load of dried hay. As José honked politely, we slowly pulled even with the youth. My heart pounded wildly. He turned his head and stared at us, touching his goad to the patient oxen.

It wasn't Juan.

Umbrilla was another clutch of stone homes, grey limestone here, huddled around a Romanesque church of the same rock. Here, too, were a few ruined houses and bullet-pocked walls. Leftist guerrillas had held out in these mountains well into the 1950s.

Above Umbrilla, tiny dairy farms cut the green land into a ragged mosaic with thousands of pieces. People milked cows, sheep and goats, and made fiercely strong blue cheese of the mingled milk, that they ripened in limestone caves and sold in local markets. For generations of peasant firstborn sons, such freeholds had been relentlessly divided and re-divided, till they were now splinters of real estate. It was this ownership of land, however fractured and impractical (the parcels' small size made modern farm machinery impractical) that distinguished the northern rural poor from the landless poor of southern Spain. In Andalucía, the Juan Dianos bent their backs as day-workers on the great latifundias, some of which dated back to Roman times — all of which were owned by families like ours.

Beyond the farms rose the Picos, sheer limestone cliffs and needles, with the 2519-meter Naranjo de Bulnes spiring in the distance, still streaked with a little snow at this time of year. Domestic stock grazed with deer and chamois on the highest alps. It was Spain's one remaining enclave of truly wild land, impenetrable save by foot or horseback. After the Civil War, a few bands of leftist guerrillas still operated up there. Even today, I had heard, a hunter might stumble on human bones in the brush along various streams.

In the village square, José and I parked near the bar, under an ancient sycamore whose top had broken in some winter storm.

Tired, my sister napped in the car while I stood looking at the church for a few minutes. An honest historian could hardly say it was built for Christian use — more likely it was a late-lingering temple school built before Christianity finally swamped these remote mountains. Along the sculptured beam-ends of the roof, humans entwined in poses that were unabashedly erotic. On the stark facade, there was no sculpture of Jesus the King — just twinings of Celtic interlace. Ireland was not far away, just 1000 kilometers north across the Bay of Biscay.

So I put on my sunglasses and forged into the bar. The bartender and his handful of customers, watching a soccer game on TV, had faces as stoney as that church outside.

"A tourist, eh? You're here to gawk at our scandalous church?" the bartender grumbled.

They didn't recognize the torero that they might have seen on that TV. But I turned on my charm, and finally they had a round of *orujo* with me. The taste of it slammed me with a powerful memory of that strong dirty hand offering me the dripping glass. I told them I was looking for my cousin Juan Diano.

Old Juan is dead now, may he rest in peace, they said. His son Manolín didn't have the patience to tear down the stone walls and put scattered bits of family land into the new farmers' collective. He abandoned the farm, went to Germany to work in a factory. Took his mother Maruca with him. The poor thing wrote one homesick letter to her neighbor. That was the last anybody heard.

Gone to West Germany? In a few days? My heart sank.

"When?" I asked.

"A year ago," the bartender said.

"My cousin doesn't have a grown son. He is around 25."

"Then you must mean Young Juan," the bar man said. "The seminarian."

"The good-good boy," someone else said. They all laughed maliciously. Seminarian? That bandit who stole a feel from me?

"Where is he now?" I asked their row of weathered faces.

"Nobody knows," said one. "After he left the seminary, he emigrated."

"The girls here don't miss him," another added.

As they all hooted with laughter, my scalp prickled. Men can be even meaner than women when they gossip.

As I left the bar, I was sure that we probably had the right man. And a cold trail. José woke up, and I told her the sad news. We completed our tour of Umbrilla by going to the tiny cemetery, and finding Old Juan's grave. Beside it were the graves of Juan's sisters, ages 2 and 4, and a grandfather who had died in 1960.

Somewhere outside of town, the Diano farm stood abandoned. We didn't have the heart to look for it.

Leaving La Montaña by another high pass over those alps, we looked for wild animals. As José drove slower, I pulled binoculars out of the glovebox and scanned the limestone crags for a glimpse of ibex with their massive curved horns. The government had grown proud of the game in this pocket of wildness, and allowed a tiny number of approved gun-owners to shoot here, even selected tourists — but at a high price per head. Few locals could afford to hunt legally. Franco liked to have newsmen photograph him with rows of dead animals.

Suddenly, as José rounded a curve near the summit, we surprised a band of dark bay horses. They were *asturcones,* a breed who have run wild on those rocky slopes since the cave of Altamira was painted. One minute, a dozen mares and foals and a stallion were grazing quietly among blue thistles near the highway. The next minute, they scudded away across the rocks, down a slope, slipping and sliding on gravel. A foal fell, scrambled up again. They splashed across a little stream. In another second, as drops of flung water still sparkled falling in the air, the last flying mane had vanished over a ridge beyond.

Suddenly my imagination could see Juan bareback on the little stallion. He had an untaught natural seat, hips thrusting with the war-horse's strides — riding wild in leather armor, brandishing a short sword and round shield with Celtic braidings on it. He and his troop of wild horsemen went racing away across that slope. They too vanished over the ridge.

José and I parked the car on the shoulder.

We jumped the stream and walked up that ridge, hoping to see the *asturcones* again. Beyond was a rocky valley, but it was empty. The weather was fine, with dapplings of white clouds across the sky, and a breeze that smelled of melting snow. Cloud shadows moved with slow dignity across the land, cooling us as they passed. As a golden eagle circled high above, his shadow scudded along the stream past us.

As José leaned on a rock, we smoked a single cigarette together in silence, listening to the rushing water.

"Dig your toes in. We'll find him," she finally said, blowing smoke.

"He probably went to Germany. I would too, if I were him. Let's go home." I dropped the cigarette and stepped on it.

She hesitated a moment.

"Before we go, I'd better tell you *my* secret," she said.

The silence moved between us, like cloud shadows across the vast slope. The question locked in my throat finally burst past my teeth, like a bubble of air from the lungs of a drowning man.

"I suppose you're...like me," I said.

"Of course."

"You reckless thing, that's what comes of sharing a womb with me," I said. "My vice rubbed off on you, eh?"

"Why did it take you so long to know about me?" she asked.

"Maybe I didn't want to know. Like I didn't want to know about myself."

She laughed, watching cloud shadows move across the rocks.

"But you always say how much you like men," I said.

She grinned. "The old broken-wing trick. You've seen a million partridge do it. I'm surprised you fell for it."

"How long have you been...this way?"

"Always, I think."

"In convent school?"

"Don't tell me," she hooted, "that you weren't giving it up at school with some brother cadet."

I sighed sadly, remembering. "You overestimate me. There was Jaime, from Galicia. It seems I go for northern men! But I never knew if... Anyway, the officers were always watching. I didn't dare do anything till later."

José chuckled. "I was with my friend under the noses of the good sisters and the entire family. Including yours."

"May I know who she is?"

She was silent a moment longer. Then:

"Serafita."

My jaw dangled with astonishment. "She...your *amiga* , all these years?"

"I've had no other."

"So...both of you so perfectly faithful?"

José was looking away, her eyes pained.

"It has grown less perfect with time," she said. "Lately we don't speak much."

"You put horns on her?" I asked drily.

"No. But I have been...mean," José's eyes moved back to mine with a strange defiant stare. "Sera was demanding that I risk everything and tell you. The pressure about the marriage is getting out of hand. We don't want it, and neither do you. The worries are affecting our friendship. I was as afraid as you."

"You two have nothing to fear from me."

"She needs to hear that from you."

I lit another cigarette and smoked, thinking. My own pulse thudded in my ears, blood pumping with deep emotion.

A tear rolled down José's cheek. "I'm afraid I...slapped her. She hasn't forgiven me yet."

"What a bastard life we have," I said.

José dried her tear, took my second cigarette and smoked it. "There is another way," she finally said.

"Go live in Denmark?" I scoffed.

"We can," José shrugged, "resort to the oldest strategy in Christendom."

"What?"

"You marry Sera. I marry your friend, if you ever settle on one. I'm not sure that I'd marry this peasant rabble of yours. But a suitable man, well...I'd marry him in a minute. And the four of us could make a secret pact to...go on as before."

Sunlight brightened across the rocky slope. Above, the eagle slid off and disappeared. I considered this tempting but terrifying option.

"You might steal my dairy-farm *majo* from me," I smiled.

"I prefer brunettes," she sniffed.

"What about children?"

"Sera and I don't want them much. And you?"

"The family demands children. You know that. Mamá and Paco, the aunts. They will be furious if no children are born."

José shrugged again.

"If I have no children," I added, "the title goes to Paco's oldest."

"Do you care?"

"No. He won't get the land, at least. The land is what matters."

"The family will have to accept our decision. For all they know, it *is* God's will. Some couples never have children."

"God's will for both couples? Such a coincidence. They may not accept the lie."

"Oh, they will eat the lie, all right."

"Either the lie," I said, "or two bullets up your *culo.*"

She shuddered at my frankness. "What do you mean?"

"I've heard rumors...how they killed poor Lorca. That's what Paco meant, the other night, when the journalists asked about *maricones.*"

"I wonder why they call us 'marys'?" she wondered.

"I'm no *maricón,* my dear."

She ignored my comment. "Curious, isn't it? All the words have Her name in them. Sera pointed that out to me. She'd love to go to school and study history."

José strolled in a slow circle, pondering.

"*María,*" she mused, going through the whole dreadful litany. "*Maricón, marica, maricona, mariposa, marimacho* ... Her holy name is in every one of the rotten words for us. Maybe we were sacred to Her once."

"Why did you and I have to turn out this way?" I protested, to no one in particular.

"Ave María, Star of the Sea...." She crushed the cigarette under her shoe, hummed the first line of the old Latin hymn, then broke off. "I don't know, 'Tonio. Look at us. Two black chick-peas in the same family. Do you suppose it's in the blood?"

"You mean...like the pepper is in the wild cattle?"

"Do you think we had...some ancestors, long ago? That maybe this was what caused some of the trouble in the family?"

My mind was moving off to the elusive Juan Diano Rodríguez again. If I were to yield to him, there would be no bloody first night, the kind that Spanish theater and films love to dramatize. All this talk of "breaking manhoods" was no different than talk of "breaking maidenheads." Both notions were an invention of patriarchal religion, which wanted to own people like cattle. The truth was, I didn't believe that true manhood lives in a man's ass, or in church fictions. Juan's love would stir my sea like an oar, and leave no mark.

She saw my imagination fly off over the slopes, like an eagle.

"Let's go home," she said, taking my arm. "Maybe we're not finding Juan Diano because he is on his way to find you."

As we drove south, José told me uncensored stories of convent school, and the start of her friendship with Sera. The stories came out with a rush. I could see her great relief at being able to tell me. Her eyes glowed, her lips trembled. Now and then, her driving was careless. My sister was a changed person, letting it be seen that she was in love.

But when we got to Madrid, and I made a casual phone call to Las Moreras to get any news, Juan wasn't there. So we visited Isaías and

Tere at their office. While José sat at the typewriter and made notes for her next column, I told the old couple that I planned to retire after Arles. They accepted the news quietly, with dry little sphinx smiles. Isaías and Tere had lived together so long that they even smiled alike.

"We expected this," he said.

"We're glad," she added. "It has made me a cardiac case, watching you struggle."

"Do you have some novice to take my place?" I wondered.

"Oh," Isaías said carelessly, "there are four or five young things dogging me. They all want to be the next El Cordobés. None of them have the gift you had." He lit a cigar. "The guy in Santander didn't show up, eh?"

"No."

"With the invitation you gave him, he wouldn't have lost a minute if he had a passion for bulls," Tere added, reaching to answer the phone.

While Tere talked on the phone, Isaías stretched, and slapped my shoulder. "Maybe it is time for me to leave the bulls too. I am losing the taste for it. The country is changing. The science, the art is vanishing. Only a few classic toreros now. The woman and I need to find something else to do."

Tere put her hand over the phone, looked at Isaías. "It's Sótano again. He wants Antonio in Vitoria," she hissed.

Isaías looked at me inquiringly.

"No," I said.

"Not even South America this winter? We have the first inquiry."

"No more contracts."

If I left Madrid without visiting Sera, the family would be all over me. After all, I had just promised them that I'd propose to her. Besides, José insisted that I put Sera's mind at rest.

So we went calling at her mother's stuffy little townhouse near the cathedral.

It was unseasonably hot. The three of us sat in their patio garden and Doña Margarita's housekeeper served us a wine cooler. José's worry over her misstep with Sera was now squeezed out of sight behind a mask of family correctness. While she chattered with Sera's mother in one corner, Sera and I sat in the opposite corner on a hard oak bench, with a discreet distance between us, and in view of the others, as a well-brought-up young couple was supposed to do do, and we had a guarded conversation. José had already told her my secret. My sister's comment about spies was keeping me nervous. Who knew if Sera's mother could read lips? I chose words that would look good to a lip-reader.

Sera and I tried to look social and relaxed. She noticed me shifting uncomfortably on the hard bench.

"Are you still feeling the thing that happened in Santander?" she asked.

"No," I said, touched at her concern. "Faisán wrenched my leg the other day. It's nothing compared to...what I am feeling right now."

Sera's hand was vibrating, almost imperceptibly, as she sipped at her glass.

"So you...know my true feelings at last," I said.

My voice was vibrating at the same frequency as her hand. I couldn't remember when I'd been so nervous in front of a bull, even one with horns like pitchforks. If I hadn't known Sera was someone like me, I couldn't have gotten the words out.

"Yes, José called me last night. She hinted," Sera said in that sweet voice that might have driven me crazy with love in another life. "Antonio, I can't believe that you...you of all men..." Her voice broke.

"Some other time, we can talk about these things," I assured her. "For now, know that I feel nothing but respect for you, and a desire to see you happy. Do you understand?"

"Yes," she murmured.

Sera raised her gaze to mine — those carefully made-up eyes, just a touch of mascara on those long eyelashes that I might have adored if I were any other man. She understood my meaning, and came close to a smile — one that I would have killed for if I was a different kind of man.

"Then let's think of the future," I said.

"It is a dangerous future."

Sera was trying to keep obvious distress out of her eyes. Her mother was on tenterhooks, working her fan, sliding sidelong glances at us, wondering if she should risk letting the Wild Man have a few moments alone with her precious only daughter, so I could give Sera a virginal peck on the lips, if that would move things more rapidly towards a formal engagement. I knew that José had mentioned to Sera the tempting and terrifying idea of the Pact.

"There is the other way," I said.

Sera's fingers tightened on the glass. With a huge effort, she kept the terror out of her eyes, and composed her face.

"Very dangerous," she said.

"More dangerous not to have a plan at all."

"I will think about it," she said. "Give me time."

"Time is passing."

"I know."

"You hesitate because you and José quarreled?"

She looked down, probably wondering if she could trust me.

"José has gotten *muy mandón,* very pushy," she said. "Sometimes I don't recognize her."

It occurred to me that, despite our growing up together, this young woman and I were strangers. What was Sera really like? Brave, certainly, if she had risked so much for so many years. I'd have to get to know her as a friend, an ally. It was awkward to be caught in the middle of her difficulties with José. I couldn't take sides against my sister. Was José that much of a man, shadowed by the old feudal attitude, thinking she had that right to command? José's pushiness had given her some great victories, but that sword cut two ways. This slapping thing was not good.

As José and I got up to leave, Sera's mother looked gloomy. Yet another formal visit by me had ended in nothing being settled.

I bent over Sera's hand and kissed it in the most gallant and bloodless way I knew.

As José and I drove off, my sister was angry at Sera's hesitation.

"¡Canastas!" she said. "What is the matter with her? The Pact is the perfect solution to our problem!"

"Perfect," I mumbled. "All I need is a friend of my own."

José dropped me at my city flat, on the Paseo de la Castellana. It was in the same building where Isaías and Tere lived. Then she went on to her own flat a few blocks away. She had writing to do. I picked up some mail, then grabbed my Volkswagen sedan out of the garage, and headed back to Las Moreras alone.

Shut in my room, I flung myself on my lonely bachelor bed and lay there wondering.

Would I have to go into exile in order to feed my nature? I could live in another country where the vice laws were less strict. France, or Netherlands, or Denmark. Could I stand it in Denmark? Even West Germany couldn't be so bad if half a million Spanish emigrants lived there now. I could have a flat in Hamburg and haunt the tenderloin every night. But it would be a lonely life. Sex with men who didn't speak my language. I tried to imagine myself falling in love with some German blueblood and living in his tiny picturebook castle in Bavaria, with his collection of armor and Gutenburg first editions. Maybe I'd get lucky and find some lonely man of Spain, a brother exile, hiding in Hamburg. Maybe I should go to New York, and live with my Red aunt, and find a manly Puerto Rican or Cuban. I couldn't imagine letting myself be fucked by some *Yanqui.*

Behind my bed, lifting a loose stone in the floor, I checked the little wooden box in its hiding place. It contained the gems that

Greatgrandmamá secretly gave me — old jewelry, a handful of investment-quality diamonds, all in chamois bags. "Always have gems," she'd said. "You never know when you'll have to run for your life. Gems are lightweight, you can sell them anywhere."

My cabuchon ring was a gift from Doña Carmen too — a public one. She gave it to me openly on the day I took the alternative as a full matador. In the face of family disapproval, it was her statement that she approved my choice of profession. The diamond had a tiny flaw, but I liked the antique cut — it added to my image of traditional torero. Along with carrying flowers, we were allowed to wear vulgar rings. In private Doña Carmen told me that it had been my greatgrandfather's ring, that three generations of Escudero men who knew the secret had worn it.

José had her own hoard.

Locking the box, I put it back in hiding.

Next afternoon, my crew glumly returned from Ciudad Real. Their novice had a bad afternoon. Desperate for solace, I called my dogs, threw my sheepskin saddle on Faisán and invited Santí to saddle another horse.

"I want to show you something," I told Santí.

Together we rode up to the *coto*. The horses hadn't been out of their stalls for days, and were looking for reasons to buck. When the dogs put up a hare, Faisán almost threw me. After the wrench he gave me, the leg started to hurt.

Our lonely power-line followed the old Roman trace from Las Moreras to the three stucco cottages at the game farm. Joaquin Pastor "El Pico" lived here primitively but comfortably with his wife Magda. A few wind-bent orchard and olive trees sheltered the little colony. No TV aerial — the Pastors didn't trust television. There was nothing tall enough for a stork nest here — everything snugged down out of the weather. Beyond the chicken coop and outdoor privy was a maze of wire-covered game-bird runs. Saddle horses lazed in a stone-walled pasture. My little mare, Mozuela, sent me a whinny.

Beyond, empty uplands of the *coto* lofted toward the sky.

As I dismounted, Old Pico came tottering out and gave me a fatherly hug. I saw him notice my limp.

"How was Santander?" he asked.

"Good enough," I said. "And you're limping as bad as me."

"It's nothing," he scoffed. "The veins in my legs hurt."

From here, the ancient trace led into the *coto,* but we never drove vehicles on it. So the old man held Faisán's head while I clambered back in the saddle, mastering the pain in my leg.

Santí and I rode over the hills, with dogs trooping along. My young picador was still a cowboy at heart, so he was happy to be out there on a saddle horse, and sang under his breath.

The country was making its last show of wild blossom, before African heat seared every rill. Overgrazed as it was, the *coto* managed to support a wilderness of deserty shrubs that sheep don't like, plus the ever-present thistles. We cantered the horses till they and the dogs got tired. Then we sat on a hilltop, leaving the horses tied to a bush, and I thought about my life while the dogs snoozed nearby in the shadow of a rock. Santí sat smoking, wondering what was on the boss's mind.

Hold on, Majín, you gorgeous guy.

Nine years ago, on a spring day like this, after my father died and I became Count of La Mora, I had come up here and ridden Faisán around on my first formal inspection as landowner.

The *coto's* degraded condition had shocked me. For generations, the village and the family had disputed the *coto's* use. The Escudero patriarchs insisted the land was ours, and shot the game to shreds. The villagers insisted the land was theirs — an ancient grazing commons, going back to some unwritten medieval agreement that our family had doubtless violated. So their goats and Merino sheep ravaged the vegetation. Trees had been cut stealthily for fodder and charcoal. With loss of vegetation, the tiny streams and springs were vanishing. Since the Civil War, land development everywhere had made it harder for La Morans to make the traditional summer stock drive to greener pastures in the north. So their animals grazed here year round, increasing pressure on the land. Here and there, a last half-dead native oak stood lonely in the scrub, stirring in the hot lonely winds and ringing silence. Only the hardiest creatures were left, and a handful of vultures.

Aristocratic land abuse was a hot political issue. In Andalucía, the Franco government had felt obliged to expropriate a couple of the most ruined properties. I wanted to make this land live again. For the first time, I knew what useful, noble thing to do with that degree in biology. When Isaías and I had thought it all out, I invited the village men and women to tour the *coto* with me. We walked around out here, and I talked and talked like I was caping whole corrals full of bulls.

"A few more years of Merinos, and it will be over," I had told them. "You and your children will have to move to Madri'th."

They had nodded, reluctantly.

"Here's what we can do," I had said. "We can settle this old dispute. You get rid of the sheep and goats. You help me improve and expand the olive groves, and I'll pay you better than my father did. We'll all get fat selling Spanish oil to the Yankees and the Frogs. Then we'll work together to restore the *coto*. There will be a board of directors and a village committee that helps run the project. We'll replant the *coto* — that'll take years and it will give you year-round work. I'll hire village men as guards. When the pigs and red deer and partridge come back, they'll make us rich all over again. People will come for the shooting. We'll have tourists. We'll shoot discreetly, so the game doesn't get destroyed again. And we'll all get to eat roast pig."

The villagers hadn't smiled. A thousand years of toil and sadness had frozen their windbeaten faces.

But they didn't say no.

So La Mora and I had signed a truce. Most of the Merinos and goats went to market, saving a few for household use.

Next came the legal stuff, which was tricky. I couldn't have the board of directors voting openly — this would look too democratic. I didn't want the regime or Paco getting the idea that this was a leftist freemason plot to bring land reform to Spain. So the Eibars and I created a *montepío,* an emergency fund, something like the Montepío de Toreros that takes care of needy bullfighters and is funded by charity. Then I went to some of my rich fans who loved to hunt, and got them to make generous donations to the Montepío del Coto Morera. At board meetings, we didn't vote, but we looked for subtle consensus. With time, if the country liberalized further, perhaps I could deed the *coto* to the Spanish people, like those national parks in the United States that I had heard about. But for the moment we had to proceed cautiously. I was glad I'd kept the title. What the public and the government saw was a threadbare member of the old aristocracy finding a creative but traditional way of solving his land-use problem.

When I had the *coto* re-surveyed, I quietly excluded the little patch of land — 200 hectares — containing the Crypt of Mercies. My excuse was that our favorite family picnicking grounds and an old family hut was there. I kept this parcel separate from the *coto* and the fund.

Then I had installed Pico, one of the best gamekeepers in Spain. Autumn after autumn, crews of well-paid villagers started planting belts of seedlings — pine, broadleaf, other vegetation. Year after year, dedicated groups of women and children motored to other areas on their Vespas, and gathered seeds of native plants and grasses, and hand-sowed them across the *coto* after the rains started. The Ministry of Agriculture helped us with a little money. I had to admit — subsidies for tree-planting were one good thing that Franco did for Spain. Now that the hard times of the 1940s and '50s were behind us, the country had the energy for a faint stirring of worry over the last tiny pockets of Spanish wildlife. The Picos alps in the north, the Coto Doñana tide marshes in the south, were already becoming objects of public pride for many Spanish people.

Now I got up creakily, and Santí and I mounted again. We rode on.

"The work is starting to show, boss. It's looking greener out here," said my picador.

Letting my gaze drift across the land, I agreed. A subtle haze of fresh green was flushing into the dry granite greys and browns.

"We've restored two springs...released a few dozen roe deer," I said. "No red deer yet — not enough feed for them. Pico is hatching his next round of partridge. Rabbits are coming back. A few hawks and wolves..."

"That's good, boss. If nobody shoots the wolves and the rabbits don't eat everything."

"Right," I said grimly.

With game returning, I'd armed a few village men with shotguns and they kept poachers out. We still had a problem with some stock-grazers over the mountains, in Pozo del Rey. They still considered the *coto* to be their grazing commons. Now and then Isaías had to drive over there and argue with them.

"Any pig yet?" Santí asked.

"Not yet. Not enough feed for them yet. I'm hoping they will come on their own. No lynx yet either. They are rare now."

I didn't mention the one thing missing from the *coto*. This was a trainee, a wildlife professional, who would succeed Pico when he died. So far, no one in the village was right for the position. I had even considered Santí for this position, but Pico had said no. He said Santí wasn't gamekeeper material, though the old man would consider him for a subordinate position. Indeed, few people in Spain were interested in this kind of *moderno* conservation work. It smacked of weepy foreign sentimentality for animals. But seeing the old man's weakness today, I was reminded that this search for a trainee couldn't be postponed longer.

I mounted Faisán again.

Farther on, we wended down into a valley, my favorite spot in the *coto*. It had been thistly and dusty in my childhood, with its stream, the Mas, shrunk to a seasonal trickle. Now the flats along the stream wore a delicate veil of new grass. A belt of new young oaks, willows, wild fruit trees, and patches of brush hesitantly shaded the rocky streambed, where water purled among the stones. From here the Mas ran north past La Mora, before it petered out. In olden times, it had emptied into the Tajo 75 kilometers away.

As I rode along the bank, Faisán shied at something, almost unseating me. A flash of pain seared through my bad leg. I calmed my horse and looked for the frightening thing. It was a dead roe deer, the oldest one on the land. Vultures and wolves had done their work. Now blue-winged magpies stopped picking bits off the bare ribs, and flew off cawing.

"Are you okay, boss?" Santí asked anxiously.

Through a haze of fresh pain, I sat looking at the fresh skeleton.

"A poacher didn't do that," Santí said. "Or he would have taken the carcass away."

"Probably wolves did it," I agreed. "When she came down to drink. Natural cycles starting to happen."

"This place is looking good, boss," Santí said. "A few more years, you'll have boar here."

I pondered how this little valley had provoked the most daring part of my dream.

"And wild cattle too, Santí," I said.

"Eh?"

"How would you like to see a little bunch of wild cows and calves out here?"

"There isn't enough feed for cattle, boss."

"But if there was?"

"Are you thinking of raising fighting bulls when you retire?" he asked, incredulous.

"No," I said. "Something very different."

A few years ago, while in southern France for a bullfight, José and I had gone to a film festival and seen a classic Yankee film, *How the West Was Won*. The scene where the North American bison do their stampede was tremendously emotional. I remembered reading somewhere how the Yankees had saved a few wild herds of their bison. For some reason I suddenly thought: Why shouldn't there be wild cattle in our *coto?* Just to be there, to inspire the human spirit, to complete the gamut of Iberian species. *Bos ibericus* was the diamond in the pinky-ring of our wildlife. The animal had roamed Spain from ancient times. Our modern fighting cattle descended from this species. As we left the theater, José felt the same way — she had grabbed my arm and babbled something about millions of wild cattle in Spain, shaking the earth as they migrated. From that day to this, José and I had dreamed together about our herd.

Now Santí knitted his brow.

"Are you planning to shoot them?" he asked.

"Of course not. Think, man! They used to be wild all over Spain. No different than wolves and deer. Of course, we'd have to build a fence around the *coto*. That would be the Great Fence of China, eh?

It would be over 80 kilometers long…cost a billion pesetas."

I had already done the arithmetic with Isaías.

Santí's first thought was practical. "Those Pozo del Rey stockraisers would be fenced out. They'd be furious."

"We'll get them on our side someday. When there is enough water and grass in these valleys, we'll get a young bull and a few heifers. How would you like to look after our little herd? Or do you want to pic bulls forever?"

Santí grinned slowly. "In ten years, when there's grass here, I'll be your man," he said.

"Good," I said. "It's settled."

We planned to get foundation stock from those few ranches that still bred the real thing. Not the cockroaches with horns that made the modern *fiesta brava* such a predictable commercial enterprise. No, sir...the kind of bearded bovine that I wouldn't want to stand in front of...not even for two million pesetas.

Paco hadn't been happy about the Montepío del Coto Morera. He considered that my decision to accept charity from outsiders was a death-blow to our family pride and our patrimony. But he couldn't find any real political grounds to make trouble for me. José supported me, and often rode with me on inspections.

Today, as I sat there on Faisán, my green flush of hope faded. All I could see was Young Juan's face, in every brief cloud that formed over the hot land. And my leg hurt badly.

That evening around 9, I headed for the chapel to pray about my misery. Mamá, Paco and Aunt Tita had returned to Toledo. Braulio stopped me in the long hallway, where José and I had removed the glowering row of family portraits and hung colorful weaves instead.

"Do you need anything before I retire?" he asked.

"No, thanks, Braulio."

"Then with your permission I'm going to watch TV. Perhaps there will be news of our king."

"Of course."

As Braulio walked away, I stared at his back for a moment. With my new paranoia, I wondered if my valet was the weak link among my men. Braulio was a Navarrese, and had worked for Emil Potrero, an old client of Isaías. When Emil retired, about the time I became matador, Isaías recommended I hire him. I considered Braulio to be part of my camouflage. He was an insufferable Old Catholic and Carlist, who managed to use the word "king" in every other sentence. The trouble was, he might be friendly with Paco behind my back. Whenever I returned from foreign trips, I was always careful to clear luggage and clothing of all evidence save that of heterosexual peccadillos.

The gloomy vaulted Gothic chapel greeted me with its aura of human majesty frozen in time. In front of the gilded high-altar was the tomb of Sanches, first Count of La Mora, who died in 1247. On the marble lid, our bloodthirsty forebear was portrayed in chain mail, hands fossilized into prayers for victory over any pagans that remained in these parts. His victories included the murder of his brother Pedro, for some reason that our family historical archive did not specify. Paco had opened the tomb, and found a few bones and scraps of leather.

But the place did have one cheery glow — at the Virgin of Mercies, where Marimarta and her 6-year-old daughter were praying right now. We had moved Her to the high altar, in place of the original Christ Triumphant, which I had sold to finance the new orchard. Her image was painted on 13th-century oak plank by some forgotten Castilian painter. In spite of tiny worm-holes, Mary of Mercies was still beautiful, enthroned between the horns of the sickle Moon, nursing her child at Her bare breast. The throne was flanked by two wild cattle, instead of the usual royal lions — their horns repeated the Moon symbol. It was a little framed color photograph of this painting that I took on the road, as my torero prayer shrine.

Now, in the blaze of candles lit by village women, Mamá's box of wedding rings sat dutifully at Mary's feet.

Head wrapped in black scarf, Marimarta lit one more candle, then came toward me, shushing her restless child.

"Dinner was wonderful tonight," I whispered. "You outdid yourself."

Marimarta grinned. She was a young La Mora widow who was left with no support after her bricklayer husband got killed in a construction accident in Toledo. José and I had heard of Marimarta's wonderful stews and fritters, and hired her. She was so pretty that my mother and Tita were convinced I was carrying on with her. I denied this, of course.

"A thousand thanks," she whispered back, then, "Shhh!" to her child.

She left, closing the outside door for the night. I heard her motorscooter start outside.

But Marimarta's footsteps echoed in my mind. What would happen to all these hundreds of people who depended on me, after I quit the bulls? Would there be enough money? Would the olive groves feed us all? Lighting a candle of my own, I knelt at the prie-dieu. Head bent, I must have been the picture of misery.

Sacred Mother, you know my harried heterodox heart....

In my mind, I kept seeing the wild blue eyes.

My human mother had my formal filial respect, but she was a prisoner of tradition. The Mother of Mercies was no one's hostage. Long ago I had abandoned all embarrassment at taking these heartbreaks to Her. Through 10 years of bulls, She had given me clear signs of her protection. She gave me food and shelter as bountifully as she did to Paco, who would call me evil. What loving Mother Deity would refuse me human love as well?

No moral scruples tore me. Like the mulberry tree outside, I was deep-rooted in that heretic rock of our history — its secrets, its hidden past. SPAIN IS DIFFERENT, said the tourist posters. I was different too. Surely my different feelings were an expression of a natural urge in some men, some women. Study of biology had given me glimpses of the infinite variety of life — the many plants and trees and animals that could live in my own *coto*. There were different species of deer, raptor birds. Why not sexual urges of different kinds? My hunger was old, rooted in the voices of children, and taste of milk, and stains of mulberries around my mouth. I had reached the point where I didn't question my hunger. The only question was how to feed it, and not get caught.

When I had finished my miserable meditation, I got awkwardly to my feet. The leg hurt from kneeling so long. Standing before Her, I lighted nine more candles for good measure.

As the new flames blazed up, there was a movement at the side door leading into the house. Braulio was standing there, with his usual noncommittal expression.

"One of the guards says some migrant has shown up," my valet told me. "The guy has your card."

Braulio smiled a small tight smile. I couldn't tell if it expressed pleasure on my behalf, or ironic disapproval.

My heart leaped like a young calf.

In the patio, the great oak door stood open on its ancient iron hinges, with my guard and his shotgun leaning in. And yes, Juan Diano Rodríguez was standing there beside the guard. He was clutching a cheap suitcase tied with rope.

5

Tired and dusty, Juan trudged through the door like he'd hoofed it clear from Madrid. I gave him a testy look. The fact is, I wanted to beat him over his peasant head with my riding whip, because of the misery he had put me through.

"You took your time," I said. "Perhaps you're not in a hurry to find destiny in the ring."

Juan met my eyes impassively.

"I had to do some things before I left," he said.

Indeed. As I studied him, it was clear that he'd hunted for bargains in new clothes. He was too proud to show up here in rags. In La Mora, he had stopped at somebody's farm pump to wash off the dust and change. Now he wore a painfully new pair of grey slacks, and a chestnut-brown Cortefiel sport jacket in last year's style. Ready-to-wear was a new thing in this country of fine tailors. No doubt he'd found it on sale at the new Santander department store. The clothes fit well, and looked good on him. This peasant kid had good taste. Or a compassionate clerk had helped him decide. He had probably blown his savings.

But new shoes were beyond his reach, so his feet wore the old hemp espadrilles and heavy village socks. His hair was neatly combed with water, and the black peasant beret stuffed in his pocket for now. Probably he'd considered whether to spend the night in the open, or arrive here at a late hour. I wanted to run my fingers through that thick, silky hair of his.

Juan's gaze held mine with fierce dignity. If I laughed at his espadrilles, he would frown and tell me to go to the devil.

"Well, then...welcome to Las Moreras," I said, putting out my hand.

As he took my hand, I expected to feel an electric current course between us. But his dry, rough fingers did not linger on mine longer than necessary. His blue gaze was clouded now, hiding expression, like a landscape with dust blowing across it.

I forced my voice to have the normal hearty tone of a man greeting a business visitor. My heart was in my throat. I still didn't dare to look directly into his eyes.

"So," I said, trying to keep myself poker-faced, "you have chosen your teacher."

"Yes," he said.

"Let's hope you've chosen well."

Casually I gave Braulio his instructions. Settle the young man in the Mudéjar Room, I said. See that he has everything he needs. Ask Marimarta to fix him a quick supper. For tomorrow, get some torero equipment together for him.

My mind was running wild with reasons why the Mudéjar Room would be the best place for him to sleep. As Braulio escorted Juan upstairs, my watch said 10:30 p.m.

Under a lamp that lit one corner of the patio arcades, I sat at the oak dining-table with our visitor and Bigotes and Manolillo. While Juan leaned gratefully over the potato omelet and sausage hastily fried by yawning Marimarta, I drank a brandy and kept my face a study in severe non-committal machismo. First Juan scanned the array of silverware, wondering which implement to use. Finally he did his own version of cutting the Gordian knot — hauled a big folding jackknife out of his pocket, and cut the chorizo sausage with it. This was a good knife with a horn haft, big enough to kill a man.

The house was quiet. Santí was in Sevilla with his working-class girlfriend Angelita. Fermín was visiting his family in Ciudad Real. Isaías was with his wife at their Madrid home, writing a brief on a contractual dispute for one of his novices. Braulio was upstairs getting the room ready.

Bigotes and Manolillo were all eyes, drinking their own brandies and watching Juan eat. Was this the long-awaited protegé?

Was I crazy? Juan Diano Rodríguez was a folly that I had set in motion, through my growing need — a father confessor would have called it "growing concupiscence." He was the precise occasion of social sin that I had avoided all these years. Ominous Catholic phrases of moral teachings resounded pitilessly in my brain, like echoes of sermons that I might have heard in a bombed-out cathedral.

Walk, Antonio.

I questioned Juan formally, and learned that he was not the typical peasant. Evidently he understood my maneuver, because he was formal also. His gaze was careful, and he kept it mostly on his plate as he wolfed the food.

"You talk like you had some schooling," I said.

"My parents wanted something better for me. They sacrificed to get me through high school. Then six months in a seminary." He was talking with his mouth full.

"How old are you?"

"Twenty-four."

I was surprised. He'd seemed older — older than me, even. One of those poor who are born old.

"Any sports training?"

"High scoring soccer player in the village. We beat the pants off Potes once."

"Do you hunt?" Everyone hunted in those mountains of his.

"We didn't butcher a nice calf if we could nab one of General Franco's deer."

The men and I kept questioning casually. Yes, his father was a small landowner and livestock breeder. Holstein milk cows and dun oxen. The best in the district. No, he'd never been around any *bravo* bulls. Except dead ones in the slaughterhouse. He'd certainly never stood in front of a charging bull.

"Except a dairy bull we had," he said slyly. "He would make all of you jump the barrier."

Done eating, he leaned back.

I had to smile. His talk had the salty eloquence that make country people of Castile sound like they are reading whole pages from Cervantes. That Montanese accent added to his charm. At the end of every other word, he dangled little suffixes like *-in* and *-ina* and *-uca*. His terrible dairy bull was a *toritín,* not a *toro.*

As he talked, there was a quietness about him. It was the same quietness that made me happy to be around animals. I felt a joy just sitting two meters away from him — the way I had felt when I saw that band of *asturcones.* Or when I saw the rare eagle flying high. Even the first crop of rabbits hopping around the *coto.* Burros and mules, my dogs and my horses. That feeling of deep comfort and completeness that the animals give us, because we know that their births and life-cycles and deaths are linked into ours. They give us food, and clothing, and tools from their bodies. We know we can't live without them.

My two subalterns were giving me dubious looks. A seminarian...milk cows... It didn't sound promising.

Bigotes remarked politely, "Well, ahem. There was one good torero who came out of La Montaña. I'm trying to remember his name."

"Go on," scoffed Manolillo. "La Montaña is more famous for cheese than bullfighters."

"Wasn't there some bull writer from La Montaña too?" Bigotes was racking his brains.

"José María de Cossío," I said. "An excellent writer. He wrote a whole encyclopedia called *The Bulls.*"

"So...Cossío and cheese," Manolillo went on scoffing.

Our visitor cleaned his plate with a piece of bread while my men insulted the taurine poverty of his homeland. I poured him a brandy.

"At 24," I added, "you are almost too old to learn the bulls."

Juan tasted the expensive brandy — a far cry from his cheap *orujo.* Then he swallowed it down.

"I learn fast," he stated calmly.

Outwardly, I was dubious. Inside, I was delighted that Juan would stay around for a couple of weeks. A vista of summer days opened before me. I would teach him how to handle bulls and swords. A few summer nights in bed with him, somehow, somewhere. He was bold enough...he'd probably teach me a thing or two. Maybe my raging hunger would be satisfied. I might even get tired of him soon, and send him on his way without regrets.

"Tomorrow we'll start you working with the cape," I said. "We'll see how you do."

While Marimarta cleared the table, my visitor said something about a shower and went upstairs. I managed not to watch him go, but my mind was nosing between his narrow peasant thighs, which moved easily in those well-cut new trousers.

For another hour, I feigned indifference and lounged in the patio with my two subalterns. Juan was probably scrubbing the dust off — settling cautiously into his room. Manolillo and Bigotes and I filled the night air with drifting cigar smoke as we talked about bulls and protegés. My men liked Juan.

"The kid has something," said Bigotes.

Manolillo agreed. "I don't know if he'll make a torero. But he has an air about him."

"You think so?" I yawned, feigning skepticism. I was the world-weary maestro who had seen many promising youngsters come to the bulls, and leave with nothing but scars.

Finally I was alone in my bedroom. The house had finally fallen silent. My alarm clock said the time was a little after 1 a.m.

My room lapped me in its history of feelings — it had been mine since the earliest winter hunts of childhood. José had brought more light and comfort here with her amateur efforts at decorating. Whitewash on the frigid stone walls, glowing oil paintings of English hunting scenes. Over the bed hung a copy of my favorite painting — Julio Romero de Torres' scandalous portrait of Juan Belmonte, showing the bullfighter nude except for the parade cape wrapped around him. To me the painting of my hero had always expressed the deep and secret vulnerability of being a man. I opened the shutters into the casement of the big window. Here my sister had put sheepskins and cushions, so I could lounge here and look through the iron grillwork into the mulberry tree outside.

Naked and barefoot, I paced around over the French rugs that she'd lovingly laid on the hard chill floor. I looked at myself in the mirror with its gold frame. There, the Wild Man was fondling himself with anguished indecision.

A kiss. I didn't want to just have him. I wanted a kiss, from those lips that had "accidentally" brushed my neck in Santander. If Juan Diano would let me kiss him, he'd do anything with me. I'd traveled out there in the great world. In other countries, kisses didn't necessarily go anywhere. But this young man would have the Spanish strictness. Kisses settle things. If he gave me his mouth, he'd give me everything. Was this too much to ask the Virgin of Mercies? A night or two of wild love on Spanish soil, in the house where I'd grown up? Where I'd gnawed my first puppy bones of fantasy? But macho men don't kiss each other that way. Ceremonial busses on the cheek in public, like General Franco greeting one of his ministers. Nothing more. No mushy stuff.

One night, one hour, might be all I'd get. Juan might wake up ashamed, and leave. He might denounce me to the police. That would be dangerous for him — I'd have to deny everything, and the police would sooner believe me than him. On the other hand, if he liked what we did, and he wasn't gifted with the cape, I'd have to find a way for him to legitimately stay in the area. Otherwise people would talk. Folly, folly.

Using the private phone in my room, I called José in Madrid. We chatted for a few minutes. Then, in case Paco had installed one of those terrible spy machines on the phone, I kept my voice casual as I mentioned that the possible protegé had shown up.

José played her part perfectly.

"Which one?" she asked. "That kid from Jaén that Isaías was talking about the other day?"

"No. The one from Santander. You remember."

"Oh, that one," she said, sounding bored. "God...are you really going to waste time on that slaughterhouse riffraff?"

Outside the iron grill of my window, the hot upland night was alive with moonlight, with the first cicadas shrilling. My legs and body vibrated insistently like cicada wings. Everything around me, and within me, all of Nature, was urging me into this journey from which there was no return. I could begin with dropping by Juan's room for two minutes, and be the gracious host making sure he was comfortable. Not for intimacy — that was too dangerous just yet. Just a few words, that might open things between us.

Walk, Antonio.

So I pulled on my terry robe and seized a towel, as if going to shower. Feeling like a fool, I peered out my door. The quadrangle of second-floor rooms, and their arches that overlooked the patio, were dark now, eerily lit by one feeble bulb. Manolillo and Bigotes had gone to bed in the room they usually used. My eyes squinted warily along the vista of closed doors.

In the old days, the quadrangle of second-floor rooms was an anthill of relatives and servants. Now, on the north side, most of those grand echoing rooms with dusty stuffed deer-heads and monastery-like furniture were used only rarely. The comfortable rooms on the south side belonged to the family. The west-side rooms were the crew's. The one closest to the bathroom was Braulio's. The modernized communal bathroom, with shower and a large tub, was located on the southwest corner. If Braulio or my subalterns came out suddenly, they would think I was on my way to bathe.

There were no secret passageways. I had spent enough time in France and England to know that noble houses might be honeycombed with hidden doors and sliding panels to permit political escapes and midnight *amoríos*. Not this house. Its stern builders had harbored no intention of easing heretic traffic between bedrooms. The solid granite walls, so glacial in winter and so refreshing in summer, were half a meter thick. The only "passageway" was on the first floor — it led to a postern door in back, for escape in wartime.

The coast was clear. So I walked silently down the corridor.

The next door was once my parents' bedroom during hunting season — José's room now. She had transformed that gloomy chamber into a well of sunlight, air, flowers, feminine comforts and bright colors, and art objects that I brought her from my travels. Next was the Rose Room. Here, the Wild Man carried on an occasional public romance with a lady. Two summers ago, an American actress spent a whole week there. The press was not too interested in my bedtime doings —

they preferred to report the romantic adventures of El Cordobés. But I did get a rich harvest of rumors among my fans — enough to keep my ID card as a *machote*. The wardrobe in the Rose Room contained a tidy trove of pornographic girlie magazines that I'd brought from Germany. I'd made sure Braulio found them. It was all part of what José called "the broken wing" maneuver.

Past the Rose Room was the Mudéjar Room. In childhood it was my sister's room, but she had hated it. Now it was just another guest room. The door was not locked. Light showed underneath.

I knocked softly, heard his voice. Then, wincing at the squeal of iron door-hinges, I peered in.

The tiny 50-watt bedside lamp picked out beams in the wooden ceiling, richly painted in a late version of the *mudéjar* style stolen from the Moors by Catholic artisans. The room was so dark and cavernous that José had been afraid of the dark, crying herself to sleep at night. A few pieces of traditional furniture threw bizarre indigo shadows — carved chests, a writing desk. The 17th-century oak bed had a baroque head-board as tall and glowering as a church facade. There, José had cowered in childhood nightmares. In one corner stood the butane heater on wheels, without which no inhabitant of this house could survive a winter.

The air smelled of water and soap — my guest must have taken a long soak.

Juan had thrown open his own shutters and was leaning against the casement, smoking a cigarette, gazing out into the mulberry tree. Save for the towel wrapped tightly around his waist, he was naked and barefoot. The lamplight picked out a deeper gold in his damp hair, and threw every muscle of that steelworker body of his into alluring relief. On either side of him, the opened shutters swung slightly in the breeze. This window lacked a grill — the ironwork had been blown off during the Civil War.

When Juan heard the door creak, he looked over his shoulder. His exhausted eyes held no surprise as I walked in. I didn't lock the door — it wouldn't look good, if Braulio was listening and heard the lock click.

"Are you comfortable?" I asked.

"Yes," he said quietly.

I dared to let my eyes rove over Juan's figure. His body pleased me. He was over-lean, needed to eat well. His good muscles were brutally corded and deep-cut by hard labor. But he was well-built. His hair was wet, and a few drops still glistened on his breasts, around full nipples that I instantly yearned to touch. Face and neck were fried to leather brown by the beating sun in the fields. Even in the dark, strong tan-lines showed at his wrists and neck. The rest of his body was starkly pale, never kissed by a fashionable resort tan. And those veins that rivered along his arms — they even laced down his belly to vanish under the tight-cinched towel, there to feed his pulsing mammalian life. I yearned to follow those veins with my own lips.

The cicadas were shrillingly, piercingly loud.

Going to the window, I leaned casually beside him — close enough to feel the heat from his body. At first he ignored me. Then he gave me a glance. We had flown together on a converging course, like two arrows shot from different bows. Now we struck quivering, side by side, into the same target.

For the first time, I dared to make full eye contact with him.

"Do you have everything you need?" I asked.

"Yes," he said, unsmiling.

Casually he rubbed the cigarette out against the casing.

Interpreting his move as a possible invitation, perhaps freeing his hands to caress me, I felt a hot flush go from my chest up to my brain, and down to my loins. It was hard to know what move to make next. The society that gave me so many paved highways and intricate road-maps leading to women had nothing to tell me about the faint, rough dirt trail that now lay before us, over a mysterious summit hidden in mists and fogs. If he was the effeminate type, I could treat him as I'd treat a Spanish woman. But he wasn't. How would I want to be treated?

To buy time, I played the tour guide and said:

"This used to be my sister's room."

I pointed out into the mulberry tree, which created its secret world against the house. Through thick foliage and half-formed fruit, a few random moonbeams picked out branches. One giant branch snaked along the granite wall, leading from this window to my own window. The branch was callused from rubbing on stone through centuries of beating wind. I smiled a little. "When José and I were bad, we were sent to our rooms. But at night we'd travel back and forth on that branch, and visit. No one knew."

Juan leaned way out the window.

"Your window has a grill on it," he said.

"When we were little, that didn't stop us. But then we got too big to crawl through."

Juan looked thoughtfully at the branch. As the cicadas shrilled in our ears, desire surged under my robe. The tension between us was now unbearable. My senses shouted at me to slide my hand inside the front of his bathtowel. My palm was callused from the hilt of my sword — he would feel that callus. His skin would quiver under its roughness, like a horse's sensitive hide. His clean male smell, the whiff of crotch odor that survives even a long bath, was driving me crazy.

He turned away from me. How could I initiate something?

"So...you came five hundred kilometers," I said.

"Yes," he said, not turning his head.

I wanted to be pressing against him, lips buried in that wet hair on the back of his neck. His skin would taste of milk and ferns. Unmoved, he stayed turned from me. This was not the slaughterhouse bandit. Maybe his own doubts were plaguing him.

"Why?" I dared to ask.

Would he give me the traditional answer, the one that sidewalk hopefuls always gave to the press? "I came because of the hunger." Or... "I came because of the very great desire I have, to cape bulls."

A long silence. He frowned into the mulberry tree.

"I came," he said icily over his shoulder, "to see if there is respect."

His extraordinary words sank into my brain. Had I heard right? What did he mean? Something in his tone warned me. Irritated, I stepped back. Then, amid disappointment, I began to feel a kind of relief. The time was not right yet. Not tonight. *Walk a little slower, Antonio.* What would tomorrow bring, if I was so loose with him tonight? Was he afraid that he'd be a rich man's convenience, used once like toilet paper and flushed away? Yes, I'd better not forget how wide the social gulf looked to him.

So I gave him a small, taut smile.

Juan turned to face me, leaning his toweled buttocks against the granite casement. He returned the small smile, and lit another of his cheap cigarettes. All this time, he hadn't moved a step. If he'd been a wild bull, he would have forced me to step back.

How opposite we were! Even his cunning at hiding his cravings was charged with a bull's forward energy, as if he were testing himself against the wall of the ring, charging full tilt and driving his master horn against the obstacle with a crash, making splinters fly. But I was more devious, a being of lures and tricks and strategies. My gift at deceit with a silk cape, convincing a bull to follow the cape past my body, had taught me how to deceive with words, deeds. If he and I were to survive this encounter, I would need to learn the art of the explosive charge...and Juan would need to learn the art of the silk.

"Respect goes both ways," I countered.

"It does," he said.

"Sleep well, then," I said, trying to get that hearty tone of the caring host back into my voice.

As I went out his door, making the normal kind of noise, Braulio was just coming out of his room with a suit of mine he'd pressed. Had he heard something, and chosen that moment to check up on me?

"Remember what I told you," I said sternly to Juan over my shoulder. "The fiesta isn't all trumpets and carnations."

"I'm ready for what comes, maestro," came Juan's voice behind me.

His tone of youthful deference to my professional severity was just right. He was going to be good at this. Better than me, maybe.

"If you need anything, speak to Braulio." I looked at my valet sternly. "Understood, Braulio?"

"At your orders, sir," said my valet.

Back in my own bed, still damp from my own hot shower, I lay there wide-awake. Would Juan take my hint about the tree branch? It was strong enough to support the weight of a grown man. So I spent an hour waiting for that stealthy rustle of mulberry leaves so familiar from childhood. Nothing happened. Nevertheless I felt a lunatic hope that the impossible thing could happen. I had maneuvered us both to a mutual allusion about it. If he felt I respected him enough, that is. And how did he define respect? What had he meant?

The next afternoon, when Juan finally got up, he joined me publicly for my leg-therapy walk. As we strolled through Las Moreras, I introduced him to my world and the people and animals in it.

This was no ordinary farmer's boy. Animals gravitated to him. My four greyhounds, Miki, Tiki, Viki and Niki, trotted after him. Faisán nosed Juan instead of trying to nip him. Out on the dirt road, we met old Aurelio Pérez with a wagon-load of charcoal that he'd made from two olive trees killed by lightning last year. While I talked to my man, the team of big mules were giving Juan their attention, nuzzling him all over while he talked to them. His hand slid down their sweaty necks, slapped their shoulders gently. I wanted his hand to slide over me like that.

From there, in the waning heat, we strolled along the first row of olive trees. My dogs competed to kiss his hands and nose his crotch. I envied their noses being so free with his person.

"Animals feel good around you," I said.

"I prefer them to people. They never judge."

A hot breeze hissed through the olive foliage, tossed our hair, fluttered our shirts against our bodies. We were in full view of the world, walking decorously with hands behind our backs. The identical *machote* mask was glued to both our faces. Juan kept bending over to study this plant, and that plant, intensely curious at being in a new province.

"What's the name of this one?" he kept asking. "That one?"

"You know a lot about plants," I commented.

"My grandfather taught me. The dairymen always asked for him instead of the vet in Santander. He treated people too. I remember a tourist guy...the doctors in Santander gave up on him, and a hotel manager sent him to Umbrilla. My grandfather gave him tea. The tourist was cured."

It was the most he'd said since arriving.

"So your grandfather was a *brujo?*"* I asked.

Brujo, bruja — witch — were words still heard in our country-side, even after 500 years of Catholic rule. Knowledge about plants and animals was dangerous knowledge, because it was older and more indigenous than the church. People had been burnt just for using herbs to freshen a cow.

"He was a great *brujo,*" Juan said.

"Did he see things too? Have visions? Know things?"

Juan shrugged. "If he did, he kept it to himself."

"Did he know the secrets of your heart?" I dared to say.

Juan flushed. "He was always good to me. Not like my mother, who was cold. It was hard when he died."

This must be the grandfather whose grave José and I had seen in Umbrilla.

Out here in the daylight, I kept noticing things about him that touched me deeply. He was close-shaven now, smelling of soap and water. Draped onto his hard-cut torso was a new Italian silk-knit pull-over. It alone must have cost him a week's wages in some Santander gentleman's emporium. No wonder he hadn't been able to afford shoes. Short sleeves bared the strong untanned arms with those sexy veins, that I could hardly keep myself from caressing. The ready-made slacks flattered his lean worker's backside. Yes, his taste in clothes was good. But his longish hair needed a barber. His skin color showed that he didn't eat well. And he smoked too much — the peasant remedy for scanty diet.

Juan looked down at himself, rubbing the silk jersey with his rough fingers. Its luxurious feel must still feel strange to him.

"How did you get here?" I asked.

"Hopped a fast freight on the TAF. Hitchhiked from Madri'th. Walked from La Mora."

"A long way to go for respect," I grinned.

Two men consumed by lust for each other, not daring more than glances. He squinted at me briefly out of the corners of those beautiful azure eyes. His sun-bleached brows and long chestnut eyelashes might have been leaves, and he an animal hiding behind them. Smiling a small crafty smile, he hurled a stick for the hounds to chase after.

"So...you followed the bulls, eh?" I pursued. "You read about me in the papers?"

He shook his head no.

"That was the first bullfight I ever saw," he said. "It was my job. I didn't know anything about you except what the slaughterhouse crew told me...what I saw that day."

Had his lust for me not flared till that accidental touching during the melee? Or had he stood there at the barrier, and looked into my heart as I was going wild with the pinto bull? Was my real nature that visible to a casual spectator? The thought terrified me.

"Why did you pick me? Why not El Cordobés?" I pursued.

"Well..." Juan was looking at the ground, moving pebbles with the toe of one espadrille.

"Tell me," I pressed him.

"Before the bullfight started, I saw you in the horse patio. You were standing alone. The big crowd was around El Cordobés. You didn't see my crew...we were standing there gawking at you. You were wrapping your parade cape around yourself, and your eyes were sad. Our chief said you were feeling the big fear. He said you were having a premonition. I thought I was going to see the bull kill you."

Lighting another of his cheap cigarettes, Juan turned away and rested his foot on the massive root of a thousand-year olive tree. Squinting into the low sunlight, he looked away at the summits of the *coto,* which were almost lost in the glare. For a moment, the smoke drifting around him looked like a deep feeling made visible in the air.

"You knew I was thirsty," I said.

We were talking double-talk now.

"The chief let me take a glass of his *orujo*. And I felt it then...that I wanted to..."

Was he going to say it?

Juan's voice faltered. "...That I wanted to do what you do...with the bulls."

I had to grin. He had passed the horns of meaning very close to him, with his own cape of words.

"So you are a *brujo* too," I said. "You know things."

"In my own way."

His gaze met mine again, then slid past me. He was pretending diffidence again, bending to touch a purple thistle-blossom with his fingers.

What were his motives? Public figures light strange fires at lonely altars in other people's hearts. There are the ones who think they own you. There are the ones who see you as their husband, friend, father, brother. They all see you as something. I thought I had seen every motive possible. Men had even discreetly touched my ass at crowded parties. But no one like Juan had ever surged out of my modest fame. What did he want from me? A stream of dark questions ran through my mind. Had he had his way with other toreros? Would he want fine clothes, money, a car? Would he try to blackmail me? Was he a spy for Paco? A shill for the secret police?

Juan's eyes stared at the distances. I could feel his own aloneness. "The chief said you got hurt bad," he said.

"That is true."

"Is the comeback going well?"

"No."

"In Santander, you looked...tired."

"The leg doesn't always obey. If a bull goes for me, I can't run for the barrier."

"You can't run?" he repeated in disbelief.

"I have to handle things where I stand," I told him.

"Jesus."

"Yes. I should retire."

"But, *hombre*...why are you still doing it?"

For a full minute, I pondered the next dangerous question. Blood hammered in my temples. Finally I asked: "Tomorrow you start working out with the cape. And if I decide you won't make a torero, then what?"

He frowned, and shrugged.

"Will you stay around if it doesn't work out?" I dared to say.

"Stay?" He repeated it as if he hadn't understood. "You mean, stay here?"

"Where will you go? Back to a nothing life in Santander? There is good work around here. Or Madrid. If you stay in the area, we might...run into each other now and then."

He looked strangely shocked at the suggestion.

"That depends," he said.

He was staring at the horizon now, his expression hostile again. I said nothing more, my throat drying up. The long vista of days with him, that I'd imagined, shrank suddenly to nothing.

As darkness fell, I showed him the chapel. Our footfalls echoed under the dusty Gothic vaults where the blaze of candles cast our two shadows huge on the walls. Juan's shadow kept its beret on. We paused at the imposing tomb of Sanches.

"He murdered his brother Pedro," I said, "who was probably a liberal."

Juan grunted. "My ancestor was the Duke of Milk."

His eyes went to the altar. Battered vases of fresh roses and dahlias from La Mora gardens banked the Virgin of Mercies. In the warmth of candle-flames, clouds of fragrance drifted round Her. Juan went to the altar, and gently touched the cow horns that guarded Her throne. I could see his ardent devotion to Her. Maybe She'd been more of a mother to him than the hard farmwoman Maruca who left him to go to Germany.

"How long since mass was said here?" he asked.

"Since 1958, when my father was alive," I said. "I am like so many — no longer Catholic."

"But you love Her."

I lit a candle. "Who doesn't love their Mother? Are you still Catholic?"

"I lost my faith in the seminary," he said.

He lighted a candle from mine. As he set it in place on the rack, he noticed the two gold wedding-rings at the Virgin's feet.

"Yours?" he wanted to know.

"I'm supposed to marry," I said wearily.

His eyes held mine, questioning. As we turned away, he noticed the narrow stairway descending into the chapel pavement. Twenty-five steps underneath Sanches' tomb, it ended at a padlocked and dusty iron-work door.

"Where does that go?" he asked.

"Some of the Escuderos call it the Crypt of the Mercies," I said. "It's just an underground room with a few coffins in it. A few more bloodthirsty ancestors."

Late that night, as everyone headed for bed, Juan walked away down the gloomy second-floor arcades. Below, in the patio dining area, Marimarta was feeding her children. As Juan passed a pot of red carnations in one of the arches, he picked one and sniffed it. A moment later, his bedroom door closed, jarred the echoes. I heard his key turn noisily in the lock. My heart sank. Nothing would happen tonight.

As the darkened house fell silent, I tossed and turned on my own bed, with its French headboard painted in hunt scenes. José had made the bed more comfortable for me, with layers of sheepskins under the mattress, to keep the floor's chill from getting to my leg. I was thirty years old, and crippled like an old man.

About 2 a. m, to my surprise, mulberry foliage rustled at the barred window.

"Psst," a voice said quietly, from outside.

My heart pounding wildly, I got up. Should I lock the door? No. If someone tried to come in, they'd think it strange. Braulio and Marimarta knew I never locked it, because I had nothing to hide in this room. Nobody would think it strange if they found me sitting in my accustomed niche in the casement. I could always say I was looking at the stars, or listening to the nightjar.

So I pulled on my robe and trousers, and went to the window. In the dark, cat-like, Juan had crept along the branch like José and I always did as children. Now he stood in the leaves, perched on the massive limb. He had put on old farm clothes — dark baggy jacket and trousers — so he wouldn't rip his new garments. His chest was even with the casement. With one hand he held onto my iron bars. In his other was the wilting carnation.

Being careful not to hurt my leg, I got up into the casement, and lay on my side in the comfortable sheepskins, leaning one elbow into the cushions. My face was half a meter from his. Between our faces were the rusted bars, glistening with cold dew, ornate as the abandoned gate of a bishop's palace.

"My door isn't locked," I said quietly. "If anyone comes in, I'll just stay here like I'm enjoying the night. You duck down in the leaves there. If they come to the window, just stay quiet ...they can't see you."

Gravely, Juan nodded. Then he thrust his free hand through the bars, offering me the carnation.

I couldn't believe my eyes. I had grown used to steady modernization in my country. So it was unsettling to confront a young man from a remote district where yeah-yeah things hadn't seeped in. Bandit he was — but an old-fashioned bandit. He had come skulking to my window at night, like the traditional swain. Patiently he held out the flower. In the moonlight, a dry peasant humor glinted in his eyes.

Taking the flower, I tucked it in my robe pocket with a flourish, next to my heart.

At that, Juan gave me a sly grin, gripping the bars with both hands. I grinned back. Yes, it was a game. The game of finding ways to court each other. Was this what he meant by "respect"? Did he want to make all the traditional moves — the ones that I was expected to make with Serafita? If he was a woman, or a man I could use like a woman, I could expect him to be a virgin. I could put him through a hell of guilt if he wasn't. He would have to be faithful to me till death and beyond, while I could put the horns of a cuckold on him if it suited me. If he ever betrayed me, even in thought, I had the right to blow his brains out in a crime of passion. Any court in Spain would let me go free, and I'd be applauded for my fine sense of honor. But he wasn't a woman. I could hardly expect to act the traditional man of honor with another honorable *machote* like myself, who had the right to blow my own brains out if I strayed. No wonder he was being cautious.

As swains had for a thousand years, we settled down on either side of the bars. Far off, on the hillside, the nightjar uttered his single bell-like call, over and over. Our warm breath condensed on the grill.

"Do you have... someone?" he whispered.

"No."

"Go on. A *majín* like you...famous and rich..."

"I don't have a soul."

"You have to be a liar," he said drily.

"If I had someone, I'd be there now, instead of sitting here behind these bars."

"Then how do you manage?"

"Whores." By using the male form of the word, I made my meaning clear.

He laughed drily. "Naturally. You can pay."

"And you? Someone?"

"No."

"Go on. A handsome lad like you."

"I can't afford anyone."

"How do *you* manage, then? The pissoirs?"

"Jesus, no. The police..."

I pressed my questioning, gaining on him step by step, as you need to do when caping a bull. "Come on now. You stole a good feel from me. Where else do you steal them?"

Even in the dark, I could see him flush.

"Migrant guys camping under bridges," he said.

"How do you manage that?"

"We're too poor for whores and girlfriends. My comrades start talking about girls. It gets them hot. Now and then somebody asks somebody for a little handwork."

"Dangerous."

"Now and then," he admitted, "somebody has second thoughts and pulls a knife." He rolled up his sleeve, and shoved his arm through the bars. In the moonlight, a few long scars gleamed on his forearm.

"Women aren't good enough for you?" I couldn't help ribbing him a little.

"I've never had one."

I tried to imagine the scene in the dark, under a bridge some-where. A modern railway bridge, a ruinous Roman bridge — it didn't matter. No campfire, so the police wouldn't know. A few shadowy men, sparse possessions in bundles or cardboard suitcases. Rough, hurried, nervous — pleasure given and taken like a whip-lash on a mule's dusty rump. He was more daring and forward than me, yet his experience was minimal. I was more cautious, yet had done more in the times I'd dared.

There was a long silence. Our faces were just centimeters apart now, and our brains were on fire. Suddenly everything got darker as the Moon set. The land went quiet — the nightjar silent now, the crickets numbed with cold dew.

"And you?" he asked. "Women, I mean?"

"Hundreds," I shrugged. "It's part of my job."

He looked disappointed. There was another long silence.

"Why did you want to be a torero?" he asked. "You had one for a friend, eh?"

How could I explain how it started? At my first bullfight, age 10, an overwhelming feeling of déjà vu, of having been there before. On reading Cossío's books, the feeling that I already knew it all. My father had those tomes in his library...*The Bulls* by Cossío. He had it because of the stuff about royal bullfights. To my father, everything royal was important. The book was full of pictures of toreros. I remembered all of them. I fell in love with all of them. Especially Juan Belmonte...doing his wonderful capework. When I realized Belmonte was dead, I cried for days. I was twelve.

"I've never had a friend," I said.

Through the bars, our foreheads almost touched grazingly. I wanted to touch his wondrous thick silky hair. His fingers, hard as horse hoof, must want to touch my cheek, feel my shaven beard. Our breath warmed each other's cheeks. As with lovers for a thousand years, a warm moist spot grew on my pants. Surely, down there against the chill granite wall, a wet spot was growing on his fly. It would be hard to see the spot on those dark peasant pants of his. Barred Spanish windows had never stopped the lust of heterosexuals — why would they stop us? I could see myself feverishly wrestling my pants down in the confines of the casement. There would be rhythmic shuddering tones in the bars as our bodies strove against them. Insistent trembling of the branch under his feet. So stark, so desperate. Not dignified. Not respectful.

Suddenly slow footsteps approached, down on the ground.

We froze, hardly breathing. One of my guards was making his rounds. In the dark, his shotgun glinted. For several minutes, he stood under the tree smoking. The smell of his cigarette drifted up to us. If he had looked up, he might have seen Juan through the foliage. But he didn't. Finally his footsteps crunched onward, around the corner of the house.

Alone again, Juan and I were both trembling with cold and fright. Then the branch trembled as he disappeared into the dark foliage, without a word.

For a while I sat alone. Finally, as the sky lightened and the first rooster crowed, I crawled down from the casement, still shivering with excitement. My legs were tottering...the bad leg would scarcely support me from hours of being in one position. All by itself, my hand went to my pocket and took out the now wilted carnation. Carefully, shakily, it put the wilted flower in front of my framed photo of Mary of the Mercies.

That hand of mine could have caressed him even if somebody cut it off at the wrist.

After a long shower to calm myself, I headed downstairs for an early coffee and ran into Braulio.

"Good morning, Antonio," my valet said.

"Good morning." My heart was hammering guiltily.

"You're up early. What a crazy night. I kept thinking I heard voices outside."

"It must have been in your head," I said.

As I watched Braulio go, I pondered him again, seemingly so loyal, so thoroughly familiar with my movements. A quiet family man with a wife and three children in Madrid. Anyone with a bribe could learn a lot about my personal habits from Braulio. Knowing this, I'd always paid him well. But was Braulio the gust of wind that lifted my cape, letting the bull see me?

––––––––––––––

Brujo — male witch. *Bruja* is a female witch.

6

"*¡Eh-heh, toro!* Over here, bull!"

In a shaded level area under the mulberry tree, six hopefuls were having torero class. Juan clutched the rose silk cape in his hands. He was learning how to shake it to catch the bull's eye. How to draw it just ahead of the bull's eyes and horns and let it ride richly on the air. How to time its movement to the bull's speed. How to do the most important thing of all: keep your feet planted and stand still, so the bull doesn't see you move. Animals see only what moves. If the bull's eye flicks from the cape to you, he will nail you like a cat nailing a mouse.

"Ha-hey, bull!"

In front of Juan was the "bull," Santí. Having spent his life around wild cattle, my picador made an excellent "bull." He knew all their tricks.

Poker-faced, I was the teacher, giving instructions.

Five boys watched Juan. It had taken several days for Isaías to round them up and get them to Las Moreras. My manager had even persuaded a photographer from the bull magazine *El Burladero* to come. Knowing they were vying for one chance to train with me, the boys wore expressions of contempt for their dairy-farm colleague. Camouflaging Juan among other hopefuls had been a good strategy. But Juan was lacking with the cape, and the other boys could see it.

They took their turns with the "bull." One kept trying to throw in fancy stuff. I tried to get his attention on a basic *veronica* but he wouldn't listen. Isaías and I exchanged looks. When hopefuls don't listen to the maestro, they wind up skewered on a horn. Isaías took him aside and told him to leave.

Yawning, the photographer left too. He hadn't seen any great promise here.

I waited till that afternoon to call José, and planned my words carefully. While I lived in an antique world of swords and mule teams, I kept in mind that modern thing called "bugging telephones."

"*Diga*... h'lo," answered my sister sleepily. She was a real citizen of the capital, still lolling in bed at 2 p.m. We chatted, careful about what we said on the phone.

"How is the training going?" José said, casually.

"One of them washed out."

"The peasant, no doubt," she drawled.

"Not yet."

My sister laughed. She understood my meaning.

For a few days, the house was noisy with five young men camping there and using the bathroom. The area under the mulberry tree got scuffed. My "bulls" got tired. Marimarta's culinary skills and Braulio's patience were taxed. To keep my mind focused, I sought solitude during the hot hours of the day — reading in my room, so I could keep from going crazy with thoughts of sex.

I had been reading Jaime de Foxá's *Solitario,* an amusing tale of a loner among wild boars, written from the pig's point of view. But suddenly it didn't fit my mood. So I grabbed one of the familiar leatherbound volumes of Cossío's *The Bulls*. Thumbing pages, I re-lived all the adolescent longing and thrills that this great monograph had stirred in me. Why had the *fiesta brava* appealed to me so powerfully? Was it just the handsome and courageous men in old photographs? Had I loved one of them in a past life? Was it more than that? The *fiesta's* rootedness in ancient times? However changed it was today, with some toreros talking about spandex breeches instead of satin ones, men — and yes, women — had been dancing with the horns of wild cattle for three thousand years.

The next night Juan sneaked to my window again. I shut off the light and took Cossío's book into the casement with me. It was a splendid night, with the Moon low in the west, visible through the mulberry foliage. We were within that sphere of glowing light and shadow. But Juan looked tired, depressed.

"I am bad with the cape, bad with my feet..." he whispered.

"Don't talk bulls here. Look at the Moon."

"I've seen the Moon a million times," he hissed.

"You haven't seen this one...this night."

Finally I got him calmed down, and he leaned back against the bars and stared at the Moon. His shoulder pressed through the bars, against my chest. At first his muscles tensed, but finally he relaxed a little. Though he wore the black jacket, he was shivering.

"Are you cold?" I dared to put my hand on his shoulder, in a neutral caring kind of way.

"A little," he said.

Somehow I got my right arm through the bars and around him, across his chest, so I could press him back against me, through the bars. As we both stared at the Moon, he allowed us to have this excuse for touching. It felt awkward but amazing. I had been so obsessed with finding a few hours' privacy for foreign adventures, that the wonder of these simple preliminaries — like having one's arm around a warm, living man — had evaded me.

So an hour passed, with me wishing that heat from our bodies could melt the damn bars. Silent, feverishly intent on our closeness, we watched the angles of a million Moon-rays change, shifting, through a million trembling mulberry leaves, listening to the calls of the nightjar far up the hillside toward the *coto*. I watched his glowing profile change as the Moon went down the sky, the shadows slowly vanishing under his brows, his nose, his upper lip, till the Moon touched the horizon and her level light shone directly between his lips, where I wanted so much to put my tongue. My nostrils were bathed in his warmth. I let my breath fan his hair. By and by, I inched my hand inside his jacket, feeling his breast through his shirt. His nipple was taut with cold and desire. I rubbed it gently.

"Don't," he whispered. He pulled my hand out of his shirt, and held it for a moment, looking at my ring. The diamond made its dark flash in the moonlight.

"That's not glass, eh?" he said. He let my hand go.

"No, it isn't glass."

"How many millions did it cost?"

"It didn't. My greatgrandmother gave it to me." Impatient for more intimacy, I was trying to hold his hand again.

"You buy everything." He pulled his hand away.

"What's the matter with you? Did someone hurt you once?"

His silence told me volumes. He shook his head.

"Tell me his name," I raged in a low voice, "so I can go find him and kill him. Was it when you were young?"

"I was fourteen...."

Had someone had him already, dishonored him? "What did you know about men, then?"

"There's nothing to tell." His voice was hoarse.

"What was his name?" I demanded to know.

With a brusque movement, Juan pulled away and vanished along the branch.

If it were winter, and time for heifer trials, I could take my five hopefuls to a friend's ranch, and toss them in front of charging heifers. It is believed that the females, not the bulls, transmit "pepper," that hot temperament in the cattle that makes them go after you. Heifers show us who the real toreros are.

But it was summer. So I called Álvaro Chaparra, a rancher in the Mancha who was a friend of mine, to see if he had weaned any bull calves yet. I'd have my own little trials right there at Las Moreras. One of my stone corrals was round — it would do for a little temporary ring.

When the crew and I went to Chaparra's to look at the calves, I casually invited Juan to go with us.

"So you can see some real *bichos,*" I said. "Not those milk cows of yours."

The Chaparra ranch was located beyond the mountains to the south, in rolling grasslands of the Mancha. When we got there, Álvaro and his foreman and vaqueros were waiting for us with saddled horses. The vaqueros armed themselves with blunt wooden lances, that they would use to tumble an animal gently in case of a charge. Then off we went in a cloud of dust. I kept Juan close by my side. The others would see this as natural — he was my responsibility. While he knew how to ride (my fantasy about his natural, untaught seat had been right), he didn't know how to handle himself or his horse around the wild stock. Nobody wanted him hurt. So it was my job to keep an eye on him.

As Álvaro gave us a tour through the different pastures, I tried to think how good it would be to see cattle dotted across the *coto.* They belonged there, like wildebeest belong on the African plains, like buffalo belong on American prairie. But sexual thoughts kept stampeding through my mind.

As our party viewed the cow herd from a safe distance, the animals surrounded us with their peppery sexuality. A cow was in season, bulling, mounting lustily onto another cow. We drew rein nearby, and watched the herd-sire go to her. He courted her with sniffs and bawls, then mounted her. This scene was observed by all of us with poker-faced respect. We toreros might joke about human estrous, but never about the estrous of these animals who could kill us. Privately, my entrails wrenched as I watched the bull's great pizzle thrust deep in the cow's vagina. Juan was watching too. What was he thinking?

Farther on, we paused to look at old Constante, one of Álvaro's best cows. She had a strong bull calf at side. We watched the little fellow butt her bag lustily, to make her let down milk. Then his eager mouth swallowed the teat. How much I wanted to swallow Juan that way.

On the weanling range, we found the calves along the north fence, in the shade of some pines. Barbed wire was a new thing to Spain — a dire necessity for modern fighting-bull ranches. We talked about choices, and then Álvaro and his men rode to the calves. Dust drifted as they quietly sorted out the ones we wanted. The vaqueros kept their lances ready — even these little guys can hurt a horse.

Meanwhile, Juan and I sat our horses some distance from the dust-cloud. To all appearances, I was explaining these professional things to my possible protegé. Now that we were alone, we exchanged a morose stare.

"Did your family know?" I asked.

"My grandfather was dead by then. I never went near girls, so people were starting to talk. My parents pretended I had a vocation. As soon as I got my school certificate, they shipped me off to the seminary like a veal to market."

I knew better than to ask further about his mystery village lover, so I said:

"Your confessor taught you Catholic morals with his hand on your antler?"

Juan grinned. "He fancied me, all right. But I didn't fancy him. After six months of me defending my honor, they threw me out. They wouldn't even give me a letter of recommendation. So I had a hard time getting a job."

"You talk so anticlerical…are you Communist?"

If Juan and I were caught together, any old Communist associations of his would be closely scrutinized by the police — and I would be guilty of association as well.

"No," he said. "The baddest political thing I ever did was go hear a Protestant missionary in Bilbao, in somebody's house. I'd never seen a Protestant before. But when he started talking about King Jesus, I left. I'm against kings."

"So, after the seminary…"

"There was the military. I was stationed in Pamplona. First Mountain Division. At least my sergeant didn't try to dishonor me."

Honor…dishonor. Pagan though he was, the old religious attitudes still warped his thinking.

"The men noticed you didn't go for girls?"

"They were always saying things. Finally one guy, Rafael Iturbe, stood up for me. 'Fael was the biggest womanizer in the unit, and everybody admired him, so they left me alone after that. Faelín and I hung around together, and I finally found out he was...you know. The whole thing with ladies was a lie."

"So," I said, feeling ready to wring his neck from jealousy, "Rafael was your mysterious friend."

"No. He wasn't."

"You hung around with him…did you go drinking together and talk about it?"

"It was the first time I knew there were other guys like…"

"How could you talk about it with him, and not want it?"

"Are you telling me I'm a liar?"

"No." I had to step back.

"After we got out of the *mili,* 'Fael went to France. It was hard after that. I was afraid to go back to Umbrilla. My family had emigrated — I almost went to find them. But a foreign country...it was scary. The idea of guys who didn't talk like me. So I drifted. Corn harvest. Wheat harvest. Highway crews. Then the slaughterhouse. I had to take shitty jobs because I didn't have a letter from a priest."

We had a long silence. My sudden subtle surge of anger and jealousy, my possessiveness, his defensiveness, had clouded the air between us. Like José said, things got less perfect with time.

"If you wash out as my protegé, what will you do?" I asked.

He frowned. "You keep asking me that. I don't know."

"What else can you do?"

"I won't work for you," he said testily.

Putting him to work in the crew — as apprentice sword-handler, for example — would be the last thing I'd do. My men were too close to me. They knew my moods, my energies. They would sense things. Especially Isaías, Santí and Braulio. And who knew how the Eibars would react if they found out?

"What did you do on the farm?" I asked.

Juan shrugged. "I was the one who looked after the animals. My father did the stock trading and kept the books."

"If you could go to university, what would you study?"

"Veterinary medicine," he said right away. "I'd like to be a vet. I could be the best vet in Spain."

"A vet who knows *brujo* stuff."

"Something like that."

"What started you thinking about that?"

"We spent a lot of money on a new cow from Holland. A big milker. She went down and died. Later I found out about this simple thing I could have done to save her. A hypodermic full of liquid calcium, right in her jugular, and *zas!* she would have been on her feet in a minute. I felt so stupid."

Álvaro's men were urging six calves gently toward the ranch buildings. Juan and I turned our horses, and followed.

A party, I thought to myself as we drove home. I should garnish the protegé trials by throwing a party. This way I could pay back some social debts, and further camouflage my interest in this young man.

Tere happily made a list, phoned invitations. *El Burladero* and *El Ruedo* reluctantly said they'd cover it. With all my failures, even the one success in Santander hadn't pushed my star higher in the sky. José, of course, would be there for *ABC*. She still had some social contempt for Juan — didn't even want to meet him. All this was costing me money. If I got him in bed just once, it would be the most expensive adventure I ever had. Even Wolfgang, a stately blond in the Hamburg red zone, who was the handsomest *puto* in West Germany, handsome enough for the SS honor guard (except he hated Hitler), had not cost me as much as Juan Diano.

That night, the bandit of the bridges came to my window, but he was not interested in the Moon. By his expression, he wanted to argue over our discussion that morning, gripping the bars with one hand.

Suddenly the rusted iron grill gave way a few centimeters, with a screechy groan. Juan's feet slipped, and he gave an involuntary exclamation. For a moment he was hanging precariously by one hand from the grill, with his hemp sandals flailing in thin air. I had a terrible flash of imagination, seeing him plunge to the ground four or five meters below — lights coming on in the house, people rushing out, his leg or arm broken, the questions and scandal.

But the iron grill now held firm on its massive rusty bolts. Muscles creaking, Juan used his strength to pull himself onto the branch again. Suddenly we both froze, as someone knocked on my bedroom door. In a flash, Juan was out of sight, crouching in the foliage. In a flash, I had calmed myself in the casement, with *The Bulls* in hand. Not for nothing had I learned to stand still as the bull charged me.

"Yes?" I called.

The door opened. "Antonio —" came Braulio's voice.

"Braulio? What are you doing up at this hour?"

My heart hammered, but my voice was even, conversational.

"Excuse me, boss...I heard a strange noise. What are you doing up in the dark?"

"I was reading…then I turned out the light to sit here and enjoy the night."

Braulio came to the window. His eyes rounded at the sight of the book in the moonlight, with shadows of iron bars across it. It took all my discipline not to glance outside the window, at the mulberry foliage just below the casement, where Juan was hiding.

"You'll ruin your eyes," he scolded me.

"Don't be silly. I'm not reading, just sitting here. What kind of noise did you hear?"

"On this side of the house. Something like a screech."

"Yes, there was some kind of night bird in the tree. Hunting, I guess. It made a strange noise. New animals are coming to us now, Braulio. Our work is changing the land."

Braulio peered out into the tree, looking dubious.

"Go to bed," I said. "You're a worry-wart."

"You go to bed too," Braulio grumbled as he left the room. "You need your rest for the trials tomorrow."

The door closed.

After a few minutes, like a startled snail cautiously uncoiling from its shell, Juan stood up out of the foliage. My arms wanted to draw him close again. But his eyes were black with emotion. Nervously, he shook his head no, and went step by careful step along the branches, back to his own window.

The trials dawned hot, with strange smoky blue skies. In the last few years, Spain had layered herself in the first brown haze. We had to admit that this was what Yankees called "smog" — penalty of the economic development so dear to our hearts. It appeared to come out of factory smokestacks and truck tail-pipes — drifting in from Madrid and Bilbao and Barcelona, cities that we at Las Moreras had once believed were far away.

That afternoon, Las Moreras filled with people and parked cars. Naturally I'd had to invite Sera and her mother. Paco had come with my mother and Tita. They hinted that my protegé thing had them worried — that I had better put spur to horse and ask for Sera's hand sooner than Arles. The situation had its black humor, with Serafita and her mamá sleeping in the Rose Room, next door to the man whose body I preferred to hers.

As Paco met the hopefuls and coolly shook Juan's hand, I felt chills galloping up and down my spine. Pray God, Goddess, Jesus, Mary and all the saints that Paco would not acquire a little *brujo* power and figure out what was going on.

José came late, and kept a professional distance from the five hopefuls. For Juan she had only a cold stare.

I tried to calm myself, and was the perfect host in my diamond studs.

Around five in the afternoon, when the heat lifted, everyone gathered at the corral with its white stucco wall. The atmosphere was serious and silent. There was no need to pic these baby beasts. My two subalterns simply broke out their capes. With my felt hat tipped at just the right rakish angle, I leaned on the wall to watch the hopefuls. Álvaro and his foreman leaned beside me, to see how their babies played.

As the gate slammed open, the first calf came racing in. He was lithe as a lynx chasing down a rabbit. Juan had drawn this one. The nervous hopeful from La Montaña stood waiting, in protective chaps that Braulio had put on him, clutching his borrowed cape. I was sure that the crowd could see every wish and fantasy of mine glowing luridly in the air around him.

"Eh-heh!" Juan called.

The calf threw up his little tail and charged.

Juan was brave enough, and stood still, as we'd taught him. But last night's incident had shaken him, and his claimed dexterity on the soccer field did not translate into dexterity with the rose-colored silk. First the calf hooked a tiny horn in the cape, and whipped it out of Juan's hands. On the next round, Juan moved just a little, and the calf ran through the cape and tossed him. Bigotes and Manolillo had to run in with their own capes, and lure the calf off. The hopeful from the Land of Cheese got up dusty and mad. The calf tossed him again.

Since this hopeful was spending more time in the air than on the ground, I barked at him to leave the ring. He clenched his jaw, but obeyed like a soldier. The other hopefuls smirked.

My manager and my crew exchanged glum looks. They had all gotten to like Juan.

"He doesn't have it," Isaías told me quietly.

"I agree," I said, pretending disappointment.

"Too bad," Tere added wistfully. "He does have something. He's got brave eyes."

When the trials were over, none of the other boys had shown real promise either. The photographers shrugged and left. Isaías shrugged too — I knew he was thinking more seriously of retiring now. Tomorrow the calves would be slaughtered, and veal distributed to every house in La Mora. I wished I could turn them loose in the *coto*. But we weren't ready for wild cattle yet.

The rest of the guests trooped back to the patio, and relaxed with drinks and food and guitar music. When darkness came, the second-story arcades were colorfully lit with Chinese paper lanterns. Juan sat silently with my crew, and had little to say to anyone. He looked sad. Bigotes and Manolillo tried to cheer him up. My family kept staring at Juan, offended that a peasant was breathing the same air as they were.

While they were staring, José took advantage of the distraction to have a moment with Sera by the fountain. I watched their calm bored expressions, their lips moving. It looked like they were discussing whether they'd meet at 3 or 4 p.m. at the Royal Tennis Club. Sera nodded.

A little later, José, Sera and I eased away from the crowd with our sherry glasses, and took a private stroll out the opened door, among everybody's parked SEATs and Mercedeses and Citröens.

"So," I said, "are you two friends again?"

"I am on bended knee," José said wearily. "And what about your friend?"

"He discovered the mulberry branch," I shrugged. "So far all we've done is talk and maneuver."

The two women kept their eyes from widening with shock. "Right in the house, under everybody's noses?" Sera queried.

José frowned. "You don't know a thing about him. How can you trust him?"

"Like I know when I can cape a bull on the right."

"Your many scars tell me that sometimes you are wrong," José said drily.

"I'm not wrong about this."

"How do you know he's not after your money?"

"I don't think he is."

"Listen," José pursued. "If you succeed with him, and we decide to carry out our Pact, this is the man you will want me to marry."

"José and I have something to say about this," Sera added, frowning.

The three of us continued to look as though we were discussing drinks after the tennis match.

"Introduce us to him," José demanded. "If anybody can sniff out a fortune-hunter, I can. Mamá has tried to make me marry enough of them."

Back inside, Juan rose from his safe corner with my crew, and awkwardly shook hands with José and Sera. He wasn't schooled enough in manners to kiss their hands. From his expression, he was being tolerant because José was my sister...he already knew her as my secret ally of the mulberry branch.

José briskly took possession of Juan. Shortly they had eased away from the crowd, strolling up and down the arcades. José was an expert interviewer, knew how to draw people out — but Juan looked uncomfortable, answering with grunts. Sera and I stayed at the fountain, managing not to watch the two of them, and I entertained my fiancée-to-be with my rousing tale of how I'd smuggled the German pump through Spanish customs.

The eyes of Paco, my aunt and my mother stayed fixed on José and Juan. All raised their eyebrows. In their eyes, the mere fact that Juan would take a turn around the patio with my sister meant that he was presuming dangerously. As they discussed it, Sera and I could hear their voices clearly.

"Humph," said my mother. "As I've said a thousand times — this is where smoking leads."

' "Jesus, Mary and Joseph, the thought that she might marry a bull-fighter," Tita added, horrified.

"As if Antonio being one isn't bad enough," Paco added. "And Josefina writing about it..."

Sera's beautiful eyes moved from Juan's distant figure to my face. Possibly her mind was digesting the revelation that our "secret vice" was not limited to the upper classes. She and I exchanged looks.

"Well," she said brightly, "when can Mamá and I expect you again in Madri'th? Maybe you'll stay long enough to have dinner next time?"

A little later, Paco took me aside. I expected him to force the subject of José. Instead he was curiously genial, confiding, wanting to talk about his latest research on the Crypt of the Mercies.

"You may be wrong," he said.

"Really?" I growled. "About what?"

Paco was pleased with himself. "The Crypt of the Mercies," he proclaimed, "is definitely *not* the one under the chapel here."

My stomach flinched a little. "How do you know?"

"I have stumbled on something interesting. Next time you're in Toledo, I'll show you."

It was almost dawn before the Chinese lanterns burned out, and the guitarist put his instrument in its case, and the last people left, or tumbled to sleep in our guest rooms. Sera and her mother went off to Toledo with my relatives. José and I stayed up like all-night revelers in Madrid and walked bleary-eyed on the road, watching the sun come up over the Montes de Toledo while the caterer cleared away crayfish shells and clattering piles of sherry bottles. Juan had gone to his room.

"Well?" I asked my sister.

"He seems innocent enough."

"Fortune-hunters always seem innocent," I said.

"He's too nervous for a fortune-hunter. He's shy around women. And he's shy with all...this. It scares him. He doesn't trust it. And you'll have to teach him some social graces."

Suddenly she laughed.

"What amuses you so much?" I asked.

"This is going to be interesting...watching you two *machotes* battling to see who gets the upper hand."

"Just as interesting as watching you and Sera duel it out."

"Don't be mean, 'Tonio. I've begged for forgiveness. She is giving me another chance."

"So...you'd consider a marriage of convenience with him?"

"Much depends on how he feels about it," she said.

"So...you approve of him?" I pressed her.

"He does have something. Your crew all think highly of him. So do Isaías and Tere."

We had turned, and were walking back. She added: "But my approval doesn't matter. He isn't even yours yet."

It was true. Juan had gone off to bed without the most casual word to me. This didn't bode well.

7

Later that afternoon, when we'd all slept in, and Juan and I were walking the greyhounds along the olive groves, he was distant and morose again.

Finally he said: "I'm leaving today."

My brain refused to understand. "It's true you were terrible in the ring, but...maybe with more practice —"

Juan cut me off.

"I didn't come for bulls," he barked. "The truth is...I don't give a fig about the bulls."

I stared into his eyes. So he had traveled 500 kilometers for — what? Only for me? If so, why had he held me off? He said he had come for respect. My respect? If so, how had I failed this test?

We kept walking, trying to look normal, playing with the dogs, talking in low voices. With skillful arguments born of desperation, I tried to persuade him to stay in the area, find some work in Madrid. Our paths would cross now and then, I promised. But the more I talked, the more he shook his head.

"I don't belong in your world," he said bluntly. "And there's too many people around you."

Now there was a tiny emptiness — a narrow and profoundly deep puncture in my spirit, like the one that is left in the bull when the sword is drawn out. Yes, this novice had killed me well, with surprising skill. A single thrust.

"Go, then," I said hoarsely. "May Our Lady guard you."

"And you," he said, fondling the dogs' ears.

114

Then he turned away and walked back towards the house. I watched him go.

While Juan packed his suitcase and tied rope around it, I scrawled him a real letter of recommendation, to help him get work. José was up now, and I quietly told her. She said little. All the men were sorry to see him go. At the patio gate, with two of the guards watching, I shook his hand formally, distantly. Everyone else shook his hand. Even for his departure, Juan wore the good jacket and slacks — proud to the last.

"Good luck," I said. "Let us know how you do."

"Sure," he said. "Maybe a postcard from Germany."

The two guards and I watched Juan strike off down the road, carrying his suitcase. Summer heat was already making the mountains shimmer. His figure grew smaller, and finally disappeared into the wavering mirages.

"What a shame," one guard said, hitching his shotgun. "What a fine kid."

"Too bad we didn't have something for him to do," added the other guard. "Sword boy or something."

"I talked to him about that," I shrugged. "He wasn't interested."

"Torero or nothing, eh?" said the first guard. "A proud kid."

Pretending boredom about the whole thing, I took another coffee and slumped into my favorite rattan chair on the patio, with one foot on an ottoman to rest my bad leg, pretending to read *The Bulls*. José didn't know what to say to me, so she just got in her car and left for Madrid, to pick up Tere. From there they were going to Barcelona — she had a bullfight to cover there.

The German pump was purring deep in the well as the gardener Eustacio dragged a hose around, washing down the flagstones. Then he hand-watered the roses and trees in their urns. There was a clean smell of water on granite and foliage, that reminded me of Juan. His sudden absence made the house feel like its roof was caving in. In just a few days, his vibrant presence had become indispensable to me. A new kind of loneliness weighed on me. I saw the falsity of my life, the frailty of the rococo facade I'd built. In my imagination, Juan's trudging figure was growing smaller, ever smaller, along the highway shoulder. A rattletrap truck stopped to give him a lift, and he climbed in. The truck disappeared around a curve, leaving a cloud of blue exhaust in the air. He was gone, back into space and time, from whence he'd come.

I tried to focus on Cossío's chapter about the different subspecies of wild cattle that were historically native to different parts of Iberia — each with its own coat color and temperament. Suddenly, out of some crevice of my brain, a stark new thought poured.

Why hadn't I offered Juan the chance to be Pico's trainee in the *coto?*

My mind had been so gnawed by lust that it wasn't thinking clearly. Suddenly I could see Juan wandering the high mountain pastures of Umbrilla, studying plants, watching chamois graze with his cows — a boy dreaming of love, listening for the scream of eagles, noticing pressed-down places in the grass where deer had slept. The Virgin of Mercies, from Her throne of cow-horns, amid Her retinue of animals, had answered my agonized prayers after the bullfight in Santander — She had sent him to cross my path a second time. And for the second time, I had thrown Juan Diano Rodríguez away. I'd been stupid — oblivious to the possibilities. A gamekeeper who had veterinary training, even a science background like mine, would be a treasure. The Lady wouldn't give me a third chance.

Pretending I wasn't in a hurry, I got my jacket and car keys.

"I'd better go to Madri'th," I yawned. "I just remembered I need fitting for a new suit of lights."

Whatever I wanted to do was fine with everybody. In the shade outside the front door, Santí looked up from a piece of leather picador equipment he was mending with rivets and a hole-punch.

"If you see Juan on the road," he said, "tell him he's a fool for leaving us."

Racing the VW sedan along that narrow highway through the hills, I drove as dangerously as José. Through my dark glasses, I desperately scanned the shimmering landscape ahead. Tires shrieked on curves. Coming off a curve, I almost hit an old woman who was trudging along with a bundle of sticks on her back. I skidded, wheels squealing. The old woman kept trudging — she didn't even notice me. Hot sweat poured down my body as I got control of the car and sped on. In my mind, Paco's voice came, cursing peasants who kept forgetting they lived in the age of automobiles now. Lucky for me, that tomorrow's headlines weren't going to read OLD WOMAN RUN OVER BY TORERO.

Slow down, you lunatic, I told myself.

All the way into La Mora — no sign of Juan. He couldn't have walked that far in an hour. So he must have hitched a ride. Halfway to Madrid by now, or Ciudad Real, or Germany. For the rest of my life, I would curse myself for this mistake. Deeply depressed, I drove ten kilometers past La Mora before finally giving up and turning around. If any day was a day to saddle Faisán and ride around the *coto* brooding on my misery, it was today. Halfway between La Mora and home, I was roaring along, scanning the olive groves with my eyes, trying to think about the harvest. Suddenly, amid the silver-grey foliage, there was a familiar flash of chestnut brown. It had to be Juan's jacket.

Had he hung himself from one of my trees?

No. He was sitting in the scant shade, suitcase beside him, with his head on his knees. Twenty-four years old. No home, no family, no job, no education, no future. And he had just walked away from me. I had been Satan, offering him the riches of the world. But he had turned his back on me and my wealth. To his way of thinking, something was lacking in what I offered. If I didn't figure out what it was, he would hold me off forever. In that moment, I began to see dimly the caliber of human being that he was. What I felt for him was no longer just a dumb craving that tore my stomach loose from its roots. What I felt for Juan Diano was respect. Was it too late to feel it?

Tires squealing, I pulled off the road, under the nearest tree, and shut off the engine.

Juan raised his head. I walked toward him, then stopped as I saw how hostile his eyes were, in the harsh shadow thrown by his beret. The space yawned between us like a canyon. Words wanted to spill out of me — honest words about how I was doing the unthinkable, how I was falling for him.

As he stood slowly up, Juan struck an aggressive pose, fists clenched. His eyes went wild with rage. I think that was the moment when I finally saw him — saw his pain, his deep feelings, his wild and lonely bravado. In a low quivering voice, he said: "I won't be your *puto,* rich man. Waiting for you in some apartment while you live your life of gold."

I lashed back at him in the same voice. "Never did I think of you that way."

"Men like you have bought and sold men like me for a thousand years," he spat. "Your money will always be between us."

Brusquely he turned away, leaning against the nearest tree. His hands clenched the trunk so hard that the silver bark almost gave under his fingers like flesh. Suddenly he smashed his fist against the tree. Yes, he too knew what was happening. What had started as simple lust for each other was changing into something more dangerous.

Furtively I looked around. No one was in sight.

I looked back at him. The wild young bull, hot and wounded, had retreated into that spot in the ring where he felt he could best defend himself. Here, he could kill me most easily if I was careless with him. I would have to be the torero of hearts, and cape him out of there. Not only that, but I would have to show respect by declaring my own feelings first.   But a lifetime of deviousness made it hard for me to talk honestly. To buy time, I patted my pockets, pulled out a little cigar, and my gold lighter, and lit it. Sitting down on a low olive limb, I smoked for a minute, collecting my thoughts, forming my strategy.

Juan walked around restlessly, kicking at rocks with the toe of his espadrille.

I finally asked him drily, "Shall I wipe your feet with my hair?"

Juan turned around and stared at me.

"I can go to the biggest pimp in Barcelona," I said, "and pick a *puto* out of a picture book. The man who has me driving these roads of God for hours, looking for him, is not in that book."

I offered him the cigar.   After hesitating a moment, Juan took it and hunkered down by me to smoke. It calmed him. He had probably never tasted good Havana leaf. His trousers stretched tight across his full crotch. I wanted to put my hand between his thighs and feel him there. My balls tickled, and my own crotch got fuller.

"What do you want?" I asked him.

"A decent life," he said.

His finger was writing in the dust.

"A good veterinarian can be a wealthy man," I said. "Richer than a doctor for humans."

"You have to be rich to get a degree. Plus living in Madrid is expensive."

My hard-on was waning as I thought about the difficulties that faced him. Spanish higher education was hard on our youth. I knew — I'd been there. In the sciences, only one in every 15 or 20 students actually graduated. In veterinary medicine, maybe 30 a year.

"You think you can finish university?" I asked.

"Yes," he said, setting his jaw.

"Were you saving for it?"

"I was hoping to have enough for this fall, for my year of pre-university. Now it's gone."

His confession gave me the perfect opening.

"There is a possibility," I said. "Will you hear it, from me?"

After a minute, he nodded.

"Your gift is not with killing animals," I said. "It's with keeping them alive.   Milk cows — wild cows too. Yes?"

His eyes went dreamy.   "I was the one who made teas for the sick cows. I bottle-raised all the orphan calves."

"You were the one who knew the magic. The things that your father didn't have patience with."

Juan nodded. Suddenly his chest heaved again, a couple of times.

He was so close to tears that he couldn't help himself.

"One time," he said, "when I was about 8, I saw my father kill some kittens that he didn't want. He stepped on their heads. He would have stepped on my head if it suited him. After that, I took over the animals from him. I protected them from him. He and my brother were glad to have me for their slave. They were the big stocktraders, drinking with their friends on market day...."

"And you love the wild places. The wild creatures."

Juan almost closed his eyes, and his answer came as a slow nod. I felt a rush of exultation.

"Listen," I said, choosing the words carefully. "There is the *coto*. The gamekeeper is old. We need him to train a professional man, to take over when he dies. The *coto* is important. Saving the lives of wild animals will be important. The pay will be high if you do well. There is a fund that can pay for your education. Biology, veterinary school... whatever is needed. You could be someone outstanding in the profession."

Juan was shaking his head no. He stood up.

"I already said I won't work for you," he barked.

Patiently I kept on. "The *coto* project doesn't belong to me. It's funded by a group of people who put up money and support the work at the *coto*."

He stood and smoked with peasant slowness, thinking. I struggled on, trying to make it look good to him.

"The project is run by nine people — something like a board of directors. They all decide how the money will be spent. My sister and I belong to it, of course. But so does the village *coto* committee, which is four people. The person who counts most is El Pico, because he is the expert. You will work with Pico for a couple of weeks. He will say yes or no to the board. If Pico doesn't want you, nothing I could say would help. He is a stubborn cantankerous old fart. In fact, I'd lose face if Pico didn't like you and I went against him."

Juan nodded slowly, considering. "How much does the job pay?" His eyes had narrowed craftily — bargaining for a good cow on market day.

"Thirty thousand pesetas a month to start, plus room and board at the *coto*."

His eyes riveted me. "That's a lot of money. Your money."

Patience, Antonio. I kept my voice quiet, even.

"No," I said. "The fund will pay you, not me. The money isn't mine. It comes from people who support what we're doing... hunters, industrialists, people of conscience who want to see ruined land rescued.

Even the government has given us some money to plant trees there. I don't have the money to do this thing." A dry little laugh escaped me. "I'm not as rich as you think."

Juan's eyes held mine studyingly. He was wondering if I was lying to him.

I added: "You walked away from a farm the size of a handkerchief. This is bigger, man. If you become the gamekeeper, you will replace Pico on the board. You would be the person in command."

A long moment went by. My heart dangled helplessly as he considered. So I stood up too, now, and stared straight into his eyes. I took the cigar from his lips, had a deep drag and went on:

"At the *coto,* I don't ask your...friendship. I ask only that you love the land, the animals. Between you and me, there will be no money."

"Word of honor?" He took the cigar back.

"Word of honor."

He blew smoke and thought, eyes on the distance.

"Where would I live?" he asked.

"For now, you stay at the *coto.* There's an empty house there. If you are accepted, you can board there. Later on, when you have money, you can live anywhere you want."

The hot wind stirred his blond forelock as he dragged thoughtfully on the cigar. His eyes, squinting against the sun, were searching mine.

"And if you and I were ever to become enemies?" he asked.

For a long moment, those wild beautiful shy eyes of his held my gaze. I understood his real question, but wasn't sure how to answer it. It seemed there were no words in our Spanish language for what we felt — that great and noble language, whose age and richness is such a source of pride to the Spanish Academy. We would have to invent a language, a civilization of two.

"Well...what do you say to this?" I pursued.

"Maybe I won't like Pico."

Of course. The peasant farmer had to look carefully at the horse's teeth before he put down his money.

It seemed proper that I should show more respect by declaring myself. This old-fashioned village bandit would want a declaration from me. He wouldn't want to be taken lightly. Acting on impulse, wanting to show him that this aristocrat would abandon all social pride and crawl in the dust for him, if necessary, I wanted to take his callused hand with its broken fingernails in my well-manicured hand with its diamond ring, and raise it to my lips. I wanted to kiss his hand very formally...as a serf kisses a lord's hand, as a common priest kisses a bishop's ring. But I didn't want to pressure him too much. He didn't have the scholarship yet, so he would continue defending his honor.

Back off, Antonio. This bull has endured enough passes.

J uan threw his miserable suitcase into the spotless trunk of my sedan. For several minutes, we sat inside the car, each of us bolt upright in our bucket seat, staring out the window beside us, not saying a word. I was shocked at how close I'd come to never seeing him again. My body was shaking all over, like after the bull died in Santander that day. So I simply jammed the key into the ignition, then sat there clutching the steering wheel and trembling. Juan was silent too. When I looked at him out of the corners of my eyes, I saw his big hands resting on his thighs. Inside the expensive but now dusty slacks, his thighs were trembling just barely. He too must be in shock.

The old woman I'd nearly hit was trudging toward us, on her endless trek to some unknown destination, with that bundle of sticks on her humped back. When the old woman crunched past the car, she didn't look at us. She couldn't have seen anything anyway — her ancient eyes were milky with cataracts. She couldn't have seen the strange sight — two men sitting side by side in a stopped car in the middle of nowhere.

W e drove straight to the *coto*. El Pico listened as I explained this sudden opportunity. The old man grumbled and growled, and looked the peasant up and down with an air of "we'll see." He showed the new hopeful to his tiny house, then to the pens, where he put him in charge of the next hatch of partridge chicks. While Juan got to work, Pico and I sat in the shade under the pear tree, and drank a glass of wine together.

"A strong young back around here," he said. "That'll be good...if he works out."

"You can even take some time off."

"No kidding. My wife has been badgering me to visit our daughter in Villarobledo. Our son-in-law just got a car. They can come and get us."

"Do it," I said, seizing the opportunity to get the farm conveniently deserted for a day. "Juan will look after things."

"I won't go five meters down the road unless I trust him. When is your next contract?"

"In ten days, at Marbella."

"The *coto* board has their next meeting that weekend. We can decide about Juan while you're gone."

"You already know what my vote is."

"Your opinion has been noted. I'll let the Committee know. Does your sister have an opinion? Tell her to let me know."

Back at Las Moreras, Santí clapped me on the shoulder when he heard that I'd run into the peasant and talked him into the *coto* deal. All the men seemed pleased that Pico had an open mind about it. Braulio remarked that it was always good to see a poor kid get a chance in this country of God.

Naturally I had mentioned Pico's decision casually to my brother, so it wouldn't seem that Juan was something I was secretive about.

"At least you're not training him for the bulls," Paco snapped.

"Yes," I said. "None of the boys worked out. It's a great disappointment."

"It's a sign of God's will that you retire."

"Indeed," I said mildly. "God's will. Do you know God that well?"

"I am still displeased with you. Don't put so much time into the *coto* now. Politics is what you need to think of. Politics, and your wife, and fathering some children."

"That is exactly my plan," I assured him. "With a young trainee there — if he works out — I can rest easy about the *coto*. Pico is old. His heart isn't strong. He could drop dead any day."

"True," Paco conceded.

"At any rate," I purred, "the Spanish voters will not fault me for the work at the *coto*. Right wing or left wing, land use is an issue. You know that, Paco. The Old Catholics will see me as the gentleman refurbishing a hunting preserve. The New Catholics will see me reviving a wasteland — creating jobs in a troubled village. Either way, politically, we can't lose."

Paco smiled broadly, baring the two prominent canine teeth that put the ferret look on his thin face.

"Now you're talking like a politician," he said. "I like that."

The ten days passed slowly. I steeled myself and stayed away from the *coto,* not wanting to be seen hovering over Juan, or pressuring Pico. The new suit of lights was delivered — a blue one. I hoped it would last through Arles. I wanted to go out in blue, the color of Juan's eyes.

Before leaving for Marbella, I still had no inkling if Pico would approve Juan. But I decided to make another risky step forward. Pulling myself together, I visited Sera's mother and asked for her daughter's hand. Doña Margarita was delighted, of course, with an air of wondering why I'd made her wait so long. But she said the customary thing — I'd have to talk to Serafita, and settle it with her. I promised Doña Margarita that if her daughter agreed, we'd get engaged after my last contract in Arles.

The wedding could take place at a fashionable time that winter. For now, I wanted both families to keep everything quiet. Not a word to the press, please. This way, I said, it wouldn't look like a publicity stunt.

Marbella is a tourist town on the Mediterranean coast, not far from Granada. The bullring there is popular with foreigners. I planned to drive there with Isaías and Tere. José wasn't with us — she had an assignment in Madrid.

We got a late start, and Isaías was grumpy. He and Tere noticed how tense I was, but we didn't talk much on the long drive south. I wondered what they would think if they knew. Would ten years of being family to me vanish if they found out?

As we neared Granada, my nervous thoughts turned to García Lorca. On an impulse I suggested we spend the night there.

Like everything else in Spain, Granada was changing — no longer the Moorish poem in stone and water that Englishmen loved to visit. The Alhambra floated in blue smog. The view of that palace on its hill was cut off by hideous blocks of apartment buildings. The hill's famous elm woods showed ominous patches of dead limbs and yellow leaves — car exhaust or foreign tree disease. We passed a steamshovel razing some beautiful old villas.

At the Hotel Albaicín, I went to bed early and spent a restless night. Waking up early, I felt another impulse. On the street, wearing sunglasses and hoping I wouldn't be recognized, I found a taxi.

"To the Fountain of Tears," I told the driver.

The driver was a crusty old Granadino, beret pulled down to his eyes, disgusted at a long fare so early in the morning. "Man, it's an hour's drive out of town. The road is not good."

I looked at my watch, calculating that I had just enough time for this trip, then drive to Marbella and dress for the ring. I offered the old man enough to make it worth his while. For almost an hour, the taxi jounced along an unpaved country road, higher into the mountains. Now and then a rock almost knocked out our oil pan.

"So," the driver said over his shoulder, "you're looking for the grave of our queer poet, eh?"

My heart almost stopped. Was I following a beaten path?

"The Fountain of Tears is celebrated by many poets," I said. "Some were Moors, some were Christians. Maybe some were queer."

The old man just laughed. As we passed through the village of Víznar, he pointed out an old manse. "That was where the Falange made their headquarters when Franco's troops came through," he said. "They say the commanding officer was the one who wanted Lorca dead."

Past Víznar, we climbed still higher, with a splendid view of the flat farmlands below where Lorca was born. Here the road came to a wide ancient ditch, built by the Moors to bring water to Granada. Pointing to a ruined mill, the old man remarked: "They say Lorca spent his last night there, with some other prisoners."

By now my thighs were trembling, like Juan's had been. Would the old man take my money, then denounce me to the police? No doubt the taxi-drivers of Granada had learned to suspect any single man who wanted to tour these hills alone. A kilometer farther, as we followed the ditch over a little aqueduct, a steep ravine yawned ahead of us, full of young pines.

"Most of the people they shot," said the old man, "they are buried up in that ravine. You can still see the low places in the ground. The fascists planted trees to try to hide the graves. But in the winter, when it rains, there's still a smell."

My heart pounded in my ears, as I looked at the young trees. Some loved lines of Lorca's came to me.

> Green, how I want you green
> Green wind, green branches
> Ship on the sea
> Horse on the mountain

Had Lorca loved some country lad? "Man," I said, "where is the Fountain of Tears? Are you taking me on a wild chase?"

We kept jouncing along the ditch.

"But they say," the old man went on, "in the first days of the rebellion, prisoners were shot in a different place. Some died in those olive groves ahead. That's where Lorca sleeps. Two toreros were shot with him. So they say."

Now olive trees passed us, the Mediterranean *picual* variety here, heavy with ripening fruit, silver foliage lifting in the breeze, silvery shadows dancing beside them. Here too, developers had left ugly chalets so newcomers could devour that magnificent view. I stuck my head out the window, daring a blast of dust and hot wind, to look. Echoes of that fatal gunfire jarred mysteriously in my heart. In my horrified mind, I could see García Lorca's limp body sprawled under the trees. It was early morning, the rumors had said, so shadows were long. His trousers had two bloody bullet-holes in the back, where they'd shot him. Or had they pulled down the great poet's pants to do it? Spread his legs and jammed the icy barrel right up his *culo?* Was he still alive when they did it? People said he was. Without effort, I felt that violation, that fatal explosion inside my own body, a thousand times more painful than what the bull did to me. The grave trench waited — they kicked me in. I fell limply, hair dusty — Spain's greatest poet — into the arms of two dead toreros whose sexual inclinations were not known. I slept, forgotten by most but not all, in a cradle of olive roots.

Spain was full of places like this now — remote spots where the earth had sunk in. Franco's German and Italian allies had chafed at him, saying the war could be won in a few weeks with blitzkrieg. But the fascists had insisted on three years of slow advance, stopping in every city and village to liquidate as many leftists and liberals as possible. How many others like me — like my sister — slept out there?

"*Señor,*" the driver was saying. "*Señor.*"

"What?" I said.

"Does the *señor* wish to stop here?" the old man asked.

Every fiber of my body wanted to stop there...to walk around, and let intuition tell me which low spot among the trees was the right one.

"No," I said. "I told you...stop at the Fountain."

How terrible that I didn't dare to identify myself as an admirer of poetry.

Two hundred meters farther down the road, we finally came to the Fountain of Tears. The old man sat in some shade and smoked a cigarette while I leaned over the balustrade and stared down into that famous cistern, built by the Moors over a thousand years ago to carry mountain water down to the thirsty city. It mirrored the balustrade, the trees around it. It mirrored a forlorn single man. Tiny bubbles rose from its depths, to sparkle on the surface — the tears of legend.

"Yes, matador," said the old man, "they always cry here."

My heart sank. He had recognized me.

"Old man, I'm incognito," I said. "Visiting this fountain in memory of someone in my family."

Back at the hotel, Isaías and Tere were cross. "Where were you?" Tere fussed. "We're going to be late."

"Looking for García Lorca's grave," I blurted.

Isaías stared at me.

How could they not know? For years the Eibars had intercepted the occasional anonymous love letters and phone calls from men. Now and then they had even joked about it. "Your invisible constituency," Isaías had called it. How could they not know?

"Since when are you interested in poetry?" Isaías exploded at me like I was a novice. "You need to get your mind on your work! Bulls, man! Bulls!"

"Our country commits suicide if she forgets our great artists," I barked back.

"I didn't hear you mention that man's name," my manager said coldly. "It's political suicide."

In Marbella, I rushed into the blue suit of lights. The damn leg was bothering me. In front of thousands of beer-drinking tourists, I stood alone in the center of the ring, and raised my hat to the crowded seats. Everyone applauded politely, thinking that I was dedicating the bull to them. Instead, I whispered to the sunlight:

"Juan Diano, this one goes for you."

From somewhere in my faltering spirit, I tried to pull another huge effort. The bull was sweet and willing. But my body knew that it was close to experiencing love. It felt an understandable urge to shrink from any rude encounters with cattle horns. At that moment, the *coto* board was probably meeting in La Mora, at the mayor's house.

Seeing me hold back, the crowd began to whistle their disapproval.

When it was time to kill, I was so drained that I stood for what seemed like several minutes in front of the tired animal. He waited patiently for death, head hanging in his own exhaustion, exposing the sweet spot between his shoulder-blades. I sighted along the curved sword-blade, willing its point to stop making a wavering little circle in the air. Finally I flung myself forward. The sword point hit bone, and the blade almost bent double. I tried again.

After three tries, the sword went in crooked. The bull choked up great splashes of blood before he finally fell over.

The tourists howled their disapproval, and threw seat-cushions and beer bottles as I left the ring. The impresario had a big fight with Isaías and didn't want to pay. Isaías threatened him, and we finally got our money. As we left town, my manager gave me another cranky lecture about keeping my mind on business. Nothing more was said about Lorca's grave.

By now, I knew that the taurine world was commenting openly on my visible shakiness in the ring. They debated my sanity in even being there. ESCUDERO FAILS IN MARBELLA, the little newspaper item would read tomorrow, at the very bottom of the page. The bullfight magazines were ignoring me. All but my most devoted fans were falling away.

Meanwhile the *coto* board had decided my fate. Isaías had mailed a yes vote to the mayor. But the rest might have voted no. If Pico or the mayor had telephones, I could have called and found out.

Stopping in Madrid with José, I talked to her about my misery. She took me to lunch, and laughed at me as she piloted her Citröen through city traffic. "It's love," she said.

"Do you think so?"

"I don't know if he loves you. But you love him."

"Love? Or lunacy?"

"You sent him to Pico because it's safer, eh? I told the mayor I voted yes, by the way."

"What do you mean, safer?"

"You want to use the Crypt of the Mercies as a meeting place, don't you?"

"I never thought about it. But...why not?"

"Only Escuderos and the most trusted spouses have known where the Crypt is. Husbands, wives spent their entire lives with us, even had our children, and never knew the secret."

"You don't need to teach me our history," I snapped.

She glanced at me briefly, gunning the Citröen around a parked truck unloading potatoes.

"Now I know you love him," she said. "You wouldn't dream of taking him into the Mercies if he wasn't worthy."

"Sera doesn't know about the Mercies?"

"Of course not. I would have asked your permission to tell her."

"Do you want to tell her?"

"If we sign the Pact, both Juan and Sera should know."

"Do you approve of my taking him there?"

She thought a moment.

"I do. But what if Pico says no? Juan will leave again, won't he?"

Exhausted, I napped at José's for a few hours, then drove back to Las Moreras. I got there around 5 a.m. with a wild urge to head on to the *coto* and wake everybody up, and ask for the news.

The dark east was turning that silver hue of dawn as I pulled into the *coto*. Parking under the apricot tree by my cottage, I got out and stretched. Instead of exhaustion from days of traveling, I was strangely and intensely awake — vibrating with anticipation.

The morning was unusually chilly. Everything was quiet. Tiny songbirds were starting to whistle and sing in the wind-bent orchard trees. Horses grazed quietly in the walled pasture. Chickens were already out and about, pecking the dirt, but I didn't see Juan. The weathered shutters of Juan's tiny house stood open to the dawn. Surely this meant he was there. If he had left, Magda would have closed the shutters. Despite the early hour, the electric lights were on in Pico's cottage. Somebody's dusty new SEAT 600 was parked in front of the house, door open, with a suitcase in the back seat. What was going on?

Inside, the old man and his wife and son-in-law were sitting down to a bit of breakfast. They had charcoal lit in the brazier to warm their old bones, and the shutters ajar to vent lethal fumes out of the room.

"Antonio, come in, come in," Magda called.

Glad of the warmth, I sat at their table. She poured me a cup of her searingly strong coffee, with a splash of milk from the bottle in the new refrigerator, her pride and joy. Toast from yesterday's bread was happening on the primitive little bread-grill over the stove's butane flame. Half of a thick Spanish omelet, "three stories tall," bursting with fried potatoes and onions and our own olive oil, remained on a plate.

"Well?" I asked Pico.

"I am not completely satisfied with Juan," said Pico.

My heart sank.

Pico chuckled, relishing my discomfort. "But he'll do."

"Stop it, old man," Magda scolded him. "This is no time for jokes." She snatched the hot toast off the grill.

"So the board —" I was feeling faint.

"The Village Committee were sticky about having an outsider," Pico said. "But finally everybody saw it my way. So we offered Juan the scholarship."

I hardly dared to ask. "Did he accept?"

"Of course. Why wouldn't he?"

Pico gave me a strange look, wiped his mouth on his hand. He and his son-in-law went out, raised the hood and fiddled with the car. Something was wrong with the wonderful Spanish-made engine, and it wouldn't start. With poetry or horses, or even olive oil, we Spanish couldn't be beaten, but now and then modern engineering defeated us.

Magda put a plate in front of me — toast, and a hunk of the omelet. "You're thin, matador. I'm going to fatten you up."

"Where is Juan this morning?"

"Sleeping in. I fed him some omelet, then sent him back to bed. He worked like a burro. He even did projects on his own...fixing things up. The poor boy. No family... I'll fatten you both up. You'll see."

Magda had raised eight children of her own, but was always ready to take on another one.

"So the suitcase in your car..." I probed.

Magda smiled. "We're going to Villarobledo to visit. My daughter is so excited! We'll be back in a few days."

She put another plate over the rest of the omelet, intending to take it to her daughter and grandchildren. Outside, the SEAT engine finally coughed to life. Pico came back in, grinning.

"For the first time in years," the old man said, "I feel like I can leave for a bit."

Juan must have made a good impression.

Half an hour later, after Magda made sure I ate every bite of omelet, Pico and Magda rode grandly off in the car with their son-in-law. I was finally alone with Juan Diano. The Lady of Mercies was looking kindly on us.

8

For appearance's sake, I went first to the small stucco guest-house that I always occupied when staying at the game farm. Its single room was as simply furnished as Pico's house. There, I opened my suitcase, hung clothes in the wardrobe, ripped open the bed as if I intended to sleep there. The sound of a motorscooter startled me, and I peered through the window. It was Marimarta, coming up from Las Moreras with fresh bread for the day. Through the closed shutters, with heart pounding, I watched her park the basket of bread on Pico's doorstep, then drive off in a cloud of dust.

Everything was quiet again. Was the coast clear?

After putting the bread inside, so the chickens wouldn't get it, I walked over to Juan's cottage, noticing little things that Juan had done. He had repaired the ancient bird-pens, cleared away a broken-down cart, pruned dead limbs out of the fruit trees. A shimmering excitement and joy filled me, clean and cold as the dew all around. I was about to push his door open when I remembered that this was his home now. Should I knock? Respect, respect. But his door was ajar. Was he expecting me? Had he known that I would visit him right away if the Committee said yes?

Inside, I shut the creaky door and locked it.

The cottage already looked lived in — it was touching to see his pride in having a place of his own. An old English shotgun and shooting gear, loaned by Pico for guarding, hung from nails in the stucco wall, alongside a cheaply framed picture of Our Lady of Mercies that Pico's wife must have given him. The wardrobe door, half open, revealed his tiny collection of clothes, along with new underwear and a pair of country boots that Pico must have advanced money for him to get. On the sink drainboard, a few dishes sat neatly washed. In the corner, the butane heater was lit to warm the room. Heating was a luxury to him. The worn tile floor was so waxed by Magda that it reflected all these furnishings like a pond.

The shutters were ajar, and through them a single ray of sun touched the metal bed, where he sprawled with the striped wool blankets half off him, head buried in the pillows. Magda's brown cat Mulata and five half-grown kittens lay curled and sunlit against him. Beyond, a back door was ajar, leading out to the privy.

I stood looking down at him, listening to him breathe. The cats stirred. I scooped them onto the floor, one by one, but they kept jumping back up. Finally Mulata looked at me with disgust and led her kittens out the back door.

Juan looked so good laying there in his underwear — tousled hair shinier, muscles already sleeker from eating Magda's good cooking. His ribs slid slowly as he breathed, one arm flung over his head. His bared breasts and nipples, the bronzed hair in his armpit, cast their shadows across his skin in the morning light. The underwear barely revealed his manhood, slack in bed-warmth and dreams. After a few minutes, he stirred, as if sensing my gaze, and one of his hands slid down to fondle himself. Gooseflesh rippled through his skin.

Quietly I stripped to my own underwear, tiles cold under my bare feet.

As I got in beside him and pulled the blankets over us, he suddenly took me in his arms. There was the shock of a man's warm flesh against mine. I returned the embrace and crushed him against me with a spasm of tenderness. Our bodies hungrily fitted themselves together, like two halves of a broken plate, as we'd done in the Santander crowd that day we met, except only two thin layers of cotton separated us now.

"Majín," he whispered in my ear in a hoarse waking-up voice. "Did you think you can sneak up on me?"

"It was hard to find you under all those kittens."

"Do you purr at night?" he teased.

I was liking this unsuspected playfulness in him. "Pico told me the news. Congratulations."

His eyes looked at me with quiet pride and happiness. I blessed myself for having been born, so that the look could be there.

"Now you will have to study like a mad Jesuit," I said.

For answer, his naked thighs gripped mine between them protectively, as they had in Santander. As he ran his callused hand up and down my back, his face pressed hungrily against mine, his stubbled cheek scratching me. My hand searched his chest, finding his nipples going hard. He let me caress him without protesting. Respect had somehow been snatched from the jaws of contempt.

"Did Pico and Magda leave already?" he whispered.

"Of course...or I wouldn't be here."

His hand slid down my back, to squeeze my hip possessively. "Marimarta was here?"

"A few minutes ago. No one else will come now."

"The Committee sometimes visits..."

But as his hands took hold of me, I could feel an icy feudal shadow creep over us, as if the morning sun had moved behind some lichened battlement. He made love to me the way he'd looked for sex under bridges. It was all he knew. So he was rough, hurrying, seeking only self-gratification, afraid that the moment would be stolen, privacy shattered. The young bull hurtled into the ring, avid to hook his horn into anything he could find. I tried to slow him, but he kept tearing the cape from my hands. I wanted to take my time, kiss him, taste him, feel him. He wanted to grab my manhood and work it hard. Under the assault of our strong bodies, the venerable bed creaked ominously. First the rough biting on my nipples that drew blood. Then he hurt my leg, and I almost cried out with the pain. I felt like a thrashing roe deer pinned to earth by a wolf trying to feed on its entrails.

"Jesus," I growled, "don't maul me."

His face showed distress, as if he couldn't help himself.

Just then, we heard voices in the distance. Juan blanched.

"Shit...I told you so," he said. "It's the Committee."

He jumped out of bed on the other side.

Through the dusty window, we glimpsed three men and a woman walking up the steep road, pushing bicycles, toward Pico's house. They were Candalaria, mayor Mercurio Fortes, and the other two members of the La Mora committee who worked directly with me and Pico on *coto* affairs. My heart pounded so heavily with fright that I felt faint.

Quickly, oblivious to my slow leg, I dressed and went out the cottage's back door. Keeping out of sight behind the bird-pens, I limped to the privy. Inside, I was so nervous that I didn't have to fake a piss. Minutes later, when I walked to my house, the Committee were leaning against my car, waiting. The men were having a smoke. They'd probably peered in my open door, and concluded I was at the privy. Calmer now, I casually adjusted my zipper, to assure them I'd just had a magnificent relief.

The villagers' wrinkled faces cracked slightly with welcoming grins. They greeted me with the slow, melodious talk of Castilian up-landers.

"Hello, Don Antonio!" said Candalaria. "You just got here, eh? Your hood's still warm."

"I wanted to know the decision. Pico told me before he and Magda left."

They didn't ask how it went in Marbella, so I knew they'd watched my disaster on the *tele*. In the distance, Juan walked to the bird-pens, tucking in his shirt-tail, Mulata riding on his shoulder. The kittens scampered after him. His hair, now combed with water, glinted in the sun. The Village Committee's eyes followed him.

"A great moment for the *coto,* eh?" I added. "Your trainee is finally here."

They hesitated, looked at each other.

"Listen, Antonio," said Mercurio the mayor, "the Committee wants to talk with you personally. It's about Juan."

"Say on." My stomach sank with apprehension. Were they about to go back on their decision? Had they sensed something about Juan's morals?

We sat in Pico's house with coffee that Magda had left for us, and some of the fresh rolls that Marimarta brought.

"In the village," said Mercurio, "people aren't happy about an outsider."

"I'm not happy about an outsider," Candalaria added.

"I understand," I said diplomatically. "All of you have the right to feel satisfied with him. Naturally, if he does not perform well, you can fire him."

"Well, we've been watching him closely," said Fermín, the bar owner.

"Very closely," added Alberto, the artisan, the one to whom I'd given the olive burls.

"First," Fermín said, "we saw him hatch out the new batch of partridge."

"And?"

"He got more chicks through the first week than Pico does," said Fermín.

"Many more," added the artisan.

"Then," Candalaria put in, "yesterday Fermín and I were up in the hills, and we saw a lynx."

"Excellent news," I said, trying to contain my excitement. This would be the first lynx seen in these parts since I was a child.

"A female." Fermín was grinning. "She has kittens."

"She is denning near that first spring we put back in," Candalaria said. "We came to tell you."

"And this is the amazing thing," the mayor mused. "Juan Diano told us a lynx would come before the month was out. He looked at what we've planted, at the number of rabbits and birds, at the Moon...and then he said it was time for a lynx to come. He said this on the day he got here."

A delicious chill flooded my skin.

"Pico says the kid's a *brujo,*" mused Alberto. "Pico ought to know."

"And Don Antonio, to think you almost wasted him as a torero," Candalaria added, with a sly twinkle in her eyes. The old edge in her voice had softened a little.

I was hardly daring to believe what I was hearing.

"So," added Mercurio, "the Committee will quiet the rest of the village about outsiders. And we'll make sure nobody shoots our lynx."

Our lynx.

I relaxed shudderingly, like when the bull is dead.

When we went outside again, Juan waved us over to the partridge pens. We walked over there. He had locked up the cats, and was unfastening one of the gates. Only I could see how shaken he still was, over interruption of our intimacy.

"Don Antonio," Juan said brusquely, "Pico told me to release the oldest ones this morning. It's time."

The "don" part hurt my feelings — that he would put that much formality between us in public, because of his fear.

So we all stood at attention while Juan opened the gate and two hundred young partridge discovered freedom. By threes and fours, they whirred away over the deeply shadowed brush, flying with that bullet speed that challenges the aim of the best shooter. Out there, they'd have all day to find their first food and water Some would die. Most would live. Life is bounty, even for human beings who deny the bounty of love to themselves and to others. It's all there for us if we fly far enough to find it. The beauty and terror of their encounter with freedom misted my eyes.

Even the Committee's hard faces softened as they watched. I had convinced them that wild things would make them rich.

"Food for the lynx," Juan said with a tight smile, as he closed the gate.

The Committee exchanged glances. Since we hadn't yet told Juan about the cat's arrival, he had already known by that mysterious way of his own. Or he had seen the cat himself.

Candalaria crossed herself. "Holy Mary of Mercies," she whispered to herself. "I hope this *brujería* is all right with You."

She moved her hand in the air slowly and elegantly, the way she talked.

Around 10 a.m., after more endless social stuff — the Committee had a brandy with us to celebrate the lynx — they left.

At the chick brooders, Juan squatted by the wooden boxes, with his back resolutely turned to me. His khaki shirt stretched tight across his muscular shoulders. I kneeled by him, wanting so much to touch him. Under the warm brooder lights, his hands were busy refilling water and food dishes, removing a few dead chicks. Then he simply crouched with his open hands laid on the earth, near the seething masses of softly cheeping partridge chicks. I watched, amazed, as chicks crowded onto his palms and nodded off to sleep in two tight clumps. Never had I seen these wary birds get so close with any human. Never had I seen my friend be so gentle. Juan was smiling a little, eyes closed with bliss at the feeling the chicks gave him.

Just as gently I laid my hand on his back, feeling him caressingly through the shirt with my own palm.

"Don't," he whispered. "You don't know who's watching."

His hands tensed. Before his clenching fingers could crush them, startled chicks scattered with tiny whirs.

"We'll spend the day in the hills," I said. "I want to show you some things."

When the chores were done, he threw sheepskin saddles on Mozuela and Faisán, while I hung a skin of wine over a saddle-horn, and thrust some fresh rolls and dry sausage in a saddle-bag.

As we headed the horses up the ancient road into the *coto,* along the first rocky slope, it was almost noon and the land glowed with a metal heat. In gullies everywhere, the new copses of brush were ever lustier. Here and there, we glimpsed a few of the young partridge. They were already doing their partridge things, enjoying their freedom. A vast sphere of shimmering stillness surrounded us. Birds, animals going quiet everywhere as the sun neared her zenith. No sound but horse hoofs against rocks.

Miles above us, a jet plane suddenly made its new sound, drawing an ugly white scar across the blue sky. Maybe it was heading for Barajas Airport at Madrid, loaded with tourists. Maybe it was going to the Yankee base at Palomares, loaded with nuclear war-heads. To get that base, and international forgiveness for his liaison with Hitler, Franco had had to let tourists come.

We reined on a hilltop, looking around. "How does it feel to own all this?" I asked.

"Good."

"But do you like it here?"

"Sometimes I miss the Picos."

"But man...this is the most beautiful place on earth." I wanted to tweak his patriotism.

"It's only missing one thing," he retorted. "The rain we have in the Picos."

"It rains here sometimes."

"When the animals and plants come back here, they will bring more rain," he said wistfully. "Yes, I like it here. The land is starting to talk to me. It will be good."

We dismounted and walked sometimes, leading the sweating horses. Partridge whirred away over the shimmering brush. I pointed here, and there. I showed him the little valley where I hoped wild cows could graze. I showed him spots where springs had once welled, that were now dry and dust-filled. In one little ravine, we dug with dry sticks in the sand, finding damp ground about 8 centimeters down. We talked about land engineering, about how to bring the spring back. I had learned some of these things on my travels.

"We'll dig it out," I said, "and fill it with loose rock. The water will leach in, and collect."

"From there, a pipe to a little catch-basin," Juan added.

"In five years it will be big enough for boars to wallow in."

We both laughed, relaxing enough to start enjoying each other's company. Now and then, a hand was laid lingeringly on the other's shoulder. We each gnawed off the same dry sausage. When he seized the *bota* from the saddle and held it up to shoot the stream of wine into his thirsty mouth, I felt a surge of joyous lust. He wiped his mouth with the back of his hand, and grinningly offered me the *bota*. Our eyes met.

"Your eyes are bread," I wanted to say, "and I am hungry."

He gave a low sexy laugh. He must have read my thought.

As the white-hot sun passed the zenith, a plateau stood ahead of us, stark against the sky. We came to the old road, leading up to the plateau. We had crossed the invisible boundary of the *coto* now, and were on the private area that I'd set aside.

On the plateau, we rode across the scrub, two lonely figures with our horses' manes and tails fanning out on the hot breeze. Colorful bee-eaters winged after insects. Here and there, little pines and oaks that the villagers had planted were taking hold.

In this lonely place, there was no visible sign that a little round building — crowned with a dome, four doors at the four directions — had stood here in ancient times. It must have been visible for kilometers. The medieval Escuderos had done a good job of razing the above-ground part of the structure, hauling away countless cart-loads of stone with teams, using it to build the Las Moreras chapel, later the house and out-buildings. After our greatgrandmother's death, José and I had spent months up here, a day at a time, pretending to picnic, quietly removing some fragments of dressed stone from amid the brush. A few at a time, we carried them in saddle-bags to the next plateau, at the next switchback of the ancient road. There, as a ruse, we scattered the rock. Future archeologists would be confused, but no matter. We hoped the ruse would confuse Paco.

Now no one would guess that, deep in the earth under our horse's hoofs, the subterranean chamber of the Mercies was still in exist-ence — a marvel to rival the painted cave of Altamira.

Near the plateau edge, amid a few wind-bent old pines, stood the stone hut built by my greatgrandfather. It was typical of the huts that you find in more remote spots in Spain, for hunters to take siesta or get out of bad weather. Beyond, a rocky ravine cut away through the land.

"We'll rest out the heat here," I said, tying my horse in the shade.

Juan's eyes met mine, now apprehensive.

The hut's plank door was not padlocked, simply shut tight to keep out animals. The villagers knew that the hut was José's and my private place, so they respectfully stayed away. Inside the low building, there was a rough floor of large unglazed tiles. On it stood two low iron-frame beds layered with sheepskins. A metal rodent-proof chest was stocked with dry blankets, matches, flashlight batteries, a can-opener, first-aid kit, tinned sardines and biscuit. On the chest stood an oil lamp.

Leaving the door open to sunlight and air, I pulled off my boots and lay down on one of the beds. Propping a pillow under my head, I lit a little cigar. Hesitantly, Juan sat by me, and we shared the smoke. The little ritual, that we'd done so often now, calmed him. Then I laid my hand on his arm. One of the horses stamped outside, and he flinched at the sound. So I stroked his hair like a horse's mane, calming him.

"I have to ask something of you," I said quietly.

"What?"

"I need you to be how you are when you hold the chicks in your hands. I have some old injuries, and can't bear any mauling. Can you think of me as a partridge chick in your hand?"

He nodded slowly, dropping his gaze.

138

"I need you to kiss me," I added in a hoarse voice.

"Kissing is for girls." He kept looking down.

"You asked me for respect. I also want respect," I said.

It was the moment to kiss his hand, and I did. The ancient gesture of homage, made harmless now. His hand opened to caress my cheek. When I took hold of his shoulders, his muscles knotted under my hands with brief resistance. Then, slowly, he let go and leaned down over me. Our hot cheeks grated together. Finally our lips touched grazingly, tasting of smoke and horses. Between my palms, I could feel him holding his breath, his whole frame trembling, as he fought to remember about partridge chicks. I kept kissing him — his cheek, his chin, his upper lip — with feather-like grazes. Finally he exhaled a slow breath of joy and his eyes closed. He liked it. This time, when a breeze rustled in the brush outside, he paid no attention. His warm lips parted with that breath, and touched mine. Our tongues touched. That newborn kiss was as fragile as a wet baby bird struggling out of its shell.

Juan Diano lay down in my arms, and gave up his mouth to me in a second kiss that went deep and hard. He liked this very much. His mouth tasted of green grass and limestone. To him, I must have tasted like hot sun and blood.

There was no sound but brush rustling, and the stamp of hoofs — the quiet sounds of our lips and tongues, and hands trying to explore through layers of corduroy and leather. Without a word, I worked the kiss of homage downwards, helping each other to unbuckle belts. I unbuttoned the fly of his old-fashioned peasant trousers. He unzipped my new English-made sporting pants. Silent, still restrained, we fondled each other's heads as our lips explored each other's necks, breasts, nipples. Pants and underwear were fumblingly pushed down around hips, just low enough. "*Ayy* Majín, how good you are," his lips murmured against the line of dark hair below my navel. For my part, I was kissing along his sensitive flank as he caressed the back of my neck. His hand shyly offered me his manhood, thick and horsey. As its smoky man-smell bathed my nostrils, I kissed it and swallowed him in.

He uttered a choking sigh of delight and humped my face roughly. But I held his hips and slowed him, timed him into my own movements — made him be the bull whose curly forehead was bathed in my cape, pass after slow pass. His lips were searching inexpertly along the scars in my groin, murmuring a few tender obscenities, to find what my own hand was offering him. I could tell this was new to him. Yes, he had never done anything but hand-jobs. It was good to know that there were still some minor trophies of innocence — an ear or two — to be taken here.

Like newborn calves, we glued our tongues around each other's members, suckling hungrily, knowing we could not live without this milk. As I let go into his throat, his twin spurt filled mine at the same instant. It was hot and rich as a mother cow's colostrum. Being famine victims, we almost fainted at the shock of this real food. We lay panting for a few minutes.

Dreamily I closed our clothing, then laughed as he sat up. His face was wet. "You'll learn to swallow," I whispered.

He looked embarrassed, as I wiped his face with my shirttail. "It took me by surprise," he growled.

We were already dozing off from the tremendous release. Days of exhaustion, travel, emotion, caught up with me. Without a word, he rose from me and slumped down on his own bed. He knew it wouldn't do for us to fall asleep together on the same bed — we might get caught that way.

We slept heavily in the fierce heat.

When I struggled awake, Juan was awake on the other bed, propped on one elbow, looking at me. In his blue eyes, the irises were black with deep emotion. "I heard voices up on the ridge," he said. "But they passed."

"Probably our guards from La Mora."

Across the space between the beds, I held my hand out to him. He took it. Late-afternoon sun, slanting into the doorway, cast a shadow of our entwined fingers on the dusty tiles. Feeling as if my wrecked body was suddenly healthier, brimming with a pure spring-water of well-being, I slid over onto his bed, back into his arms. The hot shimmering silence was still unbroken, as we lay there unwilling to end the closeness. It was amazing to listen to him breathe, study his face close up — look into his eyes, past the rich shadows of his eyelashes, into his spirit and see him liking our intimacy. He was looking at me the way I'd always imagined a man might look at a man he loved.

"Remember me telling you about the Mercies?" I asked.

"Yes."

"The entrance is here underneath us. You lift up tiles in the floor. There is a staircase...you go down into it."

He visibly felt a chill. "Is it full of dead people...like a church crypt? We did this on top of dead people?"

I laughed at his superstition. "Crypt is an old word for cave, my friend. It's not a cemetery. Just a cave. A sacred cave, like Altamira. Did you ever visit Altamira?"

"No. I was stuck on the farm."

"The Mercies is something like Altamira, only not as old. It is full of wonderful paintings of Our Lady and animals.   Another time, I'll take you down in there."

He stared at me, still uneasy, and nodded slowly. I stroked his hair to calm him. Suddenly the words came to me unbidden.

"Hombre de mi corazón," I whispered. "Man of my heart."

He stiffened a little. "That kind of talk is for girls."

"No girl gives milk like yours," I said.

A fiery flush went up his neck.

"What we feed each other," I said against his face, "becomes part of each other....bones...hair. Like any food.   Think about that."

He laughed. "Did you learn that shameless nonsense in your science class?"

We were both painfully aroused again. His big hand slid between my thighs, feeling my buttocks possessively through the cloth of my trousers. "Majín," he whispered, "I have an urge to dishonor you completely."

Was he testing me, to see how macho I really was?

"Have you ever done that ?" I asked.

"No. But I've heard that men do this sometimes."

"I suppose Rafael told you that."

"'Fael again. I already told you…"

"I know, I know. The two of you talked about it, and then he went off and did it with someone else."

"He had a friend…I never knew who it was."

I was torn between wanting this and not wanting to be thought effeminate by him, for fear he'd lose respect for me. "I suppose you gave up yours under a bridge somewhere."

He laughed. "Not under a bridge. Not anywhere. Majín, do you think I didn't chew on my tongue that first day, watching men look at you in the ring?"

I laughed too. "What about the guy in your village?"

He looked away. "What guy?"

"The one you haven't told me about."

This was still my shot in the dark. I had a feeling he'd been with someone when he was very young...not like me, who'd had only fantasy lovers. I'd had my first time thanks to a foreign *puto* when I was nineteen. I paid him some of the francs I earned on my first bullfight in France. To my surprise, Juan's eyes went wet, and his voice filled. "He was too much of a coward to try," Juan blurted.

Clearly there was huge emotion around this subject, so I let it go for the moment. Suddenly there was a sharp stirring in the brush outside. We started, and listened tensely. "It's nothing...just a falcon taking a partridge," he whispered.

Nevertheless I got off the bed. "Time to go," I said.

The day was leaving us behind. Through the hut's open door, afternoon shadows were deeper blue now, stretching farther through the brush. A light breeze stirred leaves uneasily.

"Next time we'll go down in the Mercies," I said. "No one will bother us there."

We gathered our gear, closed the hut and went to the horses. My mind went worriedly to Paco. What was my brother learning from the old records? I hadn't studied them myself. Would Paco find the Crypt on his own? Would he ever come up here looking? He had never spent much time in the *coto,* expressing contempt for the hunting that frittered away Escudero purpose. As far as I knew, he had never been to the hut.

As we rode along, Juan must have been reading my mind. He asked: "Does your sister know you told me?"

"Yes."

"Then she knows...."

"My sister and I have no secrets from each other."

At first he looked alarmed. But when I told him how José and I had driven to Santander looking for him, he burst out laughing. The look he gave me was sly and sexy.

"*Ayy,*" I said, "if I were a bull and it was spring, I would wrap my tongue around you like the first green grass."

Juan blushed. "Go to hell," he said.

Now that we'd begun this, I wanted our two lives woven together at every juncture, like one of those endless Celtic braids on the church in his village. So it seemed like the perfect moment to tell him about Sera and José, and broach the idea about marriages of convenience. Then, as I was about to open my mouth, something stopped me. This would be too much for Juan all at once. I decided to wait. Tomorrow Pico and Magda would still be gone. Juan and I could go back into the hills, to a different place this time — find some thick brush somewhere, and fuck all day long like two lynxes in heat. I would hope that Paco didn't have a spy out here with a pair of binoculars.

But back at the farm, my fantasies about tomorrow came crashing down. The SEAT 600 was parked there again. Pico's and Magda's windows glowed with light. The smell of bean stew and salt pork wafted from their door. Pico came out and gave me an embrace that was fiercely strong for a 70-year-old.

As Juan went off to lock up the chickens for the night, I told Pico about our first lynx. The old man's eyes sparkled with joy. Many were the people who thought old Pico was mad. Under his battered beret, his ragged white hair blew in the evening breeze like a wizard's.

"Pico, you came home early. Are you worried about the kid?"

"The kid is a jewel."

"Then why..."

"I'm an old worrywort, that's all. I haven't been away from here for years."

"Next time, you and Magda stay with your daughter for a few days. You need to get away. Juan won't fail you."

"So...Juan works here through September — gets to know the land. I knock the rough edges off him. After that, he'll be here on breaks from school."

"Yes. The Committee has agreed."

To keep a good appearance, I went back to Las Moreras and slept in my own bedroom that night. The memory of making love with Juan was a vivid technicolor movie running wild in every sense of mine. But when could Juan and I dare to even take all our clothes off? Spend an entire night and wake up in the morning together? When could I spend day after day with my friend? It didn't seem too much to ask for, from the Lady of Mercies.

9

Two more weeks had to pass, including one erotic siesta in the hut, and another in the brush in a remote ravine, before I dared to suggest the Pact to Juan.

It was late June now. One change of the Moon since Juan and I had met. With José's agreement, I had moved Faisán up to the farm. The old horse loved the long rides over the *coto,* calming down and getting fit. Juan was riding my roan mare, Mozuela, talking about buying his own horse. But first, he said, he wanted to buy a Vespa, so he could go places. Then his own car...someday. So he could see the world. Especially Madrid, he said.

But now, as we sat there in the shady brush and relaxed after intimacy, Juan was frowning, incredulous.

"Marry José?" he repeated.

As I'd feared, he looked shocked while I described the scheme that José, Sera and I had hatched. It was a lot for him to take in. That my sister was like me. That she had a friend too. It had never crossed Juan's mind that women could like each other that way. He and I had our clothing buttoned up now, and were looking down into a little gorge where a roe doe and her two fawns were browsing on bushes. A few ticks, feeding on them, showed as black dots. Juan was silent a long time, looking through binoculars — the ticks worried him. Finally he said: "Majín, you are full of serious proposals."

"I admit it."

"Neither of us will be free if we do this."

"It's the only way we *can* be free. Marriage is just a rubber band...it stretches around whatever you want to hold together. José will ask nothing but your name, and the protection you give. Sera will do the same with me."

"I'll think about it," he said evasively, putting the binoculars back in their case. "Things are moving so fast. A few weeks ago I didn't even know you."

"Have a heart. I'm being overrun by my family about this. Will you at least go out with José a few times, if I can arrange it?"

We were at the horses now, checking their cinches.

"Date a *woman?*" he said over his shoulder, jerking the cinch tight. The mare, Mozuela, grunted at the jerk.

"If you're going to marry her, you have to date her first."

Faisán had a tick on his chest, and I carefully picked it off.

"Who says I'm going to marry her?" Juan was indignant, climbing onto the mare.

But I was patient. "Even if you don't marry her, why not go out with her? José likes you. She's good company. To run the *coto,* you have to learn how to move in society, my friend. How to behave around society women."

"I already know how to behave around women," he said coldly. "I avoid them." He wheeled Mozuela and cantered off.

Damn! I had overstepped again. Spurring Faisán, I caught up with him. We slowed our horses to a walk.

"Besides," he said, lighting a cigarette, "women like her don't marry guys like me. Your family will have a fit."

"I'll persuade them."

He snorted. "Even that piss-ant brother of yours?"

"Juan, listen. If you don't marry, your new life will be in danger. People will talk. You already went through this hell in your village...the *mili.* The only reason I've avoided suspicion is that toreros usually don't get married till they retire. They don't put wives and children through the worry. But once I retire...if I don't gallop to the altar, people will talk. Think about it. You a bachelor, I a bachelor, the two of us spending time together... Once my family notice, the police will notice."

Juan's eyes were somber. He knew I was right.

I had saved my best pass for last. "Man, you can see Madrid this way. José loves Madrid. The high life, the clubs, restaurants. You'll have a great time with her."

"I can't afford high life." He frowned.

"José isn't as finicky as you think. Take her to the movies."

"In *her* car?"

"Why not? You'll have your own car soon enough."

To arrange things for José and Juan, I would have to work human beings with my verbal cape as never before. So the next evening, I stopped in Toledo, at my mother's house. Paco lived in the capital, because of his job, but he came here on weekends to pore over old documents in the family archives. My brother had just packed his wife and children off to their tiny villa in Santander till school started again, so he could spend weekdays researching as well. While I was looking forward to a summer between a man's legs, Paco's summer would be spent between pages of dusty books.

"*Hombre!*" he said with cheerful formality as I came into the library. "How are you?"

Piles of books, manuscripts and notes surrounded him, on the long refectory table. Under the high gloomy ceiling, with its painted beams, his solitary figure was bright-lit by a reading lamp with a magnifying lens in it. Nearby, several ancient oak chests stood open, crammed with old books and yellowed documents. Modern purists feel that these precious documents would be safer if they were kept in climate-controlled glass cabinets.

With the Spanish passion for intricate organization, Paco had the documents stuffed in labeled folders: letters, grants, estate inventories, property deeds whose earliest entries were in Arabic. There were a few yellowed genealogies from Inquisition times, with "pure" bloodlines recorded in blue ink — meaning Old Catholics of the Castilian "race," meaning Visigoth, with no "taint" of Arab, Moor, Berber, Jew. Paco proudly referred to our family as *azules,* "blues," but I happened to know that the term was an old one in the family, and had another meaning unknown to Paco. Older genealogies had disappeared, possibly with our Red aunt.

Other things had also mysteriously disappeared from this priceless collection. From my adolescent browsings, I remembered a document dated 1222, describing a church ceremony that made "brothers" of one García with Pedro, the brother of Sanches who was later murdered. These half-forgotten ceremonies were known to a few Spanish scholars, who hadn't dared to mention them since the Republic fell. Instinctively I had felt they were sanctions of sexual friendships between men, dating from an earlier, more tolerant time. The last time I'd looked for this document, it had vanished. Paco had probably destroyed it. But to inquire about its whereabouts would draw attention to myself. So I held my tongue, grabbed the crystal decanter on the vast oak cabinet, and poured myself a brandy.

"Your news about the Mercies?" I said over my shoulder.

Paco's eyes glowed hugely, spookily through his bi-focals.

"Yes. Where is that book?" he fussed. "I had it just a minute ago."

Paco dropped a page of notes, bent to fumble for it. Even with bi-focals, he could hardly see. Silently I picked the page off the floor for him. He found the right book, opened it to a bookmark.

"Now look here, at what it says about the Mercies," Paco insisted. "I never read this passage carefully before."

My stomach went nervous. This was one of the oldest books — a hand-copied leatherbound history, *Deeds of Sanches,* written with sepia ink in a peculiar Old Castilian cursive that Paco alone knew how to read. He said he'd seen books of similar manufacture in the archives at the monastery of Santo Domingo de Silos. By the material in it, this one had to be 13th century.

Now Paco's slender, fine-boned finger slid along the text.

"It mentions the old road...mentions the Crypt being near it, south of the church," he said. "But which church? The one at the castle? Or the one at Las Moreras? If it's the latter one, the Mercies would be out in the *coto* somewhere."

"Most likely it was the one near the castle," I said. "Why would it be out in the *coto,* away from protection?"

I kept silent about the real answer to this question, which was that the Mercies was far older than the castle. It dated from a time when such ceremonial practices had been widely accepted, so there was no need of a castle for protection.

Behind us, as we pored over the book, the tall glass windows framed a sunset vista of tiled Toledo roofs with myriad TV antennas. The distant silhouette of the ruined Alcázar fortress was surrounded by scaffolds — it was being rebuilt as a tourist attraction and monument to the Nationalist capture of the city. Beyond, blue shadow gathered in the Tajo River gorge that belted the city on three sides. I had been born in 1939 in this very house, just as the guns fell silent. The windows were shut tight, otherwise fumes and noise of traffic would reek in the room. Even the glorious myth of the Escuderos didn't stiffen my mother to put up with Toledo on summer weekends, when it seemed like a million German, French, Belgian and Yankee tourists and their cars invaded our city. Mamá and Tita had already fled to their tiny modern estate, "El Refugio," which I had bought them outside the city.

Paco had pulled out an old government military map of the area. I wondered where he had gotten it. He was busy adding his own markings and notes. His finger followed the Roman road, from the castle to the *coto,* and stopped on the area containing the Mercies, where he had drawn the new boundaries of the reserve parcel I'd created.

"You changed the boundaries when you made the trust," he said. "You cut off this little parcel here. Why?"

"To make a buffer zone between the private land at Las Moreras and the *coto,*" I said. "I like my privacy."

He nodded. This should seem reasonable to him.

"If the Mercies isn't the crypt at Las Moreras, then where do you think it might be?" he asked.

"The castle was the most sensible site," I shrugged.

"It's possible," said Paco. "But why?"

I shrugged. "A place of worship in the castle is logical. And the castle is the right period."

"Yes...logical also. But here on this page, the *Deeds* talks about new paintings added to the Crypt. So there were older paintings. Older than this book! Think of it, Antonio! They would be some of the oldest existing church murals in Spain. What a marvel they must be — if the Crypt still exists."

"Don't forget how the Nationalists shelled the castle," I said. "If the Mercies was there, it is pulp now."

"Why?" said Paco. "It might be hidden under fallen rock."

"Concussion of exploding shells, man." I felt impatient at Paco's lack of practical thinking. "They'd shatter the frescos underground. Anyhow, I've never had your faith in all these little pieces of paper."

"But, man," he said. "Paper is the highway of belief. How else do we have papal decrees...even our genealogy?"

"Your belief...not mine," I shrugged. "Animal breeding shows how easy it is to lie about pedigrees. All I have to do is look in the mirror to know there were Moors in our lineage. This nappy hair of mine does not come from Catholic Aryan Goths, my friend. Our mother and father were cousins. The Escuderos did line-breeding to keep the fortune together...but line-breeding exposes all the secrets."

Paco frowned. He knew that my breeder's cynicism for records extended back through church history, to the early councils, even to Scripture. Paper exists in the world of time, where humans can meddle with it. If God doesn't prevent humans from messing with each other's lives in the ugliest kind of way, then He certainly won't keep them from altering the so-called sacred texts. That was my view.

"Now really, Antonio," he said. "Grandmamá Carmen must have told you things about the Crypt. You were close with her."

"Unfortunately, José and I were too full of mischief to pay much attention to her," I said. "It's one of my greatest regrets."

But Paco kept talking, with the passion and heat of Lord Carnarvon on the trail of Tutankhamen's tomb.

"My god, yes," said Paco, staring out the window. "The Mercies might be buried under all those tons of fallen stone. What a dig I could organize, if only I had the money...."

Content for him to be racing like a pack of greyhounds along a false trail, I said:

"Well, look....if you want to organize a dig at the castle, I'll give my permission and go in with you on it. Only you must be the one to deal with the Ministry of Culture...the permit and so on. You know how I hate dealing with functionaries."

"Are you serious?" Paco looked like he didn't believe me.

"Very serious," I said. "A Yankee importer is past due on a big invoice. I'll have a little extra money."

Picking up the new *ABC* from the table, I scanned it idly. No column by José today. But an article on page 3 mentioned the CYS. I had been so engrossed in Juan that I hadn't been following CYS doings. Now, with the relaxed Press Law, a trickle of items about the terrorist group was finding its way into the papers. The beating of a Catalan liberal poet in Barcelona. In the Mediterranean resorts, vigilante activities against "unsuitable clothes and public language." Protests against yeah-yeah music. And if the CYS did this in public, they surely did things in secret, like the Black Squads of civil war days, who dragged people off to secret tortures and executions. Publicly the conservatives decried this kind of extremism. Privately, many of them probably applauded it.

"The CYS has been busy," I remarked.

"The what?" Paco was turning pages.

"The Knights of the Holy Yoke."

"Oh, that. I've been so busy, I haven't been following it."

"Five hundred years of terror," I said, "and a war that killed half the country...and they still believe that terror works."

Paco didn't reply, mumbling to himself over the book.

I finished my brandy. Time to introduce other subjects.

"Well, the *coto* looks good," I said. "Greener this year. Pico has approved our trainee. The first lynx is back."

Paco got up and stretched, stiff from hours of sitting. "So your peasant has given up the idea of being a torero."

My stomach plunged with nervousness. I had to stand very still before this kind of charging bull.

"Yes. Isaías was very disappointed," I shrugged. "All five of the boys failed. I almost let Juan Diano get away too. It was Santí who got the idea of sending him to the *coto.*"

"You think well of him, eh? What's his full name?"

"Juan Diano Rodríguez." I kept my tone mild, conversational.

"Pico and the village committee put him through a hard test before they gave him the scholarship."

"José appears to be interested in him. We all saw her walking with him at the trials."

I was relieved that Paco himself had brought up the subject.

"Poor José," I said. "She's thirty now. Marriage is on her mind too."

"I'm glad to hear that."

"In fact, José tells me that she'd like to go out with Juan."

Paco was shocked. "What?"

"You heard me."

"Putting aside the fact that he's from the slave class, he's younger than she, isn't he?"

"If he decently interests her, why should you care? You've done nothing but complain that she's not married."

"Decent?" Paco protested. "If they're seen together, he'll be taken as a gigolo and fortune-hunter."

"His fortune is already assured with the Coto Morera," I said. "Maybe he won't be rich-rich. But soon he'll be a wealthy and respected professional. He'll certainly be able to support her and a family. José wants to date him, and I've agreed."

"You can't be serious."

"I take full responsibility. After all, I introduced them."

Paco stared at me. His face, with its long eagle-beak nose and hooded dark eyes, which revealed our mixed heritage in its own way, was suddenly twisted with intense emotion. He might have been a British royal, outraged at a proposal that Princess Anne marry some commoner. I gazed impassively back, with my own hybrid face.

"Antonio, you must be joking," he said.

"Look, Paco." I sat on the edge of the refectory table. "The animal breeder is talking to you. Sera and I are third cousins. Nothing better than an outcross now and then. Eh? Otherwise the next generation of Escuderos will be born with two heads."

My brother drew himself up.

"I won't repeat your crass statement to Mamá," he said through tight lips. "But when you visit El Refugio next time, you'll find she is having a fit."

"Come on, Paco. Look at Juan. He's a better specimen of the Castilian race than I am. If you were some purist Falange father, you'd rather marry your daughter to him than me."

Paco took his final shot:

"And no family like ours ought to let in new blood without investigating it. What do you think a scrutiny of Juan Diano's family would reveal?"

In his voice, there was a subtle threat, an eerie something that I had never heard before. The bookworm sounded baleful. For a moment, my stomach took a deeper plunge. I wondered how easily Juan's unorthodox political associations would come to light, however casual they might have been.

"You'll be lucky to find his family," I shrugged. "They've emigrated."

"Families always emigrate for a reason," Paco said darkly.

"Yes," I replied. "It's called poverty."

Paco must have called Mamá immediately. Later that day, when I visited El Refugio for supper, Mamá almost said worse than *canastas* to me. I made every effort not to get into a shouting argument with her and hard-nosed Aunt Tita. I cast myself in the role of caring brother who'd introduced his sister to a man he didn't think he'd have to worry about. I even tried to use the argument of marriage for the heart's sake. Both women stared at me coldly — they had married for duty. So I started down the list of aristocrat women who got engaged to commoners since the year 1900.

"There was Princess Margaret to Peter Townsend —"

Tita cut me off. "*El* Townsend turned out badly."

The ladies shot down every morganatic marriage I mentioned, reminding me that many ended in divorce or scandal. Admittedly they were better informed on this subject than I. So I tried another tack.

"Did you know Juan is starting pre-university?" I asked.

"How will he support her as a student?" Mamá insisted. "Or will they stay engaged till he graduates? Four, five years? José is already thirty. Older women have trouble bearing children."

"Between his salary and hers, and her apartment, they should do fine."

"Her salary supporting him?" Mama spluttered. "How immoral! What decent man would allow that?"

"She won't be supporting him. He will be making good money. The *coto* scholarship is his — science and veterinary medicine."

"The scholarship?" Tita's eyebrows raised. She knew very well that it was a generous scholarship.

"The board approved it," I said. "In fact," I added, "Isaías is so happy that he's doing a little publicity about the *coto*. There is going to be an article in *ABC.*"

"José put her boss up to it, I'm sure," Tita remarked sourly.

"Isaías and Tere think he's a jewel. Ask Tere."

"Tere has no children," Mamá sniffed, "so she takes in every stray puppy that comes along."

"What else can you expect from Basque nobodies whose family smell of codfish?" Tita added.

I talked on, sketching the picture of a brilliant young wildlife expert. Juan would excel (I said) in the new wave of Spanish conservation — someday be director of the Coto Morera, traveling to prestigious international conferences. And so on. Mamá and Tita bit their lips, and wavered. They were just progressing to the point where they'd consider owning a foreign breed of dog, let alone taking it to a veterinarian. If traditional Spaniards took a sick animal anywhere, it was often to the local *bruja*. The ancient aristocrat mission of caring for game animals, however *moderno* it now sounded, had its undeniable appeal for them. Clearly Juan was not becoming a gamekeeper, whom they considered to be in the same class with a servant. He would be a *scientist* gamekeeper. Scientists, however much the Roman Catholic Church held them in contempt for discovering unpleasant facts like the Earth being round, were not servants.

I was caping with words like a lawyer in a murder trial.

"He's more of a gentleman than some men I know who claim the name," I argued. "José could do worse. And anyway...it's up to her. You know José. She may dump him next week."

"*Canastas* ...if Juan Diano is as splendid as you say," my mother retorted, "she'd be a fool to dump him."

"*I* will chaperone them, if it makes you feel better," I said. "What better chaperone than the brother who will break Juan's neck if he's disrespectful? Eh?"

They wavered further, knowing that my protectiveness of José was real and ruthless.

"Remember when I almost broke Victoriano Palma's neck?" I pressed them.

They remembered. Palma was a torero who'd taken the alternative about the same time as me. He'd presumed on his professional association with me to treat José lightly, because of the *moderna* glow around her. I had done worse to Victoriano than any bull — put him in the hospital for two weeks. The court had dropped all charges against me. Isaías had deftly played up the publicity. A torero who defenced his sister's honor was good copy with the Old Catholics. For the rest of that season, ticket sales were up 30 percent whenever I was on the bill.

"So I'll answer for Juan," I said. "And Sera ought to go with us sometimes. I've been a bad boy, I know...I plan to spend more time with her. Do you object? If I chaperone my sister and José chaperones Sera?"

My real question was a silent one. Hadn't they, and Sera's mother, always accepted José as a fit companion for Sera?

Mamá looked at Tita, asking for someone else's permission as she always did. Tita drew herself up.

"Very well," my iron aunt proclaimed. "If Sera's mamá agrees, we agree."

On his next day off, Juan had his first reluctant date with José.

In Madrid, my friend needed a place to stay, and someone to guide him on sartorial adventures. It couldn't be me. So Isaías and his wife Tere were taking him under their wing. They were profoundly impressed with Juan, with his new position at the *coto*. They had watched Juan and José talking at the trials, and were amazed and edified that he and José were seemingly intrigued with each other. Their spacious flat had two extra guest rooms, so they offered Juan the use of one room whenever he was in town, and gave him a key. This way, he wouldn't be seen anywhere near José's apartment on the Paseo de la Castellana.

It was Isaías who took Juan to a tailor, got him fitted. By the time shopping was done for one outfit of informal male town wear, including his first pair of real shoes, Juan had spent almost everything he'd already saved.

"I see," Juan grumbled, "why rich people need to be rich."

At the last minute, I couldn't go — my mind had been too far from my work. I was training like crazy for Big Week in Bilbao, and went down to Álvaro's ranch to cape some heifers. Then Sera came down with a cold. So Isaías and his wife volunteered to chaperone in our place. They invited the young couple to be their guests for an evening of high life. Their offer was acceptable to Mamá, Tita and Paco. The foursome would have drinks at the Jockey Club, dinner at the Palace Hotel, then dancing at Whisky á Go Go till Isaías and Tere folded. Then they would drop José at her flat, and Juan would go home with the Eibars.

I was anxious to hear how it went. But next day, Juan didn't call me. He just took the train to Toledo, and hitched a ride out to the *coto*. So I had no chance to talk to him.

Later that afternoon, José and I met for a late lunch in Aranjuez, halfway between our homes. We didn't trust telephones and wanted to talk privately.

Over a red wine, my sister said drily:

"Isaías and Tere did a good job. Juan was dressed exactly like a novice who's getting long in the tooth. No, really...he looked wonderful.

You couldn't have kept your hands off him. Of course Isaías and Tere and I will have to teach him everything. Socially, that is. At first he was tongue-tied and nervous. My skills were taxed, I can tell you. But he learns fast."

José had her own change of heart. "By the way, I apologize for calling him a peasant," she added. "I do like him. He has something. Better still, I trust him."

"Apology accepted."

Right away, tongues wagged in society. Was María Josefina Escudero really going out with the new assistant gamekeeper at the Coto Morera? Was María Josefina finally about to marry? Would she truly marry beneath herself? How did this Juan Diano Nobody dare to be so above himself? It sounded exactly like one of those romantic serials in the Spanish newspapers. The serials were the only reason some people read the papers, since censorship had so soured their faith in the press.

Inevitably, Sera and I had to settle things formally between us. Moreover, our quartet still had to settle details of our secret Pact. Since it was awkward for the four of us to meet for a covert discussion, we were forced to do it in the open.

It was 10 o'clock on that historic night. The weather was so hot that even tourists were laying low. We'd left Toledo simmering in heat waves on its granite mount, and drove across the Alcántara Bridge to dine at a little restaurant in the countryside, where it would be cooler. The atmosphere around us was more like an emergency summit to discuss Spain's NATO membership than engagement for two young couples being formalized.

Sera and I sat at the corner table on the terrace, where we'd have some privacy. If we'd been more relaxed, we might have found it pleasant here. A tiny breeze eased the heat, fluttering the red tablecloth around our nervous knees. The restaurant had hybridized its traditional Castilian decor by hanging Chinese lanterns from the grape arbor over our heads. These bobbed on the breeze, casting a net of foreign colors on us. Because of the late hour, tourists had already eaten, and waiters cleared tables.

José and Juan sat at the bar, having their private talk. From their own table in the center, Mamá, Tita and Serafita's mother worked their fans and watched us all like hawks. We had already had an argument with them, just to get tables that were out of their earshot.

Serafita looked over at the trio of old ladies, shivered, and pulled her light sweater around her. We hadn't ordered yet, in fact we'd hardly looked at the menu.

"So," she said, "you and Juan are..." She paused delicately.

"Yes."

"I'm glad you have someone, Antonio. José tells me he is a good person. You must have been so...lonely. I've noticed something in you for a long time. Now I know it was loneliness."

A lump rose in my throat, as I felt touched by her concern. "How are...things with you and José?"

She hesitated.

"Look," I said. "None of us have to be alone now. You have friends you can trust...me, Juan. You can talk to me. I love you and José both, and care for your welfare. My lips are sealed."

Sera sighed, twisting her wine glass. "Things are...better."

"Truly?"

"You must never tell her that I told you this," Sera said. A pulse was visible in her throat. "I told her that she can't boss me like a man. For years I watched my father slap my mother around. 'Tonio, you wouldn't...wouldn't do that to me, would you?"

I was impressed with her courage, coming as it did after five hundred years of the yoke on women's necks.

"No, I would not. How did José take your demand?"

"We'll see. She knows she has to watch herself."

"Good. I don't want to get in the middle with you and her. I'm sure you can handle it." I drew a deep breath. "Well, Serita...we need to talk of other things. The longer we go on as before, the more dangerous it is."

My head was angled so the three old terrors couldn't see my mouth move. Who knew if they could read lips?

"So what do you think of the Pact?" I asked. "We can all go on as before. Do you understand?"

Hand not trembling this time, Sera put her glass down. If she had been another girl, a tear might have streaked her camellia cheek. For many years, this young woman had played a difficult role that could have brought honor to the acting profession, to the Spanish film industry, and won her a palm at Cannes. I had underestimated the blade of spiritual steel that was hidden in her — thin as a leaf, light as a breeze, but sharp as glass, like my bull-killing sword, inside her sheath of fashion and pretty appearance.

"Yes," she said in a low voice. "I do understand. But there is one more thing. As my husband, you must indulge me in this."

"Yes?"

Sera hesitated. Was our Pact about to founder on some impossible small point?

She blurted: "I want to go to university. I don't want to live in boredom like I have. Will you allow this?"

For a moment I had a new glimpse of the battlements and closures that many women still lived behind. "I won't merely allow it, Sera. You'll do what you choose."

Her eyes flashed with joy. "Truly?"

"Truly." I had to smile. "You and Juan can help each other with homework! What do you want to study?"

"Art history," she said without hesitation. "And photography, so I can document things."

"Then you will do that. I'll put you through school."

Suddenly, for the first time, Sera smiled. It was a wide smile too, from some wide horizon hidden inside her. And I had always thought her so narrow! A bigger lump came to my throat.

"Then...everything is agreed?" I said.

"Yes, it's all settled." She kept herself from looking at Juan and José, who were visible through the door to the bar. "I want these times of fear to be over."

I sagged with relief. Now, for just a moment, the anxiety of years showed itself briefly in the young actress. She was 27, and had loved José since she was 12. Suddenly a tear did fall down her perfect cheek.

"Serita," I said quietly. "Try to look like you're crying with happiness."

"I am." Sera blotted her cheek carefully with her napkin, so she didn't smear her makeup. "Antonio, I am so grateful. I will be a devoted wife in everything that the public needs to see." She swallowed her tears, and took a dainty sip of wine.

"No husband will be more devoted or respectful than me," I said. "Listen, cheer up! Stop crying! We four are going to have a wonderful life. We're even going to have some fun. God knows we all deserve it!"

Now for the fancy social passes, that everyone needed to see. I took her tiny camellia hand in both of my sunburned hands, and held it gently. When I let it go, a gold bracelet set with a Brazilian emerald, an art nouveau piece dating from before the Civil War, rested in her palm. I had pawed through my hoard of Escudero gems, and found the one thing suitable for a fiancé's gift. The three old ladies had scrutinized it with Tita's loup, and approved it.

"'Tonio," she said, looking into my eyes. "I am afraid for you and Juan. Meeting the way you are...it's dangerous."

From a distance, it might have appeared that she was making a serious heartfelt statement about our future life together.

"Don't be silly," I said, putting the bracelet on her wrist. "Everything is going to work out. People have been making these little arrangements for a thousand years."

The bracelet-giving was the signal for José and Juan, who — judging by their sober expressions — had not yet concluded their own NATO negotiations. They came over and sat with us.

"So...it's settled?" José asked us.

"Settled," Sera said.

For public edification, José gave a little best-friend shriek, and hugged Sera decorously. Heads turned in the restaurant. Approving smiles blossomed on lantern-lit faces. Everybody loved the sight of modern young couples getting engaged. "Sera, I'm so happy for you!"

A waiter came with a tray. I had ordered a bottle of the best dry sherry and slender *caña* glasses.

"A toast," José urged us. "Everybody smile."

I poured Sera's glass. After hesitating a moment, Juan filled José's glass. I could tell that Isaías had coached him on how to pour. My friend was staring nervously at Sera's emerald bracelet. Before we drank, however, Jose and Juan still had to settle things.

"Well," said José, looking at Juan, "what about you?" Her eyes narrowed like a fox's. "An opportunity like this...it won't happen every day."

Juan sat hunched, silent. I held my breath, knowing that José was testing him one last time about interest in Escudero money.

"Things have happened so fast," he mumbled.

"Nonsense. El Cordobés was a bricklayer," José drawled. "In one month, he was an idol in the bullring. He didn't hesitate like you do."

The glasses of straw-gold sherry waited. Juan gave me a tense stare.

"Isn't it worth it?" I persisted softly.

My friend played with his untasted glass of sherry. Suddenly I could feel him remembering our first lovemaking in the hut. He drew a deep breath and nodded yes.

"Then it's settled?" José said briskly.

"Settled," Juan said.

"In a month or two," José said briskly, "Juan and I can do battle with the family, and get them to agree. It looks better if we go out a few more times. I'm sure they'll agree, now that Antonio and Sera are going ahead. If they don't, well...I'm of age, so they can't stop us. We'll elope, if we have to."

I had to smile, thinking of Juan giving José some bit of engagement jewelry. No young veterinarian would ever manipulate a syringe for the first time as nervously as Juan would a bracelet or pin. Isaías and Tere would probably help him find something suitable.

Sera picked up her sherry glass. She had now recovered complete composure, and was wearing that bright smile again.

"Chin chin…cheers," she said. "Here's to our happiness."

We lifted our glasses. "To happiness," we chorused.

Suddenly Sera was busying herself with the menu.

"Don't look," she said in a low voice, "but my mamá is coming over." Then, louder, "'Tonio darling, have you eaten here before? Do you recommend the cutlets of pork?"

"The cutlets are good," I said. "Doña Margarita, what are you ladies having to eat over there? We're discussing the cutlets."

"Cutlets?" asked Doña Margarita, coming up. "You were all looking so serious. We thought something had gone wrong."

"What could go wrong, Mamá?" said Sera brightly. She lifted her wrist, and showed her mother the bracelet.

Her mother sucked in her breath with delight.

"So it's settled?" Doña Margarita demanded.

"It's settled," I said.

"Darlings!" Doña Margarita embraced her daughter with a little scream. Over her mother's shoulder, Serafita gave the three of us a movie wink.

"Elena! Tita!" Doña Margarita called. "It's all settled!"

The three old women must be feeling the kind of relief that a torero feels when he's having the worst afternoon of his career and finally kills the bull on the last try.

"Quiet, Mamá!" hushed Sera.

"Why should they be quiet?" José commented drily. "They will want a wedding in the Toledo cathedral, with a thousand guests and the Primate of Spain tying the knot."

"Young man," said my mother, staring at Juan, "you are privileged to be in the bosom of our family at such an important moment in our history."

Juan's eyes said he knew that.

"Sit down with us, ladies." I signalled the waiter to bring chairs. "Share our toast with us. Waiter, more glasses, please."

But, between Juan and me, things were far from settled. We'd shied away from the act of sexual completeness. Our education as Spanish men had made us jumpy and jealous about that — especially Juan Diano, village conservative that he was. I had started torturing myself over whether he really cared about me...whether he was just using me for his own convenience.

We all dispersed. Juan drove back to the *coto* in Pico's son-in-law's car, which he had been ceremoniously loaned while the son-in-law and daughter were visiting at the *coto*. My mother, Tita, Sera and her mother headed for El Refugio. Hungry to talk privately, José and I headed back into Toledo. With our life-secret now shared, my sister and I were growing into new realms of psychic oneness.

Never, as on that night, did I realize how much I hated Toledo — the granite harshness of those narrow streets, those windowless señorial facades with their ornate coats-of-arms. As we crossed the square in front of the cathedral, its stained-glass windows revealed the deep lurid glow of candles dying in that Gothic prison inside. The vast armored doors were bolted shut for the night. Eerie gusting breezes seemed to carry ancient echoes across the square — a lost sound-track from a documentary film of solemn *autos de fe*. The interminable chanting and prayers. Condemned prisoners trembling on scaffolds above the crowds, hearing their sentences read. Sentences that meant years of penance, imprisonment. Sentences that meant hours of being burned alive.

But wasn't that all supposed to be in the past? Now the only swords made here were for toreros to kill bulls with, or tourists to take home. There were bright restaurant lights, throngs of strollers, Japanese tourists with cameras, the roar of powerful foreign-made auto engines. Instead of monks chanting Te Deums, we heard the latest hit songs by Marisol, the Monkees, the Carpenters.

José and I passed up the traditional taverns with their tourist patrons, and headed for our favorite bar, El Tambor. It was comfortingly modern, with tile walls and bright lights and the TV re-broadcasting a concert from the Santander Music Festival. There, we sank down at a quiet corner table. First José, then I, moved our gaze discreetly around to see if anyone had followed us in here.

"I hate this city," she said, echoing my thoughts.

"They burned people in Madrid too."

"Here, the smell lingers more."

"It's not just Catholicism. It's all religions. The ones that build empires, anyway."

"What do you mean?" she asked.

"I've seen it when I travel. First a religion yokes itself to the secular power. It teaches a set of rules, and terrifies people into obeying them. The secular power enforces the religious rules, and uses terror to do it. The terror keeps the secular power and the religion in their place. The perfect yoke — those two together."

"One of humanity's greatest dreams is to build the perfect empire. You know that," she shrugged. "They keep trying."

The waiter brought our espressos. "Juan is still scared," José said, sipping. Her angora Pulligan sweater was draped artlessly over her shoulders.

"With a bull who's gone into defensive position," I said, "you have to drag him out of it step by step."

"How confident do you feel that he'll stay with our Pact?"

"I don't know. He acts like he's crazy about me. But he won't say the words."

"Little problems with jealousies?"

"Oh....the usual things."

"Have you told him that you love him?"

"No."

"Then you're a fool. Don't complain to me."

After coffee, we walked arm in arm through the streets. A few people recognized me, but let us be. Through these very streets, the trembling prisoners who had been condemned to death were marched to the stakes.

Suddenly she said: "Do you remember the first woman's secret you ever saw?"

My sister's frankness still had the power to make me blush. "It was yours."

"We were...how old? Eleven?"

"Out in the hills, in the brush, as I recall...looking for Roman coins."

"As I recall," she said drily, "the anatomy lesson I provided was excellent. And your interests were strictly academic. You did everything but take notes."

"No man loves women more than me. I'm just not interested in relations with them."

"You obligingly showed me yours too."

"I owe you, José. It might have been another century before I learned that women have a little member of their own. The knowledge served me well, on nights when I couldn't oblige a lady otherwise."

"Who did you fantasize about, in those days?"

"Everyone who came along. And I suppose you were thinking about Sera."

"Her life and mine together," she said, "is like one of those fantastic needlework carpets, that a convent full of nuns spend their whole lives working on. I still remember her when she was eight, galloping her Welsh pony, hair flying."

I wondered how much of their devotion was forced by their lack of freedom to search for other partners. "José, I don't know how to ask this. But how do you arrange it with her? Do you...I mean...?"

"Stop being such a gentleman, 'Tonio. You want to know if I play the man with her?"

I swallowed hard.

Reaching the Tajo gorge, we leaned on the stone balustrade that keeps people from tumbling over the edge. From here, we looked down dizzy cliffs to the Tajo River, as it made its loop around the Toledo bluff, creating its perfect natural moat. On moonlit nights, the water glowed down there, currents making silvery braids amid shading poplars and willows. But tonight the river was dark, remote. That night breeze whipped our clothing now.

José shivered and pulled on her cardigan sweater.

"There are the little harnesses," said José. "But I've had to consider having my props found by the maid. So...no. Sera and I have done nicely without accoutrements."

She looked at me sharply. "Your real question is about you and Juan, isn't it? Each of you worried about being the woman."

I nodded.

"God," she swore, "you men make things so complicated. You deserve all the misery that you make your gender live in. "

"Without doubt," I said humbly.

"Think of how that belief insults women...that it's a disgrace to be the one who gives it up."

"It's more complicated than that. He's prickly about being... er...the peasant submitting to the lord."

"Then let the peasant screw the lord first," she shrugged.

Our eyes met.

"Jesus, sometimes you scare me," she said. "You'd go to any lengths for him. You'd die for him."

I turned away, staring down at the river.

"So if you'd give your life for him," she said behind me, "why are you so worried about giving him your manhood?"

It was the kind of uncomfortable question that an inquisitor might have asked.

Nearby, a local youth and a tourist girl in a miniskirt stood twined in a kiss, leaning against the balustrade. They had probably met in a bar, and were oblivious to our presence. The girl was no hippie — she looked like an escapee from some well-chaperoned student tour. Lucky for them, no police were around.

"A hundred pesetas that she slaps him before he gets his hand in her panties," José hissed.

"A hundred pesetas that she lets him," I shot back.

The youth's hand slid down and began to raise her well-tailored skirt. Before the hem passed mid-thigh, the girl slapped him. Then she stalked off, while our youth stood rubbing his cheek, angry and baffled at foreign ways. As José and I walked the winding street towards our car, I dug a 100-peseta bill out of my pocket and paid the bet.

I managed to keep myself from visiting the *coto* again till after Big Week in Bilbao. Things went so-so with my Basque fans — one ear, a few yells that I hadn't given them everything. When I saw Juan again, he was all eaten up with anxiety.

"Yes, I said it was settled," he told me. "And no, I don't want to get caught. Maybe nothing will happen to you....you have influence. But something bad might happen to me. You won't be able to save me."

"Doing things under bridges is just as dangerous."

"Well, I might change my mind."

"You're hiding something from me."

"Look, it's something that Faelín told me."

"Rafael again."

"No. Listen to me. He told me a terrible story. He knew a guy who knew someone that the CYS got their hands on. This guy got caught with some rich family's son. The family found out about it, and set the CYS on him. A CYS black squad took him away to a black house somewhere and tortured him. Hot irons on his shame. Hot irons up his *culo*. He died. Somehow it was hushed up."

Juan stared at the distant horizon.

"Where is Rafael now?" I demanded.

"I told you. He went to France. He said he didn't want to live in a country where things like that could still be done to people. God, you're jealous."

"I want to turn the street upside down, so nobody can walk on it after you."

Juan's fear was contagious — I started feeling afraid too. I decided we needed a safer situation. It was time to take him into the Crypt of Mercies.

10

The next evening I got to the game farm, I had a chance to talk to my friend alone when he was feeding the next round of partridge chicks. "Tell me again," I asked him. "Did you have any leftist or Communist associations?"

He was annoyed at me, adjusting the warm electric lights over the chicks. "Isn't it enough when I tell you things once?"

"Paco says a new family member should be investigated."

Juan shrugged. "Let him investigate."

"They can take something harmless, make it look bad."

He stared up at me. "They can invent things too."

"What about Rafael?" I persisted. "He was Basque, eh? Was he a separatist...ETA?"

"I told you...no political stuff with 'Fael. Nothing ETA, nothing Communist. All we did was go drinking together."

Shortly after dawn the next morning, Juan and I went into the hills. On this particular day, our "facade" was restoring the old spring that we'd probed last time. Pico's mule carried a load of tools and sections of pipe.

Now and then, as we dug out the moist place in the ravine, we looked at each other, and the anticipation gave us a hidden hard-on. Our wanting was as urgent as the buzz of the mole crickets, shrilling all around us in the hot air. Now and then, we saw the little creatures staring at us from their burrows. They were telling us that summer — indeed, our life — was passing swiftly. I had decided to take José's advice. To keep the peace, I'd give it up first, and be patient till Juan was willing to reciprocate. As we worked, scent of bruised wild thyme drifted around us The mule hauled buckets of broken rock for the little leach-field that would collect water.

At midmorning, a La Mora guard happened by, in his dusty brown corduroys, shotgun over shoulder. He chatted with us. He was edified at seeing the blueblood wearing a straw hat and sweating like a field worker.

"It's good for my leg," I told him.

"Eh Juanito...when will the wild pigs come back?" the guard asked my friend.

"In three years, on the last full Moon of fall," Juan grunted.

"And," the guard grinned, "what's the winning number in the next lottery?"

"If I knew," Juan shot back, "I'd buy the ticket myself."

We all chuckled.

When the guard left, I asked Juan: "How do you know for sure...about the pigs?"

"I just know. But we have to plant more oaks for them."

Juan paused to mop his brow with his sleeve, and pulled an apple out of his pocket. We both shared it. As I chewed its soft flesh, an apple of last autumn, I tried to find the taste of his saliva.

"When autumn comes and the heat breaks," he said, talking past a mouthful, "we'll get a crew from the village, and go harvest acorns, and other seeds of plants that pigs like. Over the winter, the work crew can plant everything."

"That's a good idea," I said. The La Morans would like him more for creating another paying project.

Juan had already turned away. "If we do that every winter, the old broad-leaf forest will come back faster. The plants bring water. They help each other grow."

When it started to get hot, Juan and I left the mule swishing his tail in the shade of a ledge, and walked the short distance to the stone hut. The land was incandescent, its heat seeming to glow from inside every stone, every bush. But the heat was our friend — few people walked the *coto* now, especially at midday. Even the guards were more likely to be found having a beer in the shade somewhere. I took a long look around with field-glasses, my heart hammering. No sign of Paco. No sign of anybody. We half closed the hut door, and left some of our gear outside, in the shade. This way, it would look like we had wandered away to look at something.

Inside, I took him by the shoulders and looked in his eyes.

"Swear on your life that you will never tell anyone about this," I told him. "José and Sera are the only other people who know."

Juan's voice was a little shaky. He still wondered if the Crypt was full of dead people. "I swear."

While Juan held a flashlight, I kneeled between the two beds, and used a screwdriver to pry up a section of four tiles in the floor. The tiles were glued to a square of thin old-fashioned oak panel, easily raised. Juan watched in nervous fascination. Underneath, was an ancient flagstone about a meter square, with a massive iron ring in it. It rolled aside easily on stone rollers underneath — a clever design by my greatgrandfather, who was an engineer. My hair stood on end as an echo rolled away under it. Our flashlight revealed a narrow dusty stairwell that descended into darkness. Far down there, the echo ended in a distant boom. I could sense the same chill gushing down Juan's spine.

"Huuy," said Juan softly, with awe.

"Go down ahead of me," I directed, putting the screwdriver back into the box.

Juan obeyed, sliding into the opening. I followed him, and re-placed the square of tiles over our heads, on a lip cut in the stone. It was light enough that we could raise it again from underneath. Then, squat-ting under the level of the flagstone, I seized another ring that was counter-sunk into its side, and rolled it back into place under the oak panel. After the summer buzz of crickets, that deep silence within the deep earth could be felt in our very bones.

"Very clever," Juan whispered.

"My greatgrandfather knew he needed something solid under the tiles...so there wouldn't be a hollow sound if anyone tapped on the tile floor above. And while we're down here, everything has to look normal up above."

"But supposing the stone doesn't roll? We're trapped here."

"There is another way out. And you don't need to whisper."

Below us, in the flashlight beams, that ancient stairway spiraled down. Its steep risers were worn by feet of visitors dead for a thousand years. Here and there, on the walls, ancient stone-mason's marks were barely visible in dust and cobwebs. I touched them lovingly. Had I carved one of these, in another life long past? As we moved slowly down, dust and cobwebs floated around us. Even here, there was abundant life — small spiders scuttled away into cracks. "Be careful of the spiders," I said. "They bite."

He nodded, touching the stone-mason marks.

"Was this a natural cave?" he asked.

"Yes, before people built inside it," I said. "Many of the Christian and Muslim sacred places were pagan caves."

My leg was hurting from all the exertion that day, so I sat on a step to rest it. Juan was used to my leg-rests by now, so he sat beside me, and I threw an arm over his shoulder. In that cool place, our body-warmth felt good.

"A long time ago," I explained, "a round temple used to stand above us, where the hut is. You could pray in the sanctuary above ground...or you could take this stairway into the crypt. When the Visigothic kings became Catholic, they made war on the pagans. Toledo was the capital then. The Councils of Toledo imposed new laws. They took power away from women. They outlawed men being with men. They outlawed the pagan schools and ceremonies. They killed many people...like the Falange did during the civil war. Things got so bad that our family closed the Mercies aboveground, public obedience to the Church. But the Crypt was still used secretly by some people."

Juan nodded.

"When the Muslims came in the year 712," I went on, "they were more tolerant. The Mercies re-opened for a while. But when the Catholics reoccupied this area, which was in 1085, we ran underground again like the crickets."

Juan looked dubious. "How do you know all that stuff?" he wanted to know. "Nobody's family goes back that far."

"Mine does," I grinned.

"I don't even know my greatgrandmother's name."

"Our title was created in the 13th century," I said. "It's in the old books at my mother's house."

"My head is spinning with all these dates."

"Some things don't get written down. Like your grandfather didn't write down the herbs. He just told you, right? My greatgrandmamá told me that those early Escuderos — the ones before Islam — weren't nobles. They were priestesses and priests."

As we sat on the steps, sharing our body warmth, I tried to paint clearer colors into his village-classroom picture of Spanish history. "When the Catholic Kings took over again, and the Inquisition came to Toledo, things got bad."

"The priests told me about the Inquisition."

"In the family, there were the *Azules,* Blues...the orthodox Catholics. And a few of the *Nueves,* the Nines, who knew this old stuff. Nobody knows why we were called Nines. When the Inquisition started, the family split and the Nines went underground. From around 1400 till 1853, nobody came here. One person in each generation knew the location. But it was dangerous to do anything here. My greatgrandparents were the last ones to know. When the Revolutions broke out — "

"So you are a Nine."

"Yes."

"The Revolution…you mean our civil war?"

"Starting in the 1700s, there was a bunch of civil wars. Revolutions against state religion in many countries. People hated the Catholic and Protestant monarchies. Things just boiled over. It happened in Spain too."

"My history book in school didn't talk about that."

"History books are written by the people who win the wars. We Nines worked for the First Republic. This was when my greatgrandfather and his nephew Mario built the hut here in 1853. They pretended it was a siesta and picnic place. Inside, they quietly re-excavated the old entrance. It took them years. Unfortunately, our poor country was mangled by more civil war, and the church kept its hold. Then my greatgrandfather died in 1910. My greatgrandmother and her youngest sister were left alone with the knowledge, and nobody to help them. So the Mercies was never opened again."

My leg felt better now. "Let's go on down," I said.

Juan was shaking his head. "I don't know how you remember all that stuff."

"You'll be remembering names of millions of drugs and surgical instruments," I teased him.

As we descended lower, our voices echoed more. Finally we felt ourselves to be in a vast chilly space. Echoes spread here like a million ripples of an underground lake. I shone the flashlight beam slowly around. "Holy Mary," Juan breathed in awe.

Echoes of his voice rippled away. The echo was very sensitive here. *"Mary.....Mary.......Mary....Mary....ry......ry...."*

The beam revealed a round chamber that was 20.5 meters wide. José and I had measured it. Roman-style arches slid into view, one after another, filled with mysterious shadows, their painted colors almost blinding us. Twelve columns supported the domed ceiling, their stark shadows — cast by our flashlights — striping the wall beyond. They must have been scavenged from different Roman ruins, because they didn't match. Above us, the vaulted ceiling was alarmingly crusted with mineral deposits from leaks.

As we walked, raising a bow-wave of echoes, I played the beam across the walls and ceiling. The frescos never failed to raise my hackles with excitement. Goddesses and gods, women and men, wild cattle and horses and deer and other animals, all with their young, all kinds of flowers and trees surrounding them with seeds and fruits. Scenes of birth, death, marriage, planting, hunting, teaching — all were twined together in a vision of cycles. On the northwest wall was the Lady herself, with Her child. Serene and dignified, She sat enthroned in the horns of the sickle Moon, guarded by a cow and a bull, with Her hands opened wide in a gesture of bounty and compassion. Among the human figures were several that had always excited my curiosity. A pair of young men, armed with lances, had their arms around each other's waists. And there was a similar pair of young women, armed with bows. The linked arms, seen so often in classical art, are a symbol of liaison.

The whole place was surprisingly clean, with only a light film of dust and cobwebs. Here and there, the mosaic floor had a dried puddle, where winter rains had leaked through the dome. Litter showed that small animals got in. Now and then, José and I had made twig brooms and swept the place out.

Cool fresh air moved gently past us.

Juan gazed up at the Lady, with his mouth open. Finally a tear slid down his cheek. The reverence in his eyes was that great Spanish love for the Lady. Iberians loved the Lady thousands of years ago, when a sculptor portrayed her as the Dama of Elche. The churchmen had to adopt Her, because they couldn't fight Her. Even *maricones* who have no children know they owe their lives to their mothers. "All things are born of woman," Doña Carmen had told us. "All life is birthed out of the Earth, out of the marriage of sunlight and rock, lightning and rain. Life is carried to us in the mating of earth with trees, trees with animals, so we can live in turn." Juan and I were now in the womb of the Lady, in a place where these cycles had probably been taught and celebrated.

In front of Her, on the pavement, were dozens of half-burned candles stuck into a mass of wax — relics of José's and my prayers. Pulling out his lighter, Juan lit one of them. I felt deeply touched as he stood there for a while, his lips moving.

Finally he said: "That's the painting in your chapel."

"Some artist was given a commission by the family. He copied the painting from this mural."

I was making a worried inspection of the murals. José and I had visited other Spanish sites where frescos existed, and tried to estimate the age of ours. We'd decided that the Mercies paintings could be classified into Old and New. The Old murals, on the walls of the rotunda, looked to be late Roman, before the Visigothic kings came. They were painted in brilliant gold and red, with touches of blue, black and green, in a more sophisticated style. The New murals decorated the ceilings and walls of ancillary passageways. These were medieval, maybe 12th century, maybe done during the Moorish tolerance. Their color was less good, the style and knowledge of anatomy more primitive, like the frescos in a few northern Spanish churches of that time.

But today, as I looked at the Lady of Mercies, a shocking thing happened. The whorls of air around my body were enough to make a few flakes of pigment fall from Her. Stupefied, I watched them drift down in the candle-light. Something was eating the murals away. Maybe smog was seeping in here. Maybe the chemicals could corrode paint and stone.

And that leak in the ceiling. It gave me an ominous feeling.

I pointed the flashlight beam at an alabaster doorway. Through it, a natural tunnel led away, growing narrower.

Juan had dried his tears. "How did they get everything in here? All these pillars, these huge stones..."

"Doña Carmen said they opened the ceiling and made a ramp down into the cave. When everything was done here, they closed the ceiling and just left the stairway. If you tore all this construction out, you might find older paintings on the cave walls. Maybe prehistoric, like Altamira. That tunnel is the original entrance — a natural entrance from the ravine. Later on, rocks were piled over the entrance, to hide it. But if you go to the end of that tunnel, you can see tiny bits of daylight shining through the rocks. There's a place where the rocks are not big. That's where you can break out."

"I wouldn't want to get trapped in here," he growled.

"And," I said, "the builders made sure there was enough air down here, for people in the ceremonies. I never figured out how they did it. The Mercies is alive. She breathes."

"Alive......alive....alive....ive...ive...eathes...eathes..."

Eyes rounded, Juan listened to the echo. Along with the old ideas about honor and dishonor, he was a little superstitious too. I threw my arm across his shoulders to reassure him.

"Didn't anybody ever find the other entrance?" he asked. "Herders...soldiers in the war? If the air moves, somebody outside must have felt something."

"If they did, they never said."

"Said....said....said...."

I didn't mention that José and I had found a skeleton inside the natural entrance. The rusted gun beside it was a 1930s model shotgun. Probably a wounded Republican local, who thought he could evade capture and torture by Franco's African troops. He had died there alone, in the Lady's arms, taking his secret with him. José and I had quietly buried the bones in the ravine.

Juan and I walked into the circle of Roman columns. Here

stood the altar, a massive disc of alabaster resting on the backs of twelve sturdy bulls. Half-burned candles stood stuck on it, where José and I had left them. To save our batteries, I got out my gold lighter — even its flick stirred a ripple of sound — and lit some of them. Now the darkness was softer, more velvet, dancing with mystery. Our shadows moved like two giants on the painted walls.

Juan shivered. "So...*brujas* did things here? Witches?"

"Greatgrandmother said they were people who stood for the authority of the human self. They didn't accept authority of state religion over their lives. Many were women. And a few, I guess, were...people like us. You can see them in the paintings there."

He was staring at the altar. "So...what did the *brujas* do here? Human sacrifice?"

Anti-pagan talk in the seminary had stamped its fiery cattle-brand on his mind. I had to smile a little.

"We don't know what they did," I said.

"What do you mean, you don't know?"

"The knowledge of what they did is lost. There aren't any books or documents about that. Maybe there was teaching here. And healing."

He stared at me. "Healing?"

"Doctoring...like you're going to do on the animals. Maybe spiritual healing too. It was something like a school. A prayer place too. In those days they didn't separate those two things. Imagine the singing, eh?...with the acoustics in here! José and Sera think that they doctored women here. Women wanting to have children. Women with sick children or female problems."

"Then why are animals painted here?"

"I don't know. Maybe they doctored animals too."

His eyes held mine. I took his right hand in mine, wishing that we could be transported back to that time, and joined in one of those brother ceremonies. My yearning for this, and the impossibility of it, were equally strong. I was sure that Sanches Count of La Mora had his brother Pedro killed for going through that ceremony. He probably killed poor García too, after torturing him for days.

Juan lowered his eyes, and went to pull his hand away.

I kept hold of his fingertips.

"In 1497," I said, "the last Nine woman who knew the teachings was murdered by the Blues. The Blues suspected her. They couldn't afford to have one family member noticed by the Inquisition. So they policed things on their own. That's why my brother is such a fanatic. He feels like he is the family police. He has to keep things well tied-down, as our great general Franco is always saying."

"So no Nines were ever burned at the stake."

I laughed grimly. "If that had happened, it would have caused our downfall. Our property and arms would have been confiscated. There would be no Escuderos today. Anyway, people of our rank were not burned. It was too embarrassing for the church. Other ways to get rid of noble outlaws were found."

"So your parents told Blue things to your brother."

"I don't think my mother knows anything. My father probably told Paco some of the Blue stuff."

"But your father didn't know where this place is. Your brother doesn't know."

"That's right."

"How did you find out about the Mercies?"

"My greatgrandmother brought me and José here, one day when we were seventeen. This was in 1956. We thought she was taking us on a picnic. She had me drive us in a little mule cart because she was too old to walk."

"But she didn't know much, right?"

"Not much. The one thing I remember her saying is about the Moon that the Lady is sitting in. How the Moon and the animals turn the wheels of change. But no, she was nobody like those ancient priestesses. She said we'd have to start over. Read from the Book of Life, she said. The Earth is where all the knowledge comes from...not from books. That's what she said."

"Did your greatgrandmother know about...you and José?"

I was getting tired of history lessons, and grabbed him gently by the arms. "Maybe," I said, looking into his eyes. "Maybe if she was alive today, I could take you to her, and she'd bless us."

"Bless us....bless us......bless.......bless....bluss.... us... us... us...."

Jacket zipped against the cold, Juan looked down nervously. All that talk of burning people to death, the weight of the past in this place, hadn't created a good atmosphere for love-making.

"It's too cold to undress," I said quietly. "Let's just —"

"Just...just...."

His face touched mine, but he wasn't his usual horny self.

"It doesn't feel right," he said.

Walk slow and careful, Antonio. You'll scare him.

I sighed. One more disappointment. "All right, then. Just be quiet with me here."

So we blew the dust off the altar and sat on the icy alabaster. I kept one arm around him. At first, every booming echo made him jump in my arms like a deer. The altar was hard, cold, uncomfortable — not a place designed for love. But shortly we calmed down and listened to the flames burning. Like a cape of light, the candles lapped their deep flickering around us. The animals in the paintings wavered, alive — lithe necks raised, horns gleaming, eyes flashing, leaves ruffling in some dark wind, the eyes of the Mother of Mercies on us. For some idiotic reason I was still afraid to say how much I cared, out of fear that he didn't care as much. The erotic moment had passed. I didn't feel like making love either.

"Eh!" he whispered suddenly.

"What?"

"That deer over there. I could swear it moved its head."

Suddenly, a gust of air came sweeping through the Mercies, and blew out the frail guttering candles. We were plunged into darkness, and felt around for our flashlights.

"The Lady says we've been here long enough," I said. "It isn't good to be in the hut for too long. Somebody will notice."

We left the Mercies. Blinking into the long afternoon rays, we brushed the dust and cobwebs from our clothes, until we were back to the normal dirtiness of pick and shovel work. I felt cheated of a moment of intimacy that would never come again.

While we'd been underground, the weather had changed suddenly. An erratic breeze lifted the heat. Several thunderstorms drifted over the piney hills, trailing veils of rain across the distances, wafting a faint smell of wet dust and conifers to our nostrils. One of these gusts had penetrated the Crypt and blown out our candles. As we picked up our gear, Juan pulled out his pocket-knife and dug a few little clumps of sedge grass, the kind that always grows where ground is wet. As he bent there, a breeze lifted his forelock.

"Why are you digging that up?" I asked, irritated.

"To plant at the new spring," he said impassively. "The water came."

As we walked back, our lonely mule lifted his head, and sent us a honking bray.

"Look," Juan said, pointing at the pipe we'd put in.

While we'd been down in the Mercies, the new little leach-field was already doing its work. Now, at the pipe-end, the first fragile drop of water trembled. It fell to the hot earth, and dried instantly. Then a second drop welled.

As lightning fell from the distant thunderclouds, both of us hunkered and watched the miracle with awe. My irritation faded. Juan put his fingers under the cool drip. So did I. Our earth-smeared fingers touched under the pipe. The feeling was around us, of being in a cloud charged with electricity. For a moment, I had a flash of seeing something — seeing how our feeling for each other could fuck new life into this dying land, as surely as if drops of our mingled semen had the power to fall on the ground and sprout into baby oak-trees.

"You *are* a witch," I said. He laughed, flushing a little.

We finished the job without talking much — laid the last bits of pipe, dug out the catch-basin, lined the edge of it with rocks. No one came around. As the sun set, we were two solitary figures toiling on the fiery skyline. Juan planted the clumps of sedge in the catch-basin, right where the drip now made a moist and spreading stain. I helped him firm the earth around their roots.

Pico and the Village Committee went to visit the new spring. Tracks in the mud showed that songbirds, partridge and at least one deer had already found it. They were happy about it.

The next day, driving into La Mora on *coto* business, I noticed a solitary figure at the castle ruin. It had to be Paco. Parking the car, I walked up there. The walking felt good — I'd been doing so much exercise that my bad leg was definitely stronger.

With a note pad and a camera, Paco was clambering around over tumbled rocks, looking at the rusted carcass of a 1930s field cannon. Around him, protesting, flew a shrill cloud of martins who lived in holes in the sole standing wall. "I'm doing a survey for the dig," he said. "Trying to figure out what was where — the keep, the chapel, the well…"

To keep Paco interested in the castle, I was the soul of genial helpfulness, pointing out this and that. Anything to keep him from snooping further into the *coto*. In rubble where the main gate had stood, we found half of the lichened coat-of-arms that once crowned it. The broken slab lay wedged between two larger blocks. The carving was eroded, but we could still make out the heraldic device on it: a sickle Moon cut in half by a sword. I had never been proud of that device. Paco had always maintained that it represented triumph over the Muslims, who use the Moon symbol. To me, its original meaning was probably the Blues' "killing" of the Mercies.

"What a shame," said Paco, shaking his head. "I'll look around for the other half of the shield. We can cement it together and put it somewhere."

"I prefer the real Moon," I said.

Paco stared at me. "You don't deserve the title," he said.

"I know," I said benignly.

"Are you going to keep your word on money for the dig?"

"For sure. I'm still waiting for the Yankee importer to pay me. Isaías has written him."

What with torero training and the need to publicly ignore Juan now and then, I didn't return to the *coto* for almost a week. That day Juan and I took off on horseback to scout a spot for another spring. The heat and our desire for each other were unbearable. So we were at the hut by midday, and slipped down in the Mercies.

This time, there were no history lectures. We took down a couple of blankets and a twig broom from the hut, to sweep a place in the floor and make ourselves more comfortable. The spot we chose was farthest from the drafty gusts issuing out of the tunnel, right near the Mother of Mercies mural. A single candle, stuck in its own wax, burned on the floor near us, casting our shadow hugely on the opposite wall. There, laying half-dressed, shifting to find comfortable purchase for knees and elbows, we started trying to recapture the simple pleasure of our first lovemaking in the hut.

Suddenly a loud sound, like a shot, exploded across the chamber. We both almost jumped out of our skins. The echo exploded too. Something had hit the floor beside us.

We jerked apart in our half-naked vulnerability. The candle was knocked over, and went out. Hastily we closed our clothing with trembling hands and crouched by the wall, like two soldiers on ambush.

"What the devil was that?" Juan whispered into my ear.

"That.....that......that.....at...at...t..t..."

"I don't know. An animal, maybe."

"Maybe we're not supposed to be doing this here. Maybe it's a ghost."

"Ghost...ost...ost..."

Shakily I groped for the flashlight. Hardly daring to breathe, we waited for several minutes. Maybe it was the ghost of that Civil War soldier. Nothing happened. I flicked the beam on. It blinded us, shocking our senses all over again. Finally, by the wall near us, we found what had caused the noise. It was no ghost. A piece of fresco — part of one of the Lady's beautiful eyes — had fallen from the wall, and hit the floor. In shaky fingers, I picked it up.

"She needs some care," I pondered.

"She sees us," Juan insisted. "She's telling us not to do this here."

We glared at each other. "You are too superstitious," I said.

Suddenly it was clear to me that the Lady had a different message. Our lovemaking shouldn't be hidden in this catacomb of the past. I put the piece of fresco in my jacket pocket. Shivering with nervousness, we crawled back up the long steep stairway. The flashlight beam was fading, and we got out of there just in time.

Half an hour later, riding our horses back down the old road, we were shocked all over again to see Paco's unmistakable figure just ahead.

"The Lady was warning us," I said.

With a cane walking-stick, my brother was toiling slowly up the old road, toward the plateau. He was perspiring in the heat. His bi-focal sun-glasses, his city fedora, the camera slung over his shoulder and the wrinkled map clutched in his hand, all gave him the air of an Inquisition clerk on vacation. Not physically fit, he was having a hard time. And he looked old. An old, and suddenly sinister, technician of history who was taking a purposeful holiday.

My heart was pounding. I could feel Juan wanting to bolt. We stopped our horses by Paco.

"Man," I greeted him, trying to sound playful. "What the devil are you doing out here?"

"What are *you* doing out here in the heat?" he retorted.

"Working. We're used to it...you're not. You'll get a stroke."

"Well, I was reading in the *Deeds,* about the stone that was brought from up here somewhere. The stone that was used for our buildings. This is still the old road, isn't it? They must have used this road to haul the stone out."

"Yes, this is the only way wagons could go," I agreed.

"Well, where did the stone come from?"

"I've wondered about that myself," I said wisely. "Maybe they hauled stone from the other side of the summit. There's some ruins at Pozo del Rey too...same kind of stone."

"By the way," said Paco, "you don't mind my being here?"

It wouldn't do to forbid Paco to come here. He would think I had something to hide.

"No...of course I don't mind," I said. "But next time you come, let the Committee know, or Pico...or you might find yourself looking up a guard's shotgun barrel. If something should happen to you out here, if you fall and get hurt, we need to know you're here. For your safety. Understand?"

Paco nodded unwillingly, smoke curling up past his eyes. "That is sensible."

My eyes fixed on the cigarette hanging carelessly between his lips. "Be careful with cigarettes. It's already dry. A brush fire could destroy years of our work in one hour."

"Naturally I will be careful," said Paco, looking irritated. He was eager to press on.

"Have a good walk," I said, urging my horse on.

Behind us, Paco's disquieting figure was briefly silhouetted against the sky, before he went over the ridge.

When we were well out of Paco's earshot, Juan said, "That was close." His voice was shaky.

"If he'd come to the hut while we were in the Crypt," I insisted, "he wouldn't have heard a thing."

"How about the entrance in the ravine? Can sounds from inside be heard out there?"

"Not possible. They're blocked with rocks."

"So your brother is...a Blue. And he suspects you."

"He'll finish his schoolteacher stuff up here, and move on," I scoffed. "I'll keep him running on false trails."

We reined our horses on a rocky point, looking down on the game farm. The tiny figures of Pico and Magda were moving around down there. Juan looked deeply downcast.

"The Lady hasn't given us a place to drop dead in." Juan sounded bitter.

"I pray for a room with a bed and a door we can lock. And a bathroom."

Juan was silent for a long time. Then he spurred up his horse, and started on down the slope.

"Someday," I said after him, "we can be together in the open somewhere. There'll be grass. And wildflowers. And we'll stay there all day if we feel like it."

"You swear it?"

"I swear. I promise you a meadow, on my honor."

11

Summer was passing. The Moon changed again. On July 20 — I remember the date — Yankee astronauts walked on the Moon. Our nation took this great foreign deed to its heart. Even the poorest working people stayed up all night, or got up at 4 a.m., to crowd into their neighborhood bars so they could see the telecast of that moment. Then they went off to lay bricks and sweep streets and scythe lawns and build cars with their hearts singing. Sera and her mamá watched on their set in Madrid. My mother, Tita and Paco's family watched on their *tele* in Toledo.

At our own TV in the Las Moreras patio, Juan, José, Pico, Magda, Isaías, Tere, the household staff and I watched enthralled. I pondered, listening to the astronaut's staticky voice coming across a million kilometers as he put his foot into the Moon's empty bullring and said, "One small step for a man...one giant leap for mankind."

José leaned over and squeezed my arm. I knew she'd read my mind. I understood about one small step.

Juan murmured, "I wish I could walk on the Moon."

"You will," Tere told him.

The next day, July 21 — I don't forget that date either — General Franco made another big step that got on the news. He ended years of vacillation, and signed a paper restoring the monarchy. Carlists threw their red berets in the air. Juan Carlos de Borbón was proclaimed Prince of Spain, and would take the throne after the old man died. Some liberals were less happy. For 200 years, European liberals had fought to remove lichened monarchies from power. Now the Bourbons would be back.

We had no idea what kind of king Juan Carlos was going to be. If the fascist movement was going to control him, Spain would not liberalize any further.

My Carlist valet glowed, and wore his red beret around the house for a few days.

My brother glowed even more fiercely.

"Day after tomorrow," Paco told me, "the Prince will address the Cortes. You should be there with me. I will introduce you to him. A good beginning to your political career."

"I've told you...politics doesn't interest me," I said.

"Sooner or later, politics will force itself on you," Paco said. "Franco's hand is no longer on the tiller. Man, he is 77. He is sick with Parkinson's and full of drugs. He spends most of his time fishing or watching TV. Meanwhile others fight over the carcass of Spain...the Falange with the Opus Dei, ministers with one another. Tourist immorality everywhere. A new strong hand is needed."

Paco's words sent a chill down my spine.

Two days later, at Las Moreras, I watched the TV news alone with helpless fascination. There was a long telecast while the young prince spoke to the packed chamber of Spanish legislators. Franco and Juan Carlos were fuzzy black and white images — both in uniform at the podium, the old man frail and tremulous, almost topheavy with decorations.

In the next weeks, some incidents showed the growing confidence of right-wing extremists. The newspapers seldom reported them, but I heard about them from José, who heard about them at work. Yeah-yeah thinking was to be resisted at all costs. In Madrid and Salamanca, some student longhairs were beaten up by Old Catholic thugs. In Barcelona, attacks on transvestite prostitutes stepped up. There were more wild rumors that extremists were fielding Black Squads and operating Black Houses, like they did in the awful times right after the civil war, when "cleansing" was still going on. Considering themselves above the law, they made their own arrests, dragged people off to these private jails, interrogated them, tortured them — even executed them, it was said. I was forcefully reminded of the awful story that Juan told me.

José assured me: "In the office they say the CYS is definitely behind some of these incidents."

Soon enough, it was August. By now Juan had dated my sister several times. He had gotten over being nervous with her, even enjoyed her company. He was learning to trust José, to feel the beginnings of a brother-sister comradeship with her. With a pang, I remembered seeing the graves of his little sisters in Umbrilla.

In fact, a curious friendly competition had surged up between Juan and José. Sera and I found this very funny.

By now Paco had spent several days in the *coto*. So far he paid no attention to the hut, walking on the next plateau. But my brother's intuition was leading him too close to us for comfort. I made my routine visits to the *coto* to keep an eye on the conservation work. But Juan and I stayed away from the Mercies and were too gun-shy to even touch each other in the brush.

Instead, it was my sister and Sera who went to the Mercies with me, on a day that Paco was safely tied up in Madrid with government business. José wanted to show the Mercies to her friend for the first time. My sister and I wanted to create modern documentation for the Mercies. Supposing Paco found the site, and arranged for this "pagan abomination" to be dynamited? Who could ever prove what it had looked like? Looking back on it, I think we all had a feeling of impending disaster.

José brought her camera along. In the hills, the three of us pretended to idle around on horseback, photographing each other in favorite childhood spots. Actually, we were looking for signs that Paco had discovered something. Over on the second plateau, we noticed that someone had recently rolled aside a few of the broken stones that we'd salted there. Was Paco clever enough to see that the stone didn't belong there?

At the hut, with the field-glasses telling us we were alone, we tied our horses in the shade.

Down in the Mercies, while Sera studied the murals with rapt fascination, José strode around photographing with swift professionalism. I was the assistant, handing her the rolls of film and flashbulbs, holding a flashlight for her. Again and again, the Lady and Her animals leaped at us out of the dark, like lightning in the form of paintings. In half an hour, José had several rolls of color film that documented the most important features, including the Lady's face with its piece missing.

"This is wonderful...wonderful," Sera kept saying. "Now I know why I want to study."

"But the paintings are really deteriorating." José was alarmed. "In another ten years, they'll be beyond rescue."

"Maybe we should end the secrecy," I said.

"You mean...let the government take it over as a national treasure?" Sera asked.

"Why not? They're doing a good job restoring other historic sites," I pointed out.

"But this is our holy place!" José protested.

"It's a fossil," I scoffed. "What's holy is what we know — who we are. Like Grandmamá said, we have to start over.*"*

We lighted candles on the altar, but the feeling around us was not very prayerful and reverent. I felt overcome with gloom.

"Why isn't Juan with you?" Sera asked.

"It's not going well with him."

"You're too impatient," José said. "Too jealous."

"Don't judge me. You've got your own problems."

Right there in the Mercies, José and I almost had a fight but Sera smoothed our ruffled feathers.

"Sera and I had to learn patience," José went on. "There were times when we didn't see each other for months. We'd try a meeting place once...and never again. It's the habits that give you away. And yes, we've had our bad time. I've been a burro. I'm trying to change."

Right in front of me, the two women gave each other a gentle kiss on the lips. The echoes gave the kiss back, seeming to mock me. It was more than Juan and I had dared to do in front of them.

Trust...trust...trust....rust...rust...

Back outside, the simmering landscape revealed a solitary wavering figure trudging toward us. Paco? Our hearts plunged with apprehension, and I grabbed the field-glasses. It turned out to be the mayor, Mercurio. He had already been to the farm, and was now looking for us here. His weathered face was sad.

"Someone shot our lynx," he said. "The kittens are gone."

We all felt horribly sad. If the kittens survived the trauma of capture, they'd be smuggled out of Spain and fed into the hungry black-market of exotic animals. Spanish lynx were getting rare. Live ones would command a high price from some zoo or private animal collector.

Back in Madrid, José quietly developed the films in her darkroom. She made two sets of negatives and prints, and gave me one set. I took it back to Las Moreras, and hid it in the bedroom floor, along with my diamonds and the piece of fresco.

In mid-August, two bulls faced me in San Sebastián. My next to last contract. I'd trained hard and forced Juan out of my mind. As it turned out, both animals were cowardly and fled my cape. I couldn't do a thing with them. My Basque fans saw me try, so they didn't feel too robbed. But it took a huge effort. My mind wasn't on the *fiesta brava* anymore.

More and more, it seemed like killing a bull in public was in the same class with blowing away stags for their antlers, or killing an elephant for ivory. Foreign emotion about these things had finally penetrated the Spanish press. Why do this to the creatures? If the bull was the image of my heart's desire, why was I killing him? As a torero, was I not another pagan custom appropriated by the church? Re-designed to pacify the rulers by killing the symbol of all things unconquerable in the human heart? Some Spanish historians, including Cossío, had asserted that the torero is a kind of priest. Only in state religion are sacrifices offered up. This way, the people can be inspired to sacrifice their own lives — their freedom, their art and letters, their command over their sexual powers and of course their influence with their own children — all given up to the state. Thus the Hebrews were expected to offer burnt offerings to the Lord. During the Inquisition, the church offered burnt offerings of heretics. But the Mother of Mercy does not not call for sacrifice. A loving mother, She calls for care, and understanding. No wonder that power had to be torn away from women, before the sacrificers could go to work.

Why had I become a torero anyway? Was it more than falling in love with beautiful men in old photographs ? Had I bitten an apple that was poisoned just for me? Was I a symbol of their rule? Killing an animal whose horns symbolized the irresistible powers of change? Was I just a paid executioner who wore a suit of lights instead of a black hood?

After San Sebastián, I felt like an old safari hunter who decides to shoot lions only with a camera. Arles was two weeks away — my last contract. In the French rings, the actual killing had already been outlawed. The bull is only played with capes. I'd do a few passes, and then the bull would trot from the ring alive.

After Arles, my life would center on the Coto Morera, and the Pact, and this man who had me so enthralled. But how?

Despite our lack of chances to be together, it was good to have a friend. Ordinary friendships with men I'd had — a few. Irritations and unanswered questions Juan and I had in plenty. But there was a precious unspoken closeness with him, that grew stronger every time we were together. We probed around the edges of each other's jealousy, trying to soften it. Now and then we dared to show each other candid snapshots from our hidden pasts without the fear that it might be deemed pornography. I got him to laugh at some of my adventures in foreign tenderloins. He got me to laugh at a couple of bridge stories — was more confiding when I wasn't interrogating him. I was still curious to know how a boy with his nature had survived the cruelties of conservative village life.

One day we happened to be left alone together during the construction of new bird pens. The old pens dated back to my father, and were badly built. The new ones needed to stand on fresh ground, where there was no bird disease. Pico and the village carpenter were having the satisfaction of teaching the torero how to swing a hammer. They left to drive the carpenter's truck to Toledo for supplies. Magda went with them to shop. Juan and I stayed to finish the demolition, pulling rotted posts out of the ground with our mule, piling rusted bird-wire.

We were working shirtless, very bronzed now, appreciating the sight of each other's torsos. Casually I turned the conversation to village men and their attitudes.

"The ones in Umbrilla tried everything they could think of, to get me in line," Juan grunted.

"Like what?"

"Oh, there was this girl…they actually paid her to try seducing me. They had a lottery on whether it would happen. It didn't. The ones who lost money dragged me to somebody's barn, and had her there to feel me. The bastards were going to watch…."

"Jesus," I said.

"…And of course I couldn't get it up. It occurred to me to save myself by talking about being a priest. So they got embarrassed and let me go. After that I kept talking religion like a madman, and they left me alone."

"Imagine the scandal if you'd gotten her pregnant," I said cheerfully, kicking a rotted post out of the way.

"Man, I was ignorant."

"About what? Didn't the animals teach you what men and women do?"

"I'm talking about what men do. I knew about the kid stuff. Some of the boys did it at the river, in the bushes. But I wanted…I wanted…well, to be close with someone."

"How old were you?"

"Fourteen when it happened."

"And the other guy?" I asked this casually, my back turned.

"He was around 30, I guess. He lived with his mother. His wife had left him and emigrated to Santander with her family."

Backing the mule up to another pen-post, I braced myself to hear the awful story. We'd already tried pulling posts with Pico's son-in-law's car, but the cheap little bumper almost came off.

"Was he a farmer?" My tone was mild curiosity.

"A hunter and guide. He took people up in the Picos for pay." Juan's back was turned too. He was busily rolling up rusted wire to make a neat bundle. "His name was Lin. He was *majo* like you wouldn't believe. The whole village doted on him. Every year he went out alone and got a big pig, or a stag, and everybody talked about it for the next year. He was the king."

I ground my teeth at his use of the word *majo* for somebody else, pulling the drag ropes to the post we wanted to haul out.

"A friend of your father's?"

"My father didn't like Lin. My father wasn't a bad man, but he was always in debt, always angry. He worked me and my brother hard...especially me. There was always so much to do. After my grandfather died, my father was always knocking me around. I'd think about running away, going to live with Lin and his mother. My father would come for me, and Lin would stand at the door with his shotgun...protect me from my father. I'd take care of Lin's guns and tools. I'd dress animals for him. I'd sleep in his bed at night. His mother wouldn't mind."

Feeling a horrible queasiness that the story was going to end in innocence betrayed and violated, I knotted the mule's traces in place around the pole.

Juan's magnificent shoulders flexed as he threw the roll of wire on a growing pile. "Finally I got up the guts to talk to Lin about being his gunbearer. So he invited me on his next pig hunt. We got caught in a storm up there, and stayed in a hut. We slept together to keep warm. I was in his arms...in heaven. But he didn't do anything, and I didn't have the courage to start anything. And when we got home, the bastard avoided me after that."

Juan's voice was bitter.

I pretended to be incredulous. "He didn't do anything...but he avoided you?"

"Man, I'd sit in the pasture with my cows, and cry. My parents thought I was moping over religion. I was so afraid they'd know what was really going on, I even put a little statue of Our Lady in the pasture, like a shrine. This was when my father started agreeing that I had to be a priest. Maybe he knew. And Lin and his mother moved away to Santander."

I had to laugh.

"So that's how a misfit like you got to the seminary," I said.

"No kidding. Me, a priest! I don't believe a bit of that stuff. And after the priests threw me out, I drifted, worked." Suddenly Juan laughed too. "Then a year ago, when I started working in Santander, I ran into Lin. He was back with his wife. He has four kids now. And he's fat. I couldn't believe..."

I yelled *haláaa* at the mule, who leaned into his collar, dragging the rotted post out of the ground. What a relief to know that the story ended in nothing. I believed Juan's story. It felt so good, working there with him in the sun, sweating, feeling the work healing my leg. I loved these moments. After fifteen hundred years of terror and silence, they still couldn't keep us from sharing our stories, making our pacts.

"Lin wanted something, but he was afraid," I said.

"You think so?"

"Eh," I teased, trying to keep it light, "weren't you afraid Our Lady would strike you dead with lightning for lying?"

He laughed. "I used to wonder. She had lots of chances."

It was midday — time to get out of the sun and rest. At the pump, in the shade, I poured a bucket of cold water over my head and shoulders. He carried a bucket of water to the mule. Thirstily the mule buried his nose in the bucket.

"The Lady brought you here," I said.

Juan's eyes met mine, as he poured a dipper of water over himself. I watched as streams ran sexily over his torso, down his arms where those big veins were swollen with work and heat.

"I thank Her for that," he said.

Desire shimmered like heat waves between us. I watched as he dried his torso off with an old towel. Sun was bleaching his hair and eyebrows, frying his skin dark. Complaining that this climate dried his skin out, he grabbed a little tin of my olive oil that he kept handy. Slathering a handful of the golden yellow stuff over his arms and chest, he rubbed it in his sun-bleached hair for good measure, till it shone like burnished metal. The fruity smell hung round him. He slid me one of those hungry looks. We were on the verge of going in the cottage to fall on the bed together, and use a little of that oil for another purpose, when suddenly we saw the lumbering ancient truck chugging up the road. It was so loaded with new wood and rolls of wire and sacks of concrete that the springs were flat.

Amid dust and blue exhaust, the truck stopped by the pens, and backfired as the carpenter shut off the engine. Magda was all smiles, with baskets of groceries. Pico looked grey from the heat.

"We will build these new pens well, like apartment buildings in town," the old man proclaimed, "and set the posts in concrete."

"Long live our pens," the carpenter said.

During siesta, some of the Village Committee came bicycling up the road. There was much wine and talk and joking in the shade. They visited often now. Pico's house was becoming a social center. He and Magda didn't seem to mind. Amid the chatter, Juan and I slid no more looks at each other, but that invisible mirage was trembling in the air between us like a heat wave from Africa.

The pens cost money. I'd have to make the rounds of my rich friends and get more donations into the *montepío*.

Juan spent these uneasy weeks getting tighter with the La Mora committee. We heard less mention of "the foreigner," till Candalaria was the last holdout on the committee. The *coto* was training someone like them, not some *señorito* with pull.

And things were happening. The new pens. The article in *ABC,* now posted in the La Mora bar, along with a letter from Prince Philip that I'd received. The *ABC* story had been noticed by a BBC correspondent in Madrid, who relayed it to the Prince, a dedicated conservationist, who was curious about what we were doing. The villagers had all seen Prince Philip on the telly, and they were insufferably proud. Magic was happening, and Juan Diano was part of it.

Juan tried to scoff off their gossip about his *brujo* powers. One evening, Fermín remarked that we should send Juan to Madri'th to run the government, because he knew everything that was going to happen.

Juan frowned. "I don't know everything. Just my own little things about animals."

In some mysterious way, his coming helped quench some of the last embers of civil war in La Mora. Another evening, Candalaria learned that the war had never come to Juan's village. So she marched him into an overgrazed field with an air of "I'll show the ignorant kid what went on". There she pointed out the place. In the slanting evening sunlight, shadows revealed several of those low places in the earth. The graves were not marked, but withered bouquets lay scattered around by the goats — evidence of "liberalization." For a long time, no one had dared to put flowers there, for fear of attracting police notice.

One low place was apart from the others. Only one bouquet lay there. Juan noticed it. "Who is there?" Juan asked her.

Candalaria paused a moment. "Eight women who were dishonored before they were shot."

Juan stared for a while. Finally he whispered:

"Why should those poor women be blamed for that?"

Juan couldn't have known that Candalaria's own mother lay in that grave. Candalaria couldn't have known where his peculiar understanding of honor came from. But her eyes brimmed with tears. Juan put his hand on her shoulder for a moment. Then he picked flowers off a few weeds that the goats had rejected. "With your permission?" he asked. She nodded, dabbing her eyes with her kerchief. Awkwardly he put the tiny wild bouquet in the low place. Candalaria went to her garden and picked a whole armload of flowers, and he helped her put them there.

After that, we heard no more about the "foreigner."

Juan's tiny bank account was mounting up. The Committee gave him a raise. He learned how to write checks, but didn't spend a peseta unless he had to. His check ledger was pencilled neatly with relentless high-school arithmetic. With the Coto Morera scholarship in hand, Juan applied for the year of pre-university in Madrid, and was accepted. Classes would start in October. He'd move into Madrid, where Isaías and Tere had offered him the room for the school year. This way, he wouldn't have to share some expensive apartment with a bunch of noisy students, and have no privacy. He was hoping to buy a car by then, so he'd be free to drive back and forth. For him, university acceptance was the first proof that a brilliant future was really possible for him. He was showing his grit under the iron — surging at that future with enormous will.

It was deeply moving for me to watch Juan Diano change under my eyes. Hope, good food and healthy work outdoors had put a glow on him, a quiet new ebullience. A few months ago, he had been dirt under everyone's feet. Now his gifts and his human worth were being discovered, not just by me, but by others. He was actually growing handsomer, starting to turn heads in the street. A symbol of the new Spain, with all his sensitivity and strength. Tere was right — Juan would walk on the Moon. My own personal Moon God, my male Diana, keeper of all animals and all change.

Mamá and Tita had felt obliged to invite Juan to Sunday lunches at El Refugio, so they could scrutinize him further under their moral loups. There, at the long dining table, remembering to use the right eating implement, my friend held his own with the terrible old ladies. And a miracle was happening: my mother was starting to have an opinion of her own — to appreciate Juan. With his acceptance at the University, and my steady march toward the desired marriage, she was mellowing.

"A young scientist in the family!" she told Paco. *"¡Canastas!* There's nothing wrong with that!"

José's and Juan's engagement had none of the drama that attended mine to Sera. But suddenly, at the end of one of those interminable Sunday lunches, José had a tiny moonstone bracelet dangling on her wrist. It was a gift from Juan. Tere had quietly dug into her own trove of family jewelry and gave it to him, so he didn't have to use his school money.

It was "settled." But we were going to wait till after Arles to announce both the engagements.

"Are you sure," Isaías asked me, "that you don't want to schedule one more contract, so you can retire in your own country?"

No. I wanted to fade out of the public eye without fanfare. Arles would be the end.

On the heels of these social victories, came Juan's 25th birthday. We four decided to celebrate with a little party at Las Moreras, then a weekend of high life in Madrid. Why not start having a good time to-gether? The four of us would spend a lot of time in one another's company for the next fifty years. Juan and I decided that we would grab the chance, and be together at my apartment in Madrid. Isaías and his wife wouldn't be home. They planned to go north for some badly needed vacation. So Juan could slip upstairs to my flat without being seen. One night together was safe, we were sure. As Sera had said, it was the habit that might get us caught.

Mamá and Doña Margarita were surprisingly magnanimous and gave their permission for José and Sera to spend an unchaperoned day with their fiancés, providing there was due decorum at night.

"Happy birthdaaaay!" That Saturday morning, a group of us waylaid Juan outside his house at the *coto*. He emerged, sleepy-eyed, to find us all lurking there — Pico, Magda, the Village Committee, José, Sera, the Eibars and myself. Blushing, ducking back inside to tuck in his shirt-tail, my friend came out again to find Pico offering him a gift in a small velvet case. Inside was a nice Swiss watch. Tere and Isaías had chosen it in Madrid, and everyone had put a few pesetas toward it.

Dumfounded, Juan stared at it.

"Olé for our Juan," Mercurio said.

"It's hard to know what to get a *brujo*," said Candalaria.

"But even a *brujo* can oversleep and be late for class," Pico warned.

"In this country of God, you can be late for everything, even church. But university classes — never!" I growled.

Juan was overcome at this demonstration of everyone's respect. He had never owned a watch. Carefully he put it on. A trace of tears showed in his eyes. "A thousand thanks," he whispered.

Horses, mules and burros were saddled, and the whole troop of us rode sedately into the hills to inspect our domain. There were three new springs now, all of them running well. Delicate little belts of green were sprouting around them, and all kinds of animal tracks dotted the mud. I had to smile, thinking how most in our party had no idea what urgency had driven the creation of those springs. Proudly Juan guided the tour — pointed out this, told us about that. A pair of falcons were nesting in those rocks up there, and feeding their chicks on partridge. The wolf cubs were looking healthy.

As we approached the third spring, a storm of partridge flushed with a thunder-clap of wings. Five roe deer went springing off.

"Only our lynx is missing," said Candalaria sadly, whacking her tiny burro with a stick to keep up with our horses.

"More lynx will come," Juan stated to us.

"And in three years, the pigs," added Fermín from the back of his enormous mule.

"Eh, Antonio, don't forget your promise that the whole town gets to eat roast pig," Mercurio reminded us.

"It is a solemn promise, made before the Virgin. The day we have a pig to spare," I said, "we'll shoot it and have a feast."

Everybody agreed how nice it would be to see the first litter of baby pigs, trotting after their fierce mother in all their striped camouflage.

"Do you realize," José said to everyone, "that people will travel from all over the world to see this place?"

Inspection finished, the older people were getting tired so they turned back. We two engaged couples kept on. On the plateau of the Mercies, we got frisky, spurring our horses into a gallop along the old road. José was riding Faisán. Juan had put Sera on a chestnut mare who was gentle, since Sera seldom rode now. I was on a bay, Chispa, and Juan rode Mozuela. The horses were fit, and full of energy. Perhaps they could feel our excitement about the next two days. Knowing that a rare chance for privacy was ahead gave us enormous energy.

Yes, it was time for a little fiesta. For men, traditional fiesta meant dancing a *jota* along the street with your arm around other guys' waists, getting wonderfully drunk with them, but not drunk enough to lose your dignity and fall on your face. Later, however, in some private nook, fiesta could mean opening your fly and getting wonderfully sucked off by a friend, with the understanding that both of you were too drunk to remember it later. For women, fiesta meant looking pretty, staying sober and keeping your virtue at all costs. But we were *modernos,* and it was time for modern fiesta.

José tried to make Faisán do a capriole, jumping him in the air and making him kick out behind, an old battlefield maneuver that used to be lethal in the days of horse cavalry. Juan couldn't resist tweaking her.

"That kind of *señorito* riding is useless," he said.

José rose to the bait. "Nobody from La Montaña can ride worth a peseta." She looked at Juan out of the corners of her eyes. "Except maybe riding milk cows."

"We gallop our cows up mountains," Juan retorted.

"Prove it!" José barked. "*¡Haláaaa!*"

A crack of their quirts, and the two of them were off.

Sera and I galloped close behind. I was keeping an eye on my fiancée because I didn't want to see her thrown and hurt. To my amazement, the somber Sera suddenly had a grin of fierce enjoyment on her face. Holding on for dear life, she whacked her horse and pulled ahead of me. It was wild northern riding pitted against southern school riding as we tore along with our horses' butts churning in the white dust. The horses laid their ears back and stretched out. We kept to the ancient road, not wanting to race across country and tear up new plants or nests of ground birds, or scare the devil out of our fox and deer. Juan was barely in the lead, riding like the bareback Celtic warrior in every movie we'd seen. We went rattling down the long grades, surging along the level stretches, startling echoes as we raced through the shadows in a narrow ravine.

Every time we reached the level, José urged Faisán up to Juan's girth with the old horse's magnificent mane streaming over her thighs. But Juan was more daring at hurling Mozuela downhill, so he always pulled ahead there. Careening around one curve, we almost ran over Paco, who was on another of his treks into the *coto*. My brother hastily stepped back, coughing in our dust like a cranky old man.

Not even drawing rein at the game farm, we kept going at a breakneck pace, down the dirt road leading to Las Moreras. Our horses pounded along, puffing heavily now, necks soapy with sweat. The power-line poles flew past us.

Here, we were on the level, so José laid over her horse's neck, and old Faisán found more strength. Once again, she drew even with Juan. Sera and I were racing behind them, to one side, not wanting to eat their dust. My leg was hurting, but what the hell. We flew along the olive groves where I had walked with Juan that first morning, where I'd confessed to José. As we burst into the farmyard at Las Moreras, squawking chickens scattered and dogs and cats ran for their lives. Juan had the lead again, by half a horse, as we pulled up in a spray of gravel, at the very door of the house.

The big door opened. My mother, Sera's mother and Aunt Tita stood there, alarmed.

"*¡Canastas!* What is this unseemly racket?" Tita wanted to know.

The three ladies had clambered out of their rattan chairs in the patio, where they'd been reading devotional books and watching TV. The newscaster was intoning something about the Matesa scandal. The old ladies had probably been tsk-tsking over the scandal, a textile firm that got lots of government credit by claiming fictitious foreign orders. Now the three old terrors stared at us as we milled around, letting our horses get their breath. We were teasing each other without mercy.

"Woman," Juan said to his fiancée, "even on the flat, I won."

"Rub it in, Juan," Sera hooted. "This is a historic moment. José has never lost till now."

"Yes, I'm beaten," José conceded, throwing her hands in the air. "I admit it. Thank god I'll be married to you for the next hundred years. I'll find plenty of other things to beat you at."

"Are you all right?" I asked Sera solicitously, jumping off and taking the roan's rein.

"Of course," Sera said, jumping off. I offered her my arm, and she took it, as the stable boy came running to take our horses.

Mamá, Doña Margarita and Tita exchanged looks. That Sera would take my arm, that José would let a man beat her at horse-racing — all these were good signs. Juan went up another notch in Mamá's estimation, maybe half a notch in Tita's. That the two young couples were having all this innocent fun together was another good sign. The noise could be overlooked.

But our supreme bit of theater came later. We went in the house to change and wash up for the birthday lunch in Juan's honor. Marimarta's twig fire had burned down to coals, and savory smoke was rolling up from the splendid lamb chops — marinated in our oil, garlic and rosemary — that Marimarta was tending on the grill. As we walked past Mamá and Tita sitting in their rattan chairs, Juan looked at José and said:

"You're going to put on a skirt for lunch, aren't you?"

"Of course, darling."

"Those Yankee pants are all right for riding." Juan was getting good at theater. "But I like you better in skirts."

When José came down again, she was showered and elegant in her favorite linen skirt, with hem discreetly below her knees instead of miniskirt length. The three old ladies traded a significant glance. In their eyes, Juan went up five more notches. The peasant had accomplished something that the entire Blue front of the family had failed to do.

Later that afternoon, on that fateful hot Saturday, the third Saturday in August 1969, the four of us drove to Madrid in José's Citröen. It was going to be our first night of high life.

Juan was driving, pedal to the floor. The highway was new and splendid, one of the first superhighways in Spain, and we could dare to go faster than 50 kph. Juan drove like he rode horseback — he had learned to drive during his 15 months in the Mountain Division. He was daring, if still inexpert, at the wheel. An improved highway, new-looking as a washing machine or other wondrous modern goods, the kind dangled before peasants' hungry eyes on the *tele,* was an irresistible temptation.

From afar, the four of us were the picture of youthful propriety. José was sitting in front, with Juan. I was in back with Sera. To the truckers that we whipped past, as they chugged along in their battered old post-war vehicles that belched black smoke, to the tourists in their myriad Volkswagens, to the native drivers of tiny Seat 600s who turned their heads to stare, we were two young couples of the "in set", off to the capital for some innocent fun. Only inside the Citroën could it be seen that Serafita had slipped one elegant high-heeled sandal off, and thrust her bare foot into the front seat, where it lay in her friend's lap, being stroked. On Sera's face there was a mischievous grin. I feel deeply touched, seeing Sera blossom like this. As often these days, a lump came to my throat.

I was leaning forward, as if talking to José and Juan. But I had one arm around the driver's bucket seat at waist level. The arm encircled my own friend. José kept her eyes discreetly on the highway, so she wouldn't see when my hand caressed my friend's trousered thigh. Now and then, Juan grunted with zippered discomfort.

"What's going on with you, Juanito?" José asked, eyes innocent and wide. "Is there a flea in your fly?"

"More like a scorpion," Sera drawled.

We all howled with laughter, and Juan blushed fiercely. It was always easy to make Juan blush. Lately we were finding out that Sera had a gift for sniper shots of ribald wit.

The car windows were open, and hot air blasted us. The radio was playing fast-tempo jazz from some station in France. Juan was wearing the made-to-order going-out suit that Isaías had gotten him. The warm camel-hair color brought out the burnish in his well-barbered hair, now whipping in the hot wind, and made his keen eyes look startlingly blue. He swerved out to roar skillfully past a rickety old truck loaded with jiggling pigskins of wine, and shifted into high gear.

"*Haláaa*," I said, clapping him proudly on the shoulder, feeling a surge of joyful lust.

"Look at Sera's hair," José said.

We all burst out laughing. Her exquisitely conservative hairdo, which Doña Margarita had helped her set in place before lunch with volumes of wonderful modern hair-spray, was now blown to pieces by the wind. We laughed and laughed. We were drunk with our first taste of freedom and dreams of our future.

12

In Madrid, every detail of our day enhanced our little theater performance, and heightened the anticipation of secret delights.

First we did some strategic shopping Sera had the perfect excuse — she needed baby clothes as a gift for a pregnant married friend. José was on the hunt for a new nightgown. So off went the two women to El Bebé Ingles and Nieves.

We men forged on to Armería Diana. Juan needed a good all-weather jacket, and he had hungered to buy it at this luxurious sporting establishment on Calle Serrano. Since Antonio Escudero brought him in, half the staff rushed to wait on the handsome young northerner, whom Escudero introduced as director-in-training of the Coto Morera. Juan had a wonderful time pretending he might buy a splendid shotgun and countless boxes of ammo. I didn't hover over him, because that wouldn't look good. The owner wanted to chat about bulls and partridge, so he and I strolled to the bar next door and had a whiskey.

When we came back, Juan was studying himself somberly in the mirror. He had chosen a shooting-jacket made of grey drill, with a lot of pockets. A sheepskin liner could be zipped in and out. Fall would be upon us soon enough, and I'd warned him about the icy winds that swept the *coto*. "Good enough?" he asked me.

"Good enough," I said.

As the bill was discreetly slid across the counter, my friend blanched. In his migrant days, the liner's cost alone would have fed him for a month. Standing almost at attention, he wrote the check with schoolboy care. He still had the air of a gypsy beggar woman paying for two ounces of salt pork by sliding tin *perras** across the counter one at a time. As we walked out of Armería Diana into the scorching afternoon, Juan threw a yearning glance back at the precious jacket on the counter. It would be hand-delivered to Isaías' address.

"You like running with rich people," I teased him.

"I'd like to be rich enough not to feel scared when I buy anything," he retorted.

On the corner, Juan bought a lottery ticket from a crippled veteran. The old man's legs had been blown off, so he propped himself on a little handmade cart, with strips of lottery tickets clipped to his lapels. The government had compassion on our disabled veterans, and got them jobs — the ones who fought on the fascist side, at any rate.

"If I win," Juan grinned, "I can get a white Mercedes."

At Nieves, José and Serafita were still closeted in a dressing room. Sales-ladies ran in and out, uttering little screams of delight when something looked good on the two illustrious customers. We men didn't dare be seen loitering among the dainties, so we went to the bar next door and had another whiskey and a snack. When we finally came back, the two women had arrived at the cash register. José threw in a few bits of theater, in case a police investigator came round to ask.

"Look, darling," she whispered throatily in Juan's ear. She slipped her arm around his waist, and gave him a glimpse into the paper bag, at the exquisite nightgown and negligee crafted from fine Spanish bobbin lace. "Do you like it?"

Juan stared at the delicate thing, and blushed for the hundredth time that day.

"It's…eh…very *monina,"* he said, profferring the quaintest Montanese compliment he knew. He squeezed her waist back.

"It'll look even more *monina* on the wedding night," offered Sera helpfully. The two women embraced each other with tiny squeals. "Ayy José, I'm happy for you," said Sera, weeping a little.

We four grandly swept out of the store, leaving the precious thing to be delivered to José's concierge. Behind us, the sales staff were wreathed in sentimental smiles, completely overcome by the experience. Ayyyiii, saints, if it wasn't Antonio Escudero and his fiancée! And Maria Josefina Escudero and *her* fiancé! What a marvel! How wonderful that they're our clients!   In a few months, they'll be buying baby layettes!

On the sidewalk, we burst into quiet laughter — two smart couples, feeling frisky and rebellious. People stared at us.

"And to think that the lace thing is really for Antonio's friend," José hooted.

"He will look *monino-monino* in it," Serafita hissed.

Juan was learning about repartee. "Go on," he said. "Antonio will steal that thing from me, the first chance he gets. He's the one who loves the pretty silks."

At 4 in the afternoon, our heretic quartet met Paco for a long boring lunch at El Coto Restaurant, across the street from the Stock Exchange. Paco was back in town, still irritated that our horses had almost run him down on the *coto* road.

"Who won the horse race?" he growled.

"I did," said Juan.

Paco raised his eyebrows. "And José didn't kill you?"

"Not yet," Juan said.

José smiled a fond fiancée smile at Juan. "Who knows...I might even give up smoking for him," she added.

Paco's eyebrows went higher. "You actually asked that of her?" he interrogated Juan.

"I don't like to see women smoke," said Juan calmly.

Momentarily speechless, Paco clapped his hands for the waiter and ordered more sangría.

"Did you find interesting things in the *coto* yet?" I asked.

"Not yet. We ought to go ahead with the dig. I will speak to my boss about the permit...see what archeologists are free..."

Out of my inside jacket pocket, I took a Banco de Madrid check for 100,000 pesetas that Isaías had written on my account.

"Here...as I promised you. For the dig," I said.

He pocketed the check. "I thought you'd forgotten."

"My apologies. I didn't have the money till the other day. The Yankee importer finally paid his oil invoice."

As we munched on crayfish under the shade trees, my brother sipped his sangría and scrutinized the four of us noncommittally. This lunch was a politically motivated move on our part. I wanted to keep reminding Paco that José's fiancé was made of pure gold. So we chatted about Juan's plans for higher education. Then I casually mentioned the flickers of interest being shown in our family conservation effort by the Jersey Wildlife Conservancy, who'd heard about it from Prince Philip.

Paco just grunted, and broke the tail off another crayfish. In his eyes, the Windsors were new money.

Finally we left Paco, and launched ourselves into one of those endless Madrid nights. First we were seen at the Cowboy Bar, where we ran into a couple of well-known aficionados and columnists, and invited them for drinks. Then Oliver's, where we mingled with actors and show people.

Juan grandly paid for a round of 60-peseta drinks without hardly blanching. In the crush, I contrived to let Juan be pushed against me. His arm secretly slid around my waist as we pretended to be keeping our balance.

Then we surged on to Nicca's. Despite it being August, with Madrid emptied of natives fleeing the heat, this *moderno* club was crowded with yeah-yeah young people, mostly foreigners. José and Sera were casually holding in hands in public, in a manner allowed to Spanish women — especially since each had a male escort who doted on her.

After a trip to the bathroom, I was pushing my way back to the bar, where Juan stood half a head taller than everyone, his sleek hair like a bronze helmet under the smoky lights. Suddenly I noticed an older foreign man staring at him from farther down the bar, then moving toward him. I knew that stare, astonishingly reckless for its openness and intent. If this man was not more discreet, he might find himself in a Spanish jail by morning. He was the imperial Yankee rake, who casually assumes that any young foreigner will spread his legs for him. I had met the type in New York City. A lightning blast of jealousy fried me.

Juan was laughing at some tomboy impertinence of José's. His smile, lighting up that somber face of his, was wonderful. Pushing my way among people with grim speed, I slid behind Juan, shielding him from the interloper. In the crush, I spoke quietly into his ear. "Watch your back, handsome."

Without even turning his head, Juan leaned back against me lightly. Then, over his shoulder, from narrowed eyes, he let the tourist see his look of macho contempt. Thwarted, the foreigner drifted off to look for other prey.

At midnight, we four were seen eating the latest thing — Chinese food, at the Casa de Ming. A UN diplomat friend had introduced José to this cuisine, and she couldn't get enough of it. We learned to eat with chopsticks, fed each other shrimp, and read each other's fortune-cookies with muffled bursts of laughter. We'd been laughing since morning, and were getting hoarse from it. Curiously, Juan and I both got the same fortune: LIFE BRINGS YOU A BOLD AND DASHING ADVENTURE.

By now it was 2 a.m. and we were at a nightclub where the band played deafening Latin jazz. We were all holding our liquor amazingly well, as the two frisky women tried to teach us frisky men how to rumba. Sera had never been outside of Spain, but José had gone on a press junket to Santo Domingo once, and learned the dance there. Juan was serious, trying to get the subtle hip movements just right. I was more adept, but struggling with my bad leg now and then.

By 3 a.m., flagging a little, we were at the Mayte Club for one last drink. Thank the Virgin that some celebrity actors were there — Omar Sharif, Paco Rabal, and a couple of starlets in what passed for "new wave films" under the creakily relaxed censorship laws. This meant that little attention was paid to us four, nursing our drinks in a quiet corner.

Under the table, Juan's left thigh and my right thigh were pressed gently together. In a little while, I'd be alone with him. Shadows of feudalism, dark and cold, still rose between us — how to melt them into sunlight? Penetration is the symbol of feudal ownership. It was still that delicate, uneasy question between us. He shouldn't belong to me, nor I to him. Only women belong. Children belong. Land belongs. Animals belong. Earth belongs. So says the state religion.

Finally we were back in José's Citröen, heading to our respective sleeping places. A pensive mood overcame us — a latent sadness that we would have to live in such byzantine deceptions in order to have a little freedom. José was driving. In the darkness, Serafita held José's free hand between the bucket seats. In the back seat, Juan had his hand inside my jacket, his warm palm laid gently over my breast, feeling it through my shirt.

"God, how moral and boring our high life is," said José. "When *He* dies, maybe we can have naughty movies and naughty cabarets again."

"'Tonio," said Sera, "what is high life like...out there?"

"We'll travel," I said. "We'll have wonderful times. You'll find out."

Sera looked at me in the rear-view mirror. "Are there bars for...people like us?"

"Serita, I adore how innocent you are," José said. "Of course there are bars for people like us."

"Two years ago," I said, "I was on my way to Mexico City to fight bulls, and I stopped in New York to see Aunt Pura. And I went to one of those bars."

"Are Yankees...like us?" Sera asked.

Juan was looking uncomfortable at this talk. He did not consider himself to be "different." Through my shirt, I rubbed his hand gently on my chest, and tried to explain what I had seen.

"In New York," I said, "you hear ten times the languages that you hear in Madri'th. Kinds of Spanish that I could hardly understand. Even the taxi drivers don't speak English. They're migrants like you were, Juan...just off a boat. Pakistanis, Turks.... You show them a map of the city, and point where you want to go. So I asked some discreet questions, and pointed. The United States has strict laws too. Their police are always closing those bars. Their prisons are as nasty as ours, so I'm told. Anyway, this place was a private club. When I went in, two hundred men were dancing."

"You mean...men doing the rumba together?" asked Juan, incredulous. His eyes had rounded.

"Yankees don't do those traditional dances," I said. "They do go-go stuff. You can't imagine. Guys in blue jeans, bare feet, no shirts, everybody sweating like racehorses. Wonderful bodies. Dancing in pairs, touching each other right on the dance floor. I stood at the bar watching, in my English suit and Italian tie, with a whiskey forgotten in my hand. I was... er...beyond arousal, my friend. I don't think I moved a muscle for an hour."

It was hard to explain how that club had made me feel. I launched into some passionate philosophy, fueled by alcohol. My throat had filled up with tears.

"People get sorted out like the animals," I said. "Who is wild, who is tame. Who wears the yoke. All your life, you pull a plow in the fields of belief. You plow for the churches, you plow for the people with money. The world we live in doesn't want wild animals. That's why the wild animals are being destroyed. They're a bad symbol, very bad, for the people who own the fields of belief. The people who shot Fede hung his stuffed head on the trophy wall of history. Those young Yankees I saw dancing...they have pulled their heads out of the yoke. They've gone wild again."

Night lights of Madrid were streaming past us, as my throat filled again. Tonight I wanted more. It was time.

It was now 4 a.m. on that fatal Sunday morning. The full Moon was low in the west, paled out in the city glow. José and Serafita dropped us in front of the new 14-story apartment building with its tile facade, where the Eibars and I had our flats. Then they drove on. We watched their taillights disappear down the street.

"Wonderful bodies, eh?" Juan said drily.

"That was before I met your wonderful body."

I clapped for the night watchman to come. This was the most dangerous moment of the evening — being seen entering the building together. We could have pushed the charade a bit farther, and entered separately, with the watchman having to come twice to open the door with his keys. But we were too eager, and wanted each other too fiercely, so we decided to dispense with this last touch.

While we waited, I slipped Juan a spare key to my door, and we drank in the morning air. The sky lightened. A few workers in blue coveralls were already bicycling past, on their way to some slave job that required working on Sundays. A burro cart clip-clopped by, loaded with fresh-cut fava beans. From under beetling peasant eyebrows, the cart's driver looked disapprovingly at us high-lifers. Down the street, the door of a churro shop opened, to admit a burly man bent under a huge sack of flour. Smells of hot oil and frying breakfast churros floated to our nostrils.

Finally the white-haired watchman came doddering with his big ring of keys, and opened the gate. The concierge's window was locked for the night.

My friend and I rode the elevator to the 13th floor. Each flat occupied an entire floor. With only one elevator and a staircase, the top two floors were relatively secure. Isaías had wanted it that way, so no one could go up to my door without passing his.

Juan got off at the 13th, and I rode up to the 14th.

Inside my flat, I went through motions of getting ready for bed, knowing Juan was doing the same, opening the shutters a little, yanking down bedcovers. The double bed was a modern Danish thing, plain teak, comfortable, with Irish linen sheets and a lot of pillows. I liked this room very much — I had convalesced here for a few weeks, after the Sanitorio de Toreros released me last year. My first steps on crutches had been taken out of this room. Now I put out a handful of towels. Men's love is messy, and we didn't dare leave telltale traces on the sheets, for my maid to find. Since it was Sunday, the maid would not come. Then I turned out the lights and leaned at the window, smoking a cigarette nervously, waiting. To confuse anybody watching the elevator from down below, he would take it down to the 12th floor, then quietly walk up the stairs to my landing. My knees were trembling.

Finally I heard Juan silently enter my apartment with the spare key, and lock the door. Then he loomed in the bedroom doorway, and felt his way across the room, almost falling over a chair. Finally we were going to have what civilized people have. A clean room, a locked door.

"Did you see anybody?" I whispered.

"No. No one."

Our mouths searched hungrily for that first kiss that we'd had in the hut. It had been several weeks since we'd been together. He was in a hurry. Would he be rough with me?

"Slow down," I whispered.

"Majín..." He only called me that when he wanted me very much. "Majín, don't you get tired of kissing?"

"Do I get tired of the sky? The Moon?"

Slowly we undressed each other, taking our time, and lay down side by side on the bed. We stretched luxuriously on the clean sheets. "I am so in love with you," I wanted to say, but held back, for fear that he wasn't ready to say it yet. Maybe in an hour or two. He was already holding my hips possessively, shifting our position, to make sure my leg was comfortable. The heedless young bull, who had hooked his horn into every tree he hurtled past, was maturing into a sensitive and thoughtful lover. I should be grateful for this, at least. His touches, his way of moving with me, were careful now, almost medical. He ran his hand up the inside of my thigh in the same way that he'd feel a horse's leg for a swollen tendon. Where was the predatory character that I'd dragged off the Santander street? He had studied how to give me pleasure, and gave it now, and I trusted myself into his hands.

Cool breezes from the Guadarrama mountains came gusting through the shutter louvers. The last feeble moonlight lay in camouflage stripes across our thrusting limbs. Outside, a student Tuna strolled by, singing university songs, accompanied by someone's amateurish guitar playing. At the prudery of the traditional love songs, we laughed a little. For the first time, we were protected, naked, relaxed, comfortable, uninhibited. There were hours to play, experiment, explore. I kissed him in ways, and in places, that he'd never imagined.

"Majín, you have no shame," he whispered. My answer was to kiss him more, till his body arched.

Dawn sunlight exploded through the shutters. Bars closing, people finally going home. Already workers who had to service the city on Sunday were stirring along the streets below. Car horns blew impatiently on the Castellana. The bells were ringing across Madrid, calling people vainly to the half empty churches.

I let him look between my legs, inspect the damage that the bull in Écija had done. His finger, then his lips, explored along the livid scar inside my thigh. "Jesus," he whispered, "the bull could have gutted you like a chicken."

Nearby, a church bell announced the start of early mass. Intent on intimacy, we barely listened. No wounded rose of dark guilty poetry here. For me, for us, it was three changes of the Moon now. Love drunk deep, now in the bone forever. Swift showers of summer, that brought a delicate green to land seared by a lifetime's drought. Our flesh, our minds, our emotions, our spirits, trying to grow together as the tiger-stripes of dawn brightened across us. We should be joined at the root, like Siamese twins. We had been joined in spirit since birth, since many lifetimes. I was sure, in that moment, that we had ridden those hills together many times. But I was still unable to speak my wish for union, or even the simple words of love. He didn't say them either.

In the modern bathroom, with glistening chrome and smell of French soap, we washed with blissful care. After our wild unsanitary grapplings in the mountains, it was amazing to have these comforts. Then we collapsed back onto the bed. Hungry for a cigarette now, he lit one, had a couple of drags, gave it to me. We smoked drowsily, listening to the church bells.

"I suppose," he murmured, "that José and Sera had theirs in the car somewhere... before José took her home."

"No doubt."

"Tell me. What does a woman's...you know...look like?"

"Delicate, like it's carved from live coral."

"You talk like it's beautiful."

"It is."

He got up on one elbow. "Really?" His tone was ironic.

"I went there like I'd go to the Prado to see Goya's paintings. But a museum is never a home, my friend."

Why were we still avoiding the declarations?

We fell asleep. I had a bizarre dream — José and Sera making love on a vast baroque bed, amidst a great blaze of candelabra and silken curtains and bedsheets. José was wearing her leather chaps and a magnificent dildo strapped onto her hips. It was alive-looking, pointed like a bull's pizzle. Sera had a thin red cord tied around her waist. They didn't seem to have a care in the world, laughing and giggling. Now and then they sipped from a golden chalice on a table by the bed, and nibbled bread from a golden tray. The dishes stayed full no matter how often the women partook. Watching them in grim silence were ranks of fire it archbishops. One archbishop took the dishes off the table and held them out to me — they were empty now, scratched and dented. I threw them at the old man, and he ran. José screamed with laughter and ran after him. Pulling up his vestments off his skinny butt, my sister rammed the dildo into him, and made him roll up his eyes with ecstasy, like some dewy-eyed saint in El Greco. Reappearing again, the chalice and tray had food on them again. I kept trying to get there to eat. Through a window I could see a landscape where all the wheatfields and orchards of Spain were spread like heart's desires along the edge of forever. The blue sky was shimmering with laughter, louder, louder.

Suddenly I woke with a start. Something felt wrong. Zebra stripes of midday glare lay across us, like bars, through the closed shutters. The room was so stifling hot that I could hardly breathe. The roar of midday traffic hung in the hazy sky over the capital — a dome of luminous industrial sound.

My bad feeling must have been a dream. We were still in a clean room with a locked door, my own room, both of us soaked in sweat.

Juan was beside me, flung on his back with a child's openness. My almost-fiancé, my almost-bridegroom. He had come so close to saying the fatal words, and now he was asleep.

As he breathed, his body glistened, like a rainy mountainside. His navel moved gently, with sweat pooled in it. His wet hair was separated into strands. His eyelashes were stuck to his wet cheeks. Hair in his armpits was flattened like bracken ferns by a hard rain. Stubble on his jaws made his face look thinner, and poignantly sexier. Rosy bruises of my love-bites suffused his neck and stomach. His nipples looked red-tender and well-sucked as the udder of a wild doe. One knee was raised, revealing his closed virginal buttocks, with a drop of richer sweat creeping down his crack. His organs slumped heavy across one thigh, glistening with sweat. The moisture caught glare from the shutters and glowed into a thousand rainbow colors.

I reached to turn on the fan. Its sound and cool breeze woke him. He drew a deep sigh, stretched and flexed luxuriously against me. Our arms slid around each other in the most tender, vulnerable moment we'd had. Our bellies, pressed together, were growling as one with hunger pangs. We looked in each other's eyes. I smoothed the touseled hair off his forehead, summoning courage for words.

"I want to lock up the breezes," I murmured, "so they can't touch anyone's face but yours."

His hand slid sleepily down to caress my hip. "Jealous, always jealous," he teased.

Was this the closest we were going to get? Why wouldn't he say the real words? Why wouldn't I say them?

Suddenly the telephone rang.

Shattered by the sound, we both jumped. Was it José? Two rings and a hang-up? No. It went on to a fourth, a fifth ring. Who could it be? The ringing went on and on, with an ominous insistence. Was it Mamá, demanding to know if we'd had a nice evening? Isaías, with news of a new contract? He might have called Las Moreras, and learned I was in town. Was it Paco?

"Are you going to answer it?" Juan whispered.

"No."

Finally the ringing stopped. But our spell was broken. Juan looked at his new watch. "Jesus, it's two in the afternoon."

"Is it?" I yawned.

"I never slept this late in my whole life."

While he showered, I lolled on the rumpled sheets a few more minutes. The bed looked like two wild boars had mated in it. And we were starved. Chinese food does not go as far as white beans with bacon. The refrigerator was empty. Downstairs, Isaías and Tere had heartlessly taken every scrap of food with them. Their cupboards revealed instant coffee and uncooked pasta.

"I'll go get us some churros," Juan said, toweling off, "while you clean up."

"Good idea." I headed for the shower.

Onto his damp body, Juan pulled the familiar slacks and silk jersey that he'd bought in Santander. He stuffed a 100-peseta note in his pocket with the casualness of a rich man. Before he headed for the door, he reached in the shower and cupped my wet chin in his hand. The last thing I saw, as he threw me a grin over his shoulder, was a flash from those deep blue eyes. The door slammed.

The last, of how life had been.

_____

perra — "bitch," meaning female dog. Spanish slang for the smallest denomination of Spanish coins, made of tin, valued at one tenth of a peseta.

13

Alone, I took a long shower, noticing how strong my body felt. All the walking, riding, hard work was healing me. For the first time in my life, it felt like my hunger for sex and love might someday be satisfied. Regretfully I washed the traces of love from my skin. With a towel around me, I put clean sheets on the bed and threw the old ones and the towels into the new washing machine.

Then I made two cups of instant coffee. He'd be back any minute. In a while, we'd go join the two women, find our favorite café, get some real food and an espresso with milk. My mind moved ahead, towards the Arles contract. Back to hard training tomorrow. In a week, my retinue would depart for France.

When Juan wasn't back in half an hour, I started to pace. The churro shop was just down the street. What was taking him so long? Had he met someone he knew from up north? A man who was interested in him? Had he run into Rafael, or a Lin who'd lost weight? It was amazing how fiercely jealousy flared up after such a night of abandon and tenderness and harmony. Next, the thought crossed my mind that he could have run into some random political thing in the street, a demonstration or scuffle of some kind. He and a few other bystanders might have been arrested by mistake. These things happened.

When an hour passed, then an hour and a half, my stomach began to quake deep inside.

Just then, sensing my distress from afar, José called on the telephone. I knew it was her because of the code: two rings and a hang-up,

202

then ringing back. She had almost given up on hearing from us. She was about to go join Sera and her mamá for coffee.

My sister and I talked guardedly, always concerned about the *moderno* spy equipment. Into her voice, she injected tones that were proper for a young woman worried about her fiancé.

"My god," she said, "maybe he got hit by a car. I've seen him cross streets like a soccer player, dodging cars..."

"Yes, maybe."

"I'll come right over."

If Juan was in danger, then so were José and Sera. Frantic moves on our part might give the two women away.

"No need," I said, trying to sound casual. "It might be nothing. I'll go out and look around. If there's been an accident or something, I'll call you right back."

Quickly I got dressed. My intuition about spy scrutiny was swelling to a horrifying certainty. A pistol — too bad I didn't have one. Only sporting guns were allowed, and only to certain safe civilians in this country of God. Of course, a pistol was little use against police rifles and batons. Going down in the elevator, I felt my stomach vibrating like it did when the first bull was about to burst into the ring. The feeling was a certainty. *They* — whoever they were — were waiting for me somewhere out there. *They* had been watching us in ways we hadn't suspected. Somehow we'd given ourselves away.

"Good afternoon, Don Antonio," said the concierge, getting on at the 8th floor. He was carrying a cage with an African parrot belonging to an elderly shut-in lady on that floor. As I left the building, the concierge was peacefully hanging the cage in the shaded courtyard, to give the parrot some air.

Outside, as I walked along the street, a strange black Mercedes sedan, a 1950s model, quietly pulled up beside me. My stomach clenched. This was it. Four men were in the car — enforcer types in dark suits. The back door opened for me. There was nothing to do but get in. It was the only way I'd find Juan. One of them pushed me forward, and a blindfold was roughly tied around my head.

When they jerked the blindfold off again, I was in a small untidy office. Its rough windowless stone walls gave it the look of a cellar room in some old mansion.

Sitting opposite me, at an old metal office desk, was a wiry silver-haired man. With his dark old-fashioned suit and fedora, he looked like some hardened small-time flamenco guitarist who had grown up in a sun-fried village near Cádiz and now worked Madrid clubs. Except this "musician" was wearing a black leather mask. Through the eye-slits in it, his cold grey eyes glinted. His sensual red lips, showing below the mask, gave me a horribly uneasy feeling. So did the pile of papers in front of him — two neat piles, as if one was work completed. I saw long lists of names and addresses, and files with people's names on them.

This "guitarist" was somebody's henchman — a real *sicario*.

"Good day, Your Grace," El Sicario said with an Andalucian accent. "My apologies for the inconvenience."

"Who are you?" I demanded.

"It doesn't matter who I am. Come with me."

El Sicario and two masked enforcers took my arms and marched me along an echoing corridor lined with several little storage-room offices. Inside, a few masked clerks worked under tiny lamps, amid bulging file cabinets. My stomach and skin shivered violently with apprehension. Then we went down a narrow stone stairway, into a lower level that might have been an old wine cellar. From somewhere ahead came a faint sound, something between a shout and a groan.

We entered a vaulted windowless room of stone, with a flagstone floor. Modern electric wires snaked in from the corridor — the work of some imaginative electrician. A glaring bulb lit a few wooden chairs, and a long narrow table with a scarred marble slab on it. It was the kind of cheap whitish marble used in Spain for old-fashioned kitchen counters. The table was bolted to the floor, with thick leather straps dangling along it. It smelled very bad in there — like a combination of privy and butcher shop. Instinctively, I knew why.

Beside the table, bathed in the harsh light, two more enforcer types were holding Juan between them. He gave me a wild look, then dropped his head and stared at the floor, trembling. His fine clothes were torn and dirty, and he was barefoot. Evidently he'd resisted violently — face and bare arms showed scrapes and bruises. On each of his wrists and ankles, they had put an iron shackle and a trailing chain. His watch was gone.

"We regret that you have been so stubborn," said the masked Sicario.

"Who is 'we'?" I said. My knees were almost folding beneath me. "Only cowards talk behind masks."

"Every impertinence will cost you," said El Sicario calmly. "Yes...look well at what you have caused."

"What do you want?" I demanded.

The masked one turned to the enforcers. Someone seized me by the hair, so I couldn't turn my head away.

"Strip the prisoner," El Sicario ordered.

Once I had seen a fine stallion go crazy in a horse trailer, because he was unaccustomed to modern transport. The poor animal thrashed and struggled so pitifully — breaking legs, knocking its own eyes out — that the owner was obliged to go find his hunting shotgun and blast his prize to death right there in the vehicle. Such an animal struggle was what I saw now. Juan's eyes had gone mad with outraged modesty. Heedless, he dashed himself against walls and furniture. The men might as well have put their hands on a wild buffalo — they could hardly hold his animal panic in place. When I made an instinctive lunge to help him, the two enforcers jammed me against the wall. A searing pain snaked through nerves in the old cornada — the first pain I'd felt in weeks.

Finally they had Juan twisted against the table, levering him in place with the shackles. In the silence, everyone's panting echoed in the room, as they ripped off his expensive silk pull-over. Then they yanked down his tailor-made trousers. Buttons rolled on the floor. Juan was left in nothing but his undershorts. A trickle of blood crawled down his trembling thigh.

El Sicario walked toward the victim. His eyes were on the rosy hickeys that my love-bites had left on Juan's neck and breasts.

"The woman who bit you so passionately," El Sicario purred, "you must tell me her name."

He put out his lean carbuncular hand, definitely not a guitar-player's hand, to touch Juan's chest.

With a rattle of chains, Juan tried to shake his hand off. "Don't touch me, you filth," he said in a stifled voice.

"Let him be!" I said. "Any fault here is mine!"

El Sicario turned away and gave crisp orders to his crew.

"Call the doctor down here. We must give this man a thorough examination. I wonder what other little signs of passion were left on his person by this mysterious...woman."

While one flunky went to the phone, the second put out a rude hand, grasping my friend's underwear, and attempted to tear it off him with a violent jerk. Chest heaving, Juan uttered a groan of despair and lashed out with one shackled foot like a mule, nearly dislocating the man's knee.

"Queer dogs," one of the flunkies panted. "We'll teach them to fuck like Christians."

Rage surged in me — the wildness against the iron. This was a tyrant opera, every stagey move scripted in advance, designed to crush both of us, little by little, into shivering submissive pulp. Next I would be forced to watch the rough examination of that virgin orifice into which I had wanted to invest all the love and tenderness that a human being could feel.   Ironically, there would be nothing for them to find.   But in looking for evidence, they would violate him unspeakably.   Sweat poured down my face.

"Talk to me!" I shouted at El Sicario.   Through the ringing in my eyes, my voice sounded far away.   "What do your masters want from me?"

The words had a magical effect — they let Juan go.   T h e n those fingers in my hair relaxed their grip.

Trembling violently, my poor friend held the rags of his underwear over his modesty with one hand.   Picking his half-ruined trousers off the floor with the other, he almost fell, then went to his nerveless knees with a rattle of shackles.   Finally he swayed to his feet, and leaned against the table, trying to get one shackled foot into a trouser leg.   The pants were backwards, so he fumbled to turn them around.   His thighs had gone rough with gooseflesh.

El Sicario and a flunky marched me out of the room.

Seeing me taken away, Juan must have felt the blackest despair. "Antonioooo!" he shouted out behind us, voice breaking.   He lunged after me with an awful rasp of chains, before they grabbed him and dragged him back along the stone floor.

"I'll get you out of here!" I yelled over my shoulder.

The henchmen propelled me back up the narrow stairway.   My own knees would hardly work at all.   No bull that I ever faced , not even the most terrible Tulio with horns like cathedral candlesticks, had made my limbs totter like this.

Merciless hands pushed me into an empty ballroom. Juan's shout of despair still thundered so hard in my ears that the long room seemed to be jarred by waves of sound.   Yet it was silent. The dry air reeked of musty fabric and summer heat.   One long wall was covered with fraying yellow brocade, with an endless row of gilt armchairs parked along it. Above, an endless row of gilt mirrors reflected the tall windows opposite, with their faded silk swags and weathered shutters that were locked shut but still leaked furnace air into the room.   A worn Royal Factory rug stretched endlessly away from my feet to the far wall.

There, under a titanic portrait of Philip II by some second-rate painter, a man's dark figure sat stooped at a long ormolu table cluttered with papers.   In the moldy silence, the man's typewriter tapped.

As I tottered toward the table, my leg twinged with pain.   I willed my leg to work. *One foot in front of the other.*   A little energy flowed back into me.

Where was I?   Still in Madrid, judging by the familiar traffic noise outside. But not in a prison or police building. Possibly somewhere in the old quarter, in one of those many rundown little palaces that had survived the capital's frenzy of modern apartment construction. It was the kind of minor residence that a cash-needy heir would sell to a financier or diplomat. The new owner would hire an architect and a decorator, and fix it all up, and move in with his happy family. But now and then, he and his wife and children would jump awake at night, sure they'd heard screams coming from the vaults underground. Because right now this building was apparently being used as a Black House. Juan and I had fallen into the hands of a Black Squad.

With my act of will, came a rush of adrenalin.

The man raised his head from his typewriter. Not surprisingly, it was Paco.

My brother was wearing a white shirt and loosened tie and his glasses, and looked for all the world like a graduate student at Madrid University working on a paper. An electric fan ruffled the papers. Nearby, a radio was playing something by Manuel de Falla — Paco's favorite composer because of Falla's fascist sympathies. Beside the papers, lay an item that few students would own. It was a German Luger automatic pistol, with the barrel pointed at me.

Paco gazed at me mildly.

"Man," he said, sounding like we were having lunch again. "Sit down." His slender hand indicated a frayed needlepoint French chair that sat in front of the desk. "Can I offer you something? A brandy to brace you, perhaps?"

The rage towered in me. Rage that Juan and I had each been handled so differently. That the aristocrat was kept clothed, and allowed to sit, while the peasant was stripped naked and his legs spread. I walked straight up to the desk.

Hastily my brother grabbed the pistol and aimed it inexpertly at my stomach. His bad eyesight had exempted him from military service.

"You pig," I said with icy force. "Why are you doing this to an innocent kid?"

Paco tossed a file at me with his free hand. JUAN DIANO RODRíGUEZ, it was lettered.

"Not so innocent," he said.

Leafing through it shakily, I saw copies of police and investigator documents. Paco had carried out his threat. There was the predictable report on Juan's village reputation as an "odd boy — not effeminate, but not interested in women". Alleged "perversions" practiced in the seminary with other young men — the reason for his dismissal, according to his confessor, who had been interviewed extensively. More serious was a report on Juan's "suspicious friendships" with Spanish Protestants and minor figures in the Basque liberation movement who were being sought by the state police. Among them was mention of one Rafael Iguarte, suspected of ETA membership, now known to be in West Germany.

"You aren't so innocent either," said Paco. "I know about your crimes."

"Why don't you have me examined, eh? Have your doctor take a good long look up my *culo?*"

Paco's face went dark, at my hint that the aristocrat would allow the peasant to have him.

"That won't be necessary," he said coldly. "We already know enough."

I tossed the folder back at Paco. Pages flew out of it, and whirled in the breeze from the fan. Had Juan lied to me about old "friendships" because he feared my jealousy? Or was this file fabricated to frame him?

"These are trumped-up charges," I snapped. "Do what you want with me. But let him go."

Paco chuckled.

"Ahhh…how noble you're pretending to be," he said. He got up, holding the pistol. "But where is the nobility in this animal filth where you wallow with him?"

I met my brother's eyes, understanding that the moment to step out of the feudal shadow had finally come.

"Love is noble," I said.

"Love? You dare to use that word for your vice?"

"I love him."

How was it possible that I'd said the words to Paco, and not to Juan? Paco stared at me, as if this was the last thing he'd expected me to say. Somewhere nearby, in the shimmer of hot street sounds, a church bell was ringing for the last mass of the day. Then a strange growling sound came up in my brother's throat, and he brought his fist down on the desk with a crash.

"You speak of this slave animal," he roared in a voice I'd never heard him use, "the way you ought to speak of your wife!"

His voice echoed loudly in the room, ricocheting along the mirrors. Letting him be the one to lose control, I kept speaking in an even voice.

"I have the right to love as I choose," I said.

"We say what your rights are."

"Who is we? Are you the CYS?"

"Who we are, doesn't matter. King…no king…it doesn't matter.

Who knows what will happen when Franco dies? We are committed to act no matter who governs the country. Our interest is the public moral — the sacred law. What is the life of one Red queer, weighed in the balance against the laws of Our Lord and the destiny of our family?"

"What do you want from me?"

Paco strolled around the room, playing with the pistol.

"I am more modern than you think," he said.

"Convince me," I said.

"If these were the old days, you would get the severest punish-ment. Blooded traitors like you, who betrayed the patient work of generations, were shown no mercy. Surely you know how Edward II of England, the queer king, was impaled with a hot iron. Frederick the Great, the queer emperor, whose father forced him to watch the execu-tion of his comrade in vice. Our own disgraced Count of Villamediana, who paid for his vice with his life. As for your Juan, he would have been hung by the feet with his balls tied around his neck, and burned. But...yes, I will be modern and compassionate. Do you know why?"

I was silent.

Paco paced back and forth, still holding the gun on me waver-ingly. Finally he said: "Because there is more value in reforming you than killing you."

My burning eyes followed Paco around the room.

My brother stood at one of the closed shutters, listening. Out-side, in the palace courtyard, a car door slammed, an engine started and died. Suddenly I knew they had Juan in that car, chained hand and foot. Frenzied, I went to plunge at the window. But Paco pointed the pistol at me and warned me back.

"He will never see you again," my brother said.

I hovered, immobile in agony, eyes fixed on the window, listening to the car engine below. Even terrorists had their mechanical problems. The car wouldn't start.

"From now on, your life will be regulated by his welfare," Paco said. "You will fulfill exactly, to the letter, the destiny that I lay out for you. You will be a model husband, an exemplary father, a shining states-man, a true noble. A perfect servant of our government."

Unable to believe what I was hearing, I whispered:

"Paco, are you insane? The time is over when thugs like you can run our country. Can't you feel the people's change of heart? Don't you see them staying away from church? Five hundred years of insanity. .a war in which half the country killed the other half...and you still think the old tricks work?"

It was as if my brother hadn't heard. He strolled around the room, leisurely, like a professor giving a lecture.

"Juan Diano will spend the rest of his life in our custody," he continued implacably. "If you cooperate, he will be cared for. He hasn't been hurt...yet. He will be kept in a secure place, far from you. He'll be allowed to believe that you gave him up...abandoned him. Needless to say, we will make every effort to prevent his suicide. After all, suicide is a grave sin. We cannot be party to a suicide. But for every disobedience of yours, he will suffer. Cause and effect, as St. Thomas Aquinas taught. You will be taken to where he is kept, and you will watch it done to him. He will not see you, but you will see him. A little thing — and he loses a fingerjoint. A big one, and we take a testicle. Or a foot. Or a hand. You will watch. Even if you close your eyes, you will still hear him scream and cry."

Appalled, I pressed my face against the closed shutter, hearing the car finally start. It left the patio and lost itself in traffic.

"You will begin your reform," Paco's voice went on behind me, "by taking a long retreat. I have arranged one for you, with some priests I trust. You will return to the religion of your fathers. Confess....do penance....be guided by their advice."

Was this the age-old way that the Blues had managed dissent in the family? It wasn't conceivable that Paco had learned this from my father, who had always been more humane. Perhaps from some bloodthirsty uncle?

Paco drew the curtain across the shutters, darkening the room a little, and went on.

"I will cover your tracks. I have no interest in letting this scandal be known. Mamá, Tita, Sera...even Josefina, damn her...they must never know. It's not fit for our women to hear about. Your contract in Arles will be cancelled. You will speak to Isaías, and explain about your exhaustion, your spiritual needs. He and Tere will suspect nothing. He will announce your retirement for health reasons. When we think you are ready, the marriage with Sera will take place. You will never breathe a word to her, or Juan will suffer."

"How will you explain Juan's disappearance, you fool?" I burst out. "He has become very visible. He can't just disappear."

"*You* will explain it," Paco retorted. "Tell people that his family had problems. That he went home to Santander...to Germany. No one gives a fig about a peasant's whereabouts. He'll be forgotten in a month."

"José won't forget! This is her fiancé!"

Paco laughed coldly.

"Yes, she will. I know José. She'll be furious at him for running off and leaving her. You are a monster, really...putting horns on your sister. If I weren't so modern and compassionate, I would blow your brains out."

Did Paco know about José? About the two women's liaison? My imagination saw the two women being brutalized in that vaulted room. I had heard all the stories, how lesbian women were raped in hopes they'd become interested in men. Surely they would both be treated with the modicum of respect that I was getting. Paco wouldn't have the leverage with them, because they were both upper class. Going by everything Paco said, he didn't know. Possibly his overheated moral imagination had not gotten white-hot enough to see José's fact, or our little conspiracy. *Lady of Mercies,* I was shouting at the Virgin inside my mind — *please, I beg You, spread Your mantle of protection over my two women.*

As the rage hit me, it was cold, and clear, and rational. True rage is beyond emotion. It is a thing of mine. Never did I think so strategically, as when I was raging and *bravo* in the ring. This way, I could move as close to the horn as I dared. Now the rage surged forward, calculating some way out of this situation.

"Paco," I said, "wake up. No one can do what you're asking me to do."

"You're wrong," he said briskly. "People have performed such feats of sacrifice for centuries."

"Those people didn't live in front of photographers and TV cameras like we do now," I said. "They lived hidden behind castle walls. The whole country will see my look of a broken heart. They'll know I am living a lie."

"Nothing you can do or say will alter my course."

With an air of finality, Paco sat down at his desk, and gathered his mess of papers into a neat stack. Something in the way he said this got my attention. Was he inviting me to ask if something might conceivably alter his course? Feeling the heat through the shutters, I thought about it quickly.

Then I knew what I had to do. It was a radical, and final, act. But any delay would risk my friend's life.

"I'll trade with you," I said.

Paco looked at me coldly, and stood up.

"What?" he asked.

"The title," I said. "I will abdicate in your favor. The house in Toledo, the land, the olive business — I will sign a quitclaim to you."

Paco's expression told me that I caught him by surprise. Or had I? Was this whole maneuver really about the inheritance, not about Juan? Paco had told me more than once that I'd never deserved my father's love or the inheritance. Was Juan being held for this ultimate ransom? By the slight shift of my brother's eyes, and the feeling around him, I could tell that Paco was interested in my offer. So I talked passionately, caping with words.

"*You* be the perfect servant. *You* be the statesman. No one will be more convincing than you. *Your* son will be the next Count of La Mora. And you'll be rich, Paco. Not the penniless professor that you are."

"And the *coto?*" he asked.

I had a split second to think about it. The lives of animals, the villagers' jobs, put in the balance against Juan's life.

"Only if you agree to continue the work there," I said.

"And let you go unscathed?" he protested. "Never."

"I will throw in one more thing," I said, "if you release Juan unharmed."

"You are a low-life gypsy horse-trader."

"I'll give you the Crypt of the Mercies."

Now Paco was truly surprised — more surprised than I had ever seen him. Slowly he sat down at the desk again, and stared at the stack of papers, which doubtless carried the destinies of other helpless victims of this organization.

"So you do know where the Mercies is!" he growled.

"I've known for many years."

"Liar! Ungodly deceiver!"

I was trembling violently, but plunged on.

"The Mercies is beautiful, Paco," I said. "It will take your breath away. It will fulfill all your dreams. To get the Mercies, you will give me Juan Diano unharmed. Not a scratch. He and I will go into exile and disappear."

Paco frowned, looking at the floor.

"And José?" he asked.

"She doesn't know," I said, daring to lie. "I was the only one who was told, as the heir. That's the way it has always been."

Hopefully Paco's reluctance to discuss my "vice" with José would keep him from asking her about the Mercies.

"Well," Paco said, "I don't have to spare your slave animal to find out where it is. One night with our pain technicians, and you will tell us everything."

"If you do that to me, how can you parade me in your wonderful new Spain?"

He was silent.

"Wouldn't you be more satisfied," I went on, "if I *gave* the Crypt of the Mercies to you? Isn't that a greater victory?"

His back was turned. He was pondering. I could feel the power of my lure.

"Think of it, Paco," I pressed on. *"You* can be the Escudero who gives this treasure back to Spain. Your boss will be astounded. What the hell...you might get his job because of this. You will be remembered for the Mercies. Nobody remembers the courtiers of Fernando and Isabella. But what Spaniard doesn't know the name of Professor Sautuola, who found the Cave of Altamira?"

Now Paco was shaking his head.

"No. No," he cried. "You're bluffing. You tempt me! Like the devil tempted our Lord!"

"I may be Satan," I said drily. "But you are no Jesus."

"Shut up with your insolence! What proof can you give me, that you know where the Mercies is?"

My mind leaped to think what I could show him without giving away the location.

"Tomorrow I can bring you proof," I said.

"Juan will feel his first pain if you lie to me."

"I wouldn't risk Juan's life by lying."

"What kind of proof?"

"Photographs of the Mercies," I said.

"Photos can be faked."

"If the Ministry of Culture has their experts look at them, they will know they are looking at a new national treasure. For the skeptics, I have a piece of fresco. It fell off recently. The walls are deteriorating You can have it chemically analyzed."

"Then," Paco commanded, "tomorrow you will bring me the proof."

"Not so fast. There's more." My mind raced methodically, calculating moves, the way I had to calculate with the bull.

"What?" he barked, irritated.

"In one week, is the last contract in Arles. The timing is good. I quietly leave Spain with the shirt on my back, and go to my contract. I'll tell people I am vacationing abroad for a while. I've done it before...no one will suspect anything. You will bring Juan to me in France. Make sure he has his ID and a passport. We make the exchange in France."

My lips were trembling — I could hardly speak. I didn't trust Paco to make the exchange in Spain. France was a safer choice. After World War II, France had given shelter to political refugees from Spain. I wanted gendarmes around if I needed them. Paco had to know that.

I went on: "When Juan is free, and tells me he is all right, I will give you the legal papers and directions to the Mercies. But only then.

No tricks, Paco. If you fuck with me, I will kill you."

"Futile threats, from a man in chains."

"If it takes me 20 years, or another lifetime, I will come back and tear your heart out with my bare hands."

Paco's response was a haughty smirk.

"Bring me the proof tomorrow morning at Mamá's library," he repeated. "Mamá and Tita will be in Madrid shopping for the wedding. We'll have the place to ourselves. When I've seen your proof, we'll consider your proposal."

I drew myself up as straight as I could.

"There isn't much time," I said. "Less than one week to arrange all this. Today is Sunday. Next Saturday I leave for Arles. The bullfight is next Sunday."

"You are in no position to make demands," he hissed at me. "And I trust you will mention this to no one. Not José, not Isaías, not anyone. No one can help you. It would be easy for us to turn Juan's file over to the secret police. You know how our Generalísimo feels about queers. Serious political charges could result. The firing squad. Or the garrotte, if we can make it ugly enough for him."

Paco summoned two enforcers into the room. They blindfolded me again.

When the car stopped, I was pushed out. By the time I got the blindfold off, the car had turned the corner and vanished quietly into traffic. I was in a narrow, deserted alley near Isaías' building.

At her own apartment, José would be hunched at her Olivetti portable, trying nervously to write a column. Balls of scrunched paper would litter the table, showing that she was worrying about Juan and me. Sera, suspecting nothing, was probably reading a book at her mother's house.

At all costs, I had to protect the two women's secret, if I still could. To find not one but two "traitors" in the family would be a shock that might drive Paco deeper into unreasoning action. If Paco didn't know about José and Sera, there was a chance for the two women to get out of Spain too. In spite of Paco's caution not to talk to them, I had to warn José. But at this point, I could not underestimate how closely we were being watched.

Would my sister and her friend choose exile with me...that lonely road that so many Spaniards had walked?

14

Back in Isaías' apartment, I called my sister. My hand was shaking so much, I could hardly dial the number. If the phones were tapped, Paco's colleagues knew I'd already talked to her about Juan's disappearance. In the heartiest voice I could manage, I told her:

"Juan showed up."

"Thank God! What happened?"

"News from home. Family problems. Something about the land that the family left behind. He's catching the night train to Santander. He said to give you his love and not to worry. He'll be in touch from there."

José knew the intensity of Juan's estrangement from his family. She also knew my voice. In spite of my efforts, there was something in it that my twin, and only my twin among all other human beings, would feel through the wires.

"'Tonio, are you coming down with catarrh?"

"Too much high life. I'll see you… when?"

"Wednesday. You have a dinner with your Madrid fan club, remember? They invited me."

In my panic I'd forgotten about the dinner. "Thanks for reminding me."

All the way out to Las Moreras, my mind was whirling. Who were those people at the Black House? Was Paco running the group himself? If so, how did he have the means? If not, who were his bosses?

The imagined scene came surging at me, clear as a painted mural, sharp as hallucination, out of that vaulted room now seared into my memory.

The two men were using the ankle shackles to wrest his legs apart. Juan was heaving with trembling breaths. Every tendon and muscle was vibrating with terror. His genitals shrank back into his pubic hair. The skin of his spread ass was goose-pimpled and streaked with the thin yellow feces of fear. The shit of death is runny because fright boils electrolytes out of the bloodstream into the intestines. I'd learned that from years of watching cattle die. The doctor looked down at him — elderly, stoop-shouldered, wearing rubber gloves, carrying a doctor's bag. He was all business. As the flunkies watched avidly, with their pants revealing hard-ons gotten in the name of God, the doctor took out a steel speculum and a bright little medical flashlight.

Shaking the thought away, I found myself driving that familiar potholed little highway through the Montes de Toledo.

When I got to the stretch of road where Juan had sat down to cry among the olive trees, I stopped the car and got out in the simmering heat. Finding the tree where Juan and I had talked, I leaned into its warm sunlit crotch, remembering how innocent and simple everything had looked that day. My lips glued themselves to the tree trunk. "Forgive me for not saying it before."

But how could I be forgiven? Who would forgive me? Juan? Would there be enough mercy in the Lady of Mercies for me?

The light green foliage hissed in a hot rising breeze, heavy with fruit. I would not see those olives harvested.

At Las Moreras, all the familiar things — pump purring in the well, four dogs trying to kiss me, Marimarta's voice — had suddenly turned into strange and melancholy objects in a landscape by Salvador Dalí. Braulio was talking on the downstairs phone, in a curiously quiet voice. He turned, startled at seeing me. Instantly his manner had my suspicions going.

"Antonio, you're back early," he said.

"Yes," I said. "Is the call for me?"

He hesitated just a moment before replying. "Valet stuff. Nothing you need to worry about."

Was he talking to Paco?

For a while, I kneeled in the chapel, in front of Our Lady of Mercies. But no longer than usual, and lighting only the usual number of candles. As I stared at Her image, She seemed to stand free, as if three-dimensional. Murals from my imagination's underground room loomed at me again. A shotgun barrel was shoved into his body, pumped in and out. Juan stiffened with each thrust. Raucous laughter burst out around us — honks and snorts of glee. *"Ayyy,"* said the man holding the shotgun, "my trigger finger might slip."

"The Count of La Mora shouldn't see this," said somebody. "It will upset the poor gentleman."

So a hood was pulled over my head. Half suffocating in the dark, I had to listen as Juan's groans quickened their pace. "Ay, Jesus and Mary," yelped the man with the gun, "I'm going to shoot."

"Shooot!" they cheered him. "Shooot!"

The gun roared. In the vaulted space, that sound was so shattering that my innards exploded with shock. Blackness yawned — I felt myself going down into it. Somehow I was on my knees, ears ringing. Then the hood was yanked off. They held me up, and made me look. Surely he was dead, laying there on the puddled table with his body blown apart. But no. The gunman had fired against the wall, blowing a rat-hole in the stone. They howled with laughter at their big joke.

Why wouldn't they do that to him? They had done it to Lorca. To other people, in other times, in other countries, it had been done, and done, and done. Terrorist education places the images inside a child's mind. For the rest of our lives, the images are activated by the slightest mishap. I found I was tuned into a vast, smoky, quivering collective mind of faggots through the centuries, like some invisible TV broadcast that I was fighting to turn off.

Braulio would have to go. I still wasn't sure whether he was involved. But I didn't want him on the Arles trip. In any case, it was time to start dismissing my crew. I didn't need picadors in Arles. Only Manolillo and Bigotes would be needed.

Braulio met me at the chapel door. It was 11 p.m. "Is there anything before I retire?" he asked.

"No thank you, Braulio," I said. "But we need to talk."

In the patio, I offered him a brandy and we sat. This would have to be handled delicately, so I was polite and kind.

"After Arles, I am retiring," I said.

"I've heard rumors," he nodded.

"No doubt you've seen it coming for a while," I said. "Hopefully you've already been inquiring for a new position. If you haven't, maybe Isaías can help you find something. I'll write you a letter of recommendation. It will express my appreciation for your many years of devoted service."

Braulio's chiseled mahogany face was somber, eyes on the floor. Was he embarrassed at whatever part he'd played in this ugly affair? Had he played a part at all?

"It has been an honor to spend these years with you," he said in a toneless voice.

"After Arles, I am taking a long rest. My life needs to be simple for a while. I'll have no need for a valet. Please pack a couple of suitcases for me — basic necessities. I can send for more things as I need them."

At some point during the next few days, he'd realize he wasn't going to Arles with me. I didn't need him. Isaías could help me dress for the ring.

As we got to our feet, Braulio suddenly said:

"By the way, the *señorita* Serafita called. And don't forget the dinner with your fan club in Madrid."

For much of the night, I tossed and turned. Juan was walking away down the highway, growing smaller and smaller in the wavering mirages of heat. If I had let him keep walking, he wouldn't be wearing shackles now.

Suddenly torches blazed everywhere. I was the seated majestic figure in a giant float, in the midst of a Holy Week procession. The float moved slow as a barge, with a rocking jerking rhythm, borne on the naked sweaty backs of hundreds of men. Over my head, an ornate silk canopy swayed. Banks of blazing candles and flowers pressed around me. The cloying reek of lilies and tuberoses and hot beeswax, and clouds of incense drifting past, made me nauseous.

I was encased in a white satin suit of lights that blazed with diamonds —it was so tight I could hardly breathe. Draped around me was an immense torero's parade cape, unutterably heavy, fantastically embroidered, crusted with gems and candle-drippings. Across my lap, Juan lay naked on his back. His head was pillowed against the breast of my jacket, and his legs trailed down into the cape. He was not idealized, like some handsome Christ carved by a devout sculptor. Instead, he was real — every hair, every childhood freckle, the knife scars on his arm — I could even smell his smell of crushed ferns and milk. But he was dead, of course. His body bore the marks of his passion — genitals cut away, blood still oozing between his buttocks. One limp hand trailed in the lilies.

The float moved slow as a glacier through a vast bio-mass of men in black suits, and women in their best. *"Guapo!"* they were shouting at me. "Handsome!" "Pray for us!" "Have mercy on us!" Faces glowed with sensual reverence. I tried to cry, but no tears came. Just cold diamonds that rained out of my eyes. The gems stuck to Juan's damp body till it too glittered in the fantastic light. The float seemed to be moving into a TV screen. Colors faded to black and white. The crowd was shouting in strange languages now. They were brandishing placards in

English, Russian, Chinese, Arabic. The suit of lights squeezed tighter around my chest. My lungs fought for air.

Surging out of the dream, I sat up in bed gasping for breath. Cold sweat drenched me. It was dawn. Outside the window grill, where Juan and I had tried to warm each other through the bars, birds were twittering quietly in the mulberry foliage, feeding on berries. Crawling out of bed, I threw open the shutters. After several minutes, the mulberry tree's coolness calmed me a little. Down among the farm buildings, somebody had just let out the chickens. Something frightened them and they scattered, flapping and squawking.

My mind was doing exactly what the terrorists wanted...panicking like those birds down there. I had to get myself in hand or Juan would die. Other people would die.

Walk. Push away one terrifying picture after another.

The next four days were spent in a strange isolation as I got ready for Arles.

Spain in the 1960s was a country where many things still happened at burro speed, even as jetliners sped across our land. Legal documents had to be prepared. I needed a lawyer. But Isaías and Tere would be angry if I interrupted their vacation. And I couldn't assume they would help me once they knew the truth. They might turn from me in disgust. I'd have to tell them when they met me in Arles, at the Hotel de la Sirene.

That Monday morning, I cancelled all appointments. The manila envelope containing the photos and piece of fresco came out of its hiding place. The negatives I returned to the cache. If Braulio had ever searched my room on any assignment as amateur spy, he had failed to find my cache.

At the Toledo house, Mamá and Tita were not at home. In the library, my brother spread out the photographs in the lamplight.

"Holy Mary," he said, in spite of himself. My brother was visibly shaken by what he saw.

Then, like a card player putting down his winning hand, I lay the piece of fresco in front of him.

"This fell off the north wall a few weeks ago," I said. "In that photo there, you can see the spot where it fell. Repair and restoration is badly needed. Maybe you can persuade the government to do it. They are restoring everything else in the country...why not this?"

Paco stared down at the beautiful painted eye. It was almost Egyptian in its elegance, gazing back at him implacably. My brother picked up the fragment gently, reverently, turning it over in his trembling fingers. He couldn't tear his gaze away from it. His face was radiant, eyes glistening with emotion. It was hard to believe that this appreciator of fine art was the same man who could order my friend to be butchered one limb at a time.

"I'll let you know what we decide," he said.

So he had superiors, or peers at least, to whom he had to answer.

"Time is flying," I reminded him. "You have five days till I leave for Arles. I am going to prepare the legal documents."

"How dare you dictate to me?"

"The bull season is ending. No more dates are available abroad, unless some colleague cancels and I'm asked to substitute. It's the best chance to handle this without the public noticing anything. If I have the papers ready, we can move fast."

Paco shoved the photos and fresco back in the envelope.

"With the *coto,* you'd be well advised to continue my project. Or you'll be another example of old aristocracy who don't care about land," I added.

"I'll advise you of our decision," he said curtly. "You haven't told José, I trust?"

"How could you think I would reveal this horrible thing to my sister?" I said.

"I suppose she is going to Arles."

"No, she isn't. Her boss is sending her to Barcelona, to cover Benítez, Litri and Camacho."

"You don't deserve your sister's loyalty."

I went to the door, then looked back at him. "Tell me this," I asked him. "How did you know about me and Juan?"

"I didn't," he said. "Not till you told me."

"I don't believe you," I said bitterly. "You must have spent millions of pesetas on investigators."

"Well," he said ponderingly, "for many years you did fool me. But the more liberal you got, the longer you fought with us about getting married, the more I wondered what the problem was. At first I didn't pay much attention to Juan. But that first day I walked in the *coto,* and ran into the two of you, there was a feeling around you. The suspicion crossed my mind then. When my men told me you were both finally spending the whole night in the same building, it seemed like the perfect moment to go fishing. To knock Juan around a little...see how you reacted."

I felt sick at how we'd both been taken in.

"And," Paco added, "there is history."

"What do you mean?"

"You should read those old books more carefully, dear brother. I believe that Sanches had his brother killed because Pedro was…like you."

Leaving the house, I stopped dead in the doorway as a hallucinatory picture flashed through my mind, like a waking dream. Juan was being walked into the courtyard of a prison. They had put old peasant clothes on him — baggy black trousers, rope sandals, a dingy white shirt with collar open. A low scaffold waited, draped in black cloth. Now it was surrounded by priests and army officers. He waved away the priest. They seated him there, with arms and legs bound. The iron collar of the garrotte was secured around his neck. Everyone craned their necks, to make sure they could see. As the priests intoned final prayers, the executioner began to crank the ratchet that tightened the band.

Walk. Walk.

Juan was choking, struggling, then convulsing helplessly. His face turned blue-black. The bloody tongue hung out, wagging grossly with a last twitch of life, like the bull's tongue in the sand.

Walk. Walk. Sacred Mother, help me walk.

Slamming the heavy oak door with its groaning hinges, I plunged into the glare and traffic of the narrow street.

In Madrid, it was almost siesta time. I found a public phone that worked and caught José at *ABC* just before she left for lunch. I had to talk to her. She went to someone else's phone. Paco's group might not have the resources to bug every phone in the *ABC* office. When she found an empty office and we were talking again, I told her the news, and what I planned to do.

She sucked in her breath. For the first time in my life, I could feel how frightened my twin was. The invisible energies in the air between us were screaming. Was I going to have a hysterical woman on my hands?

"Then Paco also knows about me and…" she quavered.

"I don't think he knows. In his wildest nightmares, he hasn't imagined that."

"Then, the Mercies…"

"My apologies for going ahead on that without talking to you first."

"No, no…you did the right thing." José was pulling herself together.

"You'd better be ready to dig your own toes in," I said.

"I know."

"It's a good thing you're not going to Arles. Paco might suspect that you'd flee with me."

"Unfortunately a certain person doesn't have a passport. But we'll think of something."

"I'll be staying at the Hotel de la Sirene in Arles, if you need to reach me. They mustn't know that either of you know."

"Let me worry about that. I'll see you at the dinner."

From there I went directly to Isaías' law office. It was closed for the month of August. His secretary Eva would be here on Friday to check mail and phone the Eibars about anything important. So I'd have several days to myself. After a terrible time finding a place to park, I let myself in with my key..

The office was an elegant clutter of heavy oak furniture, filing cabinets, oak shelves of law books. Around the oak clock ticking on the wall were the Eibars' "baby pictures" — photographs of torero clients, going back to novices of the 1940s that no one remembered. The two of them had fed two generations of hungry bullfighters, put them up for the night, bailed them out of countless scrapes. They'd even had a "daughter" or two — bullfighting girls on horseback. I paused before an old photo of me. The big afternoon when I cut a tail in Sevilla, April 1963 — the young hotshot passing a Domecq bull, satin pants riding high in my crack. Every man in the city must have had a hard-on for me that day.

Walk.

With the office door locked, and street noise shut out, I rifled through Tere's well-organized files for documents to use as models. Forcing my mind to tilt with legal windmills calmed me down a little.

Hours passed in this strange isolation, the clock ticking. As I scanned book pages, one case leaped up at me — the delicate subject of forcible dishonor. Suddenly my mind tried to stampede again. Deep in their most secret hearts, all men know that they are capable of sexual insanity — far more than women. Religious puritanism exists mostly to keep men in harness, with control of women only a secondary goal. Men rape and dirty each other even more willingly than they do women. Dishonoring a peer is a bigger victory and the victim is less likely than a woman to talk afterwards. Juan was being shoved into a crowded prison, the guards making sure the other prisoners knew of his nature. He would fight in self defense, inevitably he'd be overwhelmed...

No, no, Lady of my heart, I walk away from these thoughts.

My mind was getting stronger. Chain-smoking, turning pages, I sat at Isaías' monstrous black typewriter with its wide carriage, almost a museum piece, where his secretary had thumped out almost 250 contracts for me. With steady desperation, I typed with two fingers. For a man who had never done anything without the help of a secretary or a valet or a cook, I was doing reasonably well.

Suddenly the clock said 8:10 p.m. I was fainting with hunger. A phone call to the café down the block brought a waiter with a tray —

coffee, and brandy, and a couple of sandwiches made with mountain ham. I forced myself to eat. If I didn't take care of myself, I'd get killed in Arles. Then Paco's men would put a bullet into Juan's head, and they'd revile him first.

The phone rang a couple of times, but I didn't answer it.

Surging awake in the chair, I knocked over the brandy glass and broke it. It was after 10 p.m. I'd fallen asleep with my head on the typewriter. Exhausted, I went to my apartment. But the bed where I'd made love with Juan on Sunday morning was not where I wanted to sleep. The sofa was hard. Nothing but diamonds came out of my eyes.

Next morning, the concierge said, "A package came from Armería Diana for the señor Diano." It was the jacket he'd bought, so long ago, in another lifetime.

"Thank you…I'll take it to him," I said.

All the next day, Tuesday, in that strange isolation, while the great city grew and bustled around me, building its new buildings, threshing out a million personal agonies, I typed, re-typed, made notes, filled ashtrays with cigarette butts. My mind filled up with legal boilerplate, crowding out the hallucinations. It galled me to give my brother everything I'd worked for. But I kept typing. Thread-ends to tie up. What about rewarding people who had worked with me for years? Would Paco agree to go on hiring the people in La Mora? Who would take my dogs and horses?

In my legalistic frame of mind, I found that judgment, too, had been planted inside of me by the teachers of terror.

Well, look here, Antonio...you have to face the fact that they may have dishonored him already. It doesn't matter if he tried to protect himself. A fact is a fact. A mate soiled by others is no longer worthy. You know that, of course. So go ahead...do this legal thing out of nobility, out of obligation to him. Try to rescue him out of humanitarian concern. Friend or no friend, a life is a life. But if you get him back, you will have to send him on his way afterwards. He won't be worthy of your feelings. Your honor will dictate that he walk away along that highway and disappear forever.

These quiet, sneaking thoughts were more terrible than the mural pictures. By afternoon, my document of abdication and property transfer looked good. If the Spanish courts didn't like some phrase or other in my hand-made document, Paco could contact me in exile and ask for a better one.

My tired mind spawned an alternate plan. It meant getting expert help and weapons, which would be hard in this country of God where most people couldn't own any weapon but a jackknife. And it would certainly make an international desperado out of me.

Signing four copies of the document with Isaías' best old fountain pen, I shoved them into an envelope. One copy was for Paco, one for Isaías, one for me, one for the government. With it was a sheet of typed and signed instructions on how to find the Crypt of the Mercies.

Thread-ends, thread-ends. My crew would need bonuses of thanks when I dismissed them. Dragging out the big check ledger that Tere kept, I wrote five checks on my business account.

Then I locked up the office. The banks were still open, and I withdrew as much cash as I could legally take out of the country. I had the documents notarized. Finally I drove out to Las Moreras. At the *coto*, Pico and Magda were worried, wondering why their wonderful assistant had vanished.

"Some important family business in Germany came up for him, quite suddenly," I told them as casually as I could. "He went there to deal with it. He'll be back as soon as possible."

Pico was annoyed. "I've been left holding the cat by the scruff here."

"It couldn't be helped," I said humbly.

"Is everything all right?" Pico asked, peering into my eyes.

Soon enough the old wizard would know the truth, and perhaps he would curse me.

Pico was grumpily feeding the last batch of partridge that Juan had hatched in the new pen. The birds were growing strong now, putting on the first mature feathers and pinons. The old man would sadly release them alone — his fine young trainee would be gone for good. Flying level and straight, like arrows, the young birds would whir off to freedom. Juan had come flying to me like that, straight as an arrow.

But no self-respecting man will take back a wife who has been dishonored. The same goes for a friend of the same sex. In fact, I would have every right to blow his brains out, to salvage my honor. Really, if Juan were a decent man, he'd fall on his sword before I got my hands on him...like Lucretia in the Roman tale.

Third day, Wednesday. My crew came to help me with practice. I didn't need to tell them that we all had to be sharp in Arles, even in a foreign country, with foreign bulls. Braulio was packing his own effects, so I hauled out my sword case myself. Under the mulberry tree, we spent some hours at living-room bullfighting. "Hah-hey, bull!" "Huuuh, bull!" As the hot air shaped itself into silk capes, the "bull" charged till he got tired. I practiced killing, though there would be no killing in Arles. Throwing myself over the horns mounted on wheels, sinking my sword in the stuffing, felt good. Little by little, the old discipline steadied me, comforted me.

"You look good, matador," Bigotes said. "You are walking well. The best since..." Out of superstitious politeness, he didn't say the word Écija.

"I've been working hard at the *coto,*" I said. "It heals me."

"Yes, we hear the *señorito* has been sweating like a field hand," Manolillo teased.

I managed a grin — the first since Saturday. How I loved these men! Afterwards Marimarta fed us a huge meal, and I broke the news that I was retiring. I gave them the bonus checks. The crew stopped drinking brandy and went quiet. Somberly they looked down at the checks in their sunbrowned hands.

"So, matador...it ends," said Santí.

"All things end, sometime," I said.

"Good times," Fermín said. "The best I had with any maestro in these rings of God."

"Why Arles? Why aren't you retiring in Sevilla...Madrid? There's no dignity in this...retiring in the land of Frogs," Bigotes protested.

"My heart tells me to go quietly," I told them.

"You'll get the itch again. You'll do charity fights for the Montepío de Toreros," Santí said hopefully. "And you'll call us."

I knew that wouldn't be happening. But I said:

"Of course. We'll be back together for any charity stuff I do. But...what are you going to do now? There are novices out there who need you to knock some sense into their heads."

"Oh," Fermín said in his bass voice, "I've had my eye on a nice little shoe shop in Albacete, so I can be near my parents."

"Santí?"

"I hear Álvaro Chaparra is looking for an assistant foreman."

"Tonight I'll call him, and put the arm on him to hire you."

"A thousand thanks. And when there's enough grass in the *coto,*" Santí said, "I won't forget what we talked about."

"Manolillo? Bigotes?"

They shrugged.

"Emilio Puente has been trying to hire us away from you for years," Manolillo said. "He's a bastard but he pays well."

"Or maybe we'll go trout fishing up north for a while," Bigotes added.

I had opened my sword case and was inspecting my set of swords. Strangely there were no regrets as I handled those magnificent weapons with their red-wrapped hilts and leather pommels. I ran a soft cloth along the slender silken blades. You don't touch sword blades with your fingers. I didn't need them in Arles, but I'd take them anyway, to keep from feeling defenseless. After Arles, whatever happened, they would be relics of the past.

The men were all looking at me.

"Antonio," Bigotes said, "is everything all right?"

Silently I shut the sword case.

"Maestro, these last few months, you've seemed...well, in very good spirits. In spite of the afternoons when you had...bad luck. Now suddenly..." Manolillo said.

"...Now there is...er...a cloud around you," Bigotes added.

"It's nothing that a little luck can't fix," I said.

That evening my Madrid fan club — or what was left of it — feted me in a private dining room at the Cortijo, an elegant old restaurant near the Plaza Mayor. Only three dozen male members of the Peña Escudero waited at the long tables set with beef and sherry bottles. Amazing how your fans melt away when trouble comes. These die-hards wanted to cheer me up, to hear denials of rumors that I was retiring. Once again I was the picture of traditional torero — dark suit, ruffled white shirt, diamond studs, the diamond pinkie ring. Except Braulio was gone now, so my suit had a couple of wrinkles in it.

José wasn't there. She was probably busy trying to take care of a certain passport.

Amid cigar and cigarette smoke that layered its blue archeology in the air, I tried to keep my mind from screaming silent questions. Where was Juan? Still in Madrid? Had he tried to escape, been shot? Killed himself to escape the shame?

The president was making a speech more laden with rhetoric than any by Generalísimo Franco. He proclaimed:

"...Antonio Escudero has conquered one of the most glorious positions in the fiesta of today. He is a matador whose artistic horizons have been limitless, uniting the spirit of Andalucía with the spirit of Castile —"

I listened with a face chiseled from Toledo granite. How was it possible, in this stifled country where rumor was the lifeblood of news, that these men hadn't heard every crass detail of my scandal? Everyone glowed with wine, sherry, brandy and whiskey. I had to mollify them with a short speech. Hints that I was getting married, going on a long honeymoon abroad. There were cheers and toasts to the yet-unidentified fiancée.

"May she have the nine points of Spanish beauty!" called one ancient aficionado who must have been old enough to see Noah drive bulls into the Ark.

"Three black, three red, three white!" another old fart sang out.

Yes, I thought. White for his innocence, black for his despair, red for his blood.

As everyone was leaving, a waiter gave me an envelope. "A message from a *señorita,*" he said. "A fan, eh?" He grinned.

It was from José.

"If all goes well," the message said, "I'll meet you at the Hotel Bezique in Marseilles, and we'll take a little vacation."

This was a hotel where we had sometimes stayed on bullfight and film-festival jaunts in southern France.

In the men's room, I tore up her message and flushed it down the toilet. Then I made yet another long drive back to Las Moreras alone.

15

Fourth day. Thursday. More living-room bullfighting. The four men asked me no more questions. I talked to Álvaro on the phone and convinced him to hire Santí. Paco still hadn't contacted me. But that didn't mean the exchange was off. He knew where and when I'd be in France. He could call me at the Hotel de la Sirene. I tried calling all his numbers, but got no answer. His wife told me he was working overtime at the ministry. The only thing to do was go ahead. But how in the name of God and Goddess was I going to cape bulls in two days? My mind was still struggling to focus on my work.

For exile, the two suitcases that Braulio packed. Warm- and cold-weather clothes. My London Fog raincoat. The blue suit of lights, other torero gear, passport, the picture of the Lady of Mercies. My mind numbly noted the dried-up carnation still laying in front of the picture; I packed it. At the last moment, I packed the gems, photo negatives, legal papers. My envelope of cash. Nothing else. Hopefully I'd have no problems with Spanish customs. In the past, people had been arrested for taking valuables like gold coins out of the country. But usually toreros going to foreign contracts were waved through by customs officials after a few routine questions.

There'd be no goodbyes at the Toledo townhouse. My mother never liked goodbyes when I went off to the bulls — she believed it was bad luck. Depending on what happened in Arles, I might call to tell her I was staying abroad for a while, doing a little traveling. She would have no money worries — Paco would be looking after her from now on.

Swinging by the *coto,* I told Pico and Magda that Juan had called, asking for some clothes to be sent. They were deeply disgusted with him. I felt horrible that I couldn't tell them the truth. In his cottage, I threw Juan's meager possessions into an extra suitcase. I'd brought his things from his Madrid room, including the new jacket. His precious bit of hard-earned money was in the Banco de Madrid — I couldn't get it for him, but maybe Isaías could send it to him later. My hand lingered lovingly on the jackknife, before I packed it with his school documents.

Outside Juan's house, I stood in the shade of a fruit tree he'd pruned three months ago, and looked around.

Twilight was falling on the Coto Morera summits. Maybe I'd never gaze on them again. No need to carry away a handful of earth — this land was crystallized in my bones, as my friend was. But I kissed my fingers and pressed them to the ground. Halfway up the first stony slope, several young rabbits hopped about. A mother roe deer and two grown fawns peered at me over some bushes. An Egyptian vulture made one last circle before planing off to roost for the night. Never had the Coto Morera seemed so alive, so sweet, so heart-rendingly loveable. Our footprints, the hoofprints of our horses would be erased by the next rain, but not the things we'd created together — the springs, the new animals arriving. I had to hope that Paco would not destroy our work overnight.

Back at the house, I made a final prayer in the chapel, and left the Virgin's altar blazing with candles. The wedding rings glinted in the light. I decided to pack them — they were gold, and might be worth a few francs.

With a casual goodbye to the household staff, I mentioned a vacation after Arles. I didn't know how long, I said.

Friday morning. The black Mercedes pulled up at the Las Moreras door. Instead of our regular driver, Santí was at the wheel. He, Manolillo and Bigotes climbed out to help me load gear. They wore pullovers, slacks and caps.

"What are you doing here?" I asked my picador. "I don't need you."

Santí was two meters of unsmiling Andalusian brawn.

"Boss," he said evenly, "are you in some kind of political trouble?"

My heart almost stopped. I stared up into Santí's narrowed black eyes, then into the eyes of my two subalterns. It was clear that they'd talked among themselves. They weren't *brujos,* but they sensed enough to be worried. If they were that sensitive, had they sensed the friendship with Juan?

"If I were in that kind of trouble," I said, "I wouldn't ask you to take that kind of risk."

"Let us be the judge of that," Manolillo said.

"I need a little vacation myself," Santí stated. "I'm going with you…at my own expense."

In all my years in the ring, I had never gone to a contract with a bodyguard. "Where's Fermín?" I asked.

"He went home to Albacete," Bigotes said.

This was understandable. Why should Fermín choose a risk of prison over a cozy retirement in his home town?

"Let the lad come with us," Bigotes said. "No harm in having an extra hand."

"Pic men instead of bulls, eh?" Santí said, flexing his arm and making a worker's fist.

"All right," I said. A lump was in my throat.

"Who should I be keeping an eye open for?" Santí insisted.

"Oh," I said carelessly, "my brother Paco is being a bother."

"Paquito, eh?" Manolillo's voice had an edge. The brothers had never said so, but both of them disliked Paco.

"Let's go," I said.

Santí grinned, and jumped back in the driver's seat. As I got in, I tried not to look back at the house. Through the open doorway, Eustacio the gardener paused in his watering duties to call, "Good luck!"

I waved at him. When the Mercedes headed down the road, I tried not to look back.

As we headed for the Mediterranean, I stewed about the Camargue bulls that waited in Arles.

They wouldn't be the slow heavy under-age bulls that I was used to — bred to die on their first day in a Spanish ring. Camargue bulls were bred to leave the ring alive and provide years of sport in southern France. Some bulls had long careers. Young men made their names by snatching a rosette from the horns of a famous bull. Camargues were probably the closest thing to the wild *Bos ibericus* that still lived. They were lean, fast, mature — real soccer-players with horns. Only a few Spanish ranches now bred this kind of bull. Toreros that made impresarios rich were kept out of the hospital by being matched with the slowest of slow bulls. I was one of those lesser lights who took whatever was offered.

All the questions came screaming and clawing at me again.

Months ago I had accepted the Arles offer not realizing what a quandary it now put me in. My injury or death in the ring would certainly result in Juan's death as well. But cancelling Arles was unthinkable. The contract gave me a reason to leave Spain, to make the exchange on friendlier ground — and to make some extra money. Of course, I could always cancel just before the fight, saying I was sick. But now that I was poor, one more fee looked good. It would be paid in francs.

Tomorrow, Saturday, I would hope to hear from Paco at the French hotel. On Sunday afternoon I could stay alive easily. Punch the ticket, pass the bull miles away and say *adios muchachos**. Not an honorable end to my career. But justifiable under the circumstances. If I was careless, or too honorable, and got close to that fast little bull, he'd be on top of me like a lynx on a rabbit. The same discipline would be needed today as on my first day in the ring.

Manolillo must have felt my thoughts.

"Matador," he said from the front seat, "stop thinking, and take a nap."

Obediently I covered myself with the raincoat, sank my head into a pillow, and tried to sleep.

When they weren't driving, my men were quiet, dozing too. I could feel them wondering what was ahead. Could I count on them if things went bad? The many years that they had spent with me, my respect and care for them, had to count for something — the way years on the battlefield count with veteran soldiers. Memory pictures flitted through my mind. Santí's look of joy when he realized that the famous matador was going to hire him as second picador. Manolillo in debt because of his addiction to card games — I paid what he owed before he got beaten up. Bigotes needing surgery because of a terrible old cornada that hadn't healed — I paid for it. Their sister and her children evicted from her home — I helped them get it back. Did these men owe me enough? Yet hadn't they saved my ass enough times to even the score?

Had I been kind enough to them, or was I (as Juan had said) just trying to buy people again?

That night, we struck the winding highway along the sea, and crossed the French border without incident.

By the following evening, we were winding through the wetlands and sea smell of the Camargue. The season was changing — soon everything would blur with dust in fierce driving gusts of the *mistral*. There were less wild wetlands and more rice-fields than I remembered — even the French were being seduced by land development. We saw only a couple of small herds of wild cattle. Here, too, the war between tame and wild was going on.

In the outskirts of Arles, late Saturday night, we pulled up at the Hotel de la Sirene, where we had stayed five times before. It was a pleasant vine-covered stone building, with a front door done in art-nouveau glass. We got stiffly out of the car in the parking-lot, which was crowded with license-plates from half a dozen European countries. I actually had fans in this city, who would be hoping to see one or two of my *veronicas*.

At the desk, I pretended to be dissatisfied with my room, and made the staff give me a different one, just in case the CYS had managed to bug the one we'd reserved. Isaías and Tere had already checked in. My men went to their own rooms to rest.

Feeling like I was walking to my execution, I headed upstairs to the Eibars' room.

Isaías was angrier than I'd ever seen him. He prowled around the room, thinking. It wasn't clear yet what Tere felt, as she stared out the window.

Several blocks away, on the night skyline of Arles, the massive masonry of the Roman structure was garishly lit by floodlights. Two thousand years ago it functioned as an amphitheater. Who knew how many gladiators and wild animals had died there? Now it was the city's bullring and most cherished ancient monument. Tomorrow I would face two Camargue bulls there.

I had explained the situation, holding back crasser details. I didn't mention José.

Both the Eibars had blanched. Guilt by association was enough to make a person cringe. What would their association with me mean for the Eibars, politically, if it became known? Disgrace? Loss of their business? Isaías removed from the bar?

"You stupid boy," Isaías growled, prowling around.

Head bent, I felt like a whipped child.

Now it would begin — seeing the expression change in the eyes of people I loved. People who had loved and trusted me.

At odds with our mood, the hotel room was cozy and cheerful, with a huge feather-bed and flowered wallpaper. The floor was waxed hardwood planks that looked 300 years old, and creaked ominously as the old man strode around over them. He and Tere had flown to southern France and rented a Citroën because he wasn't going to drive all that way. They had arrived prepared for the poignancy of a major client's retirement. Now Isaías, who always found the right words in contract negotiations or in court, was at a loss.

Finally he sputtered: "There was one kid...his name doesn't matter...I had to keep dragging rich Americans out of his bed. But you...you fooled me completely."

"I haven't told the crew," I said in a low voice.

"Well, thank God for that."

"Santí came on his own. They sense something."

"You should have told us years ago," Isaías grumbled.

Tere shook her head. "I always knew it would come to something like this with Paco. Bad milk. Very bad milk."

"Crazy parents, who cared so little about you," Isaías raved. "Crazy God, who made you that way. Crazy Mother Mary, who let God get away with it."

"I put you both in jeopardy," I said. "I'm sorry."

Isaías thrust out his jaw. "Perhaps I could have prevented this tragedy. Advised you better."

This was encouraging talk. Something snapped inside of me, and I wept, gagging on the tears. Was I not allowed to cry in public? Toreros cried in public. They cried after two ears and a tail. I had reason enough.

Then Tere came over to me, arms spreading over me like the Mother of Mercies. I wept against her fishing-boat prow. A grown man, sobbing like a child at this touch of mother love. She and Isaías were talking in Euskera** over my head. Finally we calmed down, and Isaías called room service for a couple of stiff brandies.

I gave Isaías the envelope. "Here are the documents I wrote. Are they all right?"

My manager read swiftly, rustling pages. Then he stared at me. "In a few months," he said, "you will wake up from your trance. All you know is killing bulls. How are you going to live out there? You're not the Duke of Windsor. He gave up his title, but he kept his money...and he's ten thousand times richer than you. And what will happen when the infatuation for your Mrs. Simpson turns to boredom? Eh?"

I had no answer for this.

"And if Paco doesn't give him back to you, then what?" Tere asked. She was reading the documents now.

I rubbed my tired eyes.

"And why are you giving Paco everything?" Isaías raved on. "Everything, by God! Nine years in the ring, and you leave your motherland with *nothing?* You are crazy! You're a terrible negotiator! Why didn't you offer him a more reasonable ransom?"

"Because Paco is not a reasonable man," I burst out.

The old man thrust out his jaw, which was prickly with silver late-day stubble.

"And you're a terrible typist too," he said.

As I stood at the window, my burning eyes looked out over the night skyline of Arles. "It's not true that I have nothing," I said.

I turned and looked at the old couple. "I have my self. No one can take that unless I let them."

Isaías slipped the documents back in their envelope, and gave it to me.

"That was easy for Seneca to say," he growled. "You'd better get some rest for that self of yours. We'll see you in the morning."

I got up to leave, but couldn't bite back the question. "Are you with me, both of you? Or against me?"

"I've never understood why a man would want to...do that with another man," Isaías barked.

"Enough, eh?" Tere snapped at him. "This is a question of our children. Haven't our children come from God?"

As they left the room, the old man didn't give me the usual comforting clap on the shoulder. But Tere did kiss me lightly on the cheek. It was clear that they would have a big argument in Euskera later.

Locked in my own unbearably cozy room, I sagged into bed. Sleeping pills are out for toreros, they make you slow in the ring. But finally I called room service, and ordered another stiff shot of brandy. It mercifully put me to sleep.

---

*   *Adios muchachos* — goodbye, boys.

** Euskera — ancient non-Spanish language spoken by the Basques.

16

My last bull was making his first gallop around the oval Roman ring. This animal had worried me ever since I saw him in the corral that morning. The breeder had told me that this was the bull's first time out. His name was English — Baby. A real yeah-yeah name. Every Yankee rock and roll song I'd ever heard had a line in it about

Oh, baby, baby

But nothing was yeah-yeah about Baby. He was straight out of a prehistoric cave painting. Coal-black, slender and supple, quick as a cat, with a white star on his forehead. His horns, the distinctive horns of the Camargue breed, raked straight up at the sky. Horns like candelabra, the toreros say. We hate to see those candelabra coming out of the gate. If it catches you, that kind of horn is sure to make a tunnel through your body big enough for a truck to drive through. Give us horns that curve down, or turn in toward the head. Horns like bananas. Ripe ones, that bend easy.

I kept my eyes from sweeping the crowd sitting on the shady side of the ring. Was Paco here already?

Throwing up his long tail like a charging lion, Baby dove at Manolillo's cape, then Bigotes' cape. His master horn, the left one, thudded into the wooden wall, with a firecracker burst of splinters. When he turned, he spun on his hocks like a well-trained high-school horse. I was going to have a hard time keeping him off me.

When Baby had checked the entire perimeter, he cantered to the center of the ring, where a chalk circle was marked on the sand. Here, he stopped and craned his neck defiantly, and swung around, looking for enemies. Shiny strings of saliva trailed from his muzzle. His eyes were noble and intelligent. I hoped that some kid using his jacket for a cape had not already played Baby in the wetland pastures. If he had, Baby would already be wise to tricks of the cloth.

The packed amphitheater cheered at the sight of him. Every cranny of that ancient structure was packed with people. They even sat high on top of the old Roman wall. Rumors of my retirement had rippled into the Spanish bullfight press, so a few fans had raced here to see me one last time. Five hundred kilometers away, in Barcelona, José would be watching another torero and another bull.

Along the barrier, our row of somber eyes followed Baby. My own eyes flicked to my two subalterns. Could I trust them to cover my back, now that it was almost over?

"He favors the left. But at least he charges straight as a trolley," Isaías offered helpfully.

As if I couldn't see it.

Santí, standing in street clothes beside Isaías, moved his eyes around the stands, looking for Paco.

If anything could have driven the thought of Juan's unjust imprisonment from my mind, it was this animal. First we had to slow him down. Today there was no picador to do that. So we'd have to tire him with caping.

"Double him good," I said to Bigotes and Manolillo.

Warily my two subalterns went into the ring. They kept their distance as they made Baby run hard, spinning him on his hocks, wrenching him. Unhappy that I hadn't come out yet, the crowd started to whistle. Unmoved, I watched with narrowed eyes. Baby followed their capes like a kitten follows a pulled string. The Lady of Mercies was smiling on me. It looked like he still had his maiden. This would give me half a chance.

Finally Baby was tiring. My stomach churning, I stepped into the ring. My leg felt good — the best it had felt in a year.

The crowd quieted.

"Eheh, toro!" My voice echoed off the Roman walls.

Baby whirled to face me.

I shook the cape, catching his eye with it.

Baby dove at the moving target. I took him on his right, the safer side, and tested him with the edge of the silk. He spun on his hocks, and charged again. I barely had time to set my stance before he had his eyes on the cape again. My leg was obeying me well. Again with the edge, closer now. Baby was slowing more. My stomach quieted. Each step of mine was a prayer of pure will. No hotshot stuff this time. You can only do that with a slow and bleeding bull.

Finally Baby was just right for a *veronica* — that primal and most beautiful of the cape passes.

I called him to me. His head rushed past my leg, pushing the silk like a hot blast of mistral wind. The silk carried him hurtling past me.

"OOOOLÉ!" The French can yell olé as good as anybody. That shout of the human biomass gave me a burst of new energy.

Walk to me, Juan.

Cattle horns are alive, filled with blood vessels and nerves. Baby's horns were exploring the silk like fingers, like butterfly antennas, wondering what was behind it. Baby was smart. His eyes had told me that. On the third *veronica*, I felt his horn probe the silk. Time to quit. I finished with the half-*veronica*, catching the cape against my hip so it flared out abruptly. To follow the cape's arrested motion, Baby had to whiplash his body hard and stop in his tracks. The stop was supposed to give the matador a chance to turn his back on the bull, and walk grandly away to acknowledge the applause. But I wasn't going to turn my back on Baby.

In the next breath, Baby sprang off his hocks — straight at me.

A great scream went up from the crowd. They could see it coming — me being lashed into the air on that horn.

Cape bunched in one hand, I planted my feet where I was, very still. One last time I commanded, willed, lured, magicked Baby's eye to fix on the silk. I swung the cape one-handed past my body, making him follow it. Baby hooked at me as he plunged by. His horn raked the breast of my jacket like the point of Juan's jackknife. It tore the gilt tassel off my left epaulet.

The crowd shrieked. They could all see my tassel dancing crazily on the horn-tip.

"Look! *Mon dieu, regardez! Mira-mira!*" A thousand fingers pointed, people babbling in several languages.

Just in time, Bigotes flared his own cape from the nearest barrier. It was what I prayed my men would do. I had bound them to me with loyalty and love and, yes, pesetas so they'd do it. As Baby dived away at this new lure, I walked safely out of the ring. Hot sweat sprang out on my body. Another pass, and I would have been a dead man.

The whole amphitheater came to its feet with a roar. Everyone could see my split jacket now. The faces of Tere and Isaías were absolutely blanched. So were my crew's. I stood out and held up my cape to the people. Now was the moment to macho it a little. My career was over. I felt strangely good, almost exultant, considering how bad things were.

Juan, this bull goes for you.

Now a pack of French boys in red sashes and white pants were jumping in the ring, to play the bull. It was mayhem. Baby chased this boy, then that boy. The boys ran daringly just ahead of his horns, and made grabs at my tassel. Baby's hot breath on their kidneys inspired them to Olympic feats of speed and dexterity. To keep that awesome left horn from impaling them in an act of awful sodomy, they'd bound to the top of the barrier in a single leap, and hang there by grasping the railing beyond, till Baby hurtled on. One boy almost catapulted into Tere's lap.

Ordinarily, with my own ass now safe, I might have enjoyed this spectacle. But suddenly the emotions of that long week overcame me, and I had to put my head down on the barrier.

Now a boy had my tassel in his hand. He brandished it, triumphant and gleeful.

The crowd was going wild. Tourists and locals alike had gotten their money's worth.

By the time we were back at the hotel, it was 6:30 in the evening.

Paco hadn't shown up yet, or even called. With death by bull-horn no longer a consideration, I felt myself on the edge of insanity once again.

The usual bunch of jubilant hangers-on wanted to be in my room while I got undressed. But we locked them out for once, and asked the hotel staff to keep the hall cleared. Isaías and Tere, exhausted, dragged off to their room to take a nap. Only the crew were with me, still in their sweaty plaza clothes. In front of the Virgin of Mercies, the votive candles were burning low. While Santí helped me shed the ruined blue jacket, the subalterns' eyes followed my tired movements. By now they sensed that something terrible was happening in my world. There was their loyalty, and there was also their fear.

In the silence, we could hear the candle-flames simmer.

Just as I was about to say something to break the nerve-wracking silence, the phone rang jarringly. My body nearly jumped out of its skin. I grabbed the instrument to my ear.

"Diga," I said. "Hello."

"Antonio," said Paco's voice.

"Yes." My stomach was knotting.

"The bullring at midnight," he said. "Come to the center of the ring…and come alone. We will make the exchange there. No tricks.

Our guns will have silencers. If we have to shoot you and Juan, no one will hear."

"The bullring?" I repeated, astonished.

But the connection had already clicked off.

Shoulders hunched, I put down the telephone slowly, with chills running up and down my spine. My brother's words had called up those unpleasant historical facts…the mass executions that had taken place in bullrings. They were convenient places to deal with prisoners. Women, men and children were herded onto the sandy arena, and machine-gunned down like animals. What did Paco want? To remind me of history? Or did he want to humble me on my own ground? If so, it was a tactical error on his part. I knew that ground better than he did.

The first hope flickered in me.

"Antonio, what the demons is going on?" Bigotes asked testily.

Slowly I turned to face them. As toreros say, this was the moment of truth. My imagination had leaped ahead into the coming encounter. I was going to need their help. But I would start by trying them like bulls — skimming them past me with the very edge of the verbal silk.

"What's going on," I said, "is a bull with horns like two Yankee missiles."

"Why?"

"That was my brother," I said.

Their faces darkened. Santí frowned.

"My brother wants certain things from me." My throat constricted, but I forced the words out. "He and his little political group kidnapped Juan Diano."

Their eyes narrowed, and they all sucked in their breath.

"I don't know if they're CYS. But they are holding him hostage…hoping they can force me to do political things that they want. I am trying to ransom Juan. They want to meet me in the plaza at midnight."

The crew's minds digested the implications. They were wondering why Paco would choose Juan as a way to pressure me. They knew what the *coto* meant to me. They knew, if nothing else, that Juan had become a trusted friend and associate of mine. They also knew that I owed Juan because he'd protected me in Santander that time. All this made sense to them. And yet…and yet… I could feel their minds standing at the edge of the terrible suspicion. Loyalty and respect were trembling on a delicate balance. On the other side of the terrible question waited all the abhorrence, the moral rigor, the ridicule and the snickering.

I met their eyes, letting them see my feelings without saying the words.

"Ransom?" Santí asked. "A lot of money?"

Isaías' question had been ringing in my memory. Why should Paco get it all?

"Everything I have," I said.

"Land too?" barked Bigotes.

"Everything."

"The rotten bastard," Santí burst out.

"Pardon me, Antonio...because he's your brother," said Manolillo. "But he doesn't deserve it. You paid years of blood for what you have."

This was a good start. But I couldn't plead. The offer had to come from them.

"I don't want to give them a peseta. But if I don't cooperate, they will...injure my friend," I said quietly.

My use of the word "friend" left the door open for conjecture. And they didn't have to be told what "injury" meant. Through Spain's unending political conflicts, both sides had been free with mutilation and torture. They had all liked Juan. The thought of Paco, whom they disliked, ordering some injury done to Juan started their feelings tipping toward me, on the delicate balance. And after all, I was still the man that they'd fought with, for eight years. If I could get their sympathies, get them with me all the way, they might even offer their help tonight. Did I want to contact the French police? No. Not if I could avoid it. This affair could explode into an international incident.

Walking over to my sword case, I flipped it open. The blades gleamed there.

I lifted the long killing sword, appreciating the glint as it slid down the bent blade.

"They may try to trick me," I said. "They may take what they want, and not return Juan. They'll have guns. Probably pistols with silencers. I don't have much in the way of weapons. We toreros aren't very dangerous, eh? I have Juan's knife, which got left behind. And this..." I hefted the sword, feeling its ball hilt in my palm. "What the hell, I'll do somebody with this if I have to."

The idea of facing a band of fascist thugs with a bull sword was what finally got to them.

"Boss," said Bigotes hoarsely, "you have got balls."

"What I've got," I said hoarsely, "is a fear as big as..."

My voice broke. I could feel them seeing my feelings for Juan, my terror that they'd hurt him. Gripping the sword, I turned to them.

"You're going to need help," Manolillo said.

"That's why I came...to pic men instead of bulls," Santí repeated. He flexed his big arm again.

I looked at the others.

"How many of them?" Bigotes wanted to know.

"Not many, probably. They don't dare attract attention."

For the first time since last Sunday, I didn't feel like a helpless writhing victim. José hadn't called. I wondered briefly what was happening with her.

By now it was after 8 p.m. While the men went off to change, Santí peeled me out of my breeches. Quickly I showered, pulled on comfortable sport clothes. Then Isaías and Tere came and I gave them an update. Without saying anything specific, the old couple made it clear that they had decided to help me. Tere set her lips. Isaías's lower jaw went out like a buck salmon's — he agreed that we had no other option but to prepare for a trick.

"You should call the French police," Tere said.

"No...no police," I said.

"Antonio is right," Isaías agreed with me. "It's too tricky."

"We all have to get out of Arles tonight," I told them. "And I'm worried that my Mercedes might be recognized at the ring tonight. Why don't you both take the Mercedes and our luggage, and go on to Marseilles, to the Bezique? The boys and I will use your rental car. We'll meet you in Marseilles. If José and Sera don't show up, we'll worry about them next."

I gave the Eibars my hoard of diamonds for safekeeping.

"If something happens to me tonight," I said, "give them to José."

Back in my room, we assembled our pitiable armaments. In addition to my bull-killing weapons, the men had their own big folding pocket-knives. They had their capes. That was it.

"Capes...take them," I said. "They can be weapons."

"For sure," said Manolillo. "We can flap them over the barrier, and draw fire. Unless they have machine guns, the barrier will probably stop bullets. After all, it stops bulls..."

"Maybe they'll post guys with pistols up in the seats," said Bigotes. "The capes can make them waste a few rounds."

"Down in the alleyway, we'll be below their guns," said Santí. "We can run around down there, and they can't see us good."

"Not unless they lean over the railing..."

"Guns with silencers don't shoot far, do they?"

Everybody jumped in with ideas. I was trying hard to remember boring cadet lectures on strategy, to which I had listened fifteen years ago with only half an ear, impatient to be outdoors with animals and sunlight.

"What about your sword?" asked Bigotes.

"Walk in there with a naked *estoque* * in my hand?" I said.

So we rigged up a way of carrying the sword inside my London Fog raincoat. As the men helped, they muttered under their breath about what they'd do to the fascist bastards. The sword wound up suspended by the hilt, blade down, from my left suspender. I'd have to be careful not to poke myself in the leg with the needle-sharp point. A jerk, and it would come loose for action.

"I wonder if they trucked those bulls home yet," Santí mused.

"That," I said, reading his mind, "is an excellent idea. If the bulls are still at the ring, they'd make a good diversion...if we need one."

"That Baby would be diversion enough," growled Bigotes. "But they can shoot the bull."

"Turn loose all the bulls, then."

We couldn't assume that the CYS would run out of ammunition. But things would happen fast. They'd only get so many shots. Silencers reduced the range of pistol fire, didn't they? I'd never heard of ma-chine-guns with silencers, and prayed they wouldn't have any automatic-fire weapons. Or all our bodies would litter the sand. Since it was dark, Paco's men would have to worry about hitting each other too. We were a little bunch of crazies going up against professional killers. All we had was antique weapons, our expertness with bullfighting terrain, our closeness through so many years — and, in my case, the fanatic determi-nation that none on their side could match, not even Paco.

Plus we had another advantage. We had been in the Arles ring that afternoon. Even if Paco and his men had attended the event, and examined the scene from the seats, we still knew it better than they did.

Isaías had been listening silently, chain-smoking. Now the law-yer part of him was scared to death, and he shook his head.

"If somebody gets —" Then he bit off the words. "Forget what I said. Good luck, boys."

Now it was 10 p.m. Planning done, we had a quick snack just before the dining room closed. We finished packing up. Then we had coffee sent up from the bar, and waited tensely. I lit one last desperate candle in front of the Virgin of Mercies. When it burned down, the altar went into the luggage.

Time crawled.

At 11:30 we went downstairs with our luggage, making the nor-mal torero stir in the lobby. The hotel was used to seeing traveling bullfighters arrive and depart at odd hours of the day and night. So they just smiled and bowed, as Isaías paid the bill. I signed a couple of auto-graphs as bellhops helped us out to the waiting cars.

In case we were being watched, we didn't want to be public

about the vehicle switch. So we left the hotel in the usual vehicles, with Isaías following my Mercedes in his rental car. Near the edge of town, we swung into a deserted side street. There, with no other cars in sight, we quickly switched. Tere and Isaías got into my Mercedes. I stuck my head in the window.

"We'll see you in Marseilles," I said.

Isaías shook my hand with a fierce grip.

The crew and I jumped into Isaías's rental car.

If only my sister was here. "Dig your toes in," she would have said.

---

*   *estoque* — the matador's longest sword, used for killing the bull. Shorter swords in his kit are used for other purposes, like the coup de grace.

17

Above our heads, the menacing wall of the Roman amphitheater rose into the moonlit sky. Tall arches pierced it, like a row of eyes gone blind from watching so many centuries of pomp and death. Quietly our car circled the structure. In the back, the bull truck was still parked there. Horned shapes moved in the corral.

"All right, Santí," I said. "You're in charge of the bulls. Bigotes and Manolillo, you help him get a bull or two lined up. Then sneak into the alleyway from the back, in case I need you. Santí, be ready to dump one in the ring if you hear me yell *toro!*"

"I'm on it, boss."

We parked the rented Citroën in dark shadow, at a discreet distance from the ring. Santí slipped a flashlight in his pocket — he'd need it for his operation with the gates. The two subalterns had their folded capes inside their jackets. We got out, and listened. This countrified little city was in a waning fiesta mood. Towards the center, a last few fireworks lazed up over the roofs. The area around the ring was quiet. At a bar nearby, six little Camargue ranch horses were dozing, tied to a lamppost. Yeah-yeah music trailed out of the bar — it sounded like the Monkees. We prayed that the gendarme or night watchman on night duty at the amphitheater was paid off by Paco, or in the bar getting drunk with the vaqueros.

Just then a tiny Renault sped toward us. We bent heads together, as if lighting cigarettes, to keep our faces from being seen. The car roared past, crammed with local boys who were drunk, singing an Arlesian folk song at the top of their lungs.

244

While my three crewmen slipped away towards the rear of the plaza, I ambled casually toward the entrance. If Paco's men were watching, they could see that I was alone, wearing a raincoat. My stomach was churning. This was more than the usual nervousness before a bullfight. They might not come after all. They might try to ambush me, get their hands on the papers, then kill my friend anyway. Anything could happen. It was like any bullfight — pregnant with chaos.

The main gate stood slightly ajar, as if left open for us. When the street was empty, I slipped through and bolted it from the inside. If bulls got loose, we didn't want them all over town.

It was now exactly midnight.

The tall arched entrance, which had been so noisy with human merriment that afternoon, was silent now. My feet rustled eerily over dropped programs, food papers. The cleanup crew was too busy partying to do their job. Hundreds of times I had stood in such an entrance, after the ritual visit to the chapel, jostled by horses and well-wishers, wrapping my parade cape tightly around my body to contain the nervousness.

What had Paco's men done with the night watchman? Paid him off, killed him? How much had they done to secure the place?

I strode on through, letting my footsteps echo so Paco's thugs would know I was here. Would my leg do my bidding tonight?

Ahead was the double gate into the oval ring. That afternoon, it had swung open to let a motley spectacle of Spanish toreros and French country boys file onto the sand. Beyond it lay the oval ring — eerily empty in the moonlight. My senses, trained to note every detail of any ring, roved around keenly. Hoofprints of the last bull had not been raked from the sand, making it a trickier surface for running. Would I have to run tonight? Could I?

The Moon, almost full now, was sliding down the western sky. She cast half of the structure into purple shadow. Shadows of arches zigzagged dramatically down the tiered seats. The eye could easily be tricked here. We would have to be careful. Paco — more careful. Even in daylight, he was legally blind without his bi-focals. Along the barrier, each of the four blinds, where we toreros hide from the bull, had a white geometric design painted on it. These were easy to see in the dark.

The air was still. Capes would move as bidden.

My eyes getting used to the darkness, I expected to see several henchmen sitting in the first tier. But the seats were empty. Maybe Paco had hidden his men in the alleyway. Most likely he had only a couple of men, not wanting to attract attention by sneaking a whole squad into the amphitheater. Where were they? Probably on the other side, where the well-to-do could sit in afternoon shade. They must have Juan over there. Maybe Paco was even sitting in the president's place, so he could be the *grande* who directed this event. I had to make sure that Paco came personally down to the ring.

Hopefully my crew wouldn't find some local boys already back there, messing around with the bulls. Or a night watchman.

I waited. They were late. Even for a kidnap ransom, some Spaniards had not learned the *moderno* thing of being on time. Or maybe Paco just wanted to cause me more anxiety.

Then I froze. A dark shape was coming toward me.

It resolved into a slender man in beret and bulky jacket. In the moonlight, he looked middle-aged, with tiny intelligent eyes. That voice, those fleshy red lips were unmistakable. With a surge of angry emotion, I recognized El Sicario. He put out his hands to frisk me. At all costs, I had to keep him from touching my person, or he would find the sword under my coat. And he hadn't covered his face. I would be able to identify him later. His brazen lack of caution might mean that they intended to kill me…and Juan too…after they got their hands on the papers.

"That's right — feel me good, friend," I said, putting an insinuating tone in my voice. "Where it's hot and hard."

El Sicario hesitated. Even in the darkness, the look of loathing was visible, flooding his eyes. Instantly he didn't want to touch me. How easy it was to manipulate men who had this unreasoning fear of *maricones*.

"You criminal," he said in his Madrid dialect. "You'd better not be carrying."

"I'd be stupid to risk Juan's life. Where is he?"

"Do you have the legal papers?"

"They are right here." I patted my pocket.

"Give them to me."

"No. Paco comes to me alone with Juan. I give the papers only to Paco."

"Give them to me at once, you perverted swine!"

I was tremblingly patient, trying this bull on both sides, seeing which side he hooked toward.

"Paco needs to read them and approve them," I said. "I want to hear from him personally."

El Sicario thought, frowning. "Wait here," he said, and disappeared. When he was gone, I thought I saw Manolillo and Bigotes slip into the alleyway from the back, one man to the right, one to the left. They moved stooped and noiseless behind the barrier, and disappeared.

After a few minutes, a lone slender figure stood up in the president's box, looking down at me. Then it descended the tiers with slow dignity, and disappeared into the shadows down at ring-side. The figure was distinct in the moonlight. I'd been right — Paco had been sitting up there, where the emperor had sat in older times. Yes, Paco had that fascist love for historical pomp. It was his weakness. It was the reason why he had chosen this ground. The medieval pageant of vindicating the family honor, defeating the evil brother.

After a few minutes, El Sicario came back along the alley. Bigotes was on that side — where was he? Maybe he'd ducked through the blind till the man passed. Now Paco's man had what looked like the Luger in his hand, with a handmade pipe silencer that looked crude even in the dark, considering the fine firearms we Spanish are so proud of. Maybe he had loaned the Luger to Paco last Sunday. Paco was clearly not comfortable with firearms. Possibly he was not armed now.

"Don Francisco doesn't trust you," said El Sicario. "He says I must be present for the exchange."

My heart sank.

El Sicario left again. After a few minutes, on the other side of the ring, three dark shapes eased out of a blind, and into the moonlight. Two of them were Paco and El Sicario. The third, walking just ahead of them, was the unmistakable silhouette of Juan. His hands were not tied. But El Sicario was behind him, probably holding the silencer against my friend's kidneys. They had Juan dressed in the shabbiest black village clothing they could find. It was Paco's last dig, his silent comment on the fact that I was marrying beneath me. Juan stumbled a couple of times, as if exhausted. When they got close, I hardly recognized him. He was visibly thinner, with a strange haunted glint in his eyes. Prickly beard glinted on his jaws. They hadn't even let him shave.

We met in the middle of the ring, within that circle of chalk Juan stood with head bent, not meeting my eyes. What had they been doing to him?

"Good evening, Don Queer," Paco said, as if he was arriving at a reception.

"Let's take care of business," I said icily.

"Ah! Yes. You have some papers for me, I believe."

"Not unless Juan's papers are in order."

"Give this queer the passport," said Paco to El Sicario.

Silently the thug hauled out Juan's identity card, and a brand-new passport which they must have sped through the bowels of bureaucracy with a bribe. Flicking my lighter, I squinted at the document in the dark. It appeared to be in order. In the tiny photo, Juan looked hollow-cheeked and shockingly sad. I pocketed the documents, then held my legal papers towards Paco. The sheet of Mercies directions was still in my pocket.

"Hold them in front of me, bitch-dog, so I can read them," Paco fumed. "There had better not be any lawyer tricks in them."

Jaw tightening, I obeyed. Pulling out a little flashlight, then adjusting his bi-focals, Paco read the documents swiftly with his schoolteacher air, mumbling to himself.

My stomach tightened. I didn't dare make eye contact with Juan. But with my peripheral vision, I could see him seething with pent-up rage. Was he still strong enough for fast evasive action?

"This looks in order," said Paco. He put the papers in his jacket's inside pocket. "But it's only half the trade. The information on the Mercies, please."

"Not till Juan tells me he is unharmed, and safe behind the barrier," I said. "I already told you that."

"You see him before you."

"He needs to be safe from your guns. Let the two of us go to the exit and talk. If all is well, I'll come back and give you the Mercies information."

"Deceitful degenerate! Give me the Mercies information immediately. Or we leave and take your *puto* with us."

The time for desperate tricks was at hand. I pretended to sigh, as if submitting to his will.

"All right. I'll give it to you," I said.

My hand went to my raincoat pocket.

"If you pull a gun on us," growled El Sicario, "your *puto* is dead." The silencer muzzle pushed harder into Juan's body. Juan tensed.

"It's no gun," I said patiently. "It's the key to the Mercies."

Paco hesitated. "The key?" he said.

I pulled out my ring, and held it before El Sicario's eyes. The six-carat diamond caught the moonlight in a blaze of cold beauty. Paco's eyes widened. He knew that Doña Carmen had given me the ring, so he was immediately curious. El Sicario gaped. He probably had never seen a gem that big. Juan stared too, wondering what I was up to.

"The only key that exists," I said. "That's why I've worn it faithfully all these years."

Paco gawked at it. I went on:

"There is a stone door underground. It has a unique lock of fine steel, made by Arab locksmiths long ago. The lock is a delicate little mechanism, and it has been protected from dust and cobwebs by a little steel plate. You have to fit the facets of this stone into the lock, and turn it to the left three times. Only this stone will open the lock."

Paco's byzantine mind was captivated by this fable. But he still wavered.

"How do I know the lock still works?" he said. "Metal corrodes after hundreds of years," he said.

"How else did I get the photographs? And the piece of fresco?"

Surely Paco had profited by the several days' wait to race those photos and the bit of mural to some trusted archeologist crony in the Ministry of Culture. The expert had surely told him what I wanted him to hear.

Paco was now convinced. His eyes glowed with fervor.

. *"¡Dámelo!"* he barked, forgetting where he was and raising his voice. "Give it to me!"

I made a step forward, pretended to stumble, and "clumsily" dropped the ring near El Sicario's feet. The ring bounced on the rough sand, and disappeared into a bull's hoofprint. Paco saw his prize about to be lost in the sand.

"Damn," I said. "Sorry..."

"Get it!" Paco barked imperiously at El Sicario.

Impelled by his master's anger and greed, El Sicario did exactly what I hoped he would do. For a moment he pulled his gunpoint off Juan, and bent over to grope around for the ring. That was when I gave El Sicario a mule-kick in the head with all my strength, using the foot on my bad leg, keeping my balance with my good leg. The kick felled him. A warning twinge went through my bad leg.

Then the play of chaos was in the ring.

The Luger fell from El Sicario's hand. Juan's rage and military training had him on tenterhooks — he exploded into action and grabbed for the gun. Paco, quicker than we'd thought, lashed out blindly and hit Juan on the side of the face. My friend staggered Paco with a punch, knocking his glasses off. El Sicario was getting up, knife flashing in his hand. I grabbed the gun, covering El Sicario with it, feeling my leg pulse with pain. My hand fished in my raincoat pocket for Juan's own knife. I gave it to him, and he gratefully flicked it open. The nasty blade gleamed in the light.

"My glasses," moaned Paco.

Suddenly, at the back of the ring, there was a sound of horns on wood that made my blood jolt. The bull-gate thudded open. I hadn't given the agreed-on signal. But the lithe shape of a Camargue bull irrupted into the ring. Those upswept horns, wide as the wetlands and sharp as desire, glinted in the moonlight. Muzzle glistening, the bull shook his head threateningly and looked around.   Wild cattle see amazingly well in the dark, as boys have learned when they sneak into pastures at night to try a few passes. Even in the dark, there was no mistaking that star on his dark forehead. It was Baby.

The bull blasted his whistling snort of alert.

"Shit," swore El Sicario. His thug bravado melted into a thousand-year-old terror of bulls.

"Juan, stand very still," I said.

Finger on trigger, I clutched the Luger. I could try and shoot the bull though I had no idea if I could hit that star in his forehead with the first shot. And how many bullets would be needed to drop this hurtling comet of death?

My subalterns were on the job. "Hah-hey!" they called from the barrier. Dark capes flared there, catching the bull's eye.

"You bastard," Paco panted, hearing the voices, "you didn't come alone."

Oblivious to the bull's presence, he fell on his knees, grabbling around in the sand for his glasses.   Finally his desperate fingers found the glasses and jammed them on his face, but they were now covered with wet sand. Baby spotted his movements, and veered toward us. That animal grew in size like the Madrid-Santander overnight express train bearing down on us.

I aimed the Luger at Baby's starred forehead, praying to the Lady of Mercies like I'd never prayed before, hoping for a brain shot. Sighting a handgun on that white little target, which bobbed up and down with each stride, was difficult. I squinted, fired. The gun jammed. That damned handmade silencer was no good.

Manolillo was in the ring now, flaring his cape desperately. But the bull was too close to us to be distracted from his deadly closing rush. In a flash, I knew what would happen, a second before it did. El Sicario was the one who made the fatal move. In terror, he broke and ran for the barrier. Baby's pitiless eye caught the movement. In a burst of flying sand, he veered away from us, galloping after El Sicario.

"Juan, run!" I barked at my friend, and pointed at the blind in the opposite direction. I dropped the useless gun and whipped off the raincoat, ready to use it as a makeshift cape.

Juan raced for the blind, and safety.

Chaos now caught up with El Sicario — the deaths of his victims, packed by fate into the roiling muscles of a single wild animal. The racing bull lowered his head, and swept his master horn up. We heard El Sicario shriek as the bull caught him in the back of the thigh muscle with the "diamond" of the horn, that sharp point that the bull hones in the dirt, and whipped him into the air. So deft is the bull with this weapon that he can jab two or three separate trajectories into your flesh during those brief seconds that he has you in mid-air. The man fell over Baby's shoulder, blurred. As he hit the sand, and rolled over and over, the bull spun on his hocks, and nailed him to the ground. With technical austerity, toreros call this horrible moment the *remate* — the frosting on the cake.

We heard a strangled sound as the horn speared into El Sicario's chest. The bull flung his victim along the sand, lunged after him, and speared him yet again.

Manolillo and Bigotes were both there now, horrified, with their flapping capes. They drew the bull away from the fallen man. Quickly I picked up the gun and shoved it through my belt.

Meanwhile Paco, the fool, had been frantically grubbing around in the sand for the ring, moaning and grumbling to himself. Now sounds and movements had finally alerted him to reality.

"My god, my god…a bull is here," he said tremblingly. "You have done this! Traitor! Traitor!" he accused me. "Your word means nothing!"

Hatred and rage carried away the last shreds of my brother's common sense. He got up and lunged at me. But I had the sword in my right hand now, and raincoat in my left. I stopped my brother's forward rush with the slender bent blade, that was designed to go deep in the bull's body and cut the aorta. Right now it flexed menacingly with a little hum of metal against Paco's left lapel, right at heart level.

"*Perra,*" he spat at me. "Female dog in heat."

"Save your breath, brother of a dog. Walk…before the bull comes back."

At sword-point, I prodded Paco toward the barrier. My leg was steadily getting worse, throbbing.

In the far end of the oval ring, Manolillo and Bigotes were holding the bull, keeping his eye with little jerks of their capes. Baby's wet horn glistened in the moonlight. Nearby, El Sicario lay motionless on the sand, looking like a twisted bundle of old clothes.

"The key is lost," Paco groaned. "You stupid idiot."

At all costs, I had to retrieve the piece of jewelry. If any investigation followed, the police could easily connect the ring to me. There were jewelers in Madrid who knew that ring, to say nothing of other unfriendly members of my family. My fingerprints were on it.

At the barrier, I said to Juan, "Hold Paco here, while I find the ring."

Juan's nose was bleeding, his eye swelling. Grimly he grabbed

Paco in a stranglehold from behind, by his tie, and propelled him into the alleyway.

Thrusting the sword into my coat, spreading it wide to make the biggest possible lure, if I needed it, I ran back towards the center of the ring. I actually ran...well, jogged limpingly, trying to ignore the pain. Within that circle of chalk, my trained mind remembered right where we'd been standing. Keeping a wary eye on the bull, I stooped and ran my fingers around in the scuffed sand, trying to remember exactly where I dropped it. In the distance, a few festive firecrackers went off. Time was ticking — we had to get out of here.

I searched and searched.

"Hurry, man!" called Manolillo in a low voice.

At last! The ring's familiar shape was in my fingers. I ran painfully back to the barrier. The familiar throbbing pain filled the old re-damaged nerves, flooded my leg. Was I still that fragile?

Seeing that we were safely out of danger, my subalterns made one last maneuver. While Manolillo flared his cape at one barrier and lured Baby toward him, Bigotes grabbed El Sicario's feet and ran backwards, skidding the fallen man across the sand towards another barrier. When Bigotes was safe, Manolillo ran for the wall and vaulted over it. Now Baby ruled the ring in lonely triumph. He returned to the spot where he'd wet his horn, and sniffed the sand, then threw up his head and raised his upper lip in distaste.

In the alleyway, my enraged friend had my brother pinned to the wall in the alleyway. Paco now found himself nose to nose with centuries of *maricón* fury. Juan had Paco's tie garrotted around his throat, and his knife-point against Paco's fly. "How do *you* like this?" he hissed. He pricked Paco again and again. Paco winced.

"Go ahead and cut him," I said jokingly. "His good Catholic family is big enough."

"Please have mercy," whispered Paco.

"You had no mercy on us," I said. "Fuck you."

Reaching past Juan, into Paco's inside jacket pocket, I plucked the legal documents out and shook them before his eyes.

"You broke our agreement," I said. "You were going to kill us. So you get nothing. Have the regime dub you Count of something, if titles matter so much."

"Deceitful degenerate," mumbled Paco past bleeding lips. His eyes blazed.

I seized Paco's tie myself. My words rode on rage, as I slammed him against the wall again and again, for emphasis, and put my face to his, so he had to smell my *maricón* breath. I was on the edge of killing Paco in cold blood. But I held back from murdering my kin. His own lack of humanity would kill him. Let the Lady of Mercies be his judge. The important thing was to silence him.

"Remember…a faggot saved your life tonight. I could leave you for the bull to kill. If you ever breathe a word of this to anyone, my side of the story will be told in the foreign press. Every soul in Spain will see you being outsmarted by a faggot and squeaking for mercy. The whole country will die laughing at you."

With a last shove, I let Paco go.

"Your man is hurt over there," I said. "Better get him out of here before he dies, or the gendarmes find you. Is anyone else with you?"

"A lookout…outside," Paco said faintly.

"Get him," I said. "This is your problem now."

As I limped towards the entrance, with Juan beside me, Manolillo, Bigotes and Santí came running softly out of the dark.

"That guy is still breathing over there, but he's hurt bad," Bigotes panted.

"Paco has help on the way," I said. "Let's go."

When we left the bullring, the street still slumbered in its drunken quiet. More yeah-yeah music, the voice of Marie Osmond, could be heard. We strolled casually around the corner to where we'd parked the rented Citroën. A seventh horse was tied at the bar now. Every vaquero in the Camargue must be celebrating the day's deeds. Leisurely we got in our car — Santí driving, Bigotes in the shotgun seat, Manolillo and Juan and me crammed in the back seat. Santí stepped on the gas, and we lurched off with a little screech of tires. My heart almost stopped at the noise.

"Jesus…no movie stuff," I calmed my subaltern. "Don't attract attention."

At a discreet speed, our car wended its way through the narrow winding streets, past a few groups of late merrymakers, a few drunken French vaqueros on horseback. Manolillo was putting the sword and Luger in the sword-case under our feet. Behind us, the moonlit wall of the amphitheater disappeared behind the roofs. Now my knees were trembling, like when the bull is dead. My first thought was Juan. Grabbing him by the shoulder, I studied his haggard bloodied face in the street lights going by. Something alien was in his eyes, as if he'd walked on the Moon and seen something unimaginable to other humans.

Juan shook loose. "Don't grab me," he said hoarsely.

"Are you all right?" I insisted.

"Of course," he said curtly.

"Why did you throw the bull in the ring?" I asked Santí.

"Well…you signaled."

"I didn't."

"Boss, I heard a voice," Santí argued.

"That was Paco. He said *dámelo*," I said.

"Shit," said Santí. "From a distance, it sounded like *toro*. Sorry it was Baby. He was the easiest one to get in the pipeline." He paused. "So the bull got somebody, eh?"

"A bad guy."

"Is he dead?"

"If he is, it's Paco's problem. Good work, boys."

"Are you all right, Juan?" Bigotes asked.

"I'm fine," said Juan faintly. "Thanks to all of you."

"It was nothing," said Manolillo.

We made a quick stop at a fountain where Juan washed the blood off his face. Soon we were out of town, passing through tidelands, The Moon's reflection smearing across the water. For the last time in my life, I was driving away from a bullring. Juan Diano was with me again, and this time he would never leave. Beyond caring what anybody thought, I threw my arms around Juan. His whole body was trembling from what he'd lived through in a week. He smelled rank — his captors must not have let him bathe for all that time. He didn't hug me back. He must still be in shock.

The crew sat with eyes straight ahead. What did they sense?

Shortly Juan fell asleep with exhaustion, propped in his corner. Exhausted myself, I nodded off and slumped against Juan. Even with the growing pain in my leg, it was comforting to feel his body warmth, but something in his energy bothered me. After a while, the wind blasting through the open windows was cold. I woke to feel Santí covering Juan and me with the raincoat.

Somewhere along the highway to Marseilles, on a bridge crossing a little estuary, we pulled briefly off the road and the men raised our hood, pretending to check the engine. While they did that, I polished our fingerprints off the Luger and silencer, and hurled them into the sea. Somberly the men noticed that I was limping again.

It was the next morning before Juan and I were finally alone together, in his room at the Hotel Bezique. My room was next door, and we had opened the connecting door between. No word from José yet. I had started worrying obsessively about that. My leg was so bad that the hotel desk had secured me a cane, and I was hobbling around on it. But Isaías and Tere were on their way with the Mercedes. Security was good.

Santí was in the next room, in case we needed him. Shutters were closed against the heat.

Juan had little to say to me. He locked himself in his bathroom a long time, shaving, scrubbing away the filth. When he came out, I had my first inkling that he was no longer the same human being who had been snatched from me in Madrid.

18

As Juan rummaged in his suitcase, finding slacks and a pullover, his brief rage was lapsing into quieter edginess. With a cigarette between his lips, he roamed the room nervously, checking the locked door, checking the window, looking in the bathroom to make sure no one was there. When a car backfired in the street outside, he jumped. Sweat bathed on his face. Sharp invisible blades of emotion seemed to stick out in the air around him. His cheekbone and nose were bruised.

At first his edginess seemed only the natural result of what he'd been through. As the hours passed, however, I began to see that the single week in Paco's hands had shattered him strangely. Now he was a wraith shaped like my Juan, almost unrecognizable in those clothes he'd last worn at the *coto*. He seemed apathetic, distant, gray — a body without a spirit. Somehow I had imagined us celebrating our reunion by some kind of physical contact. If not making love right away, at least touching and comforting and calming each other.

Sitting on the edge of the bed, I smoked too, watching him. The cane leaned beside me. After the long 24 hours in Arles, I was barely holding onto my own self-discipline. I felt cold, strangely empty. And I was a cripple again. A 30-year-old man walking with a cane.

Finally Juan stood at the window, staring out through the shutters, over the vast smoggy harbor with its vista of cranes and superstructures of ships. He was staring at nothing. A tic had developed under his right eye. He said in a low flat voice:

"The bull must have killed that guy. The police will be looking for us now."

"Bigotes said he was still alive. Paco will get him to a doctor. He'll do everything he can to cover this up."

In the harbor, a ship gave a long deep hoot. The sound must have reminded Juan of the Santander harbor. Was he regretting the impulse that had brought us together?

"How did you get me out?" he asked.

I told him the story.

His jaw clenched. "So the whole world knows, eh?"

"Isaías and Tere know. I had to tell them. The crew have guessed. They're…more sympathetic than I thought."

In the dim light, his eyes made full contact with mine for the first time since he'd escaped. A little more than a week ago, I had looked into those eyes at eyelash range. They had glowed with passionate care — so close to mine that I felt I had kissed his spirit. I had felt his hands, those hands of his that knew how to hold partridge chicks, how to dig for water and plant seeds. His power to turn a wasteland green. To talk with lynx and deer. To ride the Moon. Now, in those eyes, that spirit was pulling back from me — farther, farther, ever more tiny. He didn't even express any appreciation that I'd been ready to give up everything for him.

The frenzied suspicions of the past week became a certainty in my mind. "After they took me to see Paco, what did they do to you?" I asked.

"Nothing."

"Nothing?"

"They let me put on my clothes. They sat me in one of those offices, with the shackles still on."

"Then?

"Then they took me somewhere."

"I heard a car leave."

"They drove for a long time. I don't know where. I was blindfolded. Some house in the country somewhere. It was very quiet. They kept me locked up."

"Did they torture you?"

"No. They said something about saving the fun for later."

Why would they resist the temptation to do their worst to a helpless *maricón?* To treat him with the contempt that they reserved for women of no repute? To teach the *puto* a lesson he wouldn't forget? Why did "Christian morality" pretend that heterosexual men were not capable of this degree of contempt? Conquering males had treated prisoners that way since the dawn of time, secure in their illusion of having behaved morally and defended civilization. The terrible images pulsated in my brain. And this was what he feared…that I saw the images in my mind. He even knew that I would have killed him myself, if I could have gotten to him before they did, to spare him the agony and dishonor. Sighting in on his head, squeezing the trigger, a mercy-killing no different than a soldier shooting a wounded comrade to keep him from falling into the hands of the enemy.

"A doctor should look at you," I said.

"It's not necessary."

"Let me look you over, at least."

"No, I tell you!" Juan was getting angry. "There's nothing wrong with me. Just a few scratches. And I'm starved."

I went to the phone and called room service.

If they had shamed him, he would move heaven and earth to hide the physical evidence of that shame. That was what he'd been taught to do, without it ever being stated openly. We had all been taught this secret commandment. And I'd been taught to pursue his shame avidly, verify it, confront him with it. Then the last dreadful bits of theater would happen. He would punish himself for his shame by destroying himself, no different than those women of La Mora who'd been raped by Franco's African troops. Even though what happened was not his fault, he would punish himself. And if he shrank from self-destruction, it was my own duty to destroy him. A million heterosexual dramas and films had been built on this theme.

"Why don't you ever believe me when I tell you the truth?" he asked over his shoulder.

After he'd eaten, Juan lay down on the bed with his clothes on, turning his back to me, staying on the very edge of the bed.

I went to my own room, and slept fitfully. When I got up that afternoon, Juan was still sleeping and the door was locked. So I limped downstairs and found Isaías and Tere. They had checked in and were having lunch in the dining room. I sat with them, and wordlessly put the envelope of legal documents in front of my manager.

Isaías smiled a small grim smile. "Good work," he said.

Later, in their room, we sat on their balcony with a brandy, staring over the smoky harbor. Here in France, too, those poisonous hazes layered the atmosphere. Isaías took his lighter and burned the documents one by one, including all the copies I'd made, in the ashtray. We watched them curl into black ash.

"Now we talk about what comes next," Isaías said.

"I need someone to look after my interests while I'm abroad. To make sure the *coto* moves ahead…"

The old man looked at his wife. "Leave us for a while."

Tere stood her ground, standing behind me, hands gripping my shoulders maternally, possessively. "You think this talk is too indelicate for my ears, eh? Well, I'm not going."

In the ashtray, a sea breeze lifted some of the ashes away.

"I intend to fulfill my duties here," Isaías barked. "But I will pray for understanding, because right now I don't have it. I don't understand the young man here."

"Pray to Our Mother of Mercies," Tere retorted. "Maybe She will show you mercy."

"Woman," he growled, "you are too old to be modern. Go get your typewriter, then. We have work to do."

The civilized calm and cleanness of the Bezique dining room, after that surreal savage night in Arles, was almost too much to bear. It was now the next morning. In the center of our snowy-white linen tablecloth was a bowl of fresh-cut anemones from the flower fields around Nice. Second servings of *cafe au lait* steamed in large cups. Remnants of good French butter and rolls. A bowl of pear jam. Juan's empty plate — he had devoured two ham omlettes. Lots of crumbs. Overflowing ash-trays.

Still no word from José and Sera.

Our group looked at one other blearily. We stirred our coffee, put in lumps of sugar.

Shaking his head, Isaías handed the newspaper to me.

On the third page of the Marseilles paper, there was a little item datelined Arles. Yesterday morning (it said) one of the bulls from Sunday's event had been found loose in the amphitheater. It appeared that some local delinquents had broken in and done a little night bullfighting. Human blood on the sand suggested that someone got hurt. But the boys, whoever they were, had escaped and taken their wounded comrade with them. The article cluck-clucked about the dangers of youth pranks with wild cattle. The bull, Baby, had gone back to his ranch amid celebra-tion, and was already scheduled for more appearances in Provençal rings.

Juan was silent, wearing his brown jacket, staring out the window at the pool. There, a few near-naked bikini-clad women were frolicking in the water with little shrieks. This was France, where bikinis were scantier than in Spain. Was it possible that Juan had bought that jacket in Santander only five months ago, thinking of me obsessively as he slid his bills across the counter one by one?

The diamond ring was cleaned and back on my finger. I was smoking a little cigar — the first in a while. Tere had her ledger, writing the last checks to the crew for their work. She gave me the balance of my fee in cash, large French bills in francs. I looked at the men.

"Well, boys," I said. "We've come to the end. Of bulls, anyway."

The crew looked at each other. Their minds were withdrawing now, maybe worried about what black rumors about me they'd encounter back in Spain. The Eibars had already steeled themselves against these rumors, these worries. At the end of our long meeting yesterday, we had new documents giving them the power of attorney to look after my affairs. Juan had signed a power of attorney for his tiny bank account. Spanish law limited the amount of cash or gold that could be taken out of the country, so Juan's and my funds would have to stay banked in Spain, but the Eibars would send us a small check now and then.

I told the crew:

"Isaías will make an announcement that I am retiring and getting some rest abroad. If people want to know more than that, tell them to talk to Isaías and Tere. They will be looking after all our interests, and using Las Moreras as their country house. If you have any trouble from Paco, talk to Isaías. But I don't think you will have any problems. Paco was too worried about other things, and he's so nearsighted, I don't think he recognized any of you in the dark."

"So...you're going into exile?" Bigotes asked.

His forehead wrinkled sadly. *Exilio* is a terrible word in the Spanish language. It had been uttered many times since 1930, and many more times since 1492. Jews, Arabs, Moors, Gypsies, leftists, homosexuals, packing their bare necessities and fleeing where they could. Right there in France, celebrated artists — Picasso, flamenco singers — were living because of the regime.

"At the least, we have to stay away for a while," I said.

"Till *He* dies, anyway," Isaías frowned.

"When He dies, maybe things will loosen up, " I agreed.

"Where are you going to live? Here in France?" Tere asked.

"We don't know yet," I said.

Only the Eibars knew that Juan and I were still waiting to hear from my sister. My men didn't know yet about José and Sera.

It was time for all of them to go — they had a long drive home in the Mercedes. Isaías and Tere had turned in their rented Citroën and were riding home with the crew. As I signed a bill of sale for the Mercedes, and gave it to Isaías and Tere, I told them:

"My torero gear is yours too. For your museum, if you ever have one. Or give it to some worthy novice...if you find one."

"The bulls are a closed chapter for us," Isaías growled.

He paid the check, and we left the dining room. Under the hotel's front awning, with its fake Roman decor, I shook the strong brown hands of my crew. Would the men dare to give me a parting abrazo? They would, pounding my back. They pounded Juan's back too. Who knew what was ahead for our country? They knew that they might not see us again, ever.

"Again...a thousand thanks," Juan told them in a low voice.

"Good trip," I said hoarsely. "Good luck."

The men threw their gear and luggage into the dusty old Mercedes. For once, there was no argument about where the sword-case went. Santí held the door protectively for Tere and Isaías, so they could ride in back. I helped Tere into the back seat, kissing her hand as she settled in. Her stubby hand, the hand of a tough Basque fishing dame who knew how to drive a trawler in a Biscay storm, caressed my cheek.

Then the Mercedes pulled away into the midday traffic.

Juan and I walked back into the lobby. I had a strange hollow feeling of "now what". Juan wanted to sleep some more, so I gave him the key.

"Don't let anyone in the room but me," I said.

"I know how to take care of myself," he snapped, and headed for the elevator.

It wasn't too early for a drink, so I limped to the terrace. An impeccable waiter brought me an impeccable Bombay gin on a spotless tray. There I was in my white linen slacks and silk pullover and my haggard look, complete with sun-glasses and cane — the picture of a Cote d'Azur parasite, sitting there alone to ponder some James Bond plot, except I wasn't eyeing the pretty girls in bikinis at the pool. It felt like I had stepped through a door into...nothing.

An hour later, as I was finishing the second gin and getting a little drunk, another impeccable waiter brought me a telegram. It was from José, in Lisbon. Why was she in Portugal? She said she'd be landing in Marseilles at 3:20 p.m. No mention of Sera.

As the DC8 jet parked near the terminal, I had my face pressed against the windows of the waiting area. An espresso coffee had sobered me a little. The distant tiny figure of my sister came down the airplane steps, carrying her overnight case, and crossed the tarmac. Then she was in the waiting area, in her French sunglasses and travel-wrinkled Berhayer pants suit. She gave a family kind of female shriek, more publicly appropriate for the dear cousin not seen for 10 years. Knowing her as I did, I knew she was still performing. Amid the roar of planes, she embraced me wildly.

"You got Juan?" she whispered.

"Yes. What about Sera?"

"If all goes well, she will be on the next plane from Paris. Why isn't Juan here? Where is he?"

"Resting at the hotel. How did you do it?"

She hugged me again. I could feel her trembling. I buried my nose in her perfume, my face in her Egyptian priestess wig of hair. Then we walked arm in arm, like lovers, with the skycap carrying her two bags.

"At the last moment, I persuaded my boss to send someone else to Barcelona, and have me do a report on Portuguese bullfights," she grinned. "Some of their bulls are better than ours. And what the hell…I like Mario Coehlo's *veronicas*. I filed my report by phone, and told my boss I needed a vacation. Then I grabbed the next plane to Nice. From there, to Marseilles."

"How did Sera get her passport?"

José was tensed, like a killing sword bent and tested against the barrier. She said tersely:

"One of my diamonds, for a bribe. A colleague at the paper owed me a big favor. I told him a friend of mine wanted to go shopping in Paris, but her Old Catholic mamá wouldn't let her. He believed the story. I took the photo. He took care of the passport, and left it at a drop where she could find it."

As we sat waiting in the airport bar for another hour, José chainsmoked and fidgeted. Her face fell as I told her what was going on with Juan.

"Maybe he's just in shock," she said. "He'll get over it."

When the Air France jet landed, Sera's slender figure was the fifth to come down the steps. She had been sitting in first class. Then we were hugging Sera and there were more public shrieks from both women, appropriate for long-lost sisters finding each other after ten years, and a muffled exclamation or two from me.

In the taxi, José snapped briefly and broke down, her head on Sera's knees, weeping helplessly and raving and cursing over all the years of acting and lying and tying themselves in knots. It sank into my mind that I had been so wound up in my own drama with Juan, that I had actually minimized the women's situation. The tortures and humiliations that they had felt were as serious as if they had been physical. And they had endured far longer than Juan and I had…years and years, compared to a few months. Now it was Sera who was the strong one, sitting with dignity and consoling her friend with quiet words. They held hands — their fingers looked like roots grown together. I was aghast, seeing their love so nakedly and harshly lit, as if by lightning.

The French taxi driver, who didn't understand a word of the

uproar, hunched his shoulders and kept on driving.

Back at the hotel, Juan seemed to recover briefly from his apathy as both women hugged him with a passion born of having accepted him as a best friend among males.

On the hotel terrace, we shared a bottle of champagne and Sera told her story. The escape plan had been simple, no detail that wasn't true to the mundane life of a Spanish rich girl. For days she and José had not seen each other or communicated in any way that was out of the ordinary. The previous day, on the excuse of needing a few toiletries, Sera had snatched a moment to walk alone to the neighborhood pharmacy that she and her mamá always patronized. In the apartment building next door, the concierge was holding a sealed envelope for her — the precious passport. Next day, she picked her moment to run another teeny errand that escaped chaperonage...a visit to the lingerie shop a few blocks away. "I must return this nightie I got...the idiot salesgirl delivered me the wrong size.....*Sí, sí,* I'll be back in a second."

Out the door she went breezing, with a bit of lingerie and a sweater in a Chanel shopping bag that could pass for an overnight bag. In a secret compartment in her purse, she had her jeweley and passport and some cash she'd been hoarding, nothing more. Without even a jacket on, she walked round the corner and grabbed a taxi for Barajas Airport. The most flights out of the country were to Paris, so she bought her ticket there. Sera then placed a call to Mamá, pretending to be calling from the lingerie shop, asking advice on an evening bra. Mamá was none the wiser, and advised her to buy the black lace one.

Sera had then drifted into company with a well-heeled Spanish family heading for a foreign vacation, their first ever. They were flying to Paris, then to Rome, London, New York. Sera chatted with them about joining her vacationing sister in Paris. In this manner she went past Spanish customs in a cozy intimacy with this family. No one noticed her. It was the kind of casual exit from Spain that would have been much harder before the start of *turísmo* ten years before. By the time her Mamá began worrying that her darling daughter hadn't returned from shopping, Sera's plane was taking off.

"And I did do some shopping in Paris," Sera said. "I bought some toiletries at the airport, and a raincoat at the duty-free shop. So it wasn't a lie after all." Her cheeks were flushed with mingled emotion and exultation.

José had rebuilt her fearless facade.

"Bravo," she said, squeezing Sera's hand. "Jaime Bond couldn't have done better."

"Tomorrow Jaime Bond will be homesick," Sera replied, eyes

misting. The enormity of the step she'd taken was sinking into her mind. Parental home, all the familiar things — gone now, replaced by the unknown.

"So...exile?" I said.

"Eh," José said dismissively, "the old man could die tomorrow. In a year or two, there might be democracy, and we can go home."

"Freedom is home enough," Sera added quietly.

"Easily said," I brooded.

Juan frowned. "How will we live out here?"

The next couple of days were spent consolidating our position. Sera called her mother, and let her know she was safe. Doña Margarita was furious at what she took to be a madcap thing. Shopping in France! The result of too much freedom! She demanded that Sera come home.

We were watchful, but no one from Paco's little organization showed up. Yet, in spite of all the exiles living in France, we felt uneasy about staying there. For decades, a humanized France, where the church had finally been removed from power over the state, had been a haven to Spanish refugees. After the second world war, de Gaulle had even demanded that the Allies invade Spain and end the Franco regime. But perhaps Paco's vengeful arm could stretch across the border and find us in France. So we wanted to put more countries between us and him. I called our Red aunt in New York. Without any clear explanations from us, she sensed that something calamitous had happened, and told us to come for a visit.

One evening the four of us councilled, filling a hotel room with cigarette smoke and frustration. José had been drinking hard.

"The obvious place to go is the United States," I said. "Our aunt is there. We already have a home there."

"The United States is Protestant, eh?" Juan asked.

"A lot of Catholics live there," I said. "But the state religion is Protestant."

"The Protestants burned people too," he stated with grim emphasis. "The Protestant guy I knew, the missionary in Bilbao, said so. Some Protestants are as bad as our Old Catholics."

"Yes," José said. "It's true. The main difference is, the Protestants got rid of Our Lady."

"Well, how can we go there?" Juan growled. "If the American Protestants believe in killing people as much as the Old Catholics at home?"

"At least here in France," José pointed out, "they don't believe in much of anything any more, and they leave you alone."

"It would be too easy for Paco to find us here," Sera said.

"The Yankees are changing," I insisted. "They are having their own revolution."

Finally we fell silent. José swigged a last glass of sherry and looked around at the overflowing ashtrays, at our four somber faces. Juan was sitting faced away from us, shoulders slumped.

"Since we are trying to be democratic, let's vote," José said. "Who wants to go to the United States?"

"I do," I said.

"So do I," said José. Her words were slurred.

Sera set her lips. "Then I will."

We all looked at Juan. He shrugged, outvoted.

"All right, I'll go," he said. "But I don't like it."

We discovered that we couldn't get a direct flight to New York from Marseilles. So we went to Nice. Our vacation facade was holding up nicely, but once we bought our New York tickets, we knew our cash would run out soon. It was five days now since Juan had been rescued. We still lacked a clear strategy.

And we were needing spy information on the United States.

So we cast about discreetly. Finally I met a French steward on a cruise ship. He had two day's leave between cruises, and spoke Spanish well. This man was a *maricón,* and I felt he could be trusted. I met with him in our hotel room. He thought I was a single man traveling alone. The women didn't want to identify themselves to him. As for Juan, he didn't want to hear the word *maricón* and left the room while the two of us talked.

The steward offered me some sage advice.

"When you get to customs in New York," he said, "when they look at your papers, one of the things they ask is if you are homosexual. They ask everybody this stupid question. The Americans are pretending they don't already have an army of homegrown homosexuals of their own. You must answer no. Otherwise they will not let you enter the country. As for housing, there are a few quarters in New York City where men are starting to live openly with men...and women with women. And there are a couple of homosexual *tertulias* * .....they will help you get oriented. The laws there are still strict. So you must be careful. Every state has its own different laws against homosexuals...it's like provinces here. So you can wind up in prison if you're not careful. The Tombs —that's a famous prison in New York. A friend of mine wound up there. And from there you would be deported back to Spain."

While I was shuddering at the thought of deportation, he wrote

down the address and telephone of a couple of little *maricón* organizations. There was the Mattachine Society. Casually I asked about women,
and he mentioned the Daughters of Bilitis.

"Oh, and you will need the green card to be able to work. So be
careful. And if you decide to marry an American so you can stay, watch
out! Single foreigners who try to marry there — these get scrutinized
closely by the authorities."

When he left, I took the information to the next room, where
Juan, José and Sera waited. We were still dumfounded at the idea of our
kind organizing openly and politically. So we looked at his page of notes
with our mouths open like village innocents.

"Well!" said José. "Joining forces like a Basque trade union! I
like that."

"We should go ahead and get married," Sera said. "Like we
planned. That way, we won't have trouble getting the green card."

"We can always get divorced later," I added.

Even Juan had to agree that this was a reasonable strategy for the
four of us.

So next morning I had a jeweler re-size one of the wedding rings,
and we bought two more. That afternoon, in the appropriate office of the
Nice city hall, with the French tricolor hanging on the wall, the *maricón*
quartet became two married couples. I put one ring on Sera's finger, and
Juan put the other on José's finger. The yoke would be worn in public
only — we could take it off in a trice, and use it as a club to bludgeon the
enemy. We repeated the vows in front of a Catholic priest, so the marriages would be legally good in Spain. Having copies of the documents
made, I mailed them to Isaías.

Juan went through the motions like he was sleep-walking.

That night José and Sera and I finally phoned our widowed mamás
and told them the news. Well, we had eloped! Yes, yes, we had done
this. We confessed to them that we had never wanted the big wedding in
Toledo Cathedral with a thousand guests and Mamá's antique lace bridal
veil on José's head. It was better this way. More simple, more *moderno*.
We were going to take a long honeymoon...travel a lot, have some fun.
We'd stay in touch...that is, if Mamá and Tita and Doña Margarita weren't
too angry.

Mamá took the news with surprising equanimity, better than the
other two ladies…to the point where I wondered how much she had
guessed. Maybe our mother was smarter than we'd thought. Well, at
least we were married. Thank God for that. She had to confess that she'd
worried. There were calluses on her knees from praying. Did we have
enough money? If we ran short, she'd contrive to send us some. We

should watch out for pickpockets. By the way, had we spoken with Paco? She hadn't seen him for two weeks.

"No…but give him the news for us," I said.

Our DC9 jet roared down the Nice runway, and lifted off. Gravity dragging at the stomach was something I knew from many winter trips to fight bulls in the Americas. José and Sera knew the feeling too. But Juan hated his first plane flight. As the earth fell away under us, he closed his eyes and put his hand on his queasy stomach. When he finally looked out the window, we were high above the purple-blue Mediterranean, hazed over with pollution.

"*Ayyy* mother, " he groaned.

"It's a long way to the ground, eh?" Sera teased him.

"What if the plane falls?" he wanted to know.

Sitting by José, Juan finally opened his eyes and stared dully out the window at the clouds going by. Whatever fright he felt at thinking we were now eight kilometers above the earth, and how long it would take us to fall that far if the engines stopped, was muffled by the noise of some other terror deep in his spirit.

Suddenly José said: "Look — we are flying over Spain."

With helpless remorse, we all pressed our noses to the windows. It was true. The maps in the seat-pockets in front of us showed that our route was angling us across southern Iberia. Far below were sun-soaked mountains — perhaps the Sierra Morena. We weren't far enough north to see the Montes de Toledo, or the summits of the high Cantábrico. Juan tightened his jaws and closed his eyes. But I felt as if the marrow was being dragged out of my bones with iron hooks. Would freedom ever come to Spain? Would freedom change Her enough that we could come home again? Never did I know how much I loved my country till I saw Her falling away behind the jetliner's shining tail. Far off to our right, somewhere to the northeast, out of sight beyond the horizon, was a tiny patch of hesitant green — our *coto*.

The flight was longer than a toothache. José had several drinks of whiskey. Between himself and me, Juan threw up a wall of towering thunderclouds. I was the tiny plane, flying into that storm front at my peril.

José and I had not discussed our strategy with Aunt Pura. We felt awkward about uttering the shattering words *maricón* and *maricona* to our distinguished and noble aunt. Fifteen hundred years of silence had given the words a roar like bombs falling. So we decided to "let things drift purposefully," as José put it, toward the moment when the old lady would see that she had two forbidden couples under her roof.

Would she accept us? Just because she had supported the Spanish Republic didn't mean she would tolerate such things in her family.

When we neared New York City, the cabin filled with rustling sounds as people filled out customs papers. Finally the plane banked over Manhattan Island. Juan's eyes opened wide with fright once again as concrete summits of skyscrapers and urban canyons yawned below us with terrifying nearness. Rivers of traffic moved in deep shadows between the buildings. Then we were staring down on the harbor — blue-gray water, with V's of ship wakes. Our plane's shadow was racing across the water.

"Where is Our Lady of Liberty?" José wanted to know.

"Right down there," I said. "On that little island."

"I don't see Her."

"Right there, silly."

"*Olé* Liberty," Sera cried. "There She is."

"She looks so small from here," said José.

"She is big," I said. "Very big. The first time I came to New York," I added, "I took the boat to that island to pray. I thought it was a shrine. I wanted to find out when the *romería* ** is held, so I could help carry Her out. She is too big to carry, but I thought maybe they carried out a little Liberty. But I found out the Yankees don't pray to Her. I felt sad for Her, and called Her *guapa* a few times to make Her happy. There was an old man there, selling flowers, and I bought all of them, and put them on the steps in front of Her. And an official was going to arrest me for littering."

"How do the American Protestants allow this statue of the Goddess of Liberty?" José wondered. "Do you think they have forgotten She is a pagan?"

Amid our excited babble, Juan was silent and his jaw was working nervously. I tried to calm him with a hand laid on his arm.

"Everything will be all right," I said. "You'll see."

"You told me that before," he said drily.

Our plane's tires screeched on the Yankee concrete of the runaway, at that New York airport named after a Catholic president who had been assassinated.

I thought of the man I'd seen holding partridge chicks in his cupped hands, jacket stretched tight across his broad shoulders. That man I would love always. But he was missing in action. I had no idea if he'd ever come home from his private civil war.

Customs officials loomed ahead. They were rude to us, to everyone in the line. In Spain, even with the slight fascist menace in their manner, our customs men were polite to strangers. Nervous at the rudeness, the bustle of a strange country, the clamors of strange languages around him, Juan held my sleeve like a child.

We told them we were tourists, come to visit a relative. The jewelry, divided among the four of us as "personal possessions", went through without problems. The gems were in pockets, which they failed to search. We noticed that the officials searched travelers who were dressed very yeah-yeah, but they did not bother us with our conservative Spanish tailoring.

Beyond customs, two New York friends of Aunt Pura were waiting with a handlettered sign that said ESCUDERO. They spoke heartwarming words in Castilian. From the international terminal we trudged outdoors into the fiercest, most humid heat that we'd ever felt in our lives. As the friends drove us into town to her flat on East 59th Street, we were almost suffocating.

---

tertulia — an organization or social group dedicated to a particular purpose.

**romería* — a religious excursion, usually to a shrine in the countryside.

19

Aunt Pura had air conditioning. It revived us after the hot sticky trip from the airport. The whole building seemed to vibrate with this modern wonder. Sera actually put her sweater on.

So here we were, sitting with our mythical Red aunt in her living room. In the dining room, the cook was clearing away remnants of Spanish delicacies from import shops in New York — sardines, peppers in oil, marzipans. The bread was from a French bakery. There was even a cruet of my own olive oil for the salad. Pura had known we would be homesick. Over the meal, we had recounted the latest round of gory family politics — everything but the *maricón* part. We'd had a few tense laughs over those hardheaded women, my mother and Tita.

Pura was 86 then, astonishingly vital after a long illness. She had the thinness of a long-dying Castilian poplar, with golden leaves trembling in the tiniest autumn breeze. But she relished her autumn splendor. A long dressing gown of fiery red Chinese silk clothed her brittle frame, over an old-fashioned mauve crepe dress that came down to her ankles and her old-lady black shoes. She had her own stout cane, a bamboo one, but spent more time waving it at us than leaning on it. Right now she had the cane leaning against her chair, as she fanned herself with a tortoiseshell fan.

"Canes are good for the old and the young," she had said, daring to tease me about my own cane.

Like a noble lady of old, Pura lived alone in a tower — the 20th floor of an art-deco apartment building near the East River Drive. It was what New Yorkers call a "penthouse." The cook and housekeeper came a few times a week. Outside the sliding doors we could see her tiny rooftop garden where grapevines, roses, geraniums and tall cedars survived in pots. A tiny fountain tried hard to make the space feel like a Spanish patio, even as Manhattan soot fell steadily on the red geraniums, turning them blackish purple if they weren't rinsed daily.

Indoors, her wealth was displayed not in furniture, but in human images. Her well-to-do American diplomat husband had been dead for 20 years now, even her two children both dead, and five grandchildren scattered to the winds. She had spent her twenty years of exile in passionate devotion to Spanish exiles and Spanish travelers of arts and letters. Old photographs and mementos covered the walls — framed concert programs, poems scribbled on napkins, young works by Picasso, Miró and other artists now famous. To my surprise, a photo of her with Federico García Lorca hung over the well-used record player. We had no way of knowing if Lorca's iris scent of scandal had reached my aunt's sensitive nostrils. In the picture Lorca's eyes were dark with his lifelong sadness — dark as my Juan's blue eyes were now. He sat across the coffee table from me, staring into his brandy glass.

Was it possible that only two weeks ago, Juan had been laughing, glowing, looking at me out of the corners of his eyes as the four of us learned the rumba together in a Madrid nightclub?

Brandy glasses and tableware clinked as José poured herself another shot. My aunt had already noticed José's heavy drinking.

"Auntie, I didn't know you met Lorca," José hazarded.

"Yes…when he passed through New York in 1930."

"He stayed here?"

"He visited us at the old place on East 64th Street. I gave it up after Roger died. It was too big for me. Yes," Aunt Pura said pensively, "we have had these little wars within the family from time to time…our family, the family of Spain."

She spoke a crisp educated Castilian of long ago. Listening to her was like hearing a sound track from an old movie.

Her sharp old eyes moved from me, to the young man who had been introduced to her as José's new husband. Silent and uneasy, Juan lowered his eyes. He had made an effort towards a good appearance. He wore the brown Cortefiel jacket and his best shoes, had combed his hair carefully and looked like an engineering student on vacation. But in spite of his provincial handsomeness, there was no hiding the fading bruises, now green and purple, on his face. I had a sudden violent understanding of how emotionally naked Juan and I now were: a sweet sun-ripe orange peeled by brute fingers, our juices running helplessly. For the first time, the thought crossed my mind that a long time would pass, maybe many years, before we might throw off the effects of that evil done to us.

"Well," she said, "of course you can stay here till you get on your feet. I have two little guest rooms. You will want your own apartments soon enough. I know you modern couples. And you will have to get green cards to work...visas that permit you to stay here as permanent resident aliens. I can sponsor you as a close relative. There shouldn't be a problem."

She smiled slyly at me. "But there is not much work for toreros in the United States."

"I have a degree in biology...experience with horses and game," I said. "I'll find something."

"And you, José?"

"I'll look for work in the...how do you say it?...the American mediums." My sister was pouring herself another drink.

"The word is media," Pura said, sipping at her brandy. "And you, child?" She looked at Sera, who had been introduced to her as my brand-new wife. "You don't have a degree, do you?"

"My mother wouldn't let me go to university," said Sera. "I want to go."

Before Pura got to Juan, he suddenly got up and went slamming out the sliding door, into the savage heat of the garden. We watched him leaning on the penthouse balustrade.

"He's...eh...homesick," I apologized for him.

"What is *he* going to do?" Aunt Pura wanted to know, looking at José. "He's just a country lad. Does he even have primary education?"

"Yes. He wants to study veterinary medicine," José said.

How very paltry a parchment for medical treatment of animals must look to Juan right now.

"What happened to his face?" Pura asked.

José paused before answering. "Paco roughed him up."

"Paco? Your wimpy brother?"

"He didn't approve of my marrying Juan," José said tersely.

Pura's old eyes searched our faces. Surely she knew we were hiding something.

"Well," she said, "the family needs new blood. One of the best veterinary colleges in the world is at Cornell. Your passport stamp gives you two months. Time to see if you like it here. If you stay, I can help the two students with a little money. But I'm not all that rich. They'll have to work on the side. The cost of living here is much higher than in Spain. You'll see."

Pura fussed around, settled us into our rooms as couples. Both rooms had twin beds, Pura's concession to modernity. Patiently we let her explain where everything was, knowing that we would quietly switch rooms after she had gone to bed. But in these cramped quarters we couldn't do this for long — the cook and housekeeper would start noticing little things. Outside the windows, New York roared with that titanic energy that made Madrid feel like a village. Now and then, the walls shook — Pura told us it was the distant rumble of subway trains passing. And there were other terrible wailing sounds that came and went.

"What are they?" Juan asked me. "They sound like war."

"Those are the fire sirens they have here," I told him. "There are fires all the time. So many people and buildings."

That evening, being the lawyer I had become, I called a phone number that the steward had given me, and asked some questions. *Sí, sí,* the man's voice said, there are some bad laws. No, they don't kill you here. But the state of New York will put you in prison for 20 years if they catch you. We are trying to change things, the voice said, but it is still important to be discreet.

In the coming months, I would get my first glimpses of Yankee gays, as *maricones* called themselves here. We would see them discreetly living in little apartments like husband and wife — even starting to hope that the state might legalize their liaisons someday. Their dream, big as an ocean, shocked me. My dream was small — a pebble on a beach. Juan and I had never dreamed of such a thing. The Spanish gays of Lorca's and Sanchez Mejías' generation, and mine, were gypsy horse-traders camping stealthily in the shadow of castle walls. They roamed the town at night together, visited each other discreetly, spent summers together in a faraway place if they could get away with it — as Lorca and Dalí did during their summer in Cadaqués. But sooner or later, a storm of angry knightly arrows came flying from the battlements, forcing them to strike their tents and flee. Marry Juan? My friend and I hadn't even declared ourselves. My dream was still small — freedom from injury, a safe room, a few nights of peace, and the possibility that he would say *cómo te amo, Majín.*

Late that first night, after Pura was sound asleep and we had stealthily dared the creaking old floors to change rooms, I lay listening to his breathing in the other twin bed. Would he wake up and come over to me on his own? If not for intimacy, at least for some closeness? I wondered if the two women were going at it, Será wearing the nightgown of *bolilla* lace that José had bought in Madrid, tender nipples pressed to tender nipples, hair mingled, fingers searching for the eye of the Moon. But then I heard José and Sera arguing.

Finally I turned my face into the pillow, and tried to sleep. The night passed, and he didn't come to me. The thought crossed my mind that I had given up my country and my heritage for Juan Diano Rodríguez, only to see him slip from my gaze like the sunset.

The next afternoon, José and I went out to an old diamond dealer on 57th Street that Pura knew, a Sephardic Jew named Aben Gómez. He bought two of our rose-cut diamonds, praising their cuts, and gave us $10,000 U.S. dollars in cash. Everything was expensive here. At this rate, the diamonds would not last long.

When we returned, Juan was gone from the apartment.

Still exhausted from the strain, Sera had been sleeping. She had no idea where my friend had gone. For several hours, we suffered pangs of the damned, wondering what had happened to him. José and Sera and I finally broke down and confessed to Pura something of what had happened — Paco's possible involvement with a terrorist group, the kidnapping, our efforts to free Juan, all without mentioning the *maricón* part. Pura was aghast, furious, pounding her cane on the floor.

Finally, in early evening, just as our aunt was about to call the police, Juan showed up. He was carrying his jacket, shirt grass-stained and stuck to him from the heat. He had gone for a walk, he told us curtly. He got lost in this cursed city, and couldn't see enough of the sun to find his directions. To the west he saw trees, so he went that way. It was a big city park — the smell of grass, a pond or two. He roamed there for hours, then lay on the grass. He saw animals. Horses pulling tourists in old carriages. There was even a sickening little zoo with iron bars and tigers sitting in their own filth. Finally he met some people speaking a funny kind of Spanish. They were from a place called Puerto Rico, and they helped him find his way back here.

My panic gave way to fury. No matter that what he'd done was understandable. I berated him for leaving without telling us.

At this, Juan exploded. "I'm suffocating here," he said.

Then he strode out to the garden.

I followed him, and tried an apology and quiet talk. The sun was setting into murky yellow hazes, a thousand times thicker and more poisonous than the smog blanketing Madrid. He walked around with Pura's garden hose, smoking morosely and rinsing soot off the red geraniums and begonias. The fragile smell of water moved with him — reflections of fire-red sky pooled around his feet. He looked alarmingly thin, was unshaven today. I trailed in his wake, talking to him about the years ahead, about what we might do and learn in America.

Juan stubbed out his cigarette on the parapet, bent and put his head under the hose to cool himself.

As I touched his arm, Juan's eyelids fluttered for a moment. He looked like a mask coming to life. The wild blue gaze moved to mine, expressionless. Then he looked away again, over that smoky skyline that might have been a thousand cities burning in a war.

Hair dripping, he shook away my hand.

"I feel like I'm in hell here," he said.

As he moved away, taking that smell of water with him, I leaned over the parapet. It was 20 floors down to the street. A human body, falling from here, would open fleshy petals against the sidewalk like a red geranium of death. What if Juan jumped? If he killed himself, or if he went crazy from those memories of imprisonment, whatever they were, I would go back to Spain and kill Paco. I was capable of crafting terrible revenge on my brother. He would be a whole month dying, I swore. I would invent fantastic and undreamed-of torture instruments that would be named after me and put on display in museums, like the medieval ones I had seen in Nuremburg, Germany.

How could I stir Juan's wild cantankerousness? Get him angry enough to fight back? The picador of belief had punished him beyond the limit, sitting impassive with dripping lance. The young bull swayed on his feet, dripping blood, his tongue hanging out. He had retreated onto that small patch of sand where he felt safest. How would I pull my friend out of there...make him jealous with a cape of meaning?

"'Tonio, what *is* the matter with him?" José asked me.

My sister was beginning to have her own suspicions that something had been done to him.

Later that evening, before Pura went to bed, my aunt called me into the front room to sit with her and have a brandy. She always drank a little brandy before she went to bed.

"Sit down, my boy," she said. I obeyed quietly.

"Your friend is sad," she said.

It had to be noted that she referred to him as my friend, not my sister's husband.

"Something like that," I said miserably.

"He seems like a fine boy," she said. "But sad."

Suddenly, like a sledgehammer blow, a memory of that scene in the vaulted room hit me. My skull almost caved in. My head fell forward, chin resting on my chest.

Her voice went on. "You have known him...how long? Three months?"

"I met him in May. José met him shortly after that."

"Is that time enough to know someone well?" she inquired.

"We know him well enough," I said hoarsely. My hand was shaking. My knees were trembling.

"Then you know what he needs," she said with finality, putting down her glass. "Open that desk drawer over there, and bring me the key ring that's there."

I obeyed. On the ring was a big brass key and a little silver key. She pressed the key ring into my hand.

"The big key is to my country house," she said. "It is three hours north of the city, in the Catskills. I haven't been there for a while — the trip is too hard for me now. But I will call, and have someone get the house ready for you. You need to go there with your friend. He needs to be in the country. Stay there with him as long as necessary."

My emotion caused the front of my shirt to heave slightly.

"The house is very private," she added. "You will be safe there. The gun cupboard has shotguns in it. We used to shoot pheasant up there. The small key unlocks that cupboard."

The tears I was choking back were my fear that Juan and I would come to our final parting in that house.

"José and Sera," Aunt Pura was saying, "will stay here with me. We will have a wonderful time going to concerts."

As I was leaving the room, she said:

"One more thing. In the countryside, there is an American plant with three leaves that you mustn't touch. It will make your skin break out in blisters. I'll draw you a picture."

That night, I had a terrible dream. We were on a ship, passing Gibraltar, heading into the Atlantic. I saw my friend leaning over the rail. The deck was empty, wet, with spray dashing across it. His shirtsleeves and trousers fluttered madly in the wind, and his leg was in a cast. He was staring, fascinated, into the wake boiling along the ship's side — at the crash and rip of icy foam fifty feet below.

My stomach plunged with dismay. The shame had gone so deep that he wasn't fighting it. Even his feelings for me, whatever they were, gave him no hope — in fact, they loomed as the biggest impediment. He felt he wasn't worthy of me now. He didn't want to live. I could already see him falling, blurred, down the side of the ship. Holy Mother, you can't step between another person and their sacred destiny.

Slowly he turned. His face...oh Jesus, that face I loved so much...was streaming wet, maybe with spray.

"I don't owe you anything, rich man," he said. "You owe me. I gave up everything I had. I came to you first. But you took the envelope back from Paco. Remember that."

Then suddenly his hands slid along the rail. On the wet deck, his feet were slipping. His shirt blew up, half-baring his bruised torso. I lunged toward him, holding the rail with one hand, and grabbed him with the other. He swayed against me, arms grabbing my waist. His feet were out under the railing, the leg with the cast flailing in the empty air and the blowing spray. Fifty feet below, the gray-green Atlantic gnashed and roared.

No one would see us fall. Even if someone did, and sounded the alarm, the ship couldn't turn in time to rescue us. In the darkness and rough water, with both of us so crippled, we would drown in a few minutes. In the sea. Together. *En el mar. En el mar.* A voice echoed in my head like a bell tolling. MAR...MAR...MER...MERCY...MARÍA... MARICA...MARIMACHA...MARICóN...

Gasping, I woke to fire-sirens in the Yankee dawn. Juan was startled awake in the next bed, staring at me.

Next afternoon, Aunt Pura loaned us her black Cadillac sedan. She didn't drive any more, just called a chauffeur now and then, so the car mostly sat parked in the garage next door.

"José and Sera and I will use taxis," she assured us.

Since I was the one who could read English road-signs and owned an international driver's license, I took the wheel. Other than mumbling directions from my greataunt's scribbled map, Juan didn't talk. We navigated our way fearfully north from New York City, through heavy traffic and a complicated, confusing system of highways that had many lanes. It was so confusing, it scared me more than a whole corral full of Tulio bulls. These highways were amazingly luxurious and smooth, without a single pothole, and swept us through endless wealthy suburbs and country districts that were suffocatingly green and hazed with that imponderable humidity. Even the state of New York was half as big as Spain! We were in the North American rain forest, as rainy and crowded with trees as Juan's home.

I tried to make conversation. "Yankee highway engineers are such artists," I said.

Isolated in his corner, Juan didn't answer. By evening, we were driving into low rolling mountains, through spa towns, past farms. Juicy pastures were dotted with black-and-white dairy cattle.

"The same breed as in La Montaña," I commented.

Juan just grunted.

Finally, after getting lost twice, I lost my temper at him for not paying more attention to the map. "Curse you," he barked back, and shoved the map at me. "Do it yourself."

Several times I had to pull over and flick on the overhead light, so I could study the map. By the time a mailbox finally loomed ahead, with the right street number on it, I was fuming.

For perhaps a kilometer, our headlights bored along a narrow winding drive, through dense groves of unfamiliar kinds of oaks and evergreens. Aunt Pura had said that her property was an old farm of around 483 acres.

Finally, the old wooden farmhouse loomed ahead. Our headlights threw sinister shadows along the pillared front porch littered by blown leaves. Yankees were still so rich in trees, they could afford to squander them on building houses. In our country, even in Juan's *tierra,* * where groves of oak and beech forest could still be found, they only dared to squander wood on furniture and ox-yokes. In my part of the country, where one scarcely dared to cut the few living trees, everything was made of stone and iron, even people's hearts. Nearby, under several ancient gnarled fruit trees that needed pruning, a strange kind of deer jumped away from her grazing on windfall apples. Her eyes glowed pink in the headlights before she leaped off into the dark.

In sullen silence, we carried our bags in, turned on lights, explored the cold house. Pura must have asked someone to shop — refrigerator and cupboards were freshly stocked. But neither of us was hungry. Freezing, we peered into several dank rustic bedrooms with their Yankee Victorian beds and goose-down quilts. The place smelled musty, so I flung up a couple of windows. Juan slammed the windows down again and locked them, muttering that someone would sneak in and kill us.

When I put my suitcase into the biggest guest room, thinking it would be the most comfortable for us, I was astonished to see Juan throw his bag into another smaller room. The feeling of rejection was like being gored in the stomach.

In the sitting room, someone had carefully laid a fire in the massive stone fireplace. Its mantel was cluttered with silly figurines, and an old china clock that was eerily silent. I wound the clock and jiggled it to get the pendulum swinging, but it died again. Shivering, I lit the kindling and watched flames gather as I broodingly held my hands into the warmth.

As the flickering light reminded me of being in the Crypt of the Mercies with him, homesickness and rage gathered in me like an immense herd of savage beasts. After everything we'd been through — now that we finally had time to be together, and a relatively safe place, we were going to have the fatal quarrel. One of us would say, "I'm finished with you." The living body of our oneness was now strung up by the hamstrings, on hooks, like a carcass. All the Pacos of the world held the terror in their hand, like a saw, and they were cutting us in half. A final fatal fight, two men sick with all the attitudes beaten into them for 2000 years. A strong hand grabbing a shotgun and a couple of shells from that cupboard over there. A crime of passion. Yankee police coming. The strange sirens of this land wailing for us. One of us being led away in the modern stainless-steel handcuffs they used here.

I couldn't hold back the angry stupid words.

"So — after everything, this is where we are," I said.

Suddenly Juan made two strides, his face close to mine. Rage had exploded life back into his empty eyes. He blew the words at me with hot breath, like the whistling snort of a bull at bay.

"Still trying to buy me, eh? Curse you," he barked.

"You'd rather I left you with them?"

"Better dead and free than somebody's prisoner for life."

Suddenly that strong arm lashed out, like a horse kicking. It swept every piece of bric-a-brac from the mantel and sent it crashing to the floor. The china clock hit the floor and burst in a thousand pieces, springs and flywheels flying. His eyes had absolutely gone wild. He snatched out that big pocket-knife that he'd carried ever since I'd known him. I'd seen him use it for everything from cutting rope, to cutting the apple that we shared in the *coto*. He thrust the knife at me.

"Go on, kill me," he said. "Someday that's what you'll do. So let's get it over with."

"Are you crazy?"

"Go on." He thrust the knife at me again. "We're here alone. You can bury me in the woods and tell your aunt I took off again. Nobody will know."

"Why the fuck would I kill you?"

Juan was crowding against me now, almost like a fast bull running over the top of me, trampling my cape of defensiveness. He was talking right in my face.

"Don't pretend with me. You think they dishonored me. The thought of it is driving you crazy. If you had that sword of yours, you'd run me through. Come on, torero. Finish me."

Holding him away from me, I avoided taking the knife.

"I'm not going to live by somebody else's idea of honor," I barked. "If this is your idea of honor, go cut your own throat."

I tried to walk away. He kept trying to crowd against me, blocking my way. The expression in his eyes was terrible. All the violence carefully placed in us by others, like a dynamite charge, was now about to explode against each other. I wondered if he'd actually hit me.

"What is *your* idea of honor?" he scoffed in my face.

"To keep them from winning. To leave the ring alive."

"Are you winning?"

"I don't know," I shouted. "But they got to you, I can see that. I thought you were strong...stronger than me. But you don't have the balls to live. So go ahead...cut your own throat! But don't ask for my help. I'll live another hundred years, and never forget you. But I won't obey them and live in their hell!"

An enormous silence yawned between us. The sword of death slid into me, just behind my heart, where it was supposed to be. A black anguish was bursting there inside of me, like the severed artery.

"And you lied to me about Rafael!" I shouted. "About your old associations! They had a big file on you. I saw it. They knew all about Rafael."

"I never lied about 'Fael." he yelled back. "They are the liars! You believe them and not me! You deserve your misery!"

Expertly he flicked the knife open, and put it in my hand.

"Go on," he said, voice dropping to a dead flat tone. "You've killed so many bulls. You're a good killer. One of the best, they say. You can probably find my heart on the first try. And with my dying breath I'm going to tell you they didn't do anything to me. That was part of their plan."

His words warned me of a hidden truth that I hadn't seen. I shut the knife and tremblingly placed it on the mantel.

He had turned his back on me.

"They didn't touch me," he said over his shoulder. "They didn't even take my clothes off again."

Finally, one torturous step at a time, I had gotten to the obvious question, the right question.

"Then what *did* they do to you?" I asked.

He didn't turn or look at me.

"They made me watch things," he said.

A deep gulp of tears welled into his throat. Head bowed, he choked them down. He was trembling all over, violently.

"They made me watch things they did to other people."

Suddenly truth was looming in my mind, like the bull far back in the tunnel, surging towards the harsh sunlight of the ring. I felt sick with embarrassment and dread. In fact, I suddenly wanted to crawl around on the floor on my hands and knees, and beat my head on those old American oak floor boards. My lips would hardly work as I said:

"What things?"

"Things. I closed my eyes, but I could still hear it. I could smell it. They told me that it was our fault." He pressed his hands on his head, as if he wanted to crush his own brain and blot out the memory.

"They took me to three different places, and made me watch things. Days and days. They told me they would do all these things to me another time. It was how they did their enemies. This is the real shame...that I was there. That other people suffered so much because of you and me."

Wind filled the trees outside, strange leaves rustling. How like La Montaña it smelled here — opulent trees, rich with summer life and light, bending towards golden death.

Now I believed him. Truth glared in my face, like a horror lit by headlights. My mind searched feebly for something to say, to try to rescue the situation. Then it simply fell on its side, like the pinto bull in Santander that first day.

"Tomorrow I'm gone," Juan said softly.

He took his knife off the mantel, and a shotgun and a handful of shells from the cupboard. Then he went into the bedroom he'd chosen, and shut the door.

I left the broken china where it was. After a while, I called José. She was in tears, and had a hollow tone in her voice that I'd never heard before.

"Sera and I had a terrible fight too. I had a little too much brandy and I slapped her. She moved out to a hotel. Our aunt knows, 'Tonio. And she says I'd better be careful. I'm becoming — I'm becoming — well, they call it an alcoholic here."

---

tierra — the region, within a country, where one is born and raised.

20

It was a hot sticky night. After the dry bracing air of Spain, I found it hard to breathe. The dampness in the house stirred up new aches in the old injury. Not wanting to sleep alone in the bedroom, I hauled one of those Yankee feather quilts to the warm sitting-room and went to bed on the couch, fully dressed. Shivering in the quilt, I smoked a couple of cigarettes, and watched the fire die, feeling the terrible feeling of loss and isolation that makes love look so precious by compare.

My overwrought imagination painted a new hideous mural along its endless wall. In it, Juan was leaving. He'd survive for a time. Disappear into Hispanic New York. No work permit, no green card, no education, nothing but slave jobs — a street rough again. Finally he'd be swept into one of those unsavory prisons I'd heard about — which were no better than our Spanish prisons. With his youth, he'd be prime jailbait. Held down by many hands and forced, and forced again, when the guards weren't looking. More likely killed while fighting to protect his integrity. If he survived, he'd be deported back to Spain, where Paco's men would be waiting for him.

Sera would leave too. My sister and I would be left alone.

I ground my teeth, and willed that the infernal artist stop painting these murals of dread in my inner Crypt of No Mercies.

Early next morning, the sadness woke me into remembering our situation. I felt dragged-out and unwell. One always gets sick in a foreign country. The foreign microbes get you. Now, after the strain of months and months, I was going to collapse.

Misty light greyed outside the windows. Even the earliest morning hues had a different color here, with the sky reflecting so much green instead of the grey and silver rock of the Montes de Toledo. Even in this strange land, I had an urgent sense of change — the time that had passed since Juan and I met. Instead of springtime songbirds of the *coto,* it was quiet autumn sounds of strange birds that came through the window, from the depths of the North American rain forest.   Soon it would be five months, from that first impulse on a Sunday afternoon in May. Just five months, five changes of the Moon. The seeds of our frantic, feverish summer together now lay scattered, waiting to sprout in autumn rain. Who knew what future they held?

After a while, the sitting-room windows lit with rosy lightning. A soft roll of thunder followed. Resisting the sick feeling, curious to see what our surroundings looked like, I dragged myself off the couch in my wrinkled clothes, and stiffly put on my shoes.

Outside, a heavy mist wet my face, drifting downwards in an imperceptible rain — what Juan's countrymen call a *sirimiri.* Walking with my cane, I toiled along a foot-path across an English-type lawn, into a thick belt of oak trees and unfamiliar kinds of evergreens, where a rustic bridge arced over mossy boulders. A fern-shaded stream lay over the boulders like green satin, slow and autumn-still. Beyond, I labored into the open and stood there, stunned at what I saw. Even the influenza ache now flooding my bones didn't blunt the wonder.

Returning to the house, I hobbled around to Juan's window. It was shut and latched, of course. Through the dusty glass, he was dimly visible in the bed, half-buried in quilt and pillows. Memory assailed me, of that first morning I found him at his cottage. When I tapped on the pane, he jumped awake, horribly startled. The knife was in his hand. For a moment, he thought he was back in the Black House.

"Open up," I shouted through the pane. "It's important."

After a long pause, he got up and opened the window.

"What do you want, rich man?" His hair was tousled, voice shaking.

"There's something you have to see." I tried to put some positive excitement into my voice.

"Go fuck yourself."

"Come on." I grinned like a lunatic. "Or don't you dare?"

Something in my manner caught Juan off guard, and aroused his curiosity. The dare always worked with him. Grudgingly getting into a white pullover and slacks, then running his fingers through his hair and slipping his knife in his pocket, he looked out the window at the rain, then fished in his suitcase for his old beret, and pulled it on. Finally he came outside. Now the rain was falling harder — as we walked down the path, our hair was already dripping down our necks, shirts stuck to our bodies. He drew deep breaths, sucking that fruity air into his lungs. Surely it reminded him of home.

"What is it?" he glowered.

"Follow me. You'll see."

Simmering with impatience, he walked beside me while I caned myself along. Then, beyond the tree-line, he stopped in his tracks and stared like I had. His mouth opened in astonishment, like mine had.

Before us spread an alpine meadow — ripe grasses and late wild-flowers, all bent under moisture. In my whole life, I had never seen so many green things crammed into one space. Some were strange to us, others were plants that we knew in Spain. Here was dripping goldenrod, there a patch of white yarrow, and everywhere masses of purple mar-guerites. And arcs of bronzy bracken fern, which we also knew from home. The smell of that meadow, its wet astringent herbal life, was intoxi-cating, almost overpowering. Out there in its expanse, a band of North American deer was grazing with dreamy ease — ten slippery does and fawns, and two bucks with their wet horns still in the velvet. Beyond them, the meadow sloped away to a distant fence, and a distant herd of milk-cows. Then on into dim forest and drifting mists.

The sky was lighter now. Beyond the clouds, the sun was rising. Rain was falling harder.

It was literally the first rain that had touched our lives since the night we met in Santander. I felt like I had been transported back to that Hotel Roma window on that May night, smelling the rain, knowing he smelled it too. That night, we had lain in our beds separated by half a city, thinking of each other with the smell of rain in our nostrils, and the smell of our own lonely sweat and seed. Two thousand years of terror had failed to keep us from finding each other.

Once more, lightning threw its stark shadows into the grass. Thun-der slid over us, soft as a caress.

"I promised you this meadow," I said. "Remember?"

Suddenly Juan's fists clenched so hard that his arm muscles crack-led. Blindly, he walked ahead into the trackless grass. He was wading hip deep, touching the seed-heads of the grass with his fingers. Soon he was a distant figure at the end of a lonely winding track into the grass. The deer watched him without concern. Shrugging off his shirt, he bent for a minute. When he straightened up again, he appeared to be naked — a slender white blur on the horizon of green. For a few minutes he held up his arms in the warm rain, letting it wash down over him. He rubbed his arms and his head with the rain, like he was taking a shower.

I stayed where I was. He needed to be alone. At this moment, each of us needed to be alone, face to face with the Goddess of Destiny, who was probably another Lady in disguise. A lump stuck in my throat like dry bread.

Juan lay down in the grass and disappeared.

A while went by. Dripping with rain, I watched.

Nothing. I couldn't see him.

Worried, I moved slowly forward into the grass, making my own wake through that green sea. Had he hurt himself, out there? He had the knife with him. What the devil was he doing? Was he going to stab himself? Castrate himself?

Suddenly the air roared with rain, pelting straight down. The meadow steamed. Behind a wall of steamy white, the deer disappeared.

Then he was visible, just ahead. Sleek wet, he was down on his hands and knees. His face was buried in the grass, and hands clenched in it, as if holding onto Earth's hair. Rain was exploding off his bare back, streaming down his haunches. He was tearing at the grass with his hands, choking, gagging — as if trying to puke up the poison like a wild dog. Then he pulled a handful of yarrow and grass, and started rubbing it all over his body, with frenzied method, as if it was a bar of soap. It was a ceremony, no different than any in the Mercies. Smell of herbs floating under the painted vaults. Singing, torches. He scrubbed his torso, between his thighs, with the torn plants. Crushed petals clung to his skin, then slid away on the rain. Finally his entire body was stained delicate green, even his face. He rubbed the plants into his hair. I could feel the violence of his struggle to empty himself of that memory that they had deliberately placed inside him.

It was several minutes before he quieted. Finally he swayed up onto his knees, and his hand convulsively let the mangled plants fall. Grass-seeds and petals stuck to his thighs and genitals. Rain streamed down him, washing seeds along his naked limbs. Behind him, the sky boiled with pink lightning.

After several more minutes, I realized he had forgotten I was there. Or he wanted to be alone with his healing. The deer paid no attention to our two still figures. Shortly they had drifted between us, and I could hardly see him. For a moment, the buck's antlers lined up with the top of Juan's head. One tiny isolated part of my mind wondered if he had rubbed himself with some of the deadly three-leaf plant.

He would heal himself, then he would leave me.

The sky boiled, rain roared down. Shivering, feeling worse, I started back towards the house, working my way along with the cane.

The ground and grass were slippery. Suddenly, amid the tangled plants, my left foot went down into a hidden animal burrow and I fell hard. As a searing pain flashed through the already-damaged leg nerves, I barked a curse of pure agony.

As I struggled to get up, furious with myself at being such a clumsy idiot, his naked form loomed over me. He must have heard my cry of pain. The barest flicker of concern showed in his eyes. He stared at me through the dripping hair fallen over his forehead, with that unutterably sad expression in his eyes that I saw the day I found him on the road to La Mora. The pain throbbed in my heart, my brain, my toes, my neck. It wrapped me in its flames. I wanted to embrace him, but was afraid to. How could I convince him that I now believed him?

As suddenly as it came, the rain stopped. In the silence, snorts of the grazing deer were painfully peaceful. Mist in the east suddenly lifted. A blaze of sunlight leaped across the meadow. Our eyes were dazzled by a thousand prisms of color flashing through the wet grass.

Juan grabbed my elbow and brusquely helped me up. I turned away but the leg couldn't support my weight, and I almost fell again. The familiar rage that had always surged powerfully in me, to give me courage and strength, wasn't there. I knew I was on the verge of giving up. Tying his wet shirt around his waist by its sleeves, to cover his privacy, he slung his trousers over his shoulders, like a shawl. For months I'd been obsessed with getting him naked. Now it didn't matter.

Then he helped me back to the house, pulled off my wet clothes, lay me down on the sofa, pulled the quilt over me. Fever was spiking now.

The leg seared me no matter what my position was, and the old terror of amputation came back. I'd really done it now. Some Yankee doctor would remove my leg, right at the hip joint. I could see the scalpel cutting the tendons. I'd be half a man. Something for the pain, please. Doctor, I need something for the pain. Days of pain at the Sanitorio de Toreros. While Juan went outside to look for dry firewood, I dragged myself to one bathroom, then the other, shivering with pain and fever and cold, pawing in the medicine cabinets like a madman. My aunt's old bottles of pills fell and clattered everywhere. I was looking for some old dentist painkiller. Morphine, codeine, anything. In Madrid there was a hospital orderly who slid me extra morphine out of the supply closet.

Then I tripped over the bathmat, and was falling again. Everything went soft and dark and painless.

After what seemed like a long deep nap, I woke into warm dreaminess under a goosedown quilt in my bedroom. For a moment, I thought I was home in Las Moreras. But the rain beat its tattoo on the shingle roof, making the old farmhouse sound like a drum, and the sadness came back, and I remembered where I was. Little by little, memories came — the sudden collapse of will and morale, the frantic search for painkillers. Juan must have found me half-destroyed on the bathroom floor, dragged me in here. Cautiously I felt along my body. The leg was still there, and it hurt less. No one had amputated it while I slept.

So Juan was staying a few extra hours to look after me. This was generous of him. I'd been acting like a crazy man.

The room was peaceful — one window open a crack, curtains almost drawn. Through a split in the curtains, a slice of darkening twilight showed. In the bedroom's fireplace, flames crackled peacefully, with a neat pile of dry firewood nearby. On the dresser, my picture of Our Lady of Mercies stood. I didn't remember putting it there. In spite of the embarrassment and sadness, I felt better — fever gone. Down the hallway, light shone in the kitchen, and I could hear clinks of dishes, water running. With a strange clarity of mind I lay there thinking, then drifted off to sleep again.

Suddenly I woke to Juan's hand on my shoulder. His gaze was guarded, remote. He had trimmed his hair since that morning. Why had he done that? I wondered idly. Maybe to get the plant shreds out of it.

"Did you touch the three-leaf plant?" I croaked.

"Eh?"

"The venomous ivy...did you touch it in the meadow?"

"Are you crazy? Get up. You need to eat," he said.

I struggled into my silk dressing gown, relic of the lost life at Las Moreras. I felt like a puppy just learning to walk. How could I have gotten so weak in a few hours?

"Careful," he said, eyeing me watchfully.

Then I saw myself in the mirror. A real Wild Man looked back at me. His face was shockingly thin, with a ragged beard. His hair was longer, uncombed, with five or six silver hairs in it. I stared, shocked. How long had I slept? For twenty years, like that American fable about Rip de Winkle?

We sat at the big kitchen table, two meters of space between us, eating his effort at a potato omelet — one story tall. He mumbled something about not being as good a cook as Magda. The large kitchen table wore a rustic linen cloth in bright colors. On it stood a Yankee type silver candelabra with half-burned candles in five different colors. I didn't remember seeing it there.

It occurred to me that this was the first real meal the two of us had ever eaten alone together. Here we were, two *maricones* having the impossible thing that our kind dreamed about — a table to ourselves, a country house where we could be alone for days on end — and we were sitting three chairs apart. When he opened the refrigerator door to get milk for our coffee, it revealed food that I didn't remember. On the gas stove, a copper teakettle was coming to a boil. An old Talavera bowl, that my aunt must have purchased in a moment of homesickness from a New York antique dealer, held the fruits of this land — windfall apples from the trees outside, and a few lurid orange plum-like things.

I picked up one of the "plums" suspiciously.

"What is this?" I asked.

"A per....persi....I forget. Put it back. No fruit for you."

His voice had a doctor's authority, and I obeyed. Next I picked up an antique silver salt-shaker and salted the omelet.

His eyes were on the sterling silver thing. "You have to live with somebody else's wealth now, eh?" he said drily. The kettle was boiling, and he got up to take it off the flame.

I closed my eyes. When I opened them again, his strong callused farmer hand was in front of me, holding a glass of steaming tea with a strange greenish-brown color. It smelled like swamp water. He had passed up my aunt's chipped English china teacups and hunted in the cupboards for a big heavy glass, to serve tea the way we did at home.

"Time for your medicine," he said.

On the counter, lay a fistful of strange thick-stemmed jointed plants, carefully cut with his knife. They had whorls of grass-like leaves at each joint.

"What the devil is this stuff?" I demanded to know.

He looked at me strangely. "You've been drinking it for three weeks."

I blinked. "Three weeks?"

He sat down in the chair nearest me and looked at me with concern.

"Don't you remember?" he asked.

"I was out for three weeks? A coma?"

"Not a coma. You woke up, you talked. But you didn't make much sense."

Juan explained. He had found me unconscious, head bleeding, on the bathroom floor. There he was, alone in this isolated house in a strange country with an injured man and no idea how to speak the language or do anything. But he pulled himself together and pawed through my things till he found Aunt Pura's phone number. My aunt had called the local hospital, a rural clinic. They sent a car, since they had no ambulance, and took me there and X-rayed my head. By then I was conscious, if dazed. Diagnosis: a hairline fracture and mild concussion, plus a devastating flu and boiling diarrhea. They kept me there a couple of days for observation, and next day Pura, José and Sera had driven up to see me. They took me back to the farmhouse. After a few days, the three women returned to New York City, but stayed in close touch with Juan by phone. I had actually talked to them myself. Pura still felt that something would be gained by Juan and I staying here alone. Maybe she knew that Juan and I would either kill each other here, or make peace with each other here.

Feeling in my shaggy hair, my fingers found a scab and a lump there. I was aghast. A whole painted fragment of my life had fallen away from the wall of consciousness.

"You took care of me for three weeks?" I whispered.

"A cranky old stallion with an abscessed molar was an easier patient than you."

"How do you buy food? Does Auntie call the market for you?"

The briefest pride warmed his eyes. "I have a job," he said.

"A job? How?"

"Tía Pura leased the pasture to the dairy farm next door. I helped them open up the fence. Your aunt told them I know about cows, and they hired me. They're paying me under the table till my green card comes. José got me this little book of American words. I am learning pretty fast. The farmer and his family have been kind. I ride to the store with them. They give us milk. They think I'm your cousin."

My aunt was a smart woman. Juan would feel very proud that he bought the food and supported the two of us. I noticed that he was calling her *tía,* aunt. Did his employers know that this stalwart immigrant, and his Spanish cousin, were two of those dreaded fairies against whom the U.S. government armed their customs agents, fearing them even more than the brownskinned Communists in Vietnam?

"So...this stuff I'm drinking?"

"It's *cola de caballo**. I wondered if it lived here...there are so many other medicine plants I know...yarrow, bracken. So I walked around till I found it along the stream."

"What's it for, oh great *brujo?* "

"My grandfather used it to cure scours in calves. It's poisonous for horses, though."

"I'm not a damn veal." Irritation surged.

"The Yankee doctor gave you antibiotics, and they did *nada* for you. You were shitting your guts out."

"How do you know it isn't poisonous for humans?"

Juan's eyes held mine for the first time. Suddenly he grinned crookedly, picked up the glass and drank some. "If it's poisonous, we'll die together, eh?"

Reassured, and pleased by the way he'd said this, I drank it. The powerful brackish liquid warmed my belly and filled my veins. With it came a suspicion of truth that I still denied. He wouldn't say the words of love. But he had jumped up out of his healing ceremony when he heard my fall, my cry of pain. He spent days searching the land to find some cure for me.

While Juan cleaned up the kitchen, I called New York.

"Darling!" José exclaimed, and I could almost smell her perfume through the phone. I talked with her, then with Pura for an hour, luxuriating in the warm reassuring voices of my women — my sister, greataunt and wife-in-name-only. Sera had moved back from the hotel.

"Only because I promised to go to the AA thing they have here," José said. "It seems I always hit her when I drink. I see that now. The violence comes out then. 'Tonio, I abhor violence... how did I get so violent?"

Sera got on the phone too. Her voice was calm.

"So, my little camellia," I said, "are you sorry you leaped into this adventure with us wild animals?"

"No."

"You are getting strong as oak. Stronger than any of us."

"Auntie knows everything, 'Tonio. We didn't have to tell her. She knows about me and José, and about you and Juan."

"What did she say?"

"Nothing much. Just that there are thousands of different trees and animals, so why should there be one kind of human?"

Back in the bedroom, suddenly exhausted, I struggled out of the dressing gown while Juan poked up the fire and threw a last log on it for the night. This English thing of the fireplace in the bedroom was a very good thing, very comforting, and safer than braziers too. But once again Juan looked watchful, cautious. He had obviously found my key to the gun cupboard, and now put a loaded shotgun within easy reach. I could see how fearful he still was, believing that Paco's organization could reach across the Atlantic and find us here. I was feeling a resurgence of the closeness to giving up.

"When are you leaving?" I asked him.

"What?" Juan turned and looked at me strangely.

"Well, you said you wanted to leave," I reminded him.

So much hurt was coming alive in his eyes, that I instantly wanted to take the words back. What had we talked about during those lost three weeks? Had we actually come to the point of discussing our friendship? Had I blurted my love for him? I could imagine him helping me walk, feeding me, bathing my sprawled body with a cloth and a basin of warm water. No doubt he had cleaned shit off me like I was a baby. Maybe he had even caught my flu and been sick for a few days. If it was his urge to heal that had brought us closer again, rather than a personal feeling he had for me, caring for me as some sick animal, wasn't this enough? Why did I insist on the formalities?

Years later, I would look back on that moment, as everything hung in the balance. I considered forcing the issue, saying things that I might regret.

Standing in front of the Virgin's picture on my dresser, looking dumbly at Her familiar image, I noticed that the dried carnation lay in front of Her, beside a couple of vigil candles. I didn't remember arranging my altar. Had he done it? Had he put the flower there for me? A tremendous surge of emotion came up in me, almost choking me, as I remembered the look in his eyes as he gave me the carnation, our hands and lips seeking each other's bodies the way a root grows irresistibly toward the center of the Earth. If heterosexuals are the part of humanity that grows away from gravity towards the sun, like the upper part of a plant, then Juan and I, and José and Sera, were another part of humanity that grows towards gravity, towards the core of the Earth. No human civilization has devised a law harsh enough, or a terror deep enough, or a science clever enough, to make roots grow towards the sun.

I decided to let things take their course. The way the plants and animals do, the way the Moon does. The Lady gazed up at me from Her frame, and told me this was wise.

My trembling hand lit a candle. "So," I said in a stifled voice, "it's settled then? You're staying?"

"It's settled."

Relief was draining through me. I motioned to him to light a candle of his own. His own hand was trembling, fingers red and translucent as the flame brightened.

"After all, She is yours now," I said. "Along with everything I have, which is not available to us at the moment. We may never be able to go back. I'll give it all to Isaías and Tere before I let the regime take it."

He smiled a little. "What I have is yours...my passport and jackknife and 75 dollars a week."

There, it was said. As it had been in the old missing document. I finally understood why friends had made pledges not about love, but about food and a roof over your head.

Trying to be casual, I pulled back the covers, inviting him to get in bed with me. Cautiously he stripped to his underwear and slid in beside me. As we lay quietly, I fondled his head, running my fingers through that thick, silky, straight wheat-colored hair of his, already shaped in a Yankee college-boy kind of haircut. Starting over wasn't going to be easy, with the sounds and smells of the Black House still hanging in the air around us like a dark mist. My hands explored his body with as much medical detachment of my own as I could muster, and found him as I remembered him. But that shadow was still in his eyes, and he was unaroused. He was trembling all over.

"I can't, just yet," he whispered. "Give me a little time."

I kissed his cheek in a good-night kind of way, and said quietly, "Time is all we have now."

Relieved that I wasn't going to pester him, he settled against me. As the firelight painted its murals on the walls and the candles burned down, we slept together. I slept without dreams. He slept shallowly, jerking tremblingly awake at every little sound, into my soothing voice. The expression in his eyes told me that he still woke up into his own sadness, that he needed to know I would be there when he woke, that he was not waking up in the Black House. I quieted him with caresses and knew, for the first time, that I too had a power to heal, not just manipulate and have my way. Now and then, we lay listening to the rain and the wind in the trees. Now and then, he murmured and settled heavily into a new position against me, his hair against my cheek, my arm across him, with that childlike vulnerability that he always guarded so deeply when awake. He smelled faintly of cows and grass — it was like sleeping in a warm meadow with my nose buried against the ground.

For a while I lay awake and thought about this new country where prisons in a different architectural style waited for us, with police and guards and churchmen and politicians who were Protestant and spoke English. But surely Our Lady of Liberty in the New York harbor had raised Her torch for us personally.

From those foreign trees outside, the first yellow leaves were falling. Five Moons now, since we had lain awake thinking of each other in Santander. The rain sent us the new sounds and smells of exile. From the open window, lace curtains bellied out. The peaceful sound and smell of rain filled the room. Outside, a faint stomp and snort as a few deer fed on the windfall apples. Five changes of the Moon now. Five — a hundred more if we could survive the next month. Would we have the power to fill our time with something besides sadness and lust, and memories of the terror?

Tomorrow morning, he would walk to his job across that meadow.

He would be carrying his Berlitz book and the glass jar that he brought milk home in. He had muttered something about how barbaric the Yankees were, that they sold milk in cardboard boxes instead of good honest glass bottles.

  I would watch his figure grow smaller in the vastness, surer now that he might come back.

---

* *Cola de caballo.* In English, horsetail. Nonflowering primitive plant of the genus *Equisetum,* found in many parts of the world and widely used as a medicinal herb. It grows in meadows and marshy places.

Author's Postlogue

Afternoon shadows were longer, the course of the sun farther down in the southern sky. Autumn was a month further along.

Antonio emptied his glass and sat staring sadly across the irrigated pasture. We were at the other house now, sitting in wicker chairs on the patio and drinking imported manzanilla, which has a Spanish kick equal to whiskey. Antonio's greyhounds sprawled on the flagstones at his feet. It occurred to me that he'd told the story not because of some exhibitionist need to "confess," but because he was still trying to understand it himself.

"Holy Mary," he growled, "now I understand how you know what you know about men."

"If I were Andrew Morton and you were Princess Di," I teased, "you wouldn't keep a single secret from me."

"Another drop?" he asked, picking up the bottle.

Standard love stories seldom go beyond itches of the moment. Our culture likes to frame things in the 120 minutes' running time of a movie, or a paperback left behind on the plane seat. The young things meet and mate for a night, like two lynxes in heat. Sometimes an older thing mates a young thing. There is an obsession with mechanics — who does what to whom. However happy or sad the ending might be, the story is short. Seldom are we allowed to see changes of the Moon.

So my Muse was visiting me in this seductive shape-shifting biography. Antonio and Juan, José and Serafita. She had painted the crypt of my own imagination with their images of Spanish youth of the 1960s, each image with its surprise, its twist. The lonely lusting boy in blood-stained blue coveralls, driven by his innocence and trust, impulsively holding out a drink. The blood-stained matador trudging towards him, a tired introspective Zeus thirsty from a drought of daydreams, ready to seize the cup of love from that working-class Ganymede. José the knight-errant, hazel eyes grimly clear in the shade of her Cordoban hat, cueing her war-horse through an arrogant *piaffe*. Sera, sheltered damosel, with passport and jewelry in her purse, scaling the wall of her locked garden like a ninja — the one who had turned out to be the intellect of the quartet. But all that remained of those images was the present.

Antonio's story had left me wondering if he and Juan had ever really renewed their relationship. Did they stay together for convenience…economic reasons? I hadn't even met the mythical Juan Diano yet. Juan was in Vietnam, consulting with the Vietnamese government on the gaur, that rare wild bovine that somehow survived destruction of its jungle habitat during the war. He was leaving Saigon tonight, arriving in San Diego late tomorrow.

This time I was there to travel with them for a few weeks — first to show them the buffalo they'd never seen, then to accompany them to an international wildlife conference on the Isle of Jersey. The Coto Morera was on the agenda, its conservation story to be told publicly for the first time. After Jersey, we would go on to Spain. I was excited and nervous — hadn't seen the country since 1971, when Franco was still alive. No doubt the visible changes would be shocking.

Needing to stretch our legs, Antonio and I got up and walked around, carrying our refilled glasses. In the pastures, the last spears of grass had cast their seeds. Gray-blue winter shadows stretched on and on into the afternoon. The air stirred restlessly — a new santa ana kicking up off the inland desert. Studying Antonio's profile against the boulder-strewn hills, I remembered that he was now 52. Yet right now his expression was curiously young, vulnerable. He had gotten no relief from sharing the story.

"Did Juan ever tell you what they made him watch?" I asked.

"No," Antonio said hoarsely. "And I never asked."

In daylight, with cowboy hat off, his curly hair glinted silver at the temples as he ran his fingers through it. He said:

"The land-mine Paco buried in our hearts went on exploding for years. Maybe he thought it would destroy us by remote control. To paraphrase the admirable *Señor Presidente* Lincoln, you can terrorize most of the people most of the time."

"Does Juan…accept himself like you do? Is he open?"

"The most he'll admit is that he likes sex with men. And he does…very much."

This sounded like they had never had any formal declarations. By the rules of established gay life, one is supposed to declare one's love. If one doesn't, one can't get one's green card as a gay person, so to speak.

"So the next few years of the Seventies were hard," I said.

"While everyone else was going to discos and having fun, we four Spanish knotheads were working like dogs, trying to survive. Juan was in school, so he and I were apart for long times. A cave had opened inside of him...a cave of no mercies. Now and then, he would get lost there, for a few minutes, a few days. His way of healing himself was to work. He would not lean on me for help or understanding. It was his old fanaticism about not owing me anything."

Combat veterans, death-camp survivors, men and women traumatized in maximum-security prison...all with their cave murals of memory, I thought.

"So he went to Cornell the full four years?"

"He couldn't get into Cornell. His Spanish school record wasn't good enough for them. They accepted him at U.C. Davis and University of Colorado, but we liked California more. We settled in this area, and he boarded at Davis. He worked like a mad Jesuit...learned English, got scholarships, graduated fourth in his class. The rest of us made sacrifices to keep him and Sera in school. We had a family fund, all of us supporting each other. Pura helped with some little investments she had. Without Isaías and Tere, things would have been harder."

"So the Eibars finally understood."

"Well, for a long time, Isaías was more loyal than understanding," Antonio said drily. "But they found a way to employ me as a foreign sales rep of Escudero S.A. and pay me out of a New York bank. And I did increase our sales here. Paco tried to make trouble ...went to Franco's cabinet saying that Isaías was sending money to me illegally. Spain wanted every dollar in foreign exchange that she could get. But Isaías was too good a lawyer...everything was legal. So the regime didn't intervene."

The two of us paused by the olive orchard, looking at a marble tablet in the ground. To my surprise, it read FAISÁN 1950-1979. I felt a surge of emotion. The old horse had followed his human kin to the New World, and died here in exile. Hot shimmering shadows played across the grave.

"But Isaías couldn't always send money," Antonio went on. "There were a few bad years in the olive business. Drought, poor crops. The little that came in, had to go to care for people there...and the *coto*. So I whored for money like I never did as a torero. Film consulting on Spain. The book you probably never read." He laughed. "Then it was the Eighties, and everybody in this country of God was getting rich in the stock market and the computer business while we Spanish knotheads were doing all the wrong money things."

"For instance?"

"For instance, I thought I would make a fortune importing Spanish horses." He grinned, looking at the horse's grave.

"Yes...Yankees and Spaniards share a belief that one can get rich in the horse business. I bit into that one once."

"José and I placed him with a trainer, took him to shows. He was a wonderful ambassador for the breed. But people here were infatuated with other breeds. The horse thing put me horribly in the red before it paid off. I sold the diamond out of my ring, and my diamond studs, to help Juan start his practice."

So that explained the empty bezel in his pinky ring.

Antonio dripped a libation of sherry onto the horse's grave. "Eh, old friend, don't forget to come for me when it's time."

As if in answer, a sudden gust of wind whistled through the olive trees.

We walked on. "How did José earn her share of the family fund?" I asked.

"Journalism. Everybody wanted to pay her a lot of money to write political stuff about Spain. But she said no. It might have hurt the people we left behind. So she did it the hard way. Now she sells stories to big magazines like *National Geographic...*"

"And Sera?"

"Art history and photography at UC San Diego. Then UCLA film school. Now she is José's photographer and DP. They are a good team. When American television got interested in wildlife documentaries, José and Sera got in on the ground floor."

"Are you all still married?"

"Two friendly divorces."

"Did Paco ever tell on you?"

"We don't think so."

"Was it really the CYS?"

"If it was, they probably threw him out after he failed to deliver me. Paco had hard times after that. His boss was dismissed in the next cabinet shuffle, so he lost his job. From what Mamá said, he withdrew into obsessive little historical researches. His wife opened a dressmaking business to support herself and the children. Then his youngest son Paquito insisted on getting to know me and José. Paco died of a bleeding ulcer two years ago. His widow still dresses stodgy Old Catholic ladies."

I thought of the framed clipping. "And when Franco died?"

"Much champagne…people dancing in the streets. I'm not a monarchist, but Juan Carlos has been a good king. Spain is healing. There is freedom of religion now. The old morals laws are gone. We decided to keep a foot in both countries. The chance to work with a great zoo here, that pioneered in captive wild-animal breeding…this was important. So we turned Rancho Diana into a waystation. We collect Spanish fauna from animal traders and zoo surplus. We check them for disease here, start the studbooks, and so forth. From here, the animals go back to Spain."

"What did you feel when you finally went home?"

Antonio's eyes had a faraway look. "We waited to kiss the ground till we got to the *coto*. Pico and Magda had not lived to welcome us back. Santí lives there with his family now."

"Santí…loyal too."

"Yes. We are fortunate…good people rallied around us."

"So how did Juan start in wildlife medicine?"

"Volunteering at the San Diego Zoo. Then the Wild Animal Park hired him. You can't imagine how proud he was when he started earning big money. And people were quick to recognize his gifts. His practice keeps him so busy, I have to look at his calendar to know when we can eat a meal together. He wanted to be the best vet in Spain…*¡caramba!* Now he gets called all over the world…consultant on hoofed mammals. The Chinese government just invited him to go and learn acupuncture for large animals. He's richer and more famous than I ever was."

But still a strange corrosive sadness hung around Antonio. I was about to ask if he ever felt jealous of Juan's fame, when an SUV's wheels came crunching along the long drive.

"It's José and Sera," said Antonio.

"Where have they been?" I asked him as we walked back.

"Attending a workshop on small cats."

From the first moment that Antonio talked about his twin sister and his childhood fiancée, I had known that I would like the two women. The three of us had already spent an afternoon getting acquainted over mineral water instead of manzanilla. José and Sera didn't drink any more. They were more open than Antonio, more inclined to laugh at some of their past personal dramas.

Now José's strong boisterous voice suddenly filled the patio like the first gust of a santa ana. She was the elegant dyke in a denim pants suit and cotton turtleneck, lugging a heavy briefcase. Her copper curls were cut close now, damascened with threads of silver, like her brother's. Behind her came Sera, less slender than in the old photos I'd seen, her hair streaked with white, camellia complexion now freckled and brown, narrow shoulders lugging a camera bag with the Hi-8 video camera in it. It was hard to believe that Sera had once been quiet and mousy — she was the intense brainy professional.

"*Hooo-laaaa,* Patríiiiiiiiii," José sang out.

She and Sera gave me bone-crushing hugs.

The two women filled the house with energy. José went to the patio, grabbed a few avocados and lemons off the trees. Sera swept the fruits into the kitchen and started chopping them into guacamole. She hollered from the kitchen about our laziness in making lunch. Late lunch — Madrid hours. José sank into a patio chair with a bottle of mineral water.

"How was the workshop?" Antonio asked her.

"Some interesting stuff on behavior. The curator of the Warsaw Zoo was there. And…" José paused for effect, "…he has a male Spanish lynx!"

"You don't say." Antonio's brooding eyes lit up.

"Some of us went to a bar last night. I got him drunk, and he agreed to trade the lynx for a red stag of a new bloodline."

Grinning, José got the contract out of her briefcase. They'd written the terms on a paper placemat and made copies of the improv document on the hotel xerox.

Antonio managed a chuckle. "Good work," he said.

Questions still swarmed in my mind. What was the rift between Juan and Antonio? What had happened to the Crypt of the Mercies? Towards the end of his story, Antonio hadn't mentioned the Mercies. I didn't recall reading about a sensational archeological discovery in Spain that featured goddess murals.

Now José was lighting charcoal on the American-style grill. A santa ana was definitely moving in — smoke lifted on the wind, whipped towards the horse barns. Sera set out blue-corn chips and the guacamole she'd made. Her little hand, which Antonio had described as carved from soft ivory, was now strong and callused.

"You Escuderos have learned to eat foreign food," I teased.

"When in Rome," Sera said, biting on a tortilla chip.

"It took Juan a long time to learn to eat corn," José grinned over her shoulder. "He said corn is for cows."

José kept talking like a river, while Antonio retreated back into a somber thoughtful space. They had come to love southern California, as their ancestors had. "Only this time we won't kill any Indians," she said drily. They felt a great hunger for a little piece of land. Driving here with a realtor, seeing the 300-year-old olive trees, had settled it for them.

Aunt Pura had made money gifts before she died, so they could escape paying estate tax. Her gifts bought this 300 acres, two adjoining properties with the two houses. Real estate was cheaper in the '70's! For a while, Sera and Antonio lived in this house, and Juan and José next door. When California went more liberal on gay rights, the four got divorced and switched houses.

Now Sera and José traveled too, doing features on the worldwide destruction of wild land. The Discovery Channel had just aired their documentary on village efforts to reforest in Africa. Who ran Rancho Diana when they were away? A few good volunteers, and Antonio.

"I'm the one who stays home and cleans the corrals," Antonio said drily from the other side of the patio. He got up and left, saying over his shoulder, "Time to feed the cats."

The greyhounds got up and followed him.

I looked questioningly at José and Sera. They looked at each other. José sighed.

"What's happening with him and Juan?" I asked.

"They had a big fight before Juan went to Vietnam," José said. "It was about the conference. Juan didn't want to do the presentation. He said Antonio should do it. Antonio said he had enough of being in the public eye. Then he suggested they both do it. Juan said no…he's afraid it would call attention to the *maricón* thing. Juan is still struggling with that."

"Not that José and I haven't had our own fights," Sera said.

"How did your family feel when you eloped?"

"Naturally Mamá and Tita and Sera's mamá were hurt. Then they were hurt all over again when we didn't come home from our long vacation. Paco told them to break off contact, so they did."

"The three old ladies are dead now? They never knew?"

"My mother suspected," José said. "She was always smarter than she let on. But she never asked."

"You went back after they died? Why did you wait so long?"

"Out of respect for our mothers," Sera said. "They finally defied Paco and Tita, and started writing to us. But in their social world, our coming home as open homosexuals would have been devastating for them."

"Isaías and Tere were waiting at the airport?"

José laughed, swigging mineral water.

"At Las Moreras, the house was more modern, full of life. Old friends for a welcoming fiesta. People who had put money in the *montepío* so they could shoot there. 'Tonio's old crew was there. Most of the village. Mercurio was dead by then. Candalaria is mayor now."

Sera smiled a little. "I hadn't cried so hard since the day 'Tonio and I got engaged."

"And when you finally rode through the *coto?*"

"Ayy..." José's eyes misted.

Sera added, "When we saw how green everything looked...springs everywhere, young oaks growing...."

"...Wild pig..." José's eyes gleamed.

"The first pigs came back three years later, like our *brujo* said they would," Sera explained. "And the first little herd of wild cattle was there."

A thrill raced over me. "You must have cried all over again," I said, "when you saw the cattle."

"We were beyond tears," Sera said. "Juan and Antonio went alone to that first spring they dug. They said they hardly recognized it. The ravine was full of young poplars and green grass. Places in the grass where wild cattle had bedded — cow pies everywhere."

"I suppose you sent to France to get Baby."

"Unfortunately *el famosísimo* Baby was killed in a truck accident," José explained. "We had trouble with disease too, finding stock that was clean of hoof and mouth disease. But finally we got our hands on a son of Baby's and half a dozen good cows. Now we have a nice herd, different bloodlines. We have to cull them, of course. But we don't select for *bravura* any more...just intelligence and hardiness. So the animals are getting less hot."

"Did the *coto* make the village rich? Were promises kept?"

Sera grinned. "The tourism," she said, "supports two inns, some shops, three bars and restaurants. We're on the main tourist route between Andalusia and the capital. Tourists come for a safari tour...they are thrilled to see the bulls. Hunters...we keep them happy with partridge and red-deer shooting. But they pay much to shoot. Much! We raise money that way. When we thin the animals, we get one of the best chefs in Madrid and throw a big high-life party. Society people pay to eat our game cuisine! The money goes into a fund for town improvements. The village artisan turns the hides and tusks into things they sell."

She hadn't mentioned tourism to the Crypt of the Mercies. Maybe it was still not open to the public.

Inside, the phone rang. Antonio, coming back from feeding the lynxes, went to answer it.

"Do you think democracy will last in Spain?" I asked.

Sera shrugged. "Ask if it is going to last here!"

"Already the Spanish right-wing are noisy again. They say there is too much freedom now," José said.

"Sounds like the fundamentalists in the United States."

"I've seen the same thing with extremists in other religions, all over the world." José's tone, like her brother's, was that of the weary traveler. "It is always like that. They never give up. They always believe that terror works. And wherever they hold power for a while, the land gets ruined."

"What about Communism? It ruined a lot of land."

"Communism was a substitute for state religion, no?"

I sighed. "If the fundamentalists win a majority in the United States... They don't just hate homosexuals. They hate what they call New Age religion. That's you...and me."

"Yes, it could get bad here," Sera agreed. She grinned. "You'll have a safe place in Spain, Paty."

The subject was depressing — time to lighten up. We could hear Antonio's voice inside, talking on the phone. He was upset about something.

"Your dream has been hard work," I said.

Sera grinned. "I used to worry about my nails and my hair. Now I slap cream on my blisters, and go on."

But when Antonio came back, his face was dark.

"That was Juan, from Saigon," he said. "Something has come up. So he's missing his flight. He'll meet us in Jersey."

"He'll miss seeing the buffaloes," said José, getting up and collecting glasses.

"Screw him," Antonio said. "We'll see the buffaloes ourselves. This is the old game about his independence."

"Calm down, 'Tonio," Sera said. "Why do you always think it's a game? Maybe he had a good reason to stay."

Late that night, I sat with José in the ranch office. Sera was in the next room, their library — we could hear her turning pages. José swigged a last soda as she sat at the cranky old PC. Red-deer studbook files were downloaded, and she was getting the stag's papers ready to go to Poland. The stag's forebears stretched back to 1898 — the Argentine game park had kept careful records.

"Escudero women were always keepers of the genealogies," she said. "Now we are keepers of wild-animal genealogies. Our Lady of Mercies must smile at that."

I nodded. "The same for my native American relatives. Women were always keepers of the Red Belts — the family histories."

Suddenly the computer screen froze up.

"Shit," said José. "Half an hour's work lost." She rebooted the

PC. "The Escudero files would never have survived for a thousand years if technology was that fragile in those days."

Unlocking a drawer, she pulled out a sheaf of xeroxes and plopped it in front of me. "This survived because it was written on good old paper and parchment. People carried it around in saddlebags. It froze, it fried in summer heat, it even got wet...and nothing happened to it. This was one of the few things that never got burned. The original is in a safe place."

Flipping sheets, I realized it was the Escudero genealogies.

My hair stood on end. Europe is honeycombed with this kind of closely guarded secret. To some Europeans, even today, nothing is more valuable than an ancient piece of paper proving one's family entitlement to something.

"Here is Doña Carmen here," said José, flipping pages backwards. "And her line —"

The pages went back, back, past landmark dates in U.S. history — 1812, 1776, 1620, 1492. Handwriting shifted from Victorian to Age of Enlightenment, from Renaissance to medieval script that was hard to decipher. Different genealogies overlapped. Names were inconsistently spelled.

"This is the real one," José added. "There was a fake one that the family kept to show the Inquisition. Paco always believed the fake one was the real one. It's true that we have some Berber and Morisco and Sephardic blood. Here, in 1478, is where Francisco, the youngest son, married into a Toledo Jewish family. They were learned people. It was a dynastic marriage...information was exchanged. That branch disappears into thin air. Notice the date. It was the Reconquest — all the Jews were being chased out of Spain. We don't know where they went."

My stomach took an excited plunge.

"Maybe they came to the Americas," I said.

The computer had reloaded and José opened the red-deer studbook again. "Pura always said America was the place to go when things got too hot in Europe. Even a long time ago."

José finished the red buck's pedigree, then printed it out and called out to Sera: "I have to fax Warsaw about shipping arrangements. Show Paty the library while I argue with the fax machine."

The next room was no elegant library fit for *Architectural Digest*. Industrial-steel bookshelves soared to the ceilings, crammed with books on veterinary medicine, drugs, wildlife, game management, as well as Pura's old collection of books on philosophy, spirituality, culture, linguistics. Running her hands along the backs of the books, Sera was suddenly the high priestess of the Mercies. She still had those wonderful eyes that Antonio had talked about — the eyes of a little hunting bird, a shrike maybe — clear, alert, able to calculate the parallax.

"We always had this exotic picture of Auntie Pura," Sera smiled. "We thought she knew things… occult information that nobody else in the family had. When we got here, we found out Pura didn't know much. But she had collected these books from everywhere, hoping that somebody would put the picture back together someday. She said we had to start over. Get the information from the place that the ancients got it...from Goddess and God. From the Earth. From life."

"Did you ever find out what Nine means?"

"I'm working on it. What were you saying to José about Spanish immigrants?"

"Before the Scotch-Irish Protestants settled the South," I said, "Spain tried to colonize it. Santa Elena and other colonies. There were refugees from the Inquisition, Muslims, Sephardic Jews, Castilians. They married blacks and native people, and one another. They were darkskinned, so the South classified them as 'free people of color.' They couldn't vote, couldn't own land..."

Sera stared at me. "I never knew that," she said.

"I didn't know it either. Nobody talked about the FPCs in my own family. The American Protestants like to pretend that they founded everything here. But we Americans have our own hidden histories ...our Crypt of Mercies."

Sera's pupils opened with wide with emotion. "The world is not such a big place," she said. "Time is not so long."

Fax sent, the three of us felt too restless to sleep, so we went outdoors and walked along the drive in the dark. José and Sera strolled with hands behind their backs, like European men. The santa ana was whistling through the olive trees, sweeping storms of electrons over the land. In the pasture, dim figures of red deer stood listening nervously while the horses galloped and played, feeling that rush of electrons. We looked at the olive trees, older than the United States.

"Juan taught me to look at the animals," José said. "In every herd, there are those animals who don't have young. But they help life go on in other ways. They carry plant seeds to new ranges in their guts, their coats. They destroy trees and bring in grasslands. Their bodies feed predators, keep predators alive. There are larger cycles than procreation. We help to move those larger cycles too."

"The bad guys try to saw our branches off," I agreed. "But we always grow back."

So we started the Jersey trip without Juan. Antonio had worked himself into a lather about Juan. José and Sera told him to lighten up.

A good place to see buffalo is Custer State Park in South Dakota. So the four of us flew to Bismarck. From there we rented an SUV with snow tires and chains, in case we needed them. Farther north, winter was coming early — we had to hurry, before the park closed for the season. As we drove, Antonio played a new tape of the Gipsy Kings till we were ready to scream. "World citizens, like us," he said of the refugee flamenco family.

The Wild Family calmed down a little, and there were stories about Juan's adventures as a *brujo*.

"Oh, they don't call it *brujo* here," said José. "The conservation people don't even dare call it psychic. They have to pretend that they're being scientific. They go on and on about what a good diagnostician Juan is. But sometimes..."

"...Sometimes," Antonio put in, "the zoos need to know things about their animals that test-tubes don't tell them. They hem and haw, and finally they call Juan."

"Tell Paty about the elephants at the Madrid Zoo," said Sera.

"Elephants!" I wondered.

Antonio was smiling, shaking his head, as he told it.

"Well....a cow elephant died, and the rest of the elephants were cranky. One almost killed the keeper. The staff puzzled about it. Finally the curator of mammals called Juan. Juan stood there looking at them for a few minutes. Then he told the curator that the elephants were angry because the dead cow had been taken out of the enclosure right away. The herd hadn't been able to mourn. Elephants always mourn, you know. They do it by handling the dead one's body, or bones. The zoo had already given the skeleton to a museum, so they had a hard time getting a few bones back. The keeper put them in the elephant enclosure. All the elephants came right over, and handled the bones, and passed them around, and the herd had a big meeting about it. And the trouble stopped."

"Now the zoo thinks Juan walks on water," Sera said.

"He doesn't walk on water." Antonio was annoyed. "He just pays attention to things that other people ignore."

As we neared Custer Park, the Wild Family told wild stories on each other, about their years of stormy relationships.

"Fights," said José gleefully. *"Uuuy,* our two guys have some fights."

I wondered if they hit each other. Sera read my mind.

"Words and noise," Sera said. "Like José and I do now. José, tell Paty the story about the vase."

"If you don't tell Paty," Antonio growled, "she'll Morton you till you confess."

"This was after we came to California," said José. "We were staying with friends in North Hollywood, on the 8th floor of an apartment building. It was the last time I ever got drunk. Sera got so mad at me, she walked out. I went to the balcony and waited for her to come out the front door, down below. Then I leaned off the balcony and dropped a Ming vase six stories like a bomb. It hit the sidewalk right beside her."

Sera had a steely glow in her eye. "José had to cough up a diamond to pay for that vase," she said.

José laughed. "And Juan said, 'Only the sister of a *señorito* would throw an expensive vase. I'd throw a rock. And I wouldn't miss.'"

Now and then, the talk turned to human contagions sweeping the globe. All four of them were paranoid about human diseases because some of them come from animals. This was not surprising, given their long years of dealing with animal epidemics, starting with the epidemic of *glosopeda* (hoof and mouth disease) that swept Spain in the late 1960s, and going on to swine flu and transmittable brain-wasting and tuberculosis in wild lynxes, and a thousand other spooky things. Much was explained about their fidelity to one another.

José shrugged and added:

"And we got so busy with conservation politics and sick animals that none of us ever have time to be unfaithful."

"Imagine," Antonio added, "that I'd break my neck protecting our animals from brucellosis and such, and then go out and be indiscreet with some guy when I haven't seen a health certificate on him."

"Our Lady of Mercies protects the innocent, but not the stupid," José added.

It was the perfect moment to ask another question.

"You haven't mentioned the Mercies," I said.

Their reaction was strange. Antonio looked out the window. José looked down. Sera was driving, keeping her eyes on the road.

"That is the strangest story of all," José said.

"Why?"

"The Mercies is gone."

"Gone?" I blinked.

"After Franco died," José went on, "we were getting ready to tell the Ministry of Culture about the Mercies...let them take it over and restore it. Then the winter of '77, Isaías and Tere called us up in tears. They almost didn't have the heart to tell us. The whole roof of the Mercies had fallen in."

"We couldn't believe it, even when Tere sent pictures," Sera added in. "When we finally went back to Spain, we rode up there to see. The hut was gone.   There was a big sinkhole, and a few little poplars already growing in it, from seeds that birds dropped."

I was open-mouthed. "How could it happen?"

"All the planting we did probably changed the hydrographics in the whole area," Antonio admitted. "New tree-roots, the springs.   The water table must have risen. At the old side-entrance, a spring is flowing out now."

"What a shame!" I said.   "You're not going to excavate?"

"For what?   The paintings have been destroyed by water.   Better to spend the money on caring for living people...planting more trees."

"To lose the Mercies!   After so many centuries..."

José cocked her head. "But it isn't lost. Only changed."

Those vast spaces of the American West, pale with the first faint snows, impressed my four Spanish friends as profoundly as Spain had impressed me when I saw that country for the first time.   We were approaching Custer State Park.   In the northeast, a dark lowering sky promised a storm.   The two-lane highway led us across open stretches of grassland — cured high-plains grass, rich in protein with its clinging seeds.   Somber indigo patches of pine forest loomed here and there.

Then, in the distance ahead, we saw the first brown dots near the highway.

"*Uuuuy...* " said Antonio, driving. "There they are."

In another five minutes, we were slowed to two miles an hour as hundreds of buffalo flooded around us.   The great animals were everywhere, moving at a restive amble.   Evidently the herd's collective animal mind had decided to move to shelter.   Along a nearby creek, older bulls plowed through the willow bottoms, flattening everything in their path. Young bulls came climbing up the shoulders of the road.   Cows with strong calves at side came swarming across the highway in front of us, behind us. Antonio stopped the vehicle, concerned.   We all sucked in our breath.   But the animals ignored us completely, accustomed to tourists. We drank in their beauty and power with our eyes.

"Imagine a million of them, moving as one," I said.

"*Olé* the buffalo," said José softly.

Through the open window, Sera had her Hi-8 video camera aimed into their powerful cattle smell and deep grunting calls.

Ahead of us, a lone bull — a huge beast with a hump like a mountain — was walking the white line in the middle of the highway.   We pulled even with him, staying on the shoulder at a respectful distance. He moved with purposeful stride, massive head swaying. The shaggy beard gave him a look of unutterable wisdom. It was hard to believe that these heavy animals could jump into a gallop and run like mustangs.

"Listen, 'Tonio," teased José, "how would you like to spread your cape in front of that *bicho?*"

"Not me," Antonio said.

We stopped the vehicle and watched the bull walk on — growing smaller along that lonely highway. Several buffalo cows strode past our vehicle, horns lifted into the storm. The first snowflakes were falling.

"How do the native tribes name the Lady?" Sera said, loading another magnum of film.

"White Buffalo Woman," I said.

"Juan will be sorry he missed this," José said.

Antonio didn't say anything, just drove. His eyes were wet. The flurries of snow were stronger now, pluming against our windshield. Warm motel rooms waited ahead in Rapid City.

From there to Billings, turning in our rental and almost missing our plane. Then the hop to Minneapolis, New York, the long flight to London's Gatwick airport, and the last leg on a commuter plane.

We banked over that cluster of history-worn Channel islands named after cows — Jersey, Guernsey and Aldernay — just two score miles off the French coast. Our little plane landed at the St. Helier airport. A taxi swept us past butterfly farms, fields of flowers for the florist trade, pastures dotted with sleek Jersey cows, then prosperous shops, and banks busy with offshore money business made possible by the island's Crown privilege. We arrived at the Hotel Guerdon exhausted, along with hundreds of other conference-goers.

At the desk, Antonio growled at us, "Juan hasn't checked in yet. No more planes tonight. No message either."

"There's a plane from Gatwick in the morning," José said.

"What if he's not on it?" I asked.

"Then one of us has to do the presentation. Damn him…"

"Well, we can do it," Sera pointed out. "After all, we've got the film." She thrust out her jaw. "If the three of you argue any more about who is doing it, *I'll* do it!"

That night, in hotel bars and cocktail soirees in different suites, people were already meeting informally. News was not good anywhere on Earth. Forests and grasslands were vanishing. Whole families of animals were threatened by war, poaching, loss of habitat, toxic waste, monoculture farming, swarming refugees, swelling populations everywhere. Legitimate human needs were being met by sacrificing the wild. Yet in mysterious ways that few people yet understood, the wild is part of that vast complex of cycles that supports humanity in its existence.

The Wild Family stayed closed in their own suite, hurriedly getting ready to pinch-hit the presentation. Antonio pointed out to me: "The purists don't think we should have cattle there. I'll have to talk about that."

Next morning, in the big auditorium, conference-goers came together to hear welcoming speeches by Princess Diana and the director of the Jersey Wildlife Conservancy. Antonio saved a seat for Juan beside his own, still hoping against hope. I looked nervously at the empty chair, then the program. The Coto Morera presentation was scheduled for 3 p.m.

The Princess finished amid loud applause, and flashed that famous luminous smile.

At that moment, a man came quietly down the aisle, briefcase in hand, with the sliding purposeful walk of a wild bull on his way to water. He'd probably been waiting quietly in the back till the Princess finished speaking. As he spotted the empty seat by Antonio, I recognized him from the photographs I'd seen.

Juan was the statuesque mountaineer of the Cantábrico — even at 47, in jeans and suede cowboy jacket with fringes. Heels on his hiking boots made him five foot ten. The effort to win a daily victory over memory left him looking older than Antonio, and added force to his presence. His hair was receding a little, touseled from sleeping on the plane, so silver-blond that he might have passed as a native speaker of Gaelic. His chiseled, craggy face with its day-old stubble and rough porous skin set off those clear blue eyes in their deep sockets — they seemed to see everything in the 360 degrees around him. His long muscular arms would have no trouble pregnancy-testing a cow or rolling over a sedated tiger. He limped slightly, like Antonio. How odd that the two of them were twinned this way.

Juan sat in the empty chair and looked at Antonio, then the two women, and whispered:

"I almost missed my flight out of Gatwick. I was having a heart attack that I wouldn't get here in time."

Antonio gave him a level unsmiling look, but said nothing.

José hastily made the introductions. "Juan, this is Patrí."

Juan mumbled that he was enchanted, shaking my hand. "Yes, Patrina, they've told me much about you on the phone."

He had already dangled a Montanese suffix onto my name.

Juan looked at Antonio again, a little nervously. "Well, I'm going up to shower and change." Then he disappeared back up the aisle.

As the 2 p.m. speaker finished a talk on captive breeding of lion tamarin monkeys, Juan and Antonio still hadn't exchanged a word. Juan had already given the film to the projectionist. Now he sat nervously, holding his notes for "Twenty-Two Years of Change at Coto Morera, Spain, by Juan Diano Rodríguez, director."

At 3 p.m., Juan strode down the aisle to the lectern.

Below the bright lights and the Jersey Conservancy's seal with its heraldic dodo bird, Juan looked curiously young as he nervously adjusted the mike. It was his first major conservation address. The village kid who wanted to be the best vet in Spain was now an international figure in his field. He was shaven and combed now, looking good in the dark-grey conservative European-made suit — the image of severe Spanish country man who now had a little money. A few in the audience were surely feeling a quiet kinship — they were gay, and knew he had lived with Antonio for years. I had already met a few gay and lesbian conservationists at different hotel-room parties last night. Among them was the head curator of a major U.S. zoo, a leather man, who grinningly whipped open his vest and showed me his new nipple ring.

Antonio, José and Sera sat almost at attention. Their eyes were fixed on the podium. Other people in our party had flown in from Spain together. Beside Antonio sat Santí. Next was Candalaria, who had spent twenty years fiercely renewing that land where her mother was buried. Beside José sat Paquito, who had wanted to be with his uncle and aunt on this special day. José's arm lay protectively across her nephew's shoulders.

I studied Paquito's classic Spanish profile. He looked so much like his father Paco. Yet my gaydar told me that heterodox genes might drift in his blood, just as Antonio had said.

Juan took hold of the sides of the lectern.

"Ladies and gentlemen...." he said in English. His soft tenor voice still had traces of Montanese lisp.

He looked up from his notes, and let a long shy terrible pause fall into the room. The audience tensed, wondering what was wrong. Then his next words were electrifying.

"...There is a place in Spain that looks different today than it did 22 years ago. It looks like what I love most. You can go there and see my passion, the passion of my family, the passion of my friend and colleague Antonio Escudero. Our passion to bring life back to the Coto Morera..."

It took my breath away to see how openly he had alluded to his relationship with Antonio. Sliding a glance at Antonio, then the rest of our party, I could see they were equally astonished.

Now the film was running on the screen at stage center. The first segment was black-and-white scenes from old family photos — over-grazed hills, rows of dead deer and gamebirds, a twin boy and girl pondering the devastation.

When the first color slide came up, showing the transformation, Juan smiled tensely at the audience's light patter of professional applause. Mature oak trees with foliage lifting in the hot wind. Acorns scattered on the ground. Water trickling everywhere. Wild mother pigs rooting in the cool green bottoms, with their striped piglets around them. Majestic red bucks at rutting time, squaring off with antlers locked. Wolves trotting through brush, looking suspiciously at the camera. Tiny roe deer slipping down a gorge. Birds everywhere — Egyptian vultures feasting on a deer carcass, azure-winged magpies picking last bits off the bones after the vultures left. A white stork nesting on the roof of Santí's house. Noisy flights of partridge exploding out of the bush.

Finally, the scene of the cattle release. Wooden crates unloaded from trucks, horns hitting wood inside, the door pulled up and the first animal irrupting into the open — no ring now, just the vast circle of horizon. Finally the herd was complete, standing against the horizon on a grassy tableland, perhaps 40 wild cattle staring at the camera, horns backlit by the sun. The grizzled bull, grandson of Baby, with horns raked and twisted. The lithe cows with calves at side. Yearlings with their little horns. A few roans and brindles and reds among them.

In a breathtaking helicopter shot, the herd jumped into motion, racing across the tableland like wildebeest, dust churning in their wake, past a sinkhole that might have been the tomb of the Mercies. Then the helicopter banked and let them race on into the distance, disappearing into their own dust against that ineffable Iberian sky. I had a huge lump in my throat. That one scene might go far to squelch controversy about whether the cattle belonged there.

"…And the satellite view is just as magificent," said José's voice on the voice-over.

As a LANDSAT image filled the screen, the audience caught its breath softly. No other single image told the story as well. Sprawling across the greyish summits and drainages of the Montes de Toledo, there was a ragged rectangle that was visibly greener. I looked at the faces of our party. All were struggling with tears and intense emotion. José and Sera and Antonio stared at that image, that land that the four of them had watered with the wet of labor and lovemaking. Santí, Candalaria and Paquito glowed.

I wondered how much Paquito knew, of the predator role that his father had played. Paco's actions, in the long run, only served to move the cycle onwards.

Loud applause filled the auditorium. "Bravo!" a couple of people yelled. It was one of the few moments of good news at the Jersey conference.

Afterward Juan stood talking with Prince Philip, surrounded by reporters and conference-goers. Sera hovered, flashing pictures. Antonio stayed in the background, talking quietly with Candalaria.

"You're not going to join Juan?" I asked Antonio.

Antonio turned away brusquely. "I've already met the Prince," he said. "Shooting at Sandringham thirty years ago."

He left. I knew he wanted to be alone with his thoughts over what Juan had said.

A couple of hours later, as night fell on Jersey, it was Juan who called my room. Would I join him and Antonio on their balcony for a drink? José and Sera were already downstairs, dressed for the benefit reception, circulating and doing business. In the hotel bar, over empty beer glasses, zoo curators would haggle over a hot trade — one white rhino for two scarlet macaws. Under terms of the Convention on Trade in Endangered Species, which over 100 nations had signed, no money could change hands.

Juan let me into their hotel room. He still limped slightly.

I asked, "How did you get hurt?"

"It's nothing," Juan said. "A gaur cow kicked me in the thigh again, in Vietnam. Right on the same place that I got kicked twice before. A vein hemorrhaged."

"Yes, nothing," Antonio said drily from the balcony. "He has varicose veins up and down his whole leg now. The doctor wants to remove them."

"I hate doctors," Juan said.

The three of us sat on the ninth-floor balcony. A stiff cool breeze whipped our hair. Lights winked in the little harbor as pleasure boats and fishing boats bobbed on the swell. Room service had brought a bottle of Scotch and three glasses. The change lay on the table — a Jersey coin with a milk cow on it. The two beds were still neatly made. Intuition told me that hungry lovemaking had not yet happened. Juan was sitting against the balcony railing, Antonio in a chair right by him. But a deadly tension was still in the air. Antonio was quiet, eyes on his glass. The brooding feeling around the old torero reminded me of the night we'd met in West Hollywood.

To break the tension, I fingered the coin.

"The Goddess of Horns follows us everywhere," I said, throwing a Montanese ending onto Her name.

Juan smiled a little — he still couldn't get over the fact that a Yankee lady could speak the unique Spanish of his *tierra*.

"You'll see Her in Spain," Juan said. "We'll take you to the Picos before we go home. Chamois still come right into the hay meadows. You'll see how beautiful it is. We turned the family farm into a place to stay when we're there."

"So you and your family are speaking now?"

"No," he said. "My brother died in Germany, in a factory accident. And my mother…she died of homesickness. I went to court and got claim to the land."

There was a long tense silence.

"Patrina," Juan said. "I know about the story Antonio is telling you. And he has told the truth. His truth. But you need to hear a couple of things from me. This is fair, eh? My truth."

Antonio looked at him, sudden trepidation in his eyes. Their gazes met.

"I have to confess something to Antonio," Juan said. "Something I've hidden from him all these years. You can be a witness, Patrina."

Antonio closed his eyes, clenched a fist. Oh god, I thought. Finally it's coming. The confession about Rafael, or somebody else. Irritation swept over me. I didn't want to be dragged this deep. Juan took a deep breath, as before his presentation.

"That night in the Hotel Roma," he said. "I was there."

Antonio opened his eyes. "What?"

"The night we met. I came to the Roma."

"I don't understand," Antonio said.

"After we met, I couldn't get you out of my mind. You mentioned the hotel name. So that evening I rode the trolleybus to Sardinero and hung around the Roma bar, hoping to see you. I kept out of sight behind other people."

"How did the staff let you in? Don't tell me you wore those slaughterhouse coveralls."

"No. I'd already gotten those slacks and the silk *pull*…you remember the ones. I looked good. So I just walked in. I pretended I was watching the TV…but now and then I watched you with your fans." Juan laughed. "You were overdressed, but your fans loved it. They ate you up with their eyes. That frilled shirt of yours...the diamond studs. ¡*Vaya!* But you looked sad. You didn't look well. The diamonds told me you were breathing fast, unevenly. One of them on your chest, winking in the lights. I wondered if your leg was hurting you. I wondered if you were thinking of me."

Antonio was silent, the wind working at the steely waves of his hair. "After you went upstairs," Juan went on, "I wanted to find out what room you were in. But I was too scared. So I went home, cursing myself for a coward. And the next morning, I woke up and thought how you were probably leaving town. I looked at the card you gave me, and knew I had to go find you."

Antonio was still silent, apprehensive. Juan went on:

"When you sold your diamonds to help me start my practice, it finally sank into my head that you really would give up everything for me. So I did something behind your back. I went to Aben Gómez and made a deal with him. He put the diamonds away, and I started to buy them back. Sometimes $25 a month was all I could send. Gómez died, and his son made good on the deal. With the money I just made in Vietnam, I finally paid it off. I was late getting here because I stopped in New York to cash the draft that the Vietnam government gave me. Then I picked up the diamonds."

Out of his tuxedo's inside pocket, Juan took a little manila envelope. Onto the table spilled shirt-studs and cufflinks of 22-karat gold, and the big cabuchon, which must have weighed 6 karats. Even in the subdued light from streetlights and hotel windows, the gems sparkled fiercely.

Antonio stared at the diamonds and swallowed hard. Sounds assailed us from the street below — taxis honking, a few conference-goers arguing about something at the top of their voices.

Juan had leaned against Antonio's back from behind. Gently he took Antonio's right wrist, undid the plain cufflink, replaced it with the diamond one. Then the left wrist. His fingers were as careful as if he were doing delicate sutures. One by one, he worked his way down Antonio's shift-front, replacing the studs, being careful not to wrinkle the shirt. His cheek was almost touching Antonio's.

"You doubted me many times, Majín," he said huskily as he worked. "I doubted you. We've had our civil war. It's time for peace, eh? What do you say?"

Taking Antonio's right hand, his fingers gently fitted the cabuchon back into the bezel of the ring for a moment.

Stupefied, Antonio stared down at the ring.

Juan put the loose diamond back in the envelope. Then he slid his hand inside Antonio's tuxedo and put the envelope in his friend's inside pocket.

"Tomorrow I'll find a jeweler and have him reset the stone for you," he said.

Task done, he kept his arms around Antonio, hands now resting gently on Antonio's black satin lapels. Antonio put one callused sunbrowned hand over Juan's. For the first time since I'd met him, the torero who was as good with words as with capes had nothing to say.

Just then, a knock came at the door. While Antonio wiped a suspicious trace of wetness from his eyes, Juan pulled himself together and went to open it.

Outside, in the corridor, was our whole party — José and Sera in elegant evening gowns, carrying little evening hand-bags. "Darlings!" José cried, like she hadn't seen us for months. Paquito had his arms full of champagne bottles. Candalaria in a modest dark cocktail dress, Santí in a black suit and five-o'clock shadow, twitching at his collar — both looking like village people still unaccustomed to high society. Only the Eibars were missing, too old and infirm to travel, waiting for us back at Las Moreras.

They trooped noisily in. In no time, the room was full of cigarette smoke, ice bucket rattling, champagne corks popping. With the door standing open, more people came in, including the leatherman curator, who was now in black tie. Evening wraps and purses were thrown across the neatly made bed where, later that night, when everyone had retired, the two men might passionately renew their friendship. José chugged a glass of mineral water like she was at the fair in Seville, and kissed Juan on the cheek. I had the feeling that José already knew about the diamonds. It was like one of those post-bullfight parties, with two ears and a tail on the record, and the maestro's room full of celebrants.

I found myself talking to Paquito.

"Prince Philip wants to visit Las Moreras," he confided in awe. "Maybe when my mother sees that, she'll come around."

"Is she angry that you're here?"

"Furious," the young man smiled.

Away from the uproar, Antonio still sat on the balcony, a glass of champagne fizzing untasted in front of him. He was fingering one of the diamond studs, his gaze fixed on Juan as his friend circulated through the crowd. Antonio's eyes had suddenly come alive. He drew a deep breath of relief, right down to the bottom of his lungs. A chain of firework sparkles went up his row of diamond studs, then down again as he exhaled.

I went over to him. "Are you all right?"

"Very much so," he said.

I sat down with my glass of champagne. Just then José came by, bent and kissed her brother's forehead. As always, she had been reading his thoughts.

"So…it's finally settled, eh?" she said. "I hope?"

"Settled," he said, catching his sister's hand and kissing it.

"Listen, Antonio," I said on an impulse. "What were you really doing at Numbers?"

"Woman, have you no pity?" But his eyes were sparkling like the diamonds, with sudden humor.

"None whatever."

He heaved a sigh. "Numbers...other places. Not often."

"Penance?" I asked. "For the times you tried to buy love?"

He shrugged. "Buying love isn't bad unless you do it for cowardly reasons."

"But why? You're the fox among the hens."

"Not if the fox has to go home and face the jealous bull."

"Juan knew you went there?"

"Of course. And don't fool yourself....he has been in his own dangerous places."

"Why were you there? Why Wednesdays?"

"Because Wednesday was always our day for Juan to call me from wherever he was. I'd be at the phone at 7 p.m."

"And if he didn't call?"

Antonio raised his champagne glass, an impish gleam in his eyes. *"Muñeca,"* he said, "what were *you* doing in Numbers, eh?"

"Looking for the Lady," I said.

"How is She to be found in Numbers?"

I let an impish gleam show in my own eye, and raised my own glass.

"She comes to me as a muse, in stories," I said.

"Even in Numbers?"

"Even there."

"Then here's to your muse."

We clinked glasses.

****

Notes and Acknowledgments

Today, with the U.S. religious right insisting that Americans must junk democracy and get back to God, it is a good time to tell this story of four Spanish citizens and what they experienced because Spain junked democracy and re-established state religion in 1936.

Whenever I hear Pat Robertson preach about the need for an American theocracy, I feel a deep trembling inside, and remind myself how Spanish theocrat Generalísimo Franco ignored Hitler's pressure to blitzkrieg his way across Spain. Instead, Franco's troops occupied the country a city and a village at a time, over three years, 1936-39. They systematically massacred "enemies of Catholicism and Our Lord" before they moved on. Today the Spanish speak of their Civil War as a time when "half the country killed the other half."

Such a religious civil war could happen in the United States, if enough of our own citizens don't ensure that we stay a democracy.

I first began writing this book in the late 1960s, while in and out of Spain. Had this book been published then, it would have been my first novel about gay life. To those who wonder why it's being published more than a quarter century later, I will show a little of the tapestry of long-woven thought that produced the book.

At that time, I was on assignment for the *Reader's Digest*, as a liaison with its Spanish edition *Selecciones*. As part of Spain's growing visibility on the international scene, the Digest had embarked on a joint effort with *Selecciones* to work up more editorial material that would interest both their Spanish and U.S. readers. Over several years I launched ideas for a number of book and article projects about Spain. My interest in Spain was also deeply personal, dating from 1964 when I and my (then) husband, Ukrainian poet Yurij Tarnawsky, spent two years there on leave of absence from our jobs. Our travels took us into virtually every province, including a number of visits to Toledo and its countryside.

Spain was then in stormy transition, with many citizens weary of the stagnation and strictures of fascist rule. They were agitating for liberalization. Dictator Franco was failing in health. The country was actually run by the Cabinet, yet Franco's personal brand of fierce Catholic fundamentalism still pushed the country through a series of repressions, political trials and executions. Even Spanish Catholic bishops were wakening to grave harm done the Church's credibility by its support of fascism. A few brave clerics supported the idea of religious freedom…meaning that laws would be changed to allow open worship as a Protestant, Jew or Muslim, or even profession of atheism. It was known that enemies of the Franco regime were tortured. People speculated about the number of political prisoners behind bars.

My ex-husband and I did travel to see the real-life matadors mentioned in this novel. Yuriy and I were the only "Yankee" members of Peña Taurina Montañesa, the bullfight club in Santander. I was the only woman member — always cause for Spanish male head-turning whenever I walked into the smoky downtown club on the designated meeting night.

I had arrived in Spain with a built-in interest, owing to being raised on a cattle ranch with vestigal Spanish traditions. My dad was interested in bullfighting, and collected some books including Hemingway's *Death in the Afternoon*. I read it till the pages fell out, and would have traveled clear to the Gates of Hades to see Juan Belmonte do one pass with his cape. To be sure, Papa Hemingway's stark celebration of conservative machismo was not a feminist's choice for a girl child's reading. But I, a tomboy cowgirl, had X-ray eyes, and could see the intense homo-eroticism hidden behind bullfighting's facade — and the intense femme-eroticism around the figure of the *torera,* or woman bullfighter.

When I arrived in Spain, the bullfight scene was having its own convulsions of transition. A new young matador, Manuel Benítez "El Cordobés", was busy breaking the rules of everything traditional in his profession, from haircut to headlines. Spaniards flooded to see him. To them, Benítez symbolized all the defiant modernity and change that was shaking their society like an earthquake.

But, liberal though I was, I preferred the "classic" toreros. My favorites were Santiago Martín "El Viti", Paco Camino, Diego Puerta, Jaime Ostos, Antonio Bienvenida, as well as quirky Curro Romero and worn-out Antonio Ordóñez on the rare afternoons when they were good. Ostos was an amazing man. Incredibly brave, he had been crippled by a horn wound in much the same manner as my character Antonio. The crowd always held its breath, because we knew he couldn't run from the bull if he had to.

If horseback celebrity Álvaro Domecq was on the bill, it was always a good reason to drive to an out-of-town bullfight. Domecq often rode a wonderful old stallion named Universo, a purebred Andalusian. This grey horse was old enough to have turned snow white. He had a long wavy mane that hung to his chest and a deep horn-scar in one powerful haunch. It was said that Domecq never had the bull's horns "shaved", and counted on skill to keep his horse safe…but obviously he had miscalculated on one occasion. It was hair-raising to watch Universo invite the bull's charge. The horse was not only brave, but a gorgeous show-off like the human toreros — the crowd loved him. Universo made an indelible impression, and served as inspiration for the horse in this novel, Faisán.

I might have driven clear across Spain to see Conchita Cintrón, greatest of women bullfighters. She always did it on horseback because Spanish law didn't allow women to fight on foot. Unfortunately Cintrón had retired from the ring by then. I got a paperback copy of her autobiography, Recuerdos, and read it till the pages fell out. Now and then, some new girl attempted to follow in Cintrón's hoofprints — with a rich and indulgent family covering the high cost of horses, shipping, crew, chaperones, publicity, etc. She usually came and went quickly.

In the late '60s, after the Beatles-type hysteria around Manuel Benítez "El Cordobés", every manager was trying to find the next hot kid, who might be 16 or 17. There were scads of these novilleros (novices). They got thrown in front of bulls that were supposed to be younger, but were actually older and more dangerous than what the full-fledged matadors drew.

The only novice whose name I can recall today is Sebastián Palomo "Linares." Few of these boys made it through the meatgrinder to become a matador. Most got hurt, or discouraged. It was as hard, and as expensive, to launch a career in the bullring as it was to launch a rock band. Despite being pumped by big business, bullfighting was starting to fade from the Spanish national consciousness. Soccer matches and music festivals drew bigger crowds than a corrida (run of bulls.) Inevitably, more and more modern Spaniards found it hard to defend the *fiesta brava's* antiquated cruelty and goriness — especially after they'd seen a bad bullfight.

A bad bullfight is when a fearful maestro or a trembling kid orders a bull to be virtually butchered by the picador before he will go near it. Spanish crowds are as volatile at bullfights as they are at soccer matches. They go wild with outrage, flinging seat cushions and beer bottles in the ring. Given the political instability of Spain, a disturbance at a bullring or soccer stadium could quickly escalate into anti-regime outcry. So the state police, known as the *Grises* (Greys), were routinely put on duty at bullfights. A disgraced torero might need a Grey escort on his way out.

Most of the best bulls came from Andalucía, though bull-ranches could be found in the north as well. Guardiola, Domecq, Romero and Miura were among the more distinguished breeders — in spite of the fact that the Miuras were considered to be less good than before the Civil War. It was alleged that the Miura family felt guilty — their bulls had killed two great matadors, Joselito and Manolete — so they bred a little of the "pepper" out of their stock.

In the late '60s, matadors felt the deepest tremor about bulls from the Andalusian ranch of Tulio and Isaías Vásquez. I would drive clear across Spain to see Tulios. The Vásquez brothers didn't fool around — what they shipped were mature hardened five-year-olds, not the artificially fattened three-year-olds that many other ranches produced. Like Universo, these amazing animals made an impression that three decades haven't dimmed, inspiring Baby, the bull in this story. They had the lethal speed and agility of a leopard, and the strength of a rhino. One afternoon I sat open-mouthed as a Tulio flung a 2000-pound picador's horse in the air like it was a feather pillow. The horse went high enough to turn completely over, before it hit the ground upside down, with saddle and picador underneath. (Luckily man and horse were not hurt.)

By the time I came along, the *fiesta brava* was said to have gone so commercial that it lost its soul. There was constant talk of bribes, shaved horns, underage overweight bulls, and bullrings being bought up by "chain" impresarios. When celebrity El Cordobés was on the bill, it was rumored that the three matadors did not draw lots for the bulls. El Cordobés's manager (it was said) got to pick the two animals that looked most likely for his client. The other two toreros got what was left. Big names seldom faced bulls like Tulios, who usually went to the also-rans. In this way, it was said, bullring impresarios eliminated as much risk as possible. They wanted predictable and profitable entertainment that could compete with popular new sports like soccer. The most important bullfights were broadcast live by Televisión Española. We never missed these, watching them at our favorite Santander bar over glasses of manzanilla.

The new values were geared to tourism and a new generation of Spanish fans who were not knowledgeable. This was the perennial complaint of *ABC's* noted bullfight critic, who tirelessly shot zingers of purist wit at his targets.

Danger was still present, of course, but modern medicine and antibiotics helped broaden the margin for wounded men. Only one torero was actually killed during the years I was in Spain. This was Antonio Rizo Pastor, an obscure subaltern who was spiked right in the heart by a galloping bull while doing the initial capework for his boss. Pastor was briefly mourned and eulogized, and the beat went on.

By 1970 I had seen one bad bullfight too many, and stopped following the bulls. But the story of a matador wounded in the heart was lodged in my brain like an old scar.

When not on the road to see our favorite maestros, Yuriy and I made our permanent residence in La Montaña province of northern Castile. We chose this part of Spain because there were virtually no other Americans there. At first we rented a villa in El Sardinero, the ocean-front district of Santander. Later on we bought a flat there. Having no one with whom we could speak English, whether marketing or banking or making friends, we learned Spanish fast.

La Montaña is not what Americans think of as "typically Spanish." Green, rainy, it is the only part of landlocked Castile that touches the Atlantic, between the Basque country and Asturias. It catches stormy Gulf Stream weather off the Bay of Biscay, with its magnificent range of coastal mountains called the Cantábrico. I had a love affair with this distinctive region. Over seven years, we searched out La Montaña's most remote and most piquant wonders, from its "scandalous churches" with their erotic sculptures to its Celtic sun-stones laying forgotten in cow-pastures, from the painted bison in the cave of Altamira to the live chamois scaling cliffs in the Picos de Europa, from glasses of fine wine in the capital's modern bars to shots of heady *orujo* in smoky village taverns.

With time, we came to feel *en casa* (at home) in Castile, and appreciated the cultural differences of other regions — Vascongada and Cataluña and Galicia, with their distinctive cultures and languages, and Andalucía, with its own dialect and thick Moorish overlay.

In La Montaña, and elsewhere, I came to see the love of Lady Goddess that had endured in Spain since ancient times, through numerous eras of patriarchal bias. A chance experience burned into my mind one of those indelible impressions, while visiting the Castilian monastery of Santo Domingo de Silos. It happened that the Benedictine monks were in the throes of a major archeological dig, occasioned by a routine repair of the 12th-century church floor. Under the paving stones, they had discovered rubble of an intriguing structure that was several hundred years older.

In a nearby sun-dried field, amid rows of fragments laid out by Ministry of Culture workers, the monk in charge showed us the magnificent alabaster tympanum of this temple's main doorway. It had been broken in several pieces and, along with the rest of the demolished temple, used as fill under the new 12th-century church. The tympanum had just been cleaned and reassembled. Carved in deep bas-relief in a rich detail more typical of ivory caskets carved by Arab artisans, the massive sculpture showed the Lady giving birth in a forest, assisted by a handmaiden and surrounded by wild animals — hardly the routine picture of Mary, who was usually portrayed seated in royal majesty with Her child. The structure must have served as a temple to celebrate a dark-age Lady of the Animals who was reminiscent of the goddess Diana.

Spanish folklore insisted that the spirit of Diana still roamed the highlands of Castile. Surely the 12th-century Benedictines, when settling their patriarchal system into this remote stretch of Spain, had swept an older female-oriented institution off the map, possibly with the same rigor as Franco's troops occupying a Republican village. Here was a shock to anyone who had thought of Spanish "goddess worship" as being only Mediterranean and Greco-Roman — the Dama de Elche bust with her coiled headdress.

Since that day, I had pondered why mythology would link Diana, goddess of hunting and wild animals, with the Moon, as well as with human birth and reproduction. Why were animal horns, especially a pair of cow-horns, symbolically linked to the crescent Moon and birth? Why was Diana clearly linked with Mary, who was often shown standing on the crescent Moon? Both were called "virgins" which in the ancient world did not mean "sexually innocent," but referred simply to an independent unmarried woman. What was the common factor, the link, that was so clear to the ancient mind but is now so blurred to us today?

Finally there is the burning question of why so many Spanish slang words for homosexual include Mary's name. This practice has entered American language use through Spanish-speaking gay people in the U.S. Gay men commonly call each other "Mary." Of all the hundreds of female names that could be used to denote homosexuals, why Mary? Surely the original intention was not to insult, because the insult would have redounded onto Mother Mary as well. Was the urge of some gay men to "be the woman" in a relationship seen as placing him under Her special protection? If so, why are tomboy women called "Marys" *(marimachas)* as well? Was there a time, in the ancient past, when gay men and women were held sacred to the Mother Goddess, as were the "two spirit" people among many native American tribes?

And why, since gay men and women don't always have children, might they have been sacred to the Great Mother? Stretching the symbol to its limits, were childless gay people a good choice to put in charge of animals, so that their nurturing instinct could be utilized and fulfilled? Does the natural urge to nurture living things, which is found in most humans regardless of sexual orientation, explain why so many gay people work in the conservation movement? Do they seek out a career of nurturing plants, animals and the Earth to replace the outlet they might have had with biological children?

With time, I would learn to look at Life itself, at ecology and life-processes, to begin understanding how the ancients came to create symbols, and what the symbols really mean.

In 1970, after a huge struggle and labored rewrites, the first version of this novel was completed. But I wasn't accepting my own gay nature yet, still wrestling with Catholic guilts. So I had a hard time getting an honest literary fix on my characters.

By then my first novel, *The Last Centennial*, was already accepted for publication by Dial Press. My (then) agent, Paul Reynolds Inc., showed the Spanish manuscript to editor Jim Landis at William Morrow. Landis had just leaped to his own celebrity status as the hottest new young editor in New York. Jim liked the novel…but not enough to publish it. However, he told Paul Reynolds that he wanted to see my next novel. I was not comfortable with the Spanish book as written, and felt it didn't work. So it went into a bottom drawer.

In spring 1973 the Spanish sojourn, and my marriage to Yuriy, ended when I divorced him and came out. My agent sent Landis the manuscript of my next novel, which was *The Front Runner.* Landis bought TFR immediately. Jim would be my editor through all three of my gay novels of the 1970s. Later I would bless him for his decision not to plunge on the Spanish book in its stillborn 1970 version.

Around 1985, still unhappy with the Spanish book, I fished it out of the bottom drawer and burned the manuscript.

For the next 20 years, the cast of Spanish characters hibernated in the bottom drawer of my mind.

In the 1980s, while I was researching my historical novel about native American healer women, *One Is the Sun,* I stumbled on some clues to the Mary-Diana mystery. They came to me in the Mayan number system still known to a handful of U.S. Medicine men and women. Some of these people assert that the old number system, which assigns a level of being to each integer between zero and 20, was once widely known, and distributed by trade, conquest and cultural cross-fertilization. The mathematical relationships among certain numbers — the ones assigned to humanity, sexuality, animals, the Moon and life-cycles — reveal a great deal about how the ancients created symbol as a shorthand for human relationships with all life processes. I began to understand the link between Mary, marys and wildlife. Five (humans) plus Four (animals) equals Nine (which is the Moon, and the movement of all cycles of life on Earth). Today, I think, we have lost the ability to understand ancient symbols because most cultures are no longer intimate with the life-forces that inspired symbol to begin with.

Suddenly, in late 1993, while I was taking a badly needed break from writing the *Front Runner* sequel, *Harlan's Race,* these old Spanish characters woke up and clamored at me that I was finally mature enough as an artist and a human being to listen to them, and tell their story. The "break" turned into more work, but it was exhilerating work. The new version, now titled *The Wild Man,* literally rolled out of the computer...and it finally worked.

Some bibliographical notes:

For those readers who want to know more about Spanish political turmoil of this period, Paul Preston's magnificent biography titled *Franco* (BasicBooks, Harper/Collins, 1994) is a good place to start.

For more on poet Federico García Lorca, his homosexuality and his violent death in 1936 during the first days of the Spanish Civil War, British historian Ian Gibson's *The Assassination of Federico García Lorca* (W. H. Allen, Penguin, 1971) is a must. This book was banned in Spain when it first came out, because Gibson broke the news that Lorca had been deliberately murdered by fascist insurgents. Gibson has written a number of other books about Spain, including

Lorca's Granada, for those who might want to leave their bouquet of flowers at the spot where the poet died.

Revealing Lorca material is also found in Jaime Manrique's *Eminent Maricones* (U. of Wisconsin Press, 1999).

José María de Cossío's great monograph *Los Toros*, in 12 volumes, is still the most comprehensive history of the *fiesta brava.* While living in La Montaña, I had the good fortune to know Cossío, a native of the province. He lived in a village in the mountains above Santander.

Cossío's discussion of the fighting bull as a wild animal is fascinating, complete with descriptions of the many regional strains that once ranged Iberia, from Coimbra in Portugal to the mountains of Navarra on the French border. Most bulls today are black, thanks to prevalence of a single bloodline, the Vistahermosa, with its genetically dominant black coat. But in olden times, wild cattle came in every color of the rainbow, from white through duns, reds, pintos, brindles, roans, even several shades of black (coal black, matte black, coffee black, etc.). Cossío thought that *Bos ibericus* was linked to North African cattle, on the archeological evidence of skeletal remains and horn shapes.

Spanish wildlife, and current efforts to protect it, is featured in a 1999 WGBH Boston TV six-part documentary series titled "Wild Europe."

The old number system is documented in a few native American sources on native spirituality, including Frank Waters' *Mountain Dialogues* and the writings of Hyemeyohsts Storm.

The medical uses of horsetail (*cola de caballo*) are documented in many sources dealing with herbal medicine, including an international database located at www.rain-tree.com/horsetail.htm. I say this for information only — no reader of this book should venture into herbal medicine without consulting their doctor as well as a reliable herbalist.

Early Spanish and Sephardic Jewish emigration to the American South is documented in *The Melungeons: The Resurrection of a Proud People* by N. Brent Kennedy (Mercer University Press, 1997). For more on these "free of people of color," search for www. melungeon.org on the Internet.

Some of my Spanish experiences between 1964 and 1972 are described in a short memoir titled "Throwing Carnations." It was published in the spring 1999 *Harvard Gay and Lesbian Review.*

Some of my writings on the biological/ecological basis of ancient symbol have appeared in *Mythosphere,* and in a paper presented at a 1982 UCLA conference titled "The Shining Ones: Cats as a Symbol of Light in the Ancient World."

In letters that I wrote to my parents during the late '60s, many details of Spanish life and politics were recorded. Later, this trove of letters was recovered from my parents' ranch home after my father died in 1993 — along with photographs and magazines I had sent them (such as old copies of the bullfight magazine *El Burladero,* and an issue of *Blanco y Negro,* containing a wonderful article on the Spanish wild horses called *asturcones.* These provided some timely "found" research material.

Gratitude, and acknowledgements, to the following individuals who added to my understanding of Spain, or who encouraged the writing of *The Wild Man* in some way:

•All the different Spanish people I knew in the '60s and '70s, both women and men, whose personal stories are woven into this book in some fictionalized form.

•The real-life Josefina, nicknamed José, whose memory still burns bright after thirty years.

•Jim Landis, my William Morrow editor — a wonderful craftsman on books. Jim is still a friend, now married with a family, retired from publishing and living in New England, a successful novelist in his own right.

•Spanish composer and novelist José Raúl Bernardo for his friendship, encouragement and comments. His novel *El Secreto de los toros* (Secret of the Bulls) is published by Simon & Schuster.

•Spanish playwright and novelist Carlos Miguel Suárez Radillo for his encouragement. His novel *Alguién más en el espejo* (Someone Else in the Mirror) is one of the first openly gay Spanish novels to be published in the post-Franco period.

•Internationally recognized wildlife authority Pat Quillen of S.O.S. Care, for her friendship over many years and her willingness to answer my questions about everything from studbooks to the Convention on International Trade in Endangered Species (CITES).

•Internationally recognized wildlife expert Reg Reidel for whom I was a research assistant in the 1970s, in New York State, when he was working with small cats — for his friendship and sharing of conservation information. Reg has gone on to make a name for himself in captive breeding of endangered birds, and is presently establishing a bird park in Costa Rica.

•John Graham, gay veterinarian who has a country practice in Dumfriesshire, Scotland — a great lover of wildlife and a good friend.

John was my consultant on veterinary accuracy in this book.

•Former *Selecciones* editor in chief Victor Olmos, now with EFE, for his patience in answering my many pesky questions of a Yankee journalist many years ago. Olmos first drew my attention to the Spanish government's efforts to establish wildlife refuges, like Coto Doñana in the Andalusian tide-marshes, and to reforest some of Spain's most denuded reaches.

•Former *Selecciones* book editor Angelita González, today a literary agent, for the perspective she gave me on Spanish women of the 1960s, and the challenges they faced in business and at home.

•Modas Paquita, dressmaking salon in Santander, whose owner/designer Paquita González had been born to a Spanish family living in Rio de Janeiro — for her friendship and for what she shared with me about growing up outside of Spain.

•The González brothers of Cabezón de la Sal, in La Montaña province — cabinetmakers by vocation, hunters by avocation, who helped me get acquainted with village *brujos* and Spanish hunting.

•The entire Ribalaygua family, owners of a general contracting firm that rebuilt Santander harbor and much of the downtown area after the Civil War — for their friendship, and for sharing their rich family life and their excitement at discovering the world outside Spain.

•Spanish explorer Vital Alsar, whose book about his Pacific balsa-raft voyages I edited for the Reader's Digest. It was titled *La Balsa: The Longest Raft Voage in History* (Reader's Digest/Dutton, 1973). A native of La Montaña who was then living in Mexico, Vital helped me understand the craggy conservatism of Castile.

•The scholarly monk at the monastery of Santo Domingo de Silos, whose name I have forgotten, who was in charge of the treasury at the time I visited, as well as liaison with the archeological dig. Learning that I was an archeology buff, he spent a day showing me artifacts of the discovery, as well as ancient books and objets d'art in the treasury. (As a curious footnote, a recent documentary on Santo Domingo de Silos, aired on the U.S. Hispanic channel GEMS, focused on the famous plainsong choir and the more traditional items in the treasury, with no mention of the pre-Romanesque discovery or the Lady of the Animals doorway).

•All the people I met on a 1984 trip through England, Germany, Austria, Netherlands and Switzerland while researching *One Is the Sun*. My aim was to get more acquainted with what survives of "pagan Europe." My informants included a Tyrolean village herbalist, an old German lady who was keeper of a sacred spring, a Cornish keeper of a stone circle, Little People, and a granddaughter of the last Hapsburg to rule Austria (Spanish royalty were related to the Hapsburgs.) They insisted that Europe is still riddled with historical secrets of the kind portrayed in this novel.

•Those who read the semi-final manuscript and made helpful comments, including José Raúl Bernardo, Jim Burgholzer, Joshua Chaney, Burt Coleman, Jonathan Freyberger, Michael Granville, John Selig, Carlos Sandino, Christine Soto, Bryan Wildenthal, Jesus Yanez, as well as Wildcat staffers Brandon Andersen, Eric Jensen and Lee Look. Thanks to these Wildcat people:

•Graphics artist/photographer Jay Fraley of Open Eye Studios for yet another outstanding cover. At Wildcat, we aim to avoid the "naked torso" stereotype of so many covers in our genre.

•Lee Look, for his maiden voyage as Wildcat in-house typesetter, and valiant efforts to locate the sword on the cover. We had the naïve idea that Hollywood prop houses would have bullfighter swords in stock, and we could simply rent one and photograph it. Our efforts to locate an existing suitable photograph were also in vain. We wound up ordering a real *estoque de matar* from Bermejo in Spain.

•Wildcat counsel Robert Harrison for his wise guidance.

•Eric Jensen, Wildcat controller, for his unfailing fiscal expertise.

•Last but not least, my Wildcat business partner, Tyler St. Mark, for his comments and enthusiasm for this book.

As a final note in these millennial times:

With space stations now a daily fact of life and the planet girded by an electronic nervous system called the Internet, humans still feel that irresistible primal lure to play dangerous games with wild cattle. In the last decade, a unique form of bloodless bullfighting is emerging on the U.S. rodeo circuit, being developed by rodeo clowns.

In the traditional bullriding event, professional clowns have always stood ready to lure bulls away from fallen cowboys. Bulls used in bullriding are Mexican-bred or part Brahma, and they have a fair amount of "pepper" in their blood.

In this new emerging event, the clowns "fight" young Mexican bulls specially imported for the purpose. The bulls are never ridden, but used again and again, like the ones in French bullrings. They become adept at cat-like moves, spinning, swapping ends, doing a deadly cat-and-mouse dance with their man. Judges score each clown on how closely he keeps body contact with the bull's horns. While the horns are blunted, these powerful animals can hammer a man against the ground or along the arena fence. Necks and limbs can get broken. Great Yankee bullfighters like Ron Smetz of Texas have sustained injuries and lived through crises of confidence like any Spanish matador.

The clowns even let themselves get tossed so they can leap across the bull's back like those Cretan bull-dancers of old, immortalized in some of the oldest murals known.

— Patricia Nell Warren

******

The text of this book is set in 12 pt. New Times Roman.

About the Author

Patricia Nell Warren, author of the most popular gay novel of all time, has written professionally since the age of seventeen. In over 48 years, her literary subjects have ranged from women, human rights, gay life and mixed-blood people to Earth, wildlife, and book publishing. Born in Helena, Montana to a prominent ranching family, she turns 65 this year and celebrates her 30th anniversary as a popular novelist.

Warren has published eight novels, three under her own imprint, Wildcat Press. *The Front Runner, Harlan's Race* and *Billy's Boy* are a landmark series following an evolving family through 20 years of gay life. These books have become essential gay literature for bookstores worldwide. Warren has also published two mainstream novels, *The Last Centennial* and *One Is the Sun,* as well as four books of Ukrainian poetry.

Warren's best-known book, *The Front Runner,* was first published by William Morrow in 1974 and became the first gay novel to make *The New York Time's* Bestseller List and to be mass-marketed into chain stores across America. This landmark classic about the relationship between an ex-Marine track coach and his top male runner has sold over ten million copies worldwide and been translated into ten languages. In a survey of gay bookstores nationwide by *ForeWord Magazine*, it still remains the #1 best selling gay book.

The long-awaited sequel, *Harlan's Race,* was published in June of 1994 and continued the bittersweet saga of Coach Harlan Brown. *Harlan's Race* instantly became the top-selling novel in gay bookstores nationwide, according to *Lambda Book Report*, and remained

a bestseller for over a year. *Billy's Boy*, the third book in the series, also became a gay bestseller.

Warren's political activism started during the 1960's while she was an editor at *Readers Digest* with efforts to have the American media recognize the individuality of Ukrainians and other ethnic groups in the USSR. She moved onto the battlefront for women's rights in the '70's as plaintiffs' spokesperson for *Susan Smith v. Reader's Digest,* a landmark lawsuit that resulted in a class-action victory for women. As an amateur athlete, she helped lead a group of women distance runners who forced the Amateur Athletic Union (AAU) to change discriminatory rules during the mid-70's. More recently, as a steadfast foe of censorship, Warren has been a plaintiff in both federal lawsuits over Internet censorship (*ACLU v. Reno I & II*)

Presently, Warren's activism focuses on youth. In 1994, she did volunteer teaching at EAGLES Center, a continuation program for gay and lesbian teenagers in the Los Angeles Unified School District. She served on the LAUSD Human Relations Education Commission and has helped raise funds for gay youth programs across the country. In 1995, Warren founded the Patricia Nell Warren Endowment Fund which supports gifted gay youth who are enduring economic hardship as they pursue a career in the arts.

Warren is also a political journalist and columnist. Her articles, essays, editorials and fiction have appeared in *Los Angeles Times, Reader's Digest, San Francisco Chronicle, Atlantic Monthly, A & U, Modern Maturity, Persimmon Hill, Mythosphere,* as well as *The Advocate, Gay & Lesbian Review, Washington Blade, Philadelphia Gay New* and other publications.

More information on Patricia Nell Warren can be found at www. wildcatpress.com.

Also in Print From Wildcat Press:
Other Bestselling Fiction by Patricia Nell Warren

THE FRONT RUNNER SERIES
A saga of gay family life from the '70s into the '90s

The Front Runner
1978 Walt Whitman Award for Gay Literature
A young gay athlete fears he will be outed on his way to the Olympic Games. His ex-Marine coach loves him, and fears for his life. This classic love story has 10 million copies in print worldwide, in 10 languages. Voted #1 favorite among gay novels by popular vote at publishingtriangle.org. Soon to be a major motion picture.
Hardcover $24.95   ISBN 0964109913
Trade paperback $14.95   ISBN 0964109964
Leatherbound limited edition $159.95   (specify when ordering)

Harlan's Race
Sequel to *The Front Runner*
Coach Harlan Brown struggles to heal himself of past losses, and to protect his family from anti-gay violence in the present.
Hardcover $24.95   ISBN 0964109905
Trade paperback $14.95   ISBN 0964109956

Billy's Boy
Sequel to *The Front Runner* and *Harlan's Race*
1997 Lambda Editors' Choice Award
1997 Small Press Awards, runner-up
John William, the child born in the first novel of the series, is now a questioning teenager with a powerful feeling for his best friend.
Hardcover $24.95   ISBN 0964109948
Trade paperback $14.95   ISBN 096410993X

Additional fiction titles by Warren:

The Fancy Dancer
In a conservative town, a young Catholic priest becomes painfully aware of conflict between his ministry and his sexuality.
Trade paperback $14.95   ISBN 0964109972

The Beauty Queen
Power and religion collide with a gay father's love for his born-again daughter, during an election frenzy in New York City.
Trade paperback $14.95   ISBN 0964109980

We encourage our readers to buy from, and support, their neighborhood independent bookstore. But we also appreciate the fact that our books are carried by many chain stores. Both kinds of stores have their place in a healthy book industry. If you don't find our books in any store, ask the manager to order them for you. Or contact us at wildcatprs@aol.com.

Wildcat titles are distributed by Ingram, Koen, Baker & Taylor, Bookazine, Bookpeople, Alamo Square. In Canada, by Marginal. In the UK and Europe, by Turnaround. In Australia, by Bulldog Books. Our titles are discounted on most major Internet bookselling sites, including amazon.com and barnesandnoble.com.

To obtain autographed copies, call us and place a credit-card purchase order. Or visit our Web page at wildcatpress.com and order there. Special discounts available to bookstores who buy direct from us. We have a donations program for libraries and nonprofit organizations — contact us for information.

WILDCAT PRESS
8306 Wilshire Boulevard, Box 8306
Beverly Hills, California 90211
323/966-2466 phone   323/966-2467 fax
email: wildcatpress@aol.com   web page: wildcatpress.com